AULS

Denied R.

Serniriv

KALVIV · Hadorst

Shomel

Denied R.

Zatyr

GOLDEN
SEA

Akhman

Sankar

FIRST of
CITIES

Camnan · Istas

SEA of
DREAMS · Ulsareen

Jis · Ostrisa

EMPIRE OF THE SOUTH

BY JOE ABERCROMBIE

———

HALF A KING

HALF THE WORLD

HALF THE WORLD

JOE ABERCROMBIE

HALF
THE WORLD

DEL REY • NEW YORK

Copyright © 2015 by Joe Abercrombie

Map copyright © 2015 by Nicolette Caven

All rights reserved.

Published in the United States by Del Rey,
an imprint of Random House,
a division of Random House LLC,
a Penguin Random House Company, New York.

DEL REY and the HOUSE colophon are
registered trademarks of Random House LLC.

Published in hardcover in the United Kingdom by Harper Voyager.

LIBRARY OF CONGRESS CATALOGING-IN-PUBLICATION DATA

Abercrombie, Joe.
Half the world / Joe Abercrombie.—First U.S. edition.
pages   cm.—(Shattered sea)
ISBN 978-0-8041-7842-6 (hardcover : acid-free paper)—
ISBN 978-0-8041-7844-0 (ebook)
1. Teenage girls—Fiction. 2. First loves—Fiction. I. Title.
PR6101 B49H35 2015
823'.92—dc23   2014038766

Printed in the United States of America on acid-free paper

www.delreybooks.com

9 8 7 6 5 4 3 2 1

First U.S. Edition

FOR EVE

CATTLE DIE,

KINDRED DIE,

EVERY MAN IS MORTAL:

BUT I KNOW ONE THING

THAT NEVER DIES,

THE GLORY OF THE GREAT DEED.

FROM *HÁVAMÁL*,
THE SPEECH OF THE HIGH ONE

I.

OUTCASTS

THE WORTHY

He hesitated just an instant, but long enough for Thorn to club him in the balls with the rim of her shield.

Even over the racket of the other lads all baying for her to lose, she heard Brand groan.

Thorn's father always said *the moment you pause will be the moment you die*, and she'd lived her life, for better and mostly worse, by that advice. So she bared her teeth in a fighting snarl—her favorite expression, after all—pushed up from her knees and went at Brand harder than ever.

She barged at him with her shoulder, their shields clashing and grating, sand scattering from his heels as he staggered back down the beach, face still twisted with pain. He chopped at her but she ducked his wooden sword, swept hers low and caught him full in the calf, just below his mailshirt's flapping hem.

To give Brand his due he didn't go down, didn't even cry out, just hopped back, grimacing. Thorn shook her shoulders out, waiting to see if Master Hunnan would call that a win, but he stood silent as the statues in the Godshall.

Some masters-at-arms acted as if the practice swords were real, called a halt at what would have been a finishing blow from a steel blade. But Hunnan liked to see his students put down, and hurt, and taught a hard lesson. The gods knew, Thorn had learned hard lessons enough in Hunnan's square. She was happy to teach a few.

So she gave Brand a mocking smile—her second favorite expression, after all—and screamed, "Come on, you coward!"

Brand was strong as a bull, and had plenty of fight in him, but he was limping, and tired, and Thorn had made sure the slope of the beach was on her side. She kept her eyes fixed on him, dodged one blow, and another, then slipped around a clumsy overhead to leave his side open. *The best place to sheathe a blade is in your enemy's back,* her father always said, but the side was almost as good. Her wooden sword thudded into Brand's ribs with a thwack like a log splitting, left him tottering helpless, and Thorn grinning wider than ever. There's no feeling in the world so sweet as hitting someone just right.

She planted the sole of her boot on his arse, shoved him splashing down on his hands and knees in the latest wave, and on its hissing way out it caught his sword and washed it down the beach, left it mired among the weeds.

She stepped close and Brand winced up at her, wet hair plastered to one side of his face and his teeth bloodied from the butt she gave him before. Maybe she should've felt sorry for him. But it had been a long time since Thorn could afford to feel sorry.

Instead she pressed her notched wooden blade into his neck and said, "Well?"

"All right." He waved her weakly away, hardly able to get the breath to speak. "I'm done."

"Ha!" she shouted in his face.

"Ha!" she shouted at the crestfallen lads about the square.

"Ha!" she shouted at Master Hunnan, and she thrust up her sword and shield in triumph and shook them at the spitting sky.

A few limp claps and mutters and that was it. There'd been far more generous applause for far meaner victories, but Thorn wasn't there for applause.

She was there to win.

Sometimes a girl is touched by Mother War, and put among the boys in the training square, and taught to fight. Among the smaller children there are always a few, but with each year that passes they turn to more suitable things, then are turned to them, then shouted and bullied and beaten to them, until the shameful weeds are rooted out and only the glorious flower of manhood remains.

If Vanstermen crossed the border, if Islanders landed on a raid, if thieves came in the night, the women of Gettland found blades soon enough, and fought to the death, and many of them damn well too. They always had. But the last time a woman passed the tests and swore the oaths and won a place on a raid?

There were stories. There were songs. But even Old Fen, who was the oldest person in Thorlby and, some said, the world, had never seen such a thing in all her countless days.

Not until now.

All that work. All that scorn. All that pain. But Thorn had beaten them. She closed her eyes, felt Mother Sea's salt wind kiss her sweaty face and thought how proud her father would be.

"I've passed," she whispered.

"Not yet." Thorn had never seen Master Hunnan smile. But she had never seen his frown quite so grim. "I decide the tests you'll take. I decide when you've passed." He looked over to the lads her age. The lads of sixteen, some already puffed with pride from passing their own tests. "Rauk. You'll fight Thorn next."

Rauk's brows went up, then he looked at Thorn and shrugged. "Why not?" he said, and stepped between his fellows into the square, strapping his shield tight and plucking up a practice sword.

He was a cruel one, and skillful. Not near as strong as Brand but a lot less likely to hesitate. Still, Thorn had beaten him before and she'd—

"Rauk," said Hunnan, his knobble-knuckled finger wandering on, "and Sordaf, and Edwal."

The glow of triumph drained from Thorn like the slops from a broken bath. There was a muttering among the lads as Sordaf—big, slow and with scant imagination, but a hell of a choice for stomping on someone who was down—lumbered out onto the sand, doing up the buckles on his mail with fat fingers.

Edwal—quick and narrow-shouldered with a tangle of brown curls—didn't move right off. Thorn had always thought he was one of the better ones. "Master Hunnan, three of us—"

"If you want a place on the king's raid," said Hunnan, "you'll do as you're bid."

They all wanted a place. They wanted one almost as much as Thorn did. Edwal frowned left and right, but no one spoke up. Reluctantly he slipped between the others and picked out a wooden sword.

"This isn't fair." Thorn was used to always wearing a brave face, no matter how long the odds, but her voice then was a desperate bleat. Like a lamb herded helpless to the slaughterman's knife.

Hunnan dismissed it with a snort. "This square is the battlefield, girl, and the battlefield isn't fair. Consider that your last lesson here."

There were some stray chuckles at that. Probably from some of those she'd shamed with beatings one time or another. Brand watched from behind a few loose strands of hair, one hand nursing his bloody mouth. Others kept their eyes to the ground. They all knew it wasn't fair. They didn't care.

Thorn set her jaw, put her shield hand to the pouch around her neck and squeezed it tight. It had been her against the world for longer than she could remember. If Thorn was one thing, she was a fighter. She'd give them a fight they wouldn't soon forget.

Rauk jerked his head to the others and they began to spread out, aiming to surround her. Might not be the worst thing. If she struck fast enough she could pick one off from the herd, give herself some splinter of a chance against the other two.

She looked in their eyes, trying to judge what they'd do. Edwal reluctant, hanging back. Sordaf watchful, shield up. Rauk letting his sword dangle, showing off to the crowd.

Just get rid of his smile. Turn that bloody and she'd be satisfied.

His smile buckled when she gave the fighting scream. Rauk caught her first blow on his shield, giving ground, and a second too, splinters flying, then she tricked him with her eyes so he lifted his shield high, went low at the last moment and caught him a scything blow in his hip. He cried out, twisting sideways so the back of his head was to her. She was already lifting her sword again.

There was a flicker at the corner of her eye and a sick crunch. She hardly felt as if she fell. But suddenly the sand was roughing her up pretty good, then she was staring stupidly at the sky.

There's your problem with going for one and ignoring the other two.

Gulls called above, circling.

The towers of Thorlby cut out black against the bright sky.

Best get up, her father said. *Won't win anything on your back.*

Thorn rolled, lazy, clumsy, pouch slipping from her collar and swinging on its cord, her face one great throb.

Water surged cold up the beach and around her knees and she saw Sordaf stamp down, heard a crack like a stick breaking.

She tried to scramble up and Rauk's boot thudded into her ribs and rolled her over, coughing.

The wave sucked back and sank away, blood tickling at her top lip, dripping pit-patter on the wet sand.

"Should we stop?" she heard Edwal say.

"Did I say stop?" came Hunnan's voice, and Thorn closed her fist tight around the grip of her sword, gathering one more effort.

She saw Rauk step toward her and she caught his leg as he kicked, hugged it to her chest. She jerked up hard, growling in his face, and he tumbled over backward, arms flailing.

She tottered at Edwal, more falling than charging, Mother Sea and Father Earth and Hunnan's frown and the faces of the watching lads all tipping and reeling. He caught her, more holding her up than trying to put her down. She grabbed at his shoulder, wrist twisted, sword torn from her hand as she stumbled past, floundering onto her knees and up again, her shield flapping at her side on its torn strap as she turned, spitting and cursing, and froze.

Sordaf stood, sword dangling limp, staring.

Rauk lay propped on his elbows on the wet sand, staring.

Brand stood among the other boys, mouth hanging open, all of them staring.

Edwal opened his mouth but all that came out was a strange squelch like a fart. He dropped his practice blade and lifted a clumsy hand to paw at his neck.

The hilt of Thorn's sword was there. The wooden blade had broken to leave a long shard when Sordaf stamped on it. The shard was through Edwal's throat, the point glistening red.

"Gods," someone whispered.

Edwal slumped down on his knees and drooled bloody froth onto the sand.

Master Hunnan caught him as he pitched onto his side. Brand and some of the others gathered around them, all shouting over each other. Thorn could hardly pick out the words over the thunder of her own heart.

She stood swaying, face throbbing, hair torn loose and whipping in her eyes with the wind, wondering if this was all a nightmare. Sure it must be. Praying it might be. She squeezed her eyes shut, squeezed them, squeezed them.

As she had when they led her to her father's body, white and cold beneath the dome of the Godshall.

But that had been real, and so was this.

When she snapped her eyes open the lads were still kneeling around Edwal so all she could see was his limp boots fallen outward. Black streaks came curling down the sand, then Mother Sea sent a wave and turned them red, then pink, then they were washed away and gone.

And for the first time in a long time Thorn felt truly scared.

Hunnan slowly stood, slowly turned. He always frowned, hardest of all at her. But there was a brightness in his eyes now she had never seen before.

"Thorn Bathu." He pointed at her with one red finger. "I name you a murderer."

IN THE SHADOWS

"Do good," Brand's mother said to him the day she died. "Stand in the light."

He'd hardly understood what doing good meant at six years old. He wasn't sure he was much closer at sixteen. Here he was, after all, wasting what should have been his proudest moment, still trying to puzzle out the good thing to do.

It was a high honor to stand guard on the Black Chair. To be accepted as a warrior of Gettland in the sight of gods and men. He'd struggled for it, hadn't he? Bled for it? Earned his place? As long as Brand could remember, it had been his dream to stand armed among his brothers on the hallowed stones of the Godshall.

But he didn't feel like he was standing in the light.

"I worry about this raid on the Islanders," Father Yarvi was saying, bringing the argument in a circle, as ministers always seemed to. "The High King has forbidden swords to be drawn. He will take it very ill."

"The High King forbids everything," said Queen Laithlin, one hand on her child-swollen belly, "and takes everything ill."

Beside her, King Uthil shifted forward in the Black Chair. "Meanwhile he orders the Islanders and the Vanstermen and any other curs he can bend to his bidding to draw their swords against us."

A surge of anger passed through the great men and women of Gettland gathered before the dais. A week before Brand's voice would've been loudest among them.

But all he could think of now was Edwal with the wooden sword through his neck, drooling red as he made that honking pig sound. The last he'd ever make. And Thorn, swaying on the sand with her hair stuck across her blood-smeared face, jaw hanging open as Hunnan named her a murderer.

"Two of my ships taken!" A merchant's jewelled key bounced on her chest as she shook her fist toward the dais. "And not just cargo lost but men dead!"

"And the Vanstermen have crossed the border again!" came a deep shout from the men's side of the hall, "and burned steadings and taken good folk of Gettland as slaves!"

"Grom-gil-Gorm was seen there!" someone shouted, and the mere mention of the name filled the dome of the Godshall with muttered curses. "The Breaker of Swords himself!"

"The Islanders must pay in blood," growled an old one-eyed warrior, "then the Vanstermen, and the Breaker of Swords too."

"Of course they must!" called Yarvi to the grumbling crowd, his shrivelled crab-claw of a left hand held up for calm, "but when and how is the question. The wise wait for their moment, and we are by no means ready for war with the High King."

"One is always ready for war." Uthil gently twisted the pommel of his sword so the naked blade flashed in the gloom. "Or never."

Edwal had always been ready. A man who stood for the man beside him, just as a warrior of Gettland was supposed to. Surely he hadn't deserved to die for that?

Thorn cared for nothing past the end of her own nose, and her shield rim in Brand's still-aching balls had raised her no higher in his affections. But she'd fought to the last, against the odds, just as a warrior of Gettland was supposed to. Surely she didn't deserve to be named murderer for that?

He glanced guiltily up at the great statues of the six tall gods, towering in judgment over the Black Chair. Towering in judgment over him. He squirmed as though he was the one who'd killed Edwal and named Thorn a murderer. All he'd done was watch.

Watch and do nothing.

"The High King could call half the world to war with us," Father Yarvi was saying, patiently as a master-at-arms explains the basics to children. "The Vanstermen and the Throvenmen are sworn to him, the Inglings and the Lowlanders are praying to his One God, Grandmother Wexen is forging alliances in the south as well. We are hedged in by enemies and we must have friends to—"

"Steel is the answer." King Uthil cut his minister off with a voice sharp as a blade. "Steel must always be the answer. Gather the men of Gettland. We will teach these carrion-pecking Islanders a lesson they will not soon forget." On the right side of the hall the frowning men beat their approval on mailed chests, and on the left the women with their oiled hair shining murmured their angry support.

Father Yarvi bowed his head. It was his task to speak for Father Peace but even he was out of words. Mother War ruled today. "Steel it is."

Brand should've thrilled at that. A great raid, like in the songs, and him with a warrior's place in it! But he was still trapped beside the training square, picking at the scab of what he could've done differently.

If he hadn't hesitated. If he'd struck without pity, like a warrior was supposed to, he could've beaten Thorn, and there it would've ended. Or if he'd spoken up with Edwal when Hunnan set three on one, perhaps together they could've stopped it. But he hadn't spoken up. Facing an enemy on the battlefield took courage, but you had your friends beside you. Standing alone against your friends, that was a different kind of courage. One Brand didn't pretend to have.

"And then we have the matter of Hild Bathu," said Father Yarvi, the name bringing Brand's head jerking up like a thief's caught with his hand round a purse.

"Who?" asked the king.

"Storn Headland's daughter," said Queen Laithlin. "She calls herself Thorn."

"She's done more than prick a finger," said Father Yarvi. "She killed a boy in the training square and is named a murderer."

"Who names her so?" called Uthil.

"I do." Master Hunnan's golden cloak-buckle gleamed as he stepped into the shaft of light at the foot of the dais.

"Master Hunnan." A rare smile touched the corner of the king's mouth. "I remember well our bouts together in the training square."

"Treasured memories, my king, though painful ones for me."

"Ha! You saw this killing?"

"I was testing my eldest students to judge those worthy to join your raid. Thorn Bathu was among them."

"She embarrasses herself, trying to take a warrior's place!" one woman called.

"She embarrasses us all," said another.

"A woman has no place on the battlefield!" came a gruff voice from among the men, and heads nodded on both sides of the room.

"Is Mother War herself not a woman?" The king pointed up at the Tall Gods looming over them. "We only offer her the choice. The Mother of Crows picks the worthy."

"And she did not pick Thorn Bathu," said Hunnan. "The girl has a poisonous temper." Very true. "She failed the test I set her." Partly true. "She lashed out against my judgment and killed the boy Edwal." Brand blinked. Not quite a lie, but far from all the truth. Hunnan's gray beard wagged as he shook his head. "And so I lost two pupils."

"Careless of you," said Father Yarvi.

The master-at-arms bunched his fists but Queen Laithlin spoke first. "What would be the punishment for such a murder?"

"To be crushed with stones, my queen." The minister spoke calmly, as if they considered crushing a beetle, not a person, and that a person Brand had known most of his life. One he'd disliked almost as long, but even so.

"Will anyone here speak for Thorn Bathu?" thundered the king.

The echoes of his voice faded to leave the silence of a tomb. Now was the time to tell the truth. To do good. To stand in the light. Brand looked across the Godshall, the words tickling at his lips. He saw Rauk in his place, smiling. Sordaf too, his doughy face a mask. They didn't make the faintest sound.

And nor did Brand.

"It is a heavy thing to order the death of one so young." Uthil stood from the Black Chair, mail rattling and skirts rustling as everyone but the queen knelt. "But we cannot turn from the right thing simply because it is a painful thing."

Father Yarvi bowed still lower. "I will dispense your justice according to the law."

Uthil held his hand out to Laithlin, and together they came down the steps of the dais. On the subject of Thorn Bathu, crushing with rocks was the last word.

Brand stared in sick disbelief. He'd been sure among all those lads someone would speak, for they were honest enough. Or Hunnan would tell his part in it, for he was a respected master-at-arms. The king or the queen would draw out the truth, for they were wise and righteous. The gods wouldn't allow such an injustice to pass. Someone would do something.

Maybe, like him, they were all waiting for someone else to put things right.

The king walked stiffly, drawn sword cradled in his arms, his iron-gray stare wavering neither right nor left. The queen's slightest nods were received like gifts, and with the odd word she let it be known that this person or that should enjoy the favor of visiting her counting house upon some deep business. They came closer, and closer yet.

Brand's heart beat loud in his ears. His mouth opened. The queen turned her freezing gaze on him for an instant, and in shamed and shameful silence he let the pair of them sweep past.

His sister was always telling him it wasn't up to him to put the world right. But if not him, who?

"Father Yarvi!" he blurted, far too loud, and then, as the minister turned toward him, croaked far too soft, "I need to speak to you."

"What about, Brand?" That gave him pause. He hadn't thought Yarvi would have the vaguest notion who he was.

"About Thorn Bathu."

A long silence. The minister might only have been a few years older than Brand, pale-skinned and pale-haired as if the color was washed out of him, so gaunt a stiff breeze might blow him away and with a crippled hand besides, but close up there was something chilling in the minister's eye. Something that caused Brand to wilt under his gaze.

But there was no going back, now. "She's no murderer," he muttered.

"The king thinks she is."

Gods, his throat felt dry, but Brand pressed on, the way a warrior was supposed to. "The king wasn't on the sands. The king didn't see what I saw."

"What did you see?"

"We were fighting to win places on the raid—"

"Never again tell me what I already know."

This wasn't running near as smoothly as Brand had hoped. But so it goes, with hopes. "Thorn fought me, and I hesitated . . . she should've won her place. But Master Hunnan set three others on her."

Yarvi glanced toward the people flowing steadily out of the Gods-hall, and eased a little closer. "Three at once?"

"Edwal was one of them. She never meant to kill him—"

"How did she do against those three?"

Brand blinked, wrong-footed. "Well . . . she killed more of them than they did of her."

"That's in no doubt. I was but lately consoling Edwal's parents, and promising them justice. She is sixteen winters, then?"

"Thorn?" Brand wasn't sure what that had to do with her sentence. "I . . . think she is."

"And has held her own in the square all this time against the boys?" He gave Brand a look up and down. "Against the men?"

"Usually she does better than hold her own."

"She must be very fierce. Very determined. Very hard-headed."

"From what I can tell her head's bone all the way through." Brand realized he wasn't helping and mumbled weakly, "but . . . she's not a bad person."

"None are, to their mothers." Father Yarvi pushed out a heavy sigh. "What would you have me do?"

"What . . . would I what?"

"Do I free this troublesome girl and make enemies of Hunnan and the boy's family, or crush her with stones and appease them? Your solution?"

Brand hadn't expected to give a solution. "I suppose . . . you should follow the law?"

"The law?" Father Yarvi snorted. "The law is more Mother Sea than Father Earth, always shifting. The law is a mummer's puppet, Brand, it says what I say it says."

"Just thought I should tell someone . . . well . . . the truth?"

"As if the truth is precious. I can find a thousand truths under every autumn leaf, Brand: everyone has their own. But you thought no further than passing the burden of your truth to me, did you? My epic thanks, preventing Gettland sliding into war with the whole Shattered Sea gives me not enough to do."

"I thought . . . this was doing good." Doing good seemed of a sudden less a burning light before him, clear as Mother Sun, and more a tricking glimmer in the murk of the Godshall.

"Whose good? Mine? Edwal's? Yours? As we each have our own truth so we each have our own good." Yarvi edged a little closer, spoke a little softer. "Master Hunnan may guess you shared your truth with me, what then? Have you thought on the consequences?"

They settled on Brand now, cold as a fall of fresh snow. He looked up, saw the gleam of Rauk's eye in the shadows of the emptying hall.

"A man who gives all his thought to doing good, but no thought to the consequences . . ." Father Yarvi lifted his withered hand and pressed its one crooked finger into Brand's chest. "That is a dangerous man."

And the minister turned away, the butt of his elf staff tapping against stones polished to glass by the passage of years, leaving Brand to stare wide-eyed into the gloom, more worried than ever.

He didn't feel like he was standing in the light at all.

JUSTICE

Thorn sat and stared down at her filthy toes, pale as maggots in the darkness.

She had no notion why they took her boots. She was hardly going to run, chained by her left ankle to one damp-oozing wall and her right wrist to the other. She could scarcely reach the gate of her cell, let alone rip it from its hinges. Apart from picking the scabs under her broken nose till they bled, all she could do was sit and think.

Her two least favorite activities.

She heaved in a ragged breath. Gods, the place stank. The rotten straw and the rat droppings stank and the bucket they never bothered to empty stank and the mold and rusting iron stank and after two nights in there she stank worst of all.

Any other day she would've been swimming in the bay, fighting Mother Sea, or climbing the cliffs, fighting Father Earth, or running or rowing or practicing with her father's old sword in the yard of their house, fighting the blade-scarred posts and pretending they were Gettland's enemies as the splinters flew—Grom-gil-Gorm, or Styr of the Islands, or even the High King himself.

But she would swing no sword today. She was starting to think she had swung her last. It seemed a long, hard way from fair. But then, as Hunnan said, fair wasn't a thing a warrior could rely on.

"You've a visitor," said the key-keeper, a weighty lump of a woman with a dozen rattling chains about her neck and a face like a bag of axes. "But you'll have to make it quick." And she hauled the heavy door squealing open.

"Hild!"

This once Thorn didn't tell her mother she'd given that name up at six years old, when she pricked her father with his own dagger and he called her "thorn." It took all the strength she had to unfold her legs and stand, sore and tired and suddenly, pointlessly ashamed of the state she was in. Even if she hardly cared for how things looked, she knew her mother did.

When Thorn shuffled into the light her mother pressed one pale hand to her mouth. "Gods, what did they do to you?"

Thorn waved at her face, chains rattling. "This happened in the square."

Her mother came close to the bars, eyes rimmed with weepy pink. "They say you murdered a boy."

"It wasn't murder."

"You killed a boy, though?"

Thorn swallowed, dry throat clicking. "Edwal."

"Gods," whispered her mother again, lip trembling. "Oh, gods, Hild, why couldn't you . . ."

"Be someone else?" Thorn finished for her. Someone easy, someone normal. A daughter who wanted to wield nothing weightier than a needle, dress in southern silk instead of mail, and harbor no dreams beyond wearing some rich man's key.

"I saw this coming," said her mother, bitterly. "Ever since you went to the square. Ever since we saw your father dead, I saw this coming."

Thorn felt her cheek twitch. "You can take comfort in how right you were."

"You think there's any comfort for me in this? They say they're going to crush my only child with stones!"

Thorn felt cold then, very cold. It was an effort to take a breath. As though they were piling the rocks on her already. "Who said?"

"Everyone says."

"Father Yarvi?" The minister spoke the law. The minister would speak the judgment.

"I don't know. I don't think so. Not yet."

Not yet, that was the limit of her hopes. Thorn felt so weak she could hardly grip the bars. She was used to wearing a brave face, however scared she was. But Death is a hard mistress to face bravely. The hardest.

"You'd best go." The key-keeper started to pull Thorn's mother away.

"I'll pray," she called, tears streaking her face. "I'll pray to Father Peace for you!"

Thorn wanted to say, "Damn Father Peace," but she could not find the breath. She had given up on the gods when they let her father die in spite of all her prayers, but a miracle was looking like her best chance.

"Sorry," said the key-keeper, shouldering shut the door.

"Not near as sorry as me." Thorn closed her eyes and let her forehead fall against the bars, squeezed hard at the pouch under her dirty shirt. The pouch that held her father's fingerbones.

We don't get much time, and time feeling sorry for yourself is time wasted. She kept every word he'd said close to her heart, but if there'd ever been a moment for feeling sorry for herself, this had to be the one. Hardly seemed like justice. Hardly seemed fair. But try telling Edwal about fair. However you shared out the blame, she'd killed him. Wasn't his blood crusted up her sleeve?

She'd killed Edwal. Now they'd kill her.

She heard talking, faint beyond the door. Her mother's voice— pleading, wheedling, weeping. Then a man's, cold and level. She couldn't quite catch the words, but they sounded like hard ones. She flinched as the door opened, jerking back into the darkness of her cell, and Father Yarvi stepped over the threshold.

He was a strange one. A man in a minister's place was almost as rare as a woman in the training square. He was only a few years Thorn's elder but he had an old eye. An eye that had seen things. They told strange stories of him. That he had sat in the Black Chair, but given it up. That he had sworn a deep-rooted oath of vengeance. That he had killed his Uncle Odem with the curved sword he always wore. They said he was cunning as Father Moon, a man rarely to be trusted and never to be crossed. And in his hands—or in his one good one, for the other was a crooked lump—her life now rested.

"Thorn Bathu," he said. "You are named a murderer."

All she could do was nod, her breath coming fast.

"Have you anything to say?"

Perhaps she should've spat her defiance. Laughed at Death. They said that was what her father did, when he lay bleeding his last at the feet of Grom-gil-Gorm. But all she wanted was to live.

"I didn't mean to kill him," she gurgled up. "Master Hunnan set three of them on me. It wasn't murder!"

"A fine distinction to Edwal."

True enough, she knew. She was blinking back tears, shamed at her own cowardice, but couldn't help it. How she wished she'd never gone to the square now, and learned to smile well and count coins like her mother always wanted. But you'll buy nothing with wishes.

"Please, Father Yarvi, give me a chance." She looked into his calm, cold, gray-blue eyes. "I'll take any punishment. I'll do any penance. I swear it!"

He raised one pale brow. "You should be careful what oaths you make, Thorn. Each one is a chain about you. I swore to be revenged on the killers of my father and the oath still weighs heavy on me. That one might come to weigh heavy on you."

"Heavier than the stones they'll crush me with?" She held her open palms out, as close to him as the chains would allow. "I swear a sun-oath and a moon-oath. I'll do whatever service you think fit."

The minister frowned at her dirty hands, reaching, reaching. He frowned at the desperate tears leaking down her face. He cocked his head slowly on one side, as though he was a merchant judging her value. Finally he gave a long, unhappy sigh. "Oh, very well."

There was a silence then, while Thorn turned over what he'd said. "You're not going to crush me with stones?"

He waved his crippled hand so the one finger flopped back and forth. "I have trouble lifting the big ones."

More silence, long enough for relief to give way to suspicion. "So . . . what's the sentence?"

"I'll think of something. Release her."

The jailer sucked her teeth as if opening any lock left a wound, but did as she was bid. Thorn rubbed at the chafe-marks the iron cuff left on her wrist, feeling strangely light without its weight. So light she wondered if she was dreaming. She squeezed her eyes shut, then grunted as the key-keeper tossed her boots over and they hit her in the belly. Not a dream, then.

She couldn't stop herself smiling as she pulled them on.

"Your nose looks broken," said Father Yarvi.

"Not the first time." If she got away from this with no worse than a broken nose she would count herself blessed indeed.

"Let me see."

A minister was a healer first, so Thorn didn't flinch when he came close, prodded gently at the bones under her eyes, brow wrinkled with concentration.

"Ah," she muttered.

"Sorry, did that hurt?"

"Just a litt—"

He jabbed one finger up her nostril, pressing his thumb mercilessly into the bridge of her nose. Thorn gasped, forced down onto her knees, there was a crack and a white-hot pain in her face, tears flooding more freely than ever.

"That got it," he said, wiping his hand on her shirt.

"Gods!" she whimpered, clutching her throbbing face.

"Sometimes a little pain now can save a great deal later." Father Yarvi was already walking for the door, so Thorn tottered up and, still wondering if this was some trick, crept after him.

"Thanks for your kindness," she muttered as she passed the key-keeper

The woman glared back. "I hope you never need it again."

"No offense, but so do I." And Thorn followed Father Yarvi along the dim corridor and up the steps, blinking into the light.

He might have had one hand but his legs worked well enough, setting quite a pace as he stalked across the yard of the citadel, the breeze making the branches of the old cedar whisper above them.

"I should speak to my mother—" she said, hurrying to catch up.

"I already have. I told her I had found you innocent of murder but you had sworn an oath to serve me."

"But . . . how did you know I'd—"

"It is a minister's place to know what people will do." Father Yarvi snorted. "As yet you are not too deep a well to fathom, Thorn Bathu."

They passed beneath the Screaming Gate, out of the citadel and into the city, down from the great rock and toward Mother Sea. They went by switching steps and narrow ways, sloping steeply between tight-crammed houses and the people tight-crammed between them.

"I'm not going on King Uthil's raid, am I?" A fool's question, doubtless, but now Thorn had stepped from Death's shadow there was light enough to mourn her ruined dreams.

Father Yarvi was not in a mourning mood. "Be thankful you're not going in the ground."

They passed down the Street of Anvils, where Thorn had spent long hours gazing greedily at weapons like a beggar child at pastries. Where she had ridden on her father's shoulders, giddy-proud as the smiths begged him to notice their work. But the bright metal set out before the forges only seemed to mock her now.

"I'll never be a warrior of Gettland." She said it soft and sorry, but Yarvi's ears were sharp.

"As long as you live, what you might come to be is in your own hands, first of all." The minister rubbed gently at some faded marks on his neck. "There is always a way, Queen Laithlin used to tell me."

Thorn found herself walking a little taller at the name alone. Laithlin might not be a fighter, but Thorn could think of no one she admired more. "The Golden Queen is a woman no man dares take lightly," she said.

"So she is." Yarvi looked at Thorn sidelong. "Learn to temper stubbornness with sense and maybe one day you will be the same."

It seemed that day was still some way off. Wherever they passed people bowed, and muttered softly, "Father Yarvi," and stepped aside to give the minister of Gettland room, but shook their heads darkly at Thorn as she skulked after him, filthy and disgraced, through the gates of the city and out onto the swarming dockside. They wove between sailors and merchants from every nation around the Shattered Sea and some much farther off, Thorn ducking under fishermen's dripping nets and around their glittering, squirming catches.

"Where are we going?" she asked.

"Skekenhouse."

She stopped short, gaping, and was nearly knocked flat by a passing barrow. She had never in her life been further than a half-day's walk from Thorlby.

"Or you could stay here," Yarvi tossed over his shoulder. "They have the stones ready."

She swallowed, then hurried again to catch him up. "I'll come."

"You are as wise as you are beautiful, Thorn Bathu."

That was either a double compliment or a double insult, and she suspected the latter. The old planks of the wharf clonked under their boots, salt water slapping at the green-furred supports below. A ship rocked beside it, small but sleek and with white-painted doves mounted at high prow and stern. Judging by the bright shields ranged down each side, it was manned and ready to sail.

"We're going now?" she asked.

"I am summoned by the High King."

"The High . . . King?" She looked down at her clothes, stiff with dungeon filth, crusted with her blood and Edwal's. "Can I change, at least?"

"I have no time for your vanity."

"I stink."

"We will haul you behind the ship to wash away the reek."

"You will?"

The minister raised one brow at her. "You have no sense of humor, do you?"

"Facing Death can sap your taste for jokes," she muttered.

"That's the time you need it most." A thickset old man was busy casting off the prow rope, and tossed it aboard as they walked up. "But don't worry. Mother Sea will have given you more washing than you can stomach by the time we reach Skekenhouse." He was a fighter: Thorn could tell that from the way he stood, his broad face battered by weather and war.

"The gods saw fit to take my strong left hand." Yarvi held up his twisted claw and wiggled the one finger. "But they gave me Rulf instead." He clapped it down on the old man's meaty shoulder. "Though it hasn't always been easy, I find myself content with the bargain."

Rulf raised one tangled brow. "D'you want to know how I feel about it?"

"No," said Yarvi, hopping aboard the ship. Thorn could only shrug at the gray-bearded warrior and hop after. "Welcome to the *South Wind*."

She worked her mouth and spat over the side. "I don't feel too welcome."

Perhaps forty grizzled-looking oarsmen sat upon their sea chests, glaring at her, and she had no doubts what they were thinking. *What is this girl doing here?*

"Some ugly patterns keep repeating," she murmured.

Father Yarvi nodded. "Such is life. It is a rare mistake you make only once."

"Can I ask a question?"

"I have the sense that if I said no, you would ask anyway."

"I'm not too deep a well to fathom, I reckon."

"Then speak."

"What am I doing here?"

"Why, holy men and deep-cunning women have been asking that question for a thousand years and never come near an answer."

"Try talking to Brinyolf the Prayer-Weaver on the subject," grunted Rulf, pushing them clear of the wharf with the butt of a spear. "He'll bore your ears off with his talk of whys and wherefores."

"Who is it indeed," muttered Yarvi, frowning off toward the far horizon as though he could see the answers written in the clouds, "that can plumb the gods' grand design? Might as well ask where the elves went!" And the old man and the young grinned at each other. Plainly this act was not new to them.

"Very good," said Thorn. "I mean, why have you brought me onto this ship?"

"Ah." Yarvi turned to Rulf. "Why do you think, rather than taking the easy road and crushing her, I have endangered all our lives by bringing the notorious killer Thorn Bathu onto my ship?"

Rulf leaned on his spear a moment, scratching at his beard. "I've really no idea."

Yarvi looked at Thorn with his eyes very wide. "If I don't share my thinking with my own left hand, why ever would I share it with the likes of you? I mean to say, you stink."

Thorn rubbed at her temples. "I need to sit down."

Rulf put a fatherly hand on her shoulder. "I understand." He shoved her onto the nearest chest so hard she went squawking over the back of it and into the lap of the man behind. "This is your oar."

FAMILY

"You're late."

Rin was right. Father Moon was smiling bright, and his children the stars twinkling on heaven's cloth, and the narrow hovel was lit only by the embers of the fire when Brand ducked through the low doorway.

"Sorry, sister." He went in a stoop to his bench and sank down with a long groan, worked his aching feet from his boots and spread his toes at the warmth. "But Harper had more peat to cut, then Old Fen needed help carrying some logs in. Wasn't like she was chopping them herself, and her ax was blunt so I had to sharpen it, and on the way back Lem's cart had broke an axle so a few of us helped out—"

"Your trouble is you make everyone's trouble your trouble."

"You help folk, maybe when you need it they'll help you."

"Maybe." Rin nodded toward the pot sitting over the embers of the fire. "There's dinner. The gods know, leaving some hasn't been easy."

He slapped her on the knee as he leaned to get it. "But bless you for it, sister." Brand was fearsome hungry, but he remembered to mutter a thanks to Father Earth for the food. He remembered how it felt to have none.

"It's good," he said, forcing it down.

"It was better right after I cooked it."

"It's still good."

"No, it's not."

He shrugged as he scraped the pot out, wishing there was more. "Things'll be different now I've passed the tests. Folk come back rich from a raid like this one."

"Folk come to the forge before every raid telling us how rich they're going to be. Sometimes they don't come back."

Brand grinned at her. "You won't get rid of me that easily."

"I'm not aiming to. Fool though y'are, you're all the family I've got." She dug something from behind her and held it out. A bundle of animal skin, stained and tattered.

"For me?" he said, reaching through the warmth above the dying fire for it.

"To keep you company on your high adventures. To remind you of home. To remind you of your family. Such as it is."

"You're all the family I need." There was a knife inside the bundle, polished steel gleaming. A fighting dagger with a long, straight blade, crosspiece worked like a pair of twined snakes and the pommel a snarling dragon's head.

Rin sat up, keen to see how her gift would sit with him. "I'll make you a sword one day. For now this was the best I could manage."

"You made this?"

"Gaden gave me some help with the hilt. But the steel's all mine."

"It's fine work, Rin." The closer he looked the better it got, every scale on the snakes picked out, the dragon baring little teeth at him, the steel bright as silver and holding a deadly edge too. He hardly dared touch it. It seemed too good a thing for his dirty hands. "Gods, it's master's work."

She sat back, careless, as though she'd known that all along. "I think I've found a better way to do the smelting. A hotter way. In a clay jar, sort of. Bone and charcoal to bind the iron into steel, sand and glass to coax the dirt out and leave it pure. But it's all about the heat . . . You're not listening."

Brand gave a sorry shrug. "I can swing a hammer all right but I don't understand the magic of it. You're ten times the smith I ever was."

"Gaden says I'm touched by She who Strikes the Anvil."

"She must be happy as the breeze I quit the forge and she got you as an apprentice."

"I've a gift."

"The gift of modesty."

"Modesty is for folk with nothing to boast of."

He weighed the dagger in his hand, feeling out the fine heft and balance to it. "My little sister, mistress of the forge. I never had a better gift." Not that he'd had many. "Wish I had something to give you in return."

She lay back on her bench and shook her threadbare blanket over her legs. "You've given me everything I've got."

He winced. "Not much, is it?"

"I've no complaints." She reached across the fire with her strong hand, scabbed and calloused from forge-work, and he took it, and they gave each other a squeeze.

He cleared his throat, looking at the hard-packed earth of the floor. "Will you be all right while I'm gone on this raid?"

"I'll be like a swimmer who just shrugged her armor off." She gave him the scornful face but he saw straight through it. She was fifteen years old, and he was all the family she had, and she was scared, and that made him scared too. Scared of fighting. Scared of leaving home. Scared of leaving her alone.

"I'll be back, Rin. Before you know it."

"Loaded with treasures, no doubt."

He winked. "Songs sung of my high deeds and a dozen fine Islander slaves to my name."

"Where will they sleep?"

"In the great stone house I'll buy you up near the citadel."

"I'll have a room for my clothes," she said, stroking at the wattle wall with her fingertips. Wasn't much of a home they had, but the gods knew they were grateful for it. There'd been times they had nothing over their heads but weather.

Brand lay down too, knees bent since his legs hung way off the end of his bench these days, started unrolling his own smelly scrap of blanket.

"Rin," he found he'd said, "I might've done a stupid thing." He wasn't much at keeping secrets. Especially from her.

"What this time?"

He set to picking at one of the holes in his blanket. "Told the truth."

"What about?"

"Thorn Bathu."

Rin clapped her hands over her face. "What is it with you and her?"

"What d'you mean? I don't even like her."

"No one likes her. She's a splinter in the world's arse. But you can't seem to stop picking at her."

"The gods have a habit of pushing us together, I reckon."

"Have you tried walking the other way? She killed Edwal. She killed him. He's dead, Brand."

"I know. I was there. But it wasn't murder. What should I have done, tell me that, since you're the clever one. Kept my mouth shut with everyone else? Kept my mouth shut and let her be crushed with rocks? I couldn't carry the weight of that!" He realized he was near-shouting, anger bubbling up, and he pressed his voice back down. "I couldn't."

A silence, then, while they frowned at each other, and the fire sagged, sending up a puff of sparks. "Why does it always fall to you to put things right?" she asked.

"I guess no one else is doing it."

"You always were a good boy." Rin stared up toward the smoke-hole and the chink of starry sky showing through it. "Now you're a good man. That's your trouble. I never saw a better man for doing good things and getting bad results. Who'd you tell your tale to?"

He swallowed, finding the smoke-hole mightily interesting himself. "Father Yarvi."

"Oh, gods, Brand! You don't like half measures, do you?"

"Never saw the point of them," he muttered. "Dare say it'll all work out, though?" wheedling, desperate for her to tell him yes.

She just lay staring at the ceiling, so he picked her dagger up again, watched the bright steel shine with the colors of fire.

"Really is fine work, Rin."

"Go to sleep, Brand."

KNEELING

"If in doubt, kneel." Rulf's place as helmsman was the platform at the *South Wind*'s stern, steering oar wedged under one arm. "Kneel low and kneel often."

"Kneel," muttered Thorn. "Got it." She had one of the back oars, the place of most work and least honor, right beneath his ever-watchful eye. She kept twisting about, straining over her shoulder in her eagerness to see Skekenhouse, but there was a rainy mist in the air and she could make out nothing but ghosts in the murk. The looming phantoms of the famous elf-walls. The faintest wraith of the vast Tower of the Ministry.

"You might be best just shuffling around on your knees the whole time you're here," said Rulf. "And by the gods, keep your tongue still. Cause Grandmother Wexen some offense and crushing with stones will seem light duty."

Thorn saw figures gathered on the dock as they glided closer. The figures became men. The men became warriors. An honor guard, though they had more the flavor of a prison escort as the *South Wind* was tied off and Father Yarvi and his bedraggled crew clambered onto the rain-slick quay.

At sixteen winters Thorn was taller than most men but the one who stepped forward now might easily have been reckoned a giant, a full head taller than she was at least. His long hair and beard were darkened by rain and streaked with gray, the white fur about his shoulders beaded with dew.

"Why, Father Yarvi." His sing-song voice was strangely at odds with that mighty frame. "The seasons have turned too often since we traded words."

"Three years," said Yarvi, bowing. "That day in the Godshall, my king."

Thorn blinked. She had heard the High King was a withered old man, half-blind and scared of his own food. That assessment seemed decidedly unfair. She had learned to judge the strength of a man in the training square and she doubted she had ever seen one stronger. A warrior too, from his scars, and the many blades sheathed at his gold-buckled belt. Here was a man who looked a king indeed.

"I remember well," he said. "Everyone was so very, very rude to me. The hospitality of Gettlanders, eh, Mother Scaer?" A shaven-headed woman at his shoulder glowered at Yarvi and his crew as if they were heaps of dung. "And who is this?" he asked, eyes falling on Thorn.

At starting fights she was an expert, but all other etiquette was a mystery. When her mother had tried to explain how a girl should behave, when to bow and when to kneel and when to hold your key, she'd nodded along and thought about swords. But Rulf had said kneel, so she dropped clumsily down on the wet stones of the dock, scraping her sodden hair out of her face and nearly tripping over her own feet.

"My king. My high . . . king, that is—"

Yarvi snorted. "This is Thorn Bathu. My new jester."

"How is she working out?"

"Few laughs as yet."

The giant grinned. "I am but a low king, child. I am the little king of Vansterland, and my name is Grom-gil-Gorm."

Thorn felt her guts turn over. For years she had dreamed of meeting the man who killed her father. None of the dreams had worked out quite like this. She had knelt at the feet of the Breaker of Swords, the Maker of Orphans, Gettland's bitterest enemy, who even now was ordering raids across the border. About his thick neck she saw the chain, four times looped, of pommels twisted from the swords of his fallen enemies. One of them, she knew, from the sword she kept at home. Her most prized possession.

She slowly stood, trying to gather every shred of her ruined dignity. She had no sword-hilt to prop her hand on, but she thrust her chin up at him just as if it was a blade.

The King of Vansterland peered down like a great hound at a bristling kitten. "I am well accustomed to the scorn of Gettlanders, but this one has a cold eye upon her."

"As if she has a score to settle," said Mother Scaer.

Thorn gripped the pouch about her neck. "You killed my father."

"Ah." Gorm shrugged. "There are many children who might say so. What was his name?"

"Storn Headland."

She had expected taunts, threats, fury, but instead his craggy face lit up. "Ah, but that was a duel to sing of! I remember every step and cut of it. Headland was a great warrior, a worthy enemy! On chill mornings like that one I still feel the wound he gave me in my leg. But Mother War was by my side. She breathed upon me in my crib. It has been foreseen that no man can kill me, and so it has proved." He beamed down at Thorn, spinning one of the pommels idly around and around on his chain between great finger and thumb. "Storn Headland's daughter, grown so tall! The years turn, eh, Mother Scaer?"

"Always," said the minister, staring at Thorn through blue, blue narrowed eyes.

"But we cannot pick over old glories all day." Gorm swept his hand out with a flourish to offer them the way. "The High King awaits, Father Yarvi."

Grom-gil-Gorm led them across the wet docks and Thorn slunk after, cold, wet, bitter, and powerless, the excitement of seeing the Shattered Sea's greatest city all stolen away. If you could kill a man by frowning at his back, the Breaker of Swords would have fallen bloody through the Last Door that day, but a frown is no blade, and Thorn's hatred cut no one but her.

Through a pair of towering doors trudged the *South Wind*'s crew, into a hallway whose walls were covered from polished floor to lofty ceiling with weapons. Ancient swords, eaten with rust. Spears with hafts shattered. Shields hacked and splintered. The weapons that once belonged to the mountain of corpses Bail the Builder climbed to his place as the first High King. The weapons of armies his successors butchered spreading their power from Yutmark into the Lowlands, out to Inglefold and halfway around the Shattered Sea. Hundreds of years of victories, and though swords and axes and cloven helms had no voice, together they spoke a message more eloquent than any minister's whisper, more deafening than any master-at-arms' bellow.

Resisting the High King is a very poor idea.

"I must say it surprises me," Father Yarvi was saying, "to find the Breaker of Swords serving as the High King's doorman."

Gorm frowned sideways. "We all must kneel to someone."

"Some of us kneel more easily than others, though."

Gorm frowned harder but his minister spoke first. "Grandmother Wexen can be most persuasive."

"Has she persuaded you to pray to the One God, yet?" asked Yarvi.

Scaer gave a snort so explosive it was a wonder she didn't blow snot down her chest.

"Nothing will pry me from the bloody embrace of Mother War," growled Gorm. "That much I promise you."

Yarvi smiled as if he chatted with friends. "My uncle uses just

those words. There is so much that unites Gettland and Vansterland.
We pray the same way, speak the same way, fight the same way. Only
a narrow river separates us."

"And hundreds of years of dead fathers and dead sons," muttered
Thorn, under her breath.

"Shush," hissed Rulf, beside her.

"We have a bloody past," said Yarvi. "But good leaders must put
the past at their backs and look to the future. The more I think on it,
the more it seems our struggles only weaken us both and profit others."

"So after all our battles shall we link arms?" Thorn saw the corner
of Gorm's mouth twisted in a smile. "And dance over our dead together into your brave future?"

Smiles, and dancing, and Thorn glanced to the weapons on the
walls, wondering whether she could tear a sword from its brackets
and stove Gorm's skull in before Rulf stopped her. There would be a
deed worthy of a warrior of Gettland.

But then Thorn wasn't a warrior of Gettland, and never would be.

"You weave a pretty dream, Father Yarvi." Gorm puffed out a
sigh. "But you wove pretty dreams for me once before. We all must
wake, and whether it pleases us to kneel or no, the dawn belongs to
the High King."

"And to his minister," said Mother Scaer.

"To her most of all." And the Breaker of Swords pushed wide the
great doors at the hallway's end.

Thorn remembered the one time she had stood in Gettland's
Godshall, staring at her father's pale, cold corpse, trying to squeeze
her mother's hand hard enough that she would stop sobbing. It had
seemed the biggest room in the world, too big for man's hands to have
built. But elf hands had built the Chamber of Whispers. Five Gods-
halls could have fit inside with floor left over to plant a decent crop of
barley. Its walls of smooth elf-stone and black elf-glass rose up, and
up, and were lost in the dizzying gloom above.

Six towering statues of the tall gods frowned down, but the High

King had turned from their worship and his masons had been busy. Now a seventh stood above them all. The southerners' god, the One God, neither man nor woman, neither smiling nor weeping, arms spread wide in a smothering embrace, gazing down with bland indifference upon the petty doings of mankind.

People were crowded about the far-off edges of the floor, and around a balcony of gray elf-metal at ten times the height of a man, and a ring of tiny faces at another as far above again. Thorn saw Vanstermen with braids in their long hair, Throvenmen with silver ring-money stacked high on their arms. She saw Islanders with weathered faces, stout Lowlanders and wild-bearded Inglings. She saw lean women she reckoned Shends and plump merchants of Sagenmark. She saw dark-faced emissaries from Catalia, or the Empire of the South, or even further off, maybe.

All the people in the world, it seemed, gathered with the one purpose of licking the High King's arse.

"Greatest of men!" called Father Yarvi, "between gods and kings! I prostrate myself before you!" And he near threw himself on his face, the echoes of his voice bouncing from the galleries above and shattering into the thousand thousand whispers which gave the hall its name.

The rumors had in fact been overly generous to the greatest of men. The High King was a shrivelled remnant in his outsize throne, withered face sagging off the bone, beard a few gray straggles. Only his eyes showed some sign of life, bright and flinty hard as he glared down at Gettland's minister.

"Now you kneel, fool!" hissed Rulf, dragging Thorn down beside him by her belt. And only just in time. An old woman was already walking out across the expanse of floor toward them.

She was round-faced and motherly, with deep laughter lines about her twinkling eyes, white hair cut short, her coarse gray gown dragging upon the floor so heavily its hem was frayed to dirty tatters. About her neck upon the finest chain, crackling papers scrawled with runes were threaded.

"We understand Queen Laithlin is with child." She might have looked no hero, but by the gods she spoke with a hero's voice. Deep, soft, effortlessly powerful. A voice that demanded attention. A voice that commanded obedience.

Even on his knees, Yarvi found a way to bow lower. "The gods have blessed her, most honored Grandmother Wexen."

"An heir to the Black Chair, perhaps?"

"We can but hope."

"Convey our warm congratulations to King Uthil," scratched out the High King, no trace of either warmth or congratulation on his withered face.

"I will be delighted to convey them, and they to receive them. May I rise?"

The first of ministers gave the warmest smile, and raised one palm, and tattooed upon it Thorn saw circles within circles of tiny writing.

"I like you there," she said.

"We hear troubling tales from the north," croaked out the High King, and curling back his lip licked at a yawning gap in his front teeth. "We hear King Uthil plans a great raid against the Islanders."

"A raid, my king?" Yarvi seemed baffled by what was common knowledge in Thorlby. "Against our much-loved fellows on the Islands of the Shattered Sea?" He waved his arm so his crippled hand flopped dismissively. "King Uthil is of a warlike temper, and speaks often in the Godshall of raiding this or that. It always comes to nothing for, believe me, I am ever at his side, smoothing the path for Father Peace, as Mother Gundring taught me."

Grandmother Wexen threw her head back and gave a peal of laughter, rich and sweet as treacle, echoes ringing out as if she were a chuckling army. "Oh, you're a funny one, Yarvi."

She struck him with a snake's speed. With an open hand, but hard enough to knock him on his side. The sound of it bounced from the balconies above sharp as a whip cracks.

Thorn's eyes went wide and without thinking she sprang to her feet. Or halfway there, at least. Rulf's hand shot out and caught a fistful of her damp shirt, dragging her back to her knees, her curse cut off in an ugly squawk.

"Down," he growled under his breath.

It felt suddenly a very lonely place, the center of that huge, empty floor, and Thorn realized how many armed men were gathered about it, and came over very dry in the mouth and very wet in the bladder.

Grandmother Wexen looked at her, neither scared nor angry. Mildly curious, as though at a kind of ant she did not recognize. "Who is this . . . person?"

"A humble halfwit, sworn to my service." Yarvi pushed himself back up as far as his knees, good hand to his bloody mouth. "Forgive her impudence, she suffers from too little sense and too much loyalty."

Grandmother Wexen beamed down as warmly as Mother Sun, but the ice in her voice froze Thorn to her bones. "Loyalty can be a great blessing or a terrible curse, child. It all depends on to whom one is loyal. There is a right order to things. There *must be* a right order, and you Gettlanders forget your place in it. The High King has forbidden swords to be drawn."

"I have forbidden it," echoed the High King, his own voice dwindled to a reedy rustling, hardly heard in the vastness.

"If you make war upon the Islanders you make war upon the High King and his ministry," said Grandmother Wexen. "You make war upon the Inglings and the Lowlanders, upon the Throvenmen and the Vanstermen, upon Grom-gil-Gorm, the Breaker of Swords, whom it has been foreseen no man can kill." She pointed out the murderer of Thorn's father beside the door, seeming far from comfortable on one great knee. "You even make war upon the Empress of the South, who has but lately pledged an alliance with us." Grandmother Wexen spread her arms wide to encompass the whole vast chamber, and its legion of occupants, and Father Yarvi and his shabby crew looked a feeble flock before them indeed. "Would you make war on half the world, Gettlanders?"

Father Yarvi grinned like a simpleton. "Since we are faithful servants of the High King, his many powerful friends can only be a reassurance."

"Then tell your uncle to stop rattling his sword. If he should draw it without the High King's blessing—"

"Steel shall be my answer," croaked the High King, watery eyes bulging.

Grandmother Wexen's voice took on an edge that made the hairs on Thorn's neck prickle. "And there shall be such a reckoning as has not been seen since the Breaking of the World."

Yarvi bowed so low he nearly nosed the floor. "Oh, highest and most gracious, who would wish to see such wrath released? Might I now stand?"

"First one more thing," came a soft voice from behind. A young woman walked toward them with quick steps, thin and yellow-haired and with a brittle smile.

"You know Sister Isriun, I think?" said Grandmother Wexen.

It was the first time Thorn had seen Yarvi lost for words. "I . . . you . . . joined the Ministry?"

"It is a fine place for the broken and dispossessed. You should know that." And Isriun pulled out a cloth and dabbed the blood from the corner of Yarvi's mouth. Gentle, her touch, but the look in her eye was anything but. "Now we are all one family, once again."

"She passed the test three months ago without one question wrong," said Grandmother Wexen. "She is already greatly knowledgeable on the subject of elf-relics."

Yarvi swallowed. "Fancy that."

"It is the Ministry's most solemn duty to protect them," said Isriun. "And to protect the world from a second breaking." Her thin hands fussed one with the other. "Do you know the thief and killer, Skifr?"

Yarvi blinked as though he scarcely understood the question. "I may have heard the name . . ."

"She is wanted by the Ministry." Isriun's expression had grown even deadlier. "She entered the elf-ruins of Strokom, and brought out relics from within."

A gasp hissed around the chamber, a fearful whispering echoed among the balconies. Folk made holy signs upon their chests, murmured prayers, shook their heads in horror.

"What times are we living in?" whispered Father Yarvi. "You have my solemn word, if I hear but the breath of this Skifr's passing, my doves will be with you upon the instant."

"Such a relief," said Isriun, "Because if anyone were to strike a deal with her, I would have to see them burned alive." She twisted her fingers together, gripping eagerly until the knuckles were white. "And you know how much I would hate to see you burn."

"So we have that in common too," said Yarvi. "May I now depart, oh, greatest of men?"

The High King appeared to have nodded sideways, quite possibly off to sleep.

"I will take that as a yes." Yarvi stood, and Rulf and his crew stood with him, and Thorn struggled up last. She seemed always to be kneeling when she had better stand and standing when she had better kneel.

"It is not too late to make of the fist an open hand, Father Yarvi." Grandmother Wexen sadly shook her head. "I once had high hopes for you."

"Alas, as Sister Isriun can tell you, I have often been a sore disappointment." There was just the slightest iron in Yarvi's voice as he turned. "I struggle daily to improve."

Outside the rain was falling hard, still making gray ghosts of Skekenhouse.

"Who was that woman, Isriun?" Thorn asked as she hurried to catch up.

"She was once my cousin." The muscles worked on the gaunt side of Yarvi's face. "Then we were betrothed. Then she swore to see me dead."

Thorn raised her brows at that. "You must be quite a lover."

"We cannot all have your gentle touch." He frowned sideways at her. "Next time you might think before leaping to my defense."

"The moment you pause will be the moment you die," she muttered.

"The moment you didn't pause you nearly killed the lot of us."

She knew he was right, but it still nettled her. "It might not have come to that if you'd told them the Islanders have attacked us, and the Vanstermen too, that they've given us no choice but to—"

"They know that well enough. It was Grandmother Wexen set them on."

"How do you—"

"She spoke thunderously in the words she did not say. She means to crush us, and I can put her off no longer."

Thorn rubbed at her temples. Ministers seemed never to mean quite what they said. "If she's our enemy, why didn't she just kill us where we knelt?"

"Because Grandmother Wexen does not want her children dead. She wants them to obey. First she sends the Islanders against us, then the Vanstermen. She hopes to lure us into rash action and King Uthil is about to oblige her. It will take time for her to gather her forces, but only because she has so many to call on. In time, she will send half the world against us. If we are to resist her, we need allies."

"Where do we find allies?"

Father Yarvi smiled. "Among our enemies, where else?"

DEAD MAN'S MAIL

The boys were gathered.

The *men* were gathered, Brand realized. There might not be much beard among them, but if they weren't men now they'd passed their tests and were about to swear their oaths, when would they be?

They were gathered one last time with Master Hunnan, who'd taught them, and tested them, and hammered them into shape like Brand used to hammer iron at Gaden's forge. They were gathered on the beach where they'd trained so often, but the blades weren't wooden now.

They were gathered in their new war-gear, bright-eyed and breathless at the thought of sailing on their first raid. Of leaving Father Peace at their backs and giving themselves guts and sinew to his red-mouthed wife, Mother War. Of winning fame and glory, a place at the king's table and in the warriors' songs.

Oh, and coming back rich.

Some were buckled up prettily as heroes already, blessed with family who'd bought them fine mail, and good swords, and new gear all aglitter. Though he counted her more blessing than he deserved,

Brand had only Rin, so he'd borrowed his mail from Gaden in return for a tenth share of aught he took—dead man's mail, tarnished with use, hastily resized and still loose under the arms. But his ax was good and true and polished sharp as a razor, and his shield that he'd saved a year for was fresh painted by Rin with a dragon's head and looked well as anyone's.

"Why a dragon?" Rauk asked him, one mocking eyebrow high.

Brand laughed it off. "Why not a dragon?" It'd take more than that fool's scorn to spoil the day of his first raid.

And it wasn't just any raid. It was the biggest in living memory. Bigger even that the one King Uthrik led to Sagenmark. Brand went up on tiptoe again to see the gathered men stretched far off down the shore, metal twinkling in the sun and the smoke from their fires smudging the sky. Five thousand, Hunnan had said, and Brand stared at his fingers, trying to reckon each a thousand men. It made him as dizzy as looking down a long drop.

Five thousand. Gods, how big the world must be.

There were men well-funded by tradesmen or merchants and ragged brotherhoods spilled down from the mountains. There were proud-faced men with silvered sword-hilts and dirty-faced men with spears of flint. There were men with a lifetime of scars and men who'd never shed blood in their lives.

It was a sight you didn't see often, and half of Thorlby was gathered on the slopes outside the city walls to watch. Mothers and fathers, wives and children, there to see off their boys and husbands and pray for their safe and enriched return. Brand's family would be there too, no doubt. Which meant Rin, on her own. He bunched his fists, staring up into the wind.

He'd make her proud. He swore he would.

The feeling was more of wedding-feast than war, the air thick with smoke and excitement, the clamor of songs, and jests, and arguments. Prayer-Weavers wove their own paths through the throng speaking blessings for a payment, and merchants too, spinning lies about how all great warriors carried an extra belt to war. It wasn't just warriors hoping to turn a coin from King Uthil's raid.

"For a copper I'll bring you weaponluck," said a beggar-woman, selling lucky kisses, "for another I'll bring you weatherluck too. For a third—"

"Shut up," snapped Master Hunnan, shooing her off. "The king speaks."

There was a clattering of gear as every man turned westward. Toward the barrows of long-dead rulers above the beach, dwindling away to the north into wind-flattened humps.

King Uthil stood tall before them on the dunes, the long grass twitching at his boots, cradling gently as a sick child his sword of plain gray steel. He needed no ornaments but the scars of countless battles on his face. Needed no jewels but the wild brightness in his eye. Here was a man who knew neither fear nor mercy. Here was a king that any warrior would be proud to follow to the very threshold of the Last Door and beyond.

Queen Laithlin stood beside him, hands on her swollen belly, golden key upon her chest, golden hair taken by the breeze and torn like a banner, showing no more fear or mercy than her husband. They said it was her gold that bought half these men and most of these ships, and she wasn't a woman to take her eye off an investment.

The king took two slow, swaggering steps forward, letting the breathless silence stretch out, excitement building until Brand could hear his own blood surging in his ears.

"Do I see some men of Gettland?" he roared.

Brand and his little knot of newly-minted warriors were lucky to be close enough to hear him. Further off the captains of each ship passed on the king's words to their crews, wind-blown echoes rippling down the long sweep of the shore.

A great clamor burst from the gathered warriors, weapons thrust up toward Mother Sun in a glittering forest. All united, all belonging. All ready to die for the man at their shoulder. Perhaps Brand had only one sister, but he felt then he had five thousand brothers with him on the sand, a sweet mixture of rage and love that wetted his eyes and warmed his heart and seemed in that moment a feeling worth dying for.

King Uthil raised his hand for silence. "How it gladdens me to see so many brothers! Wise old warriors often tested on the battlefield, and bold young warriors lately tested in the square. All gathered with good cause in the sight of the gods, in the sight of my forefathers." He spread his arms toward the ancient barrows. "And can they ever have looked on so mighty a host?"

"No!" someone screamed, and there was laughter, and others joined him, shouting wildly, "No!" Until the king raised his hand for silence again.

"The Islanders have sent ships against us. They have stolen from us, and made our children slaves, and spilled our blood on our good soil." A muttering of anger began. "It is they who turned their backs on Father Peace, they who opened the door to Mother War, they who made her our guest." The muttering grew, and swelled, an animal growling that found its way to Brand's own throat. "But the High King says we of Gettland must not be good hosts to the Mother of Crows! The High King says *our* swords must stay sheathed. The High King says we must suffer these insults in silence! Tell me, men of Gettland, what should be our answer?"

The word came from five thousand mouths as one deafening roar, Brand's voice cracking with it. "Steel!"

"Yes." Uthil cradled his sword close, pressing the plain hilt to his deep-lined cheek as if it was a lover's face. "Steel must be the answer! Let us bring the Islanders a red day, brothers. A day they will weep at the memory of!"

With that he stalked toward Mother Sea, his closest captains and the warriors of his household behind him, storied men with famous names, men Brand dreamed of one day joining. Folk whose names had yet to trouble the bards crowded about the king's path for a glimpse of him, for a touch of his cloak, a glance of his gray eye. Shouts came of, "The Iron King!" and "Uthil!" until it became a chant, "Uthil! Uthil!" each beat marked with the steely clash of weapons.

"Time to choose your futures, boys."

Master Hunnan shook a canvas bag so the markers clattered within. The lads crowded him, shoving and honking like hogs at feeding time, and Hunnan reached inside with his gnarled fingers and one by one pressed a marker into every eager palm. Discs of wood, each with a sign carved into it that matched the prow-beasts on the many ships, telling each boy—or each man—which captain he'd swear his oath to, which crew he'd sail with, row with, fight with.

Those given their signs held them high and whooped in triumph, and some argued over who'd got the better ship or the better captain, and some laughed and hugged each other, finding the favor of Mother War had made them oarmates.

Brand waited, hand out and heart thumping. Drunk with excitement at the king's words, and the thought of the raid coming, and of being a boy no more, being poor no more, being alone no more. Drunk on the thought of doing good, and standing in the light, and having a family of warriors always about him.

Brand waited as his fellows were given their places—lads he liked and lads he didn't, good fighters and not. He waited as the markers grew fewer in the bag, and let himself wonder if he was left till last because he'd won an oar on the king's own ship, no place more coveted. The more often Hunnan passed him over, the more he allowed himself to hope. He'd earned it, hadn't he? Worked for it, deserved it? Done what a warrior of Gettland was supposed to?

Rauk was the last of them, forcing a smile onto his crestfallen face when Hunnan brought wood from the bag for him, not silver. Then it was just Brand left. His the only hand still out, the fingers trembling. The lads fell silent.

And Hunnan smiled. Brand had never seen him smile before, and he felt himself smile too.

"This for you," said the master-at-arms as he slowly, slowly drew out his battle-scarred hand. Drew out his hand to show . . .

Nothing.

No glint of the king's silver. No wood neither. Only the empty bag, turned inside out to show the ragged stitching.

"Did you think I wouldn't know?" said Hunnan.

Brand let his hand drop. Every eye was upon him now and he felt his cheeks burning like he'd been slapped.

"Know what?" he muttered, though he knew well enough.

"That you spoke to that cripple about what happened in my training square."

A silence, while Brand felt as if his guts dropped into his arse. "Thorn's no murderer," he managed to say.

"Edwal's dead and she killed him."

"You set her a test she couldn't pass."

"I set the tests," said Hunnan. "Passing them is up to you. And you failed this one."

"I did the right thing."

Hunnan's brows went up. Not angry. Surprised. "Tell yourself that if it helps. But I've my own right thing to look to. The right thing for the men I teach to fight. In the training square we pit you against each other, but on the battlefield you have to stand together, and Thorn Bathu fights everyone. Men would have died so she could play with swords. They're better off without her. And they're better off without you."

"Mother War picks who fights," said Brand.

Hunnan only shrugged. "She can find a ship for you, then. You're a good fighter, Brand, but you're not a good man. A good man stands for his shoulder-man. A good man holds the line."

Maybe Brand should've snarled, "It isn't fair," as Thorn had when Hunnan broke her hopes. But Brand wasn't much of a talker, and he had no words then. No anger in him when he actually needed it. He didn't make even a mouse's squeak while Hunnan turned and walked away. Didn't even bunch his fists while the lads followed their master-at-arms toward the sea. The lads he'd trained with these ten years.

Some looked at him with scorn, some with surprise. One or two even gave him a sorry pat on the shoulder as they passed. But they all passed. Down the beach, toward the breaking waves and their hard-won places on the ships that rocked there. Down to their oaths of loyalty and off on the raid that Brand had dreamed of all his life. It was Rauk who went last, one hand slack on the hilt of his fine new sword, grinning over his shoulder.

"See you when we get back."

Brand stood alone for a long time, not moving. Alone, in his borrowed mail, with the gulls crying over that vast stretch of sand, empty apart from the bootprints of the men he'd thought his brothers. Alone, long after the last ship had pushed off from the shore and out to sea, carrying Brand's hopes away with it.

So it goes, with hopes.

POISON

She Who Sings the Wind sang one hell of a wind on the way over from Skekenhouse and they were washed leagues off-course.

They rowed like fury while Rulf roared abuse at them until his voice was hoarse and their oars were all tangled and every one of them was blowing like a fish and soaked with Mother Sea's salt spray. Thorn was quite extremely terrified but she put a brave face on. The only faces she had were brave, though this was a green one, as the thrashing of the ship like an unbroken horse soon made her sick as she'd never been sick in her life. It felt as if everything she'd ever eaten went over the side, over her oar, or over her knees, and half that through her nose.

Thorn had a fair storm blowing on the inside too. The giddy wave of gratitude at being given back her life had soon soaked away, leaving her chewing over the bitter truth that she had traded a future as a proud warrior for one as a minister's slave, collared by her own over-hasty oath, for purposes Father Yarvi had no intention of sharing.

To make matters even worse, she could feel her blood coming and her guts were stabbed through with aches and her chest was sore and she had a rage in her even beyond the usual. The mocking laughter of the crew at her puking might've moved her to murder if she could've unpeeled her death-gripping fingers from the oar.

So it was on wobbling legs she staggered onto the wharf at Yale-toft, the stones of Throvenland pocked with puddles from last night's storm, twinkling in this morning's sun. She blundered through the crowds with her shoulders hunched around her ears, every hawker's squawk and seagull's call, every wagon's rattle and barrel's clatter a knife in her, the over-hearty slaps on the back and snide chuckles of the men who were supposed to be her fellows cutting deeper still.

She knew what they were thinking. *What do you expect if you put a girl in a man's place?* And she muttered curses and swore elaborate revenges, but didn't dare lift her head in case she spewed again.

Some revenge that would be.

"Don't be sick in front of King Fynn," said Rulf, as they approached the looming hall, its mighty roof beams wonderfully carved and gilded. "The man's famous for his temper."

But it was not King Fynn but his minister, Mother Kyre, who greeted them at the dozen steps, each one cut of a different-colored marble. She was a handsome woman, tall and slender with a ready smile that did not quite reach her eyes. She reminded Thorn of her mother, which was a dark mark against her from the off. Thorn trusted few enough people, but hardly any had ready smiles and none at all looked like her mother.

"Greetings, Father Yarvi," said King Fynn's handsome minister. "You are ever welcome in Yaletoft, but I fear the king cannot see you."

"I fear you have advised him not to see me," answered Father Yarvi, planting one damp boot on the lowest step. Mother Kyre did not deny it. "Perhaps I might see Princess Skara? She can have been no more than ten years old when we last met. We were cousins then, before I took the Minister's Test—"

"But you did take the test," said Mother Kyre, "and gave up all your family but the Ministry, as did I. In any case, the princess is away."

"I fear you sent her away when you heard I was coming."

Mother Kyre did not deny that either. "Grandmother Wexen has sent me an eagle, and I know why you are here. I am not without sympathy."

"Your sympathy is sweet, Mother Kyre, but King Fynn's help in the trouble that comes would be far sweeter yet. It might prevent the trouble altogether."

Mother Kyre winced the way someone does who has no intention of helping. The way Thorn's mother used to wince when Thorn spoke of her hero's hopes.

"You know my master loves you and his niece Queen Laithlin," she said. "You know he would stand against half the world to stand with you. But you know he cannot stand against the wishes of the High King." A sea of words, this woman, but that was ministers for you. Father Yarvi was hardly a straight talker. "So he sends me, wretched with regret, to deny you audience, but to humbly offer you all food, warmth, and shelter beneath his roof."

Which, apart from the food, sounded well enough to Thorn.

King Fynn's hall was called the Forest for it was filled with a thicket of grand columns, said to have been floated down the Divine River from Kalyiv, beautifully carved and painted with scenes from the history of Throvenland. Somewhat less beautiful were the many, many guards, closely watching the *South Wind*'s disheveled crew as they shuffled past, Thorn most disheveled of all, one hand clutched to her aching belly.

"Our reception in Skekenhouse was . . . not warm." Yarvi leaned close to Mother Kyre and Thorn heard his whisper. "If I didn't know better I might say I am in danger."

"No danger will find you here, Father Yarvi, I assure you." Mother Kyre gestured at two of the most unreassuring guards Thorn had ever seen, flanking the door to a common room that stank of stale smoke.

"Here you have water." She pointed out a barrel as if it was the highest of gifts. "Slaves will bring food and ale. A room for your crew to sleep in is made ready. No doubt you will wish to be away with the first glimpse of Mother Sun, to catch the tide and carry your news to King Uthil."

Yarvi scrubbed unhappily at his pale hair with the heel of his twisted hand. "It seems you have thought of everything."

"A good minister is always prepared." And Mother Kyre shut the door as she left them, lacking only the turning of a key to mark them out as prisoners.

"As warm a welcome as you thought we'd get," grunted Rulf.

"Fynn and his minister are predictable as Father Moon. They are cautious. They live in the shadow of the High King's power, after all."

"A long shadow, that," said Rulf.

"Lengthening all the time. You look a little green, Thorn Bathu."

"I'm sick with disappointment to find no allies in Throvenland," she said.

Father Yarvi had the slightest smile. "We shall see."

THORN'S EYES SNAPPED OPEN in the fizzing darkness.

She was chilly with sweat under her blanket, kicked it off, felt the sticky wetness of blood between her legs and hissed a curse.

Beside her Rulf gave a particularly ripping snore then rolled over. She could hear the rest of the crew breathing, wriggling, muttering in their sleep, squashed in close together on dirty mats, tight as the fresh catch on market day.

They had made no special arrangements for her and she had asked for none. She wanted none. None except a fresh cloth down her trousers, anyway.

She stumbled down the corridor, hair in a tangle and guts in an aching knot, her belt undone with the buckle slapping at her thighs and one hand shoved down her trousers to feel how bad the bleeding was. All she needed to stop the mocking was a great stain around her crotch, and she cursed He Who Sprouts the Seed for inflicting this stupid business on her, and she cursed the stupid women who thought it was something to celebrate, her stupid mother first among them, and she cursed—

There was a man in the shadows of the common room.

He was dressed in black and standing near the water butt. In one hand he held its lid. In the other a little jar. As if he'd just poured something in. The place was lit by only one guttering candle and he had a bad squint, but Thorn got the distinct feeling he was staring right at her.

They stood unmoving, he with his jar over the water, she with her hand down her trousers, then the man said, "Who are you?"

"Who am I? Who are you?"

Know where your nearest weapon is, her father used to tell her, and her eyes flickered to the table where the wreckage of their evening meal was scattered. An eating knife was wedged into the wood, short blade faintly gleaming. Hardly a hero's blade, but when surprised at night with your belt open you take what you can get.

She gently eased her hand out of her trousers, gently eased toward the table and the knife. The man gently eased the jar away, eyes fixed on her, or at least somewhere near her.

"You're not supposed to be here," he said.

"*I'm* not? What're you putting in our water?"

"What're you doing with that knife?"

She wrenched it from the table and held it out, somewhat shaky, her voice high. "Is that poison?"

The man tossed down the barrel's lid and stepped toward her. "Now don't do anything stupid, girl." As he turned she saw he had a sword at his belt, his right hand reaching for the hilt.

Perhaps she panicked then. Or perhaps she thought more clearly than she ever had. Before she knew it she sprang at him, caught his wrist with one hand and drove the knife into his chest with the other.

It wasn't hard to do. Much easier than you'd think.

He heaved in a wheezing breath, sword no more than quarter drawn, eyes more crossed than ever, pawing at her shoulder.

"You . . ." And he crashed over on his back, dragging her on top of him.

Thorn tore his limp hand away and struggled up. His black clothes turned blacker as blood soaked them, the eating knife wedged in his heart to the handle.

She squeezed her eyes shut, but when she opened them, he was still there.

Not a dream.

"Oh, gods," she whispered.

"They rarely help." Father Yarvi stood frowning in the doorway. "What happened?"

"He had poison," muttered Thorn, pointing weakly at the fallen jar. "Or . . . I think he did . . ."

The minister squatted beside the dead man. "You have a habit of killing people, Thorn Bathu."

"That's a bad thing," she said in a voice very small.

"It does rather depend on who you kill." Yarvi slowly stood, looked about the room, walked over to her, peering at her face. "He hit you?"

"Well . . . no—"

"Yes." He punched her in the mouth and she sprawled against the table. By then he was already throwing the door wide. "Bloodshed in King Fynn's Hall! To arms! To arms!"

First came Rulf, who blinked down at the corpse and softly said, "That works."

Then came guards, who blinked down at the corpse and made their weapons ready.

Then came the crew, who shook their shaggy heads and rubbed their stubbled jaws and murmured prayers.

And finally came King Fynn.

Thorn had moved among the powerful since she killed Edwal. She had met five ministers and three kings, one of them High, and the only one to impress her was the one who killed her father. Fynn might have been famed for his anger, but the first thing that struck Thorn was what a strangely shapeless man the King of Throvenland was. His chin melted into his neck, his neck into his shoulders, his shoulders into his belly, his sparse gray hairs in wafting disarray from the royal bed.

"Kneeling isn't your strength, is it?" hissed Rulf, dragging Thorn down along with everyone else. "And for the gods' sake fasten your damn belt!"

"What happened here?" roared the king, spraying his wincing guards with spit.

Thorn kept her eyes down as she fumbled with her buckle. Crushing with rocks looked inevitable now. Certainly for her. Possibly for the rest of the crew too. She saw the looks on their faces. *This is what happens if you give a girl a blade. Even a little one.*

Mother Kyre, immaculate even in her nightclothes, took up the fallen jar between finger and thumb, sniffed at it and wrinkled her nose. "Ugh! Poison, my king."

"By the gods!" Yarvi put his hand on Thorn's shoulder. The same hand he had just punched her with. "If it wasn't for this girl's quick thinking, I and my crew might have passed through the Last Door before morning."

"Search every corner of my hall!" bellowed King Fynn. "Tell me how this bastard got in!"

A warrior who had knelt to root through the dead man's clothes held out his palm, silver glinting. "Coins, my king. Minted in Skekenhouse."

"There is altogether too much from Skekenhouse in my hall of late." Fynn's quivering jowls had a pink flush. "Grandmother Wexen's coins, Grandmother Wexen's eagles, Grandmother Wexen's demands too. Demands of me, the King of Throvenland!"

"But think of your people's welfare, my king," coaxed Mother Kyre, still clinging to her smile, but it hardly touched her mouth now, let alone her eyes. "Think of Father Peace, Father of Doves, who makes of the fist—"

"I have suffered many indignities on behalf of Father Peace." The flush had spread to King Fynn's cheeks. "Once the High King was the first among brothers. Now he gives a father's commands. How men should fight. How women should trade. How all should pray. Temples to the One God spring up across Throvenland like mushrooms after the rains, and I have held my tongue!"

"You were wise to do so," said Mother Kyre, "and would be wise to—"

"Now Grandmother Wexen sends assassins to my land?"

"My king, we have no proof at all—"

Fynn bellowed over his minister, doughy face heating from pink to blazing crimson. "To my very house? To poison my guests?" He stabbed at the corpse with one sausage of a finger. "Beneath my own roof and under my protection?"

"I would counsel caution—"

"You always do, Mother Kyre, but there is a limit on my forbearance, and the High King has stepped over it!" With face now fully purple he seized Father Yarvi's good hand. "Tell my beloved niece Queen Laithlin and her honored husband that they have a friend in me. A friend whatever the costs! I swear it!"

Mother Kyre had no smile ready for this moment, but Father Yarvi certainly did. "Your friendship is all they ask for." And he lifted King Fynn's hand high.

The guards cheered this unexpected alliance between Throvenland and Gettland with some surprise, the *South Wind*'s crew with great relief, and Thorn Bathu should no doubt have applauded loudest of all. Killing a man by accident had made her a villain. Killing another on purpose had made her a hero.

But all she could do was frown at the body as they dragged it out, and feel there was something very odd in all this.

LOST AND FOUND

Brand was proper drunk.

He often had been, lately.

Lifting on the docks was the best work he could find, and a day of that was thirsty work indeed. So he'd started drinking, and found he'd a real gift for it. Seemed he'd inherited something from his father after all.

The raid had been a mighty success. The Islanders were so sure the High King's favor would protect them they were taken unawares, half their ships captured and half the rest burned. Brand had watched the warriors of Gettland swagger up through the twisting streets of Thorlby when they landed, laden with booty and covered in glory and cheered from every window. He heard Rauk took two slaves, and Sordaf got himself a silver arm-ring. He heard Uthil dragged old King Styr naked from his hall, made him kneel and swear a sun-oath and a moon-oath never to draw a blade against another Gettlander.

All heroes' news, like something from the songs, but there's nothing like others' successes to make your own failures sting the worse.

Brand walked the crooked walk down some alley or other, between some houses or other, and shouted at the stars. Someone shouted back. Maybe the stars, maybe from a window. He didn't care. He didn't know where he was going. Didn't seem to matter anymore.

He was lost.

"I'm worried," Rin had said.

"Try having all your dreams stolen," he'd spat at her.

What could she say to that?

He tried to give her the dagger back. "I don't need it and I don't deserve it."

"I made it for you," she'd said. "I'm proud of you whatever." Nothing made her cry but she had tears in her eyes then, and they hurt worse than any beating he'd ever taken and he'd taken plenty.

So he asked Fridlif to fill his cup again. And again. And again. And Fridlif shook her gray head to see a young life wasted and all, but it was hardly the first time. Filling cups was what she did.

At least when he was drunk Brand could pretend other people were to blame. Hunnan, Thorn, Rauk, Father Yarvi, the gods, the stars above, the stones under his feet. Sober, he got to thinking he'd brought this on himself.

He blundered into a wall in the darkness and it spun him about, the anger flared up hot and he roared, "I did good!" He threw a punch at the wall and missed, which was lucky, and fell in the gutter, which wasn't.

Then he was sick on his hands.

"Are you Brand?"

"I was," he said, rocking back on his knees and seeing the outline of a man, or maybe two.

"The same Brand who trained with Thorn Bathu?"

He snorted at that, but his snorting tasted of sick and nearly made him spew again. "Sadly."

"Then this is for you."

Cold water slapped him in the face and he spluttered on it, tried to scramble up and slipped over in the gutter. An empty bucket skittered away across the cobbles. Brand scraped the wet hair out of his eyes, saw a strip of lamplight across an old face, creased and lined, scarred and bearded.

"I should hit you for that, you old bastard," he said, but getting up hardly seemed worth the effort.

"But then I'd hit you back, and a broken face won't mend your troubles. I know. I've tried it." The old man put hands on knees and leaned down close. "Thorn said you were the best she used to train with. You don't look like the best of anything to me, boy."

"Time hasn't been kind."

"Time never is. A fighter keeps fighting even so. Thought you were a fighter?"

"I was," said Brand.

The old man held out his broad hand. "Good. My name's Rulf, and I've got a fight for you."

THEY'D MADE THE TORCHLIT storehouse up like a training square, ropes on the old boards marking the edge. There wasn't as big an audience as Brand was used to, but what there was made him want to be sick again.

On one of the stools, with the key to the kingdom's treasury gleaming on her chest, sat Laithlin, Golden Queen of Gettland. Beside her was the man who had once been her son and was now her minister, Father Yarvi. Behind them were four silver-collared slaves—two huge Inglings with hard axes at their belts and even harder frowns on their rock-chiselled faces, and two girls like as the halves of a walnut, each with braids so long they had them looped around and around one arm.

And leaning against the far wall with one boot up on the stonework and that mocking little lop-sided smile on her lips was Brand's least favorite sparring partner, Thorn Bathu.

And the strange thing was, though he'd spent long drunk hours blaming her for all his woes, Brand was happy to see her face. Happier than he'd been in a long while. Not because he liked her so much, but because the sight of her reminded him of a time when he liked himself. When he could see his future, and liked what he saw. When his hopes stood tall and the world seemed full of dares.

"Thought you'd never get here." She worked her arm into the straps of a shield and picked out a wooden sword.

"Thought they crushed you with rocks," said Brand.

"It's still very much a possibility," said Father Yarvi.

Rulf gave Brand a shove between the shoulderblades and sent him tottering into the square. "Get to it, then, lad."

Brand knew he didn't have the fastest mind, and it was far from its fastest then, but he got the gist. He walked almost a straight line to the practice weapons and picked out a sword and shield, keenly aware of the queen's cold eyes judging his every movement.

Thorn was already taking her mark. "You're a sorry bloody sight," she said.

Brand looked down at his vest, soaked and somewhat sick-stained, and had to nod. "Aye."

That wrinkle to her mouth twisted into a full sneer. "Weren't you always telling me you'd be a rich man after your first raid?"

That stung. "I didn't go."

"Hadn't marked you for a coward."

That stung more. She'd always known how to sting him. "I didn't get picked," he grunted.

Thorn burst out laughing, no doubt showing off in front of the queen. She'd never tired of spouting how much she admired the woman. "Here's me full of envy, expecting you all puffed up like a hero, and what do I find but some drunk beggar-boy?"

Brand felt a cold flush through him then, sweeping the drink away more surely than any ice water. He'd done more than his share of begging, that was true. But it's the true ones that sting.

Thorn was still chuckling at her cleverness. "You always were an idiot. Hunnan stole my place, how did you toss yours away?"

Brand would've liked to tell her how he'd lost his place. He would've liked to scream it in her face, but he couldn't get the words out because he'd started growling like an animal, growling louder and louder until the room throbbed with it, and his chest hummed with it, his lips curled back and his jaw clenched so hard it seemed his teeth would shatter, and Thorn was frowning at him over the rim of her shield like he'd gone mad. Maybe he had.

"Begin!" shouted Rulf, and he was on her, hacked her sword away, struck back so hard he sent splinters from her shield. She twisted, quick, she'd always been deadly quick, made enough space to swing but he wasn't hesitating this time.

He shrugged the blow off his shoulder, barely felt it, bellowed as he pressed in blindly, driving her staggering back, shield-rims grinding together, almost lifting her as she tripped over the rope and crashed into the wall. She tried to twist her sword free but he still had it pinned useless over his shoulder, and he caught her shield with his left hand and dragged it down. Too close for weapons, he flung his practice blade away and started punching her, all his anger and his disappointment in it, as if she was Hunnan, and Yarvi, and all those so-called friends of his who'd done so well from doing nothing, stolen his place, stolen his future.

He hit her in the side and heard her groan, hit her again and she folded up, eyes bulging, hit her again and she went down hard, coughing and retching at his feet. He might've been about to set to kicking her when Rulf caught him around the neck with one thick forearm and dragged him back.

"That's enough, I reckon."

"Aye," he muttered, going limp. "More'n enough."

He shook the shield off his arm, shocked of a sudden at what he'd done and nowhere near proud of it, knowing full well what it felt like on the other side of a beating like that. Maybe there was more than one thing he'd inherited from his father. He didn't feel like he was standing in the light right then. Not at all.

Queen Laithlin gave a long sigh, Thorn's coughing and dribbling in the background, and turned on her stool. "I was wondering when you'd arrive."

And it was only then Brand noticed another watcher, slouched in the shadows of a corner in a cloak of rags every shade of gray. "Always when I am sorest needed and least expected." A woman's voice from within the hood and a strange accent on it. "Or hungry."

"Did you see it?" asked Yarvi.

"I had that questionable privilege."

"What do you think?"

"She is wretched. She is all pride and anger. She has too much confidence and too little. She does not know herself." The figure pushed back her hood. A black-skinned old woman with a face lean as famine and hair shaved to gray fuzz. She picked her nose with one long forefinger, carefully examined the results, then flicked them away. "The girl is stupid as a stump. Worse. Most stumps have the dignity to rot quietly without causing offense."

"I'm right here," Thorn managed to hiss from her hands and knees.

"Just where the drunk boy put you." The woman flashed a smile at Brand that seemed to have too many teeth. "I like him, though: he is pretty and desperate. My favorite combination."

"Can anything be done with her?" asked Yarvi.

"Something can always be done, given enough effort." The woman peeled herself away from the wall. She had the strangest way of walking—wriggling, jerking, strutting—as though she was dancing to music only she could hear. "How much effort will you pay for me to waste upon her worthless carcass, is the question? You owe me already, after all." A long arm snaked from her cloak with something in the hand.

It was a box perhaps the size of a child's head—dark, square, perfect, with golden writing etched into the lid. Brand found his eyes drawn to it. It took an effort not to step closer, to look closer. Thorn was staring too. And Rulf. And the queen's thralls. All fascinated and afraid at once, as if by the sight of a terrible wound. None of them could read, of course, but you did not have to be a minister to know those were elf-letters on the box. Letters written before the Breaking of God.

Father Yarvi swallowed, and with the one finger of his crippled hand eased the box open. Whatever was inside, a pale light shone from it. A light that picked out the hollows of the minister's face as his mouth fell open, that reflected in Queen Laithlin's widening eyes which a moment before Brand had thought nothing could surprise.

"By the gods," she whispered. "You have it."

The woman gave an extravagant bow, the hem of her cloak sending up a wash of straw-dust from the storehouse floor. "I deliver what I promise, my most gilded of queens."

"Then it still works?"

"Shall I make it turn?"

"No," said Father Yarvi. "Make it turn for the Empress of the South, not before."

"There is the question of—"

Without taking her eyes from the box, the Queen held out a folded paper. "Your debts are all canceled."

"The very question I had in mind." The black-skinned woman frowned as she took it between two fingers. "I have been called a witch before but here is sorcery indeed, to trap such a weight of gold in a scrap of paper."

"We live in changing times," murmured Father Yarvi, and he snapped the box shut, putting the light out with it. Only then Brand realized he'd been holding his breath, and slowly let it out. "Find us a crew, Rulf, you know the kind."

"Hard ones, I'm guessing," said the old warrior.

"Oarsmen and fighters. The outcasts and the desperate. Men who don't get weak at the thought of blood or the sight of it. The journey is long and the stakes could not be higher. I want men with nothing to lose."

"My kind of crew!" The black-skinned woman slapped her thigh. "Sign me up first!" She slipped between the stools and strutted over toward Brand, and for a moment her cloak of rags came open and he saw the glint of steel. "Can I buy you a drink, young man?"

"I think the boy has drunk enough." Queen Laithlin's gray eyes were on him, and the eyes of her four slaves as well, and Brand swallowed, his sick-tasting mouth suddenly very dry. "Though my first husband gave me two sons, for which I will always be grateful, he drank too much. It spoils a bad man. It ruins a good one."

"I . . . have decided to stop, my queen," mumbled Brand. He knew then he wasn't going back. Not to the ale-cup, nor to begging, nor to lifting on the docks.

The black woman puffed out her cheeks in disappointment as she made for the door. "Young people these days have no ambition in them."

Laithlin ignored her. "The way you fight reminds me of an old friend."

"Thank you—"

"Don't. I had to kill him." And the queen of Gettland swept out, her slaves following in her wake.

"I've a crew to gather." Rulf took Brand under the arm. "And no doubt your gutter's missing you—"

"It'll manage without me." Rulf was strong but Brand wouldn't be moved. He'd remembered how it felt to fight, and how it felt to win, and he was more sure of the good thing to do than he'd ever been in his life. "Luck's with you, old man," he said. "Now you need to gather one less."

Rulf snorted. "This ain't no two-day jaunt, boy, nor even a raid to the Islands. We're headed far up the Divine River and down the Denied, over the tall hauls and beyond. We go to speak to the Prince of Kalyiv. To seek an audience with the Empress of the South in the First of Cities, even! All kinds of dangers on that journey, even if you're not seeking allies against the most powerful man in the world. We'll be gone months. If we come back at all."

Brand swallowed. Dangers, no doubt, but opportunities too. Men won glory on the Divine. Men won fortunes beyond it. "You need oarsmen?" he said. "I can pull an oar. You need loads lifted? I can lift a load. You need fighters?" Brand nodded toward Thorn, who'd managed to stand, wincing as she kneaded at her battered ribs. "I can fight. You want men with nothing to lose? Look no further."

Rulf opened his mouth but Father Yarvi spoke over him. "The way may be hard, but we go to smooth the path for Father Peace. We go to find allies." The minister gave Brand the slightest nod. "We might need one man aboard who spares some thought for doing good. Give him a marker, Rulf."

The old warrior scratched at his gray beard. "Yours'll be the lowest place, boy. The worst work for the thinnest rewards. Back oar." He jerked his head over at Thorn. "Opposite that article."

Thorn gave Brand a long, hard frown and spat, but it only made him smile wider. He saw his future once again, and he liked what he saw. Compared to lifting loads on the docks, he liked it a lot.

"Looking forward to it." He plucked the marker from Rulf's hand, the minister's dove carved into the face, and he wrapped his fingers painfully tight about it.

It seemed Mother War had found a crew for him after all. Or Father Peace had.

II.

DIVINE
AND DENIED

THE FIRST
LESSON

The *South Wind* rocked on the tide, boasting new oars and a new sail, freshly painted and freshly provisioned, lean and sleek as a racing dog and with minister's doves gleaming white at high prow and stern. It was, without doubt, a beautiful ship. A ship fit for high deeds and heroes' songs.

Sadly, her new crew were not quite of that caliber.

"They seem a . . ." Thorn's mother always found a pretty way to put things, but even she was stumped. "*Varied* group."

" 'Fearsome' is the word I'd have reached for," grunted Thorn.

She might well have tripped over "desperate," "disgusting" or "axbitten" on the way. All three seemed apt for the gathering of the damned crawling over the *South Wind* and the wharf beside it, hefting sacks and barrels, hauling at ropes, shoving, bellowing, laughing, threatening, all under Father Yarvi's watchful eye.

Fighting men, these, but more like bandits than warriors. Men with many scars and few scruples. Men with beards forked and braided and shaved in strange patches and dyed hair chopped into spikes. Men whose clothes were ragged but whose muscled arms and thick necks and calloused fingers glittered with gold and silver ring-money, proclaiming to the world the high value they put on themselves.

Thorn wondered what mountain of corpses this lot might have heaped up between them, but she wasn't one to be easily intimidated. Especially when she had no choice. She set down her sea-chest, everything she had inside, her father's old sword wrapped in an oilcloth on top. She put on her bravest face, stepped up to the biggest man she could see and tapped him on the arm.

"I'm Thorn Bathu."

"I am Dosduvoi." She found herself staring sharply up at one of the biggest heads she ever saw, tiny features squeezed into the center of its doughy expanse, looming so high above her that at first she thought its owner must be standing on a box. "What bad luck brings you here, girl?" he asked, with a faintly tragic quiver to his voice.

She wished she had a different answer, but snapped out, "I'm sailing with you."

His face retreated into an even tinier portion of his head as he frowned. "Along the Divine River, to Kalyiv and beyond?"

She thrust her chin up at him in the usual manner. "If the boat floats with so much meat aboard."

"Reckon we'll have to balance the benches with some little ones." This from a man small and hard as Dosduvoi was huge and soft. He had the spikiest shag of red hair and the maddest eyes, bright blue, shining wet and sunken in dark sockets. "My name is Odda, famed about the Shattered Sea."

"Famed for what?"

"All kinds of things." He flashed a yellow wolf-smile and she saw his teeth were filed across the front with killer's grooves. "Can't wait to sail with you."

"Likewise," Thorn managed to croak, stepping back despite herself and nearly tripping over someone else. He looked up as she turned and, brave face or no, she shrank back the other way. A huge scar started at the corner of one eye, all dragged out of shape to show the pink lid, angled across his stubbled cheek and through both lips. To make matters worse, she realized from his hair, long and braided back around his face, that they would be sailing with a Vansterman.

He met her ill-concealed horror with a mutilated blankness more terrible than any snarl and said mildly, "I am Fror."

It was either bluster or look weak and Thorn reckoned that no choice at all, so she puffed herself up and snapped out, "How did you get the scar?"

"How did *you* get the scar?"

Thorn frowned. "What scar?"

"That's the face the gods gave you?" And with the faintest of smiles the Vansterman went back to coiling rope.

"Father Peace protect us," squeaked Thorn's mother as she edged past. "Fearsome is a fair word for them."

"They'll be the ones scared of me soon enough," said Thorn, wishing, and not for the first time, that saying a thing firmly enough makes it so.

"That's a good thing?" Her mother stared at a shaven-headed man with runes stating his crimes tattooed on his face, laughing jaggedly with a bony fellow whose arms were covered in flaking sores. "To be feared by men like these?"

"Better to be feared than afraid." Her father's words and, as always, her mother was ready for them.

"Are those life's only two choices?"

"They're a warrior's two choices." Whenever Thorn traded more than ten words with her mother she somehow ended up defending an indefensible position. She knew what came next. *Why fight so hard to be a warrior if all you can win is fear?* But her mother only shut her mouth, and looked pale and scared, and piled guilt on Thorn's simmering anger. As ever.

"You can always go back to the house," snapped Thorn.

"I want to see my only child on her way. Can't you give me that? Father Yarvi says you might be gone a year." Her mother's voice took on an infuriating quiver. "If you come back at all—"

"Fear not, my doves!" Thorn jumped as someone flung an arm

around her shoulders. The strange woman who had watched Thorn fight Brand a few days before thrust her gray-stubbled skull between her and her mother. "For the wise Father Yarvi has placed your daughter's education in my dextrous hands."

Thorn hadn't thought her spirits could drop any lower, but the gods had found a way. "Education?"

The woman hugged them tighter, her smell a heady mix of sweat, incense, herbs and piss. "It's where I teach and you learn."

"And who . . ." Thorn's mother gave the ragged woman a nervous look, "or what . . . are you?"

"Lately, a thief." When that sharpened nervousness into alarm she added brightly, "but also an experienced killer! And navigator, wrestler, stargazer, explorer, historian, poet, blackmailer, brewer . . . I may have forgotten a few. Not to mention an accomplished amateur prophet!"

The old woman scraped a spatter of fresh bird-droppings from a post, tested its texture with her thumb, smelled it closely, seemed on the point of tasting it, then decided against and wiped the mess on her ragged cloak.

"Inauspicious," she grunted, peering up at the wheeling gulls. "Add to all that my unchallenged expertise in . . ." she gave a suggestive wiggling of the hips, "*the romantic arts* and you can see, my doves, there are few areas of interest to the modern girl in which I am not richly qualified to instruct your daughter."

Thorn should have enjoyed the rare sight of her mother rendered speechless, but was, for once, speechless herself.

"Thorn Bathu!" Rulf shouldered his way through the bustle. "You're late! Get your skinny arse down the wharf and start shifting those sacks. Your friend Brand has already . . ." He swallowed. "I didn't know you had a sister."

Thorn sourly worked her tongue. "Mother."

"Surely not!" Rulf combed at his beard with his fingers in a vain attempt to tame the brown-and-gray tangle. "If you can suffer a compliment from a plain old fighting man, your beauty lights these docks up like a lamp at twilight." He glanced at the silver key on her chest. "Your husband must be—"

Thorn's mother could suffer the compliment. Indeed she clutched it with both hands. "Dead," she said quickly. "Eight years, now, since we howed him up."

"Sorry to hear that." Though Rulf sounded, in fact, anything but sorry. "I'm Rulf, helmsman of the *South Wind*. The crew may seem rough but I've learned never to trust a smooth one. I picked these men and each knows his business. Thorn'll be rowing right beneath my beard and I'll treat her with just as soft a heart and firm a hand as I would my own daughter."

Thorn rolled her eyes, but it was wasted effort. "You have children?" her mother asked.

"Two sons, but it's years since I saw them. The gods parted me from my family for too long."

"Any chance they could part you from mine?" grunted Thorn.

"Shush," hissed her mother, without taking her eyes from Rulf, and the thick-linked golden chain he wore in particular. "It will be a great comfort to know that a man of your quality looks to my daughter's welfare. Prickly though she may be, Hild is all I have."

A lot of strong wind and no doubt not a little strong ale had rendered Rulf ruddy about the cheeks already, but Thorn thought she saw him blush even so. "As for being a man of quality you'll find many to disagree, but as to looking to your daughter's welfare I promise to do my best."

Thorn's mother flashed a simpering smile. "What else can any of us promise?"

"Gods," hissed Thorn, turning away. The one thing she hated worse than being fussed over was being ignored.

Brinyolf the Prayer-Weaver had wrought murder on some unwitting animal and was daubing its blood on the *South Wind*'s prow-beast, red to the wrists as he wailed out a blessing to Mother Sea and She Who Finds the Course and He Who Steers the Arrow and a dozen other small gods whose names Thorn had never even heard before. She'd never been much for prayers and had her doubts the weather was that interested in them either.

"How does a girl end up on a fighting crew?"

She turned to see a young lad had stolen up on her. Thorn judged him maybe fourteen years, slight, with a bright eye and a twitchy quickness to him, a mop of sandy hair and the first hints of beard on his sharp jaw.

She frowned back. "You saying I shouldn't be?"

"Not up to me who gets picked." He shrugged, neither scared nor scornful. "I'm just asking how you did."

"Leave her be!" A small, lean woman gave the lad a neat cuff around the ear. "Didn't I tell you to make yourself useful?" Some bronze weights swung on a cord around her neck while she herded him off toward the *South Wind,* which made her a merchant, or a storekeeper, trusted to measure fairly.

"I'm Safrit," she said, planting her hands on her hips. "The lad with all the questions is my son Koll. He's yet to realize that the more you learn the more you understand the size of your own ignorance. He means no harm."

"Nor do I," said Thorn, "but I seem to cause a lot even so."

Safrit grinned. "It's a habit with some of us. I'm along to mind the stores, and cook, and watch the cargo. Fingers off, understand?"

"I thought we were aiming to win friends for Gettland? We're carrying cargo too?"

"Furs and tree-tears and walrus ivory among . . . other things." Safrit frowned toward an iron-shod chest chained up near the mast. "Our first mission is to talk for Father Peace but Queen Laithlin paid for this expedition."

"Ha! And there's a woman who never in her life missed out on a profit!"

"Why would I?"

Thorn turned again to find herself looking straight into the queen's face at a distance of no more than a stride. Some folk are more impressive from far off but Laithlin was the opposite, as radiant as

Mother Sun and stern as Mother War, the great key to the treasury shining on her chest, her thralls and guards and servants in a disapproving press behind her.

"Oh, gods . . . I mean, forgive me, my queen." Thorn wobbled down to one knee, lost her balance and nearly caught Laithlin's silken skirts to steady herself. "Sorry, I've never been much good at kneeling—"

"Perhaps you should practice." The queen was about as unlike Thorn's mother as was possible for two women of an age—not soppy soft and circumspect but hard and brilliant as a cut diamond, direct as a punch in the face.

"It's an honor to sail with you as patron," Thorn blathered. "I swear I'll give your son the very best service—Father Yarvi, that is," realizing he wasn't supposed to be her son any longer. "I'll give your minister the very best service—"

"You are the girl who swore to give that boy a beating just before he gave you one." The Golden Queen raised a brow. "Fools boast of what they will do. Heroes do it." She summoned one of her servants with a snap of her fingers and was already murmuring instructions as she swept past.

Thorn might never have got off her knees had Safrit not hooked her under the arm and dragged her up. "I'd say she likes you."

"How does she treat folk she doesn't like?"

"Pray you never find out." Safrit clutched at her head as she saw her son had swarmed up the mast nimbly as a monkey and was perched on the yard high above, checking the knots that held the sail. "Gods damn it, Koll, get down from there!"

"You told me to be useful!" he called back, letting go the beam with both hands to give an extravagant shrug.

"And how useful will you be when you plummet to your doom, you fool?"

"I'm so pleased to see you're joining us." Thorn turned once more to find Father Yarvi at her side, the old bald woman with him.

"Swore an oath, didn't I?" Thorn muttered back.

"To do whatever service I think fit, as I recall."

The black woman chuckled softly to herself. "Oooh, but that wording's awfully vague."

"Isn't it?" said Yarvi. "Glad to see you're making yourself known to the crew."

Thorn glanced around at them, worked her mouth sourly as she saw her mother and Rulf still deep in conversation. "They seem a noble fellowship."

"Nobility is overrated. You met Skifr, did you?"

"You're Skifr?" Thorn stared at the black-skinned woman with new eyes. "The thief of elf-relics? The murderer? The one sorely wanted by Grandmother Wexen?"

Skifr sniffed at her fingers, still slightly smeared with gray, and frowned as though she could not guess how bird droppings might have got there. "As for being a thief, the relics were just lying in Strokom. Let the elves impeach me! As for being a murderer, well, the difference between murderer and hero is all in the standing of the dead. As for being wanted, well, my sunny disposition has made me always popular. Father Yarvi has hired me to do . . . various things, but among them, for reasons best known to himself," and she pressed her long forefinger into Thorn's chest, "to teach you to fight."

"I can fight," growled Thorn, drawing herself up to her most fighting height.

Skifr threw back her shaved head and laughed. "Not that risible stomping about I saw. Father Yarvi is paying me to make you deadly." And with blinding speed Skifr slapped Thorn across the face, hard enough to knock her against a barrel.

"What was that for?" she said, one hand to her stinging cheek.

"Your first lesson. Always be ready. If I can hit you, you deserve to be hit."

"I suppose the same would go for you."

Skifr gave a huge smile. "Of course."

Thorn dived at her but caught only air. She stumbled, her arm suddenly twisted behind her, and the slimy boards of the wharf smashed her in the face. Her fighting scream became a wheeze of shock and then, as her little finger was savagely twisted, a long moan of pain.

"Do you still suppose I have nothing to teach you?"

"No! No!" whimpered Thorn, writhing helplessly as fire shot through every joint in her arm. "I'm keen to learn!"

"And your first lesson?"

"If I can be hit I deserve it!"

Her finger was released. "Pain is the best schoolmaster, as you will soon discover."

Thorn clambered to her knees, shaking out her throbbing arm, to find her old friend Brand standing over her, a sack on his shoulder and a grin on his face.

Skifr grinned back. "Funny, eh?"

"Little bit," said Brand.

Skifr slapped him across the cheek and he tottered against a post, dropped his sack on his foot, and was left stupidly blinking. "Are you teaching me to fight?"

"No. But I see no reason you shouldn't be ready too."

"Thorn?" Her mother was offering a hand to help her up. "What happened?"

Thorn pointedly didn't take it. "I suppose you'd know if you'd been seeing your daughter off instead of snaring our helmsman."

"Gods, Hild, you've no forgiving in you at all, have you?"

"My father called me Thorn, damn it!"

"Oh, your father, yes, him you'll forgive anything—"

"Maybe because he's dead."

Thorn's mother's eyes were already brimming with tears, as usual. "Sometimes I think you'd be happier if I joined him."

"Sometimes I think I would be!" And Thorn dragged up her sea-chest, her father's sword rattling inside as she swung it onto her shoulder and stomped toward the ship.

"I like that contrary temperament of hers," she heard Skifr saying behind her. "We'll soon have that flowing down the right channels."

One by one they clambered aboard and set their sea-chests at their places. Much to Thorn's disgust Brand took the other back oar, the two of them wedged almost into each other's laps by the tapering of the ship's sides.

"Just don't jog my elbow," she growled, in a filthier mood than ever.

Brand wearily shook his head. "I'll just throw myself in the sea, shall I?"

"Could you? That'd be perfect."

"Gods," muttered Rulf, at his place on the steering platform above them. "Will I have to listen to you two snap at each other all the way up the Divine like a pair of mating cats?"

"More than likely," said Father Yarvi, squinting up. The sky was thick with cloud, Mother Sun barely even a smudge. "Poor weather for picking out a course."

"Bad weatherluck," moaned Dosduvoi, from his oar somewhere near the middle of the boat. "Awful weatherluck."

Rulf puffed out his grizzled cheeks. "Times like this I wish Sumael was here."

"Times like this and every other time," said Father Yarvi, with a heavy sigh.

"Who's Sumael?" muttered Brand.

Thorn shrugged. "How the hell should I know who he is? No one tells me anything."

Queen Laithlin watched them push away with one palm on her child-swollen belly, gave Father Yarvi a terse nod, then turned and was gone toward the city, her gaggle of thralls and servants scurrying after. This crew were men who blew with the wind, so there was only a sorry little gathering left to wave them off. Thorn's mother was one, tears streaking her cheeks and her hand raised in farewell until the wharf was a distant speck, then the citadel of Thorlby only a jagged notching, then Gettland fading into the gray distance above the gray line of Mother Sea.

The thing about rowing, you face backward. Always looking into the past, never the future. Always seeing what you're losing, never what you've got to gain.

Thorn put a brave face on it, as always, but a brave face can be a brittle thing. Rulf's narrowed eyes were fixed ahead on the horizon. Brand kept to his stroke. If either of them saw her dashing the tears on her sleeve they had nothing to say about it.

THE SECOND
LESSON

Roystock was a reeking spew of wooden shops, piled one on the other and crammed onto a rotting island at the mouth of the Divine River. The place spilled over with yammering beggars and swaggering raiders, rough-handed dockers and smooth-talking merchants. Its teetering wharves were choked by strange boats with strange crews and stranger cargoes, taking on food and water, selling off goods and slaves.

"Gods damn it I need a drink!" snarled Odda, as the *South Wind* scraped alongside her wharf and Koll sprang ashore to make her fast.

"I might be persuaded to join you," said Dosduvoi. "As long as there are no dice involved. I have no luck at dice." Brand could have sworn the *South Wind* rose a few fingers in the water when he heaved himself ashore. "Care to join us, boy?"

It was a sore temptation after the hell of hard work and hard words, bad weather and bad tempers they'd been through on the way across the Shattered Sea. Brand's hopes for the wondrous voyage had so far proved a great deal more wondrous than the voyage itself, the crew less a family bound tight by a common goal than a sackful of snakes, spitting poison at each other as though their journey was a struggle that could have only one winner.

Brand licked his lips as he remembered the taste of Fridlif's ale going down. Then he caught sight of Rulf's disapproving face, and remembered the taste of Fridlif's ale coming back up, and chose to stand in the light. "I'd best not."

Odda spat in disgust. "One drink never hurt anyone!"

"One didn't," said Rulf.

"Stopping at one is my problem," said Brand.

"Besides, I have a better use for him." Skifr slipped between Brand and Thorn, one long arm hooking each of their necks. "Fetch weapons, my sprouts. It is past time the education began!"

Brand groaned. The last thing he wanted to do was fight. Especially to fight Thorn, who'd been jostling his oar at every stroke and sneering at his every word since they left Thorlby, no doubt desperate to even the score. If the crew were snakes, she was the most venomous of the lot.

"I want you all back here before midday!" yelled Yarvi as most of his crew began to melt away into the mazy alleys of Roystock, then muttered under his breath to Rulf, "We stop overnight we'll never get this lot started again. Safrit, make sure none of them kill anyone. Especially not each other."

Safrit was in the midst of buckling on a knife only just this side of a sword, and a well-used one at that. "A man bent on self-destruction will find his way there sooner or later."

"Then make sure it's later."

"Don't suppose you've a notion how I do that?"

"Your tongue's sharp enough to goad a tree to movement." Which brought a mad giggle from Koll as he knotted the rope. "But if that fails you, we both know you're not too shy to stick them with your dagger instead."

"All right, but I swear no oaths." Safrit nodded to Brand. "Try and keep my Death-flirting son off that mast, will you?"

Brand looked at Koll, and the lad flashed him a mischief-loving grin. "Don't suppose you've a notion how I do that?"

"If only," snorted Safrit, and with a sigh she headed into town, while Rulf set a few who'd drawn short lots to scrubbing down the deck.

Brand clambered onto the wharf, firm boards seeming treacherous after so long on the shifting water, groaning as he stretched out muscles stiff from rowing and shook out clothes stiff with salt.

Skifr was frowning at Thorn with hands on hips. "Do we need to strap down your chest?"

"What?"

"A woman's chest can make trouble in a fight, swinging about like sacks of sand." Skifr snaked her hand out and before Thorn could wriggle away gave her chest an assessing squeeze. "Never mind. That won't be a problem for you."

Thorn glared at her. "Thanks for that."

"No need for thanks, I am paid to teach you!" The old woman hopped back aboard the *South Wind*, leaving Brand and Thorn facing each other once again, wooden weapons in hand, he nearest to the town, she with the sea at her back.

"Well, children? Do you await an invitation by eagle?"

"Here?" Thorn frowned down at the few paces of narrow wharf between them, cold Mother Sea slapping at the supports below.

"Where else? Fight!"

With a growl Thorn set to work, but with so little space all she could do was jab at him. It was easy for Brand to fend her efforts off with his shield, pushing her back a quarter-step each time.

"Don't tickle him!" barked Skifr, "Kill him!"

Thorn's eyes darted about for an opening but Brand gave her no room, easing forward, herding her toward the end of the wharf. She came at him with her usual savagery, their shields clashing, grating, but he was ready, used his weight to doggedly shove her back. She snarled and spat, her boots scraping at the mossy boards, flailed at him with her sword but the blows were weak.

It was inevitable. With a despairing cry Thorn toppled off the end of the wharf and splashed into the welcoming arms of Mother Sea. Brand winced after her, very much doubting this would make a year of rowing beside her any easier.

Kalyiv was a long, long way off, but it was starting to seem farther than ever.

The crew chuckled to each other over the result. Koll, who'd shinned up to the *South Wind*'s yard as usual in spite of his mother's warnings, whooped from above.

Skifr put long finger and thumb to her temples and gently rubbed at them. "Inauspicious."

Thorn flung her shield onto the wharf and dragged herself up by a barnacle-crusted ladder, soaked to the skin and white with fury.

"You seem distressed," said Skifr. "Is the test not fair?"

Thorn forced through her clenched teeth, "The battlefield is not fair."

"Such wisdom in one so young!" Skifr offered out Thorn's fallen practice sword. "Another go?"

The second time she went into the sea even faster. The third she ended up on her back tangled with the *South Wind*'s oars. The fourth she beat at Brand's shield so hard she broke off the end of her practice sword. Then he barged her off the wharf again.

By now a merry crowd had gathered on the docks to watch. Some crew from their ship, some crew from others, some folk from the town come to laugh at the girl being knocked into the sea. There was even some lively betting on the result.

"Let's stop," begged Brand. "Please." The only outcomes he could see were enraging her further or going into the sea himself, and neither particularly appealed.

"Damn your please!" snarled Thorn, setting herself for another round. No doubt she'd still have been tumbling into the sea by the light of Father Moon if she'd been given the chance, but Skifr steered her broken sword down with a gentle fingertip.

"I think you have entertained the good folk of Roystock enough. You are tall and you are strong."

Thorn stuck her jaw out. "Stronger than most men."

"Stronger than most boys in the training square, but . . ." Skifr flopped one lazy hand out toward Brand. "What is the lesson?"

Thorn spat on the boards, and wiped a little stray spit from her chin, and kept sullen silence.

"Do you like the taste of salt so much you wish to try him again?" Skifr walked to Brand and seized him by the arms. "Look at his neck. Look at his shoulders. What is the lesson?"

"That he is stronger." Fror stood with his forearms dangling over the *South Wind*'s rail, rag and block in his hands. Might've been the first time Brand had heard him speak.

"Exactly so!" called Skifr. "I daresay this tight-lipped Vansterman knows battle. How did you get that scar, my dove?"

"I was milking a reindeer and she fell on me," said Fror. "She was ever so sorry afterward, but the damage was done." And Brand wondered if he winked his misshapen eye.

"Truly a hero's mark, then," grunted Thorn, curling her lip.

Fror shrugged. "Someone must bring in the milk."

"And someone must hold my coat." Skifr whipped off her cloak of rags and tossed it to him.

She was lean as a whip, narrow-waisted as a wasp, wound about with strips of cloth, coiled with belts and straps, bristling with knives and hooks, pouches and picks, scrags, rods, papers and devices Brand could not guess at the purpose of.

"Have you never seen a grandmother without her cloak before?" And from behind her back she brought an ax with a shaft of dark wood and a thin, bearded blade. A beautiful weapon, snakes of strange letters etched into the bright steel. She held up her other hand, thumb folded in and fingers pressed together. "Here is my sword. A blade fit for the songs, no? Put me in the sea, boy, if you can."

Skifr began to move. It was a baffling performance, lurching like a drunkard, floppy as a doll, and she swung that ax back and forth, knocking the boards and striking splinters. Brand watched her over his shield's rim, trying to find some pattern to it, but he'd no idea where her next footstep might fall. So he waited for the ax to swing wide, then aimed a cautious swipe at her.

He could hardly believe how fast she moved. His wooden blade missed her by a hair as she darted in, caught the rim of his shield with that hooked ax and dragged it away, slipped past his sword arm and jabbed him hard in the chest with her fingertips, making him grunt and stagger back on his heels.

"You are dead," she said.

The ax flashed down and Brand jerked his shield up to meet it. But the blow never came. Instead he winced as Skifr's fingers jabbed him in the groin, and looking down saw her smirking face beneath the bottom rim of his shield.

"You are dead twice."

He tried to barge her away but he might as well have barged the breeze. She somehow slipped around him, fingers jabbing under his ear and making his whole side throb.

"Dead."

She chopped him in the kidneys with the edge of her hand as he tried to turn.

"Dead."

He reeled around, teeth bared, sword flashing at neck height but she was gone. Something trapped his ankle, turning his war cry to a gurgle of shock, and he kept spinning, balance gone, lurching off the edge of the wharf—

He stopped, choking as something caught him around the neck.

"You are the deadest boy in Roystock."

Skifr had one foot on his heel, the bearded blade of her ax hooked into his collar to keep him from falling, leaning sharply away to balance his weight. He was held helpless, teetering over the cold sea. The watching crowd had fallen silent, almost as dumbstruck at Skifr's display as Brand was.

"You will not beat a strong man with strength any more than I will beat you with youth," Skifr hissed at Thorn. "You must be quicker to strike and quicker when you do. You must be tougher and cleverer, you must always look to attack, and you must fight without honor, without conscience, without pity. Do you understand?"

Thorn slowly nodded. Of all those in the training square, she'd been the one who hated most being taught. But she'd been the one quickest to learn.

"Whatever happened here?" Dosduvoi had strolled up and stood staring at Brand as he dangled spluttering over the water.

"They're training," called Koll, who'd leaned out from the mast to flip a copper coin nimbly across his knuckles. "Why are you back so soon?"

"I lost terribly at dice." He rubbed sadly at his great forearm, where a couple of silver rings had gone missing. "Awful luck, it was."

Skifr gave a disgusted hiss. "Those with bad luck should at least attempt to balance it with good sense." She twisted her wrist. The ax blade tore through Brand's shirt collar and it was his turn to plunge flailing into cold water. His turn to drag himself up the ladder. His turn to stand dripping under the scorn of the crowd.

He found he enjoyed his turn even less than he had Thorn's.

The Vansterman threw Skifr's ragged cloak back to her. "An impressive performance."

"Like magic!" Koll tossed his coin high but fumbled it on the way back so it flickered down toward the sea.

"Magic?" The old woman darted out a hand to pluck Koll's coin from the air between finger and thumb. "That was training, and experience, and discipline. Perhaps I will show you magic another day, but let us all hope not." She flicked the coin spinning far into the air and Koll laughed as he caught it. "Magic has costs you will not wish to pay."

Skifr shrugged her coat back on with a snapping of cloth. "This style of fighting you have learned," she said to Thorn, "standing in a row with shield and mail and heavy blade, it does not suit you. It is not meant to suit you." Skifr dragged the shield from Thorn's arm and tossed it rattling among the chests on the *South Wind*. "You will fight with lighter, quicker weapons. You will fight in lighter armor."

"How will I stand in the shield wall without a shield?"

"Stand?" Skifr's eyes went wide as cups. "You are a killer, girl! You are the storm, always moving! You rush to meet your enemy, or you trick him into meeting you, and on the ground of your choosing, in the manner of your choosing, you *kill him*."

"My father was a famous warrior, he always said—"

"Where is your father?"

Thorn frowned for a moment, mouth half open, then touched her hand to a lump in her damp shirt, and slowly shut it. "Dead."

"So much for his expertise." Skifr tossed over the long ax and Thorn plucked it from the air, and weighed it in her hand, and swished it cautiously one way and the other. "What do the letters on the blade mean?"

"They say in five languages, 'to the fighter everything must be a weapon.' Good advice, if you are wise enough to take it."

Thorn nodded, frowning. "I am the storm."

"As yet, more of a drizzle," said Skifr. "But we are only beginning."

THE THIRD
LESSON

The Divine River.

Thorn remembered listening entranced to her father's stories of journeys up it and down its sister, the Denied, his eyes bright as he whispered of desperate battles against strange peoples, and proud brotherhoods forged in the crucible of danger, and hoards of gold to be won. Ever since she had dreamed of her own voyage, the names of those far places like the words of a magic spell, bursting with power and mystery: the tall hauls, Kalyiv, the First of Cities.

Strange to say, her dreams had not included arse and hands chafed raw from rowing, nor endless clouds of biting midges, nor fog so thick you only got fleeting glimpses of the fabled land, and those of bitter bog and tangled forest, the joys of which were hardly rare in Gettland.

"I was hoping for more excitement," grunted Thorn.

"So it is with hopes," muttered Brand.

She was a long way from forgiving him for humiliating her in front of Queen Laithlin, or for all those drops into Roystock's cold harbor, but she had to give a grim snort of agreement.

"There'll be excitement enough before we're back this way," said

Rulf, giving a nudge to the steering oar. "Excitement enough you'll be begging for boredom. If you live through it."

Mother Sun was sinking toward the ragged treetops when Father Yarvi ordered the *South Wind* grounded for the night and Thorn could finally ship her oar, flinging it roughly across Brand's knees and rubbing at her blistered palms.

They dragged the ship from the water by the prow rope in a stumbling, straining crowd, the ground so boggy it was hard to tell where river ended and earth began.

"Gather some wood for a fire," called Safrit.

"Dry wood?" asked Koll, kicking through the rotten flotsam clogged on the bank.

"It does tend to burn more easily."

"Not you, Thorn." Skifr was leaning on one of the ship's spare oars, the blade high above her head. "In the day you belong to Rulf, but at dawn and dusk you are mine. Whenever there is light, we must seize every chance to train."

Thorn squinted at the gloomy sky, huddled low over the gloomy land. "You call this light?"

"Will your enemies wait for morning if they can kill you in the dark?"

"What enemies?"

Skifr narrowed her eyes. "The true fighter must reckon everyone their enemy."

The sort of thing Thorn used to airily proclaim to her mother. Heard from someone else, it sounded like no fun at all. "When do I rest, then?"

"In the songs of great heroes, do you hear often of resting?"

She watched Safrit tossing flat loaves among the crew, and her mouth flooded with spit. "You sometimes hear of eating."

"Training on a full stomach is unlucky."

Even Thorn had precious little fight left after a long day competing with Brand at the oar. But she supposed the sooner they started, the sooner they'd finish. "What do we do?"

"I will try to hit you. You will try not to be hit."

"With an oar?"

"Why not? To hit and not be hit is the essence of fighting."

"There's no way I could work this stuff out on my own," grunted Thorn.

She didn't even gasp when Skifr darted out a hand and cuffed her across the cheek. She was getting used to it.

"You will be struck, and when you are, the force of it must not stagger you, the pain of it must not slow you, the shock of it must not cause you to doubt. You must learn to strike without pity. You must learn to be struck without fear." Skifr lowered the oar so that the blade hovered near Thorn's chest. "Though I advise you to get out of the way. If you can."

She certainly tried. Thorn dodged, wove, sprang, rolled, then she stumbled, lurched, slipped, floundered. To begin with she hoped to get around the oar and bring Skifr down, but she soon found just staying out of its way took every grain of wit and energy. The oar darted at her from everywhere, cracked her on the head, on the shoulders, poked her in the ribs, in the stomach, made her grunt, and gasp, and whoop as it swept her feet away and sent her tumbling.

The smell of Safrit's cooking tugged at her groaning belly, and the crew ate and drank, spreading their fingers to the warmth of the fire, propping themselves easily on their elbows, watching, chuckling, making bets on how long she could last. Until the sun was a watery glow on the western horizon and Thorn was soaked through and mud-caked from head to toe, throbbing with bruises, each breath ripping at her heaving chest.

"Would you like the chance to hit me back?" asked Skifr.

If there was one thing that could have made Thorn enthusiastic about holding an oar again, it was the chance to club Skifr with one.

But the old woman had other ideas. "Brand, bring me that bar."

He scraped the last juice from his bowl, stood up wrapped in a blanket and brought something over, licking at his teeth. A bar of rough-forged iron, about the length of a sword but easily five times the weight.

"Thanks," said Thorn, voice poisonous with sarcasm.

"What can I do?"

All she could think of was him wearing that same helpless look on the beach below Thorlby, as Hunnan sent three lads to kill her dreams. "What do you ever do?" Not fair, maybe, but she wasn't feeling too fair. Wasn't as if anyone was ever fair to her.

His brow furrowed, and he opened his mouth as if to snap something at her. Then he seemed to think better of it, and turned back to the fire, dragging his blanket tight over his hunched shoulders.

"Aye!" she called after him, "you go and sit down!" A feeble sort of jibe, since she would have liked nothing better.

Skifr slid a shield onto her arm. "Well, then? Hit me."

"With this?" It took an effort just to lift the damn thing. "I'd rather use the oar."

"To a fighter, everything must be a weapon, remember?" Skifr rapped Thorn on the forehead with her knuckles. "Everything. The ground. The water. That rock. Dosduvoi's head."

"Eh?" grunted the giant, looking up.

"Dosduvoi's head would make a fearsome weapon, mark you," said Odda. "Hard as stone and solid right through."

Some chuckling at that, though laughter seemed a foreign tongue to Thorn as she weighed that length of iron in her hand.

"For now, that is your weapon. It will build strength."

"I thought I couldn't win with strength."

"You can lose with weakness. If you can move that bar fast enough to hit me, your sword will be quick as lightning and just as deadly. Begin." Skifr opened her eyes very wide and said in a piping mimicry of Thorn's voice. "Or is the task not fair?"

Thorn set her jaw even harder than usual, planted her feet, and with a fighting growl went to work. It was far from pretty. A few swings and her arm was burning from neck to fingertips. She reeled about after the bar, struck great clods of mud from the ground, one landing in the fire and sending up a shower of sparks and a howl of upset from the crew.

Skifr danced her lurching dance, dodging Thorn's clumsy efforts with pitiful ease and letting her lumber past, occasionally knocking the bar away with a nudge of her shield, barking out instructions Thorn could barely understand, let alone obey.

"No, you are trying to lead the way, you must follow the weapon. No, more wrist. No, elbow in. The weapon is part of you! No, angled, angled, like so. No, shoulder up. No, feet wider. This is your ground! Own it! You are queen of this mud! Try again. No. Try again. No. Try again. No, no, no, no, no. No!"

Thorn gave a shriek and flung the bar to the wet earth, and Skifr shrieked back, crashed into her with the shield, and sent her sprawling. "Never lower your guard! That is the moment you die. Do you understand?"

"I understand," Thorn hissed back through her gritted teeth, tasting a little blood.

"Good. Let us see if your left hand has more spice in it."

By the time Skifr called a grudging halt Father Moon was smiling in the sky and the night was noisy with the strange music of frogs. Apart from a handful keeping watch the crew was sleeping soundly, bundled in blankets, in furs and fleeces, and in the luckiest cases bags of seal-skin, sending up a thunder of snores and a smoking of breath in the ruddy light of the dying fire.

Safrit sat crosslegged, Koll sleeping with his head in her lap and her hand on his sandy hair, eyelids flickering as he dreamed. She handed up a bowl. "I saved you some."

Thorn hung her head, face crushed up tight. Against scorn, and pain, and anger she was well-armored, but that shred of kindness brought a sudden choking sob from her.

"It'll be all right," said Safrit, patting her knee. "You'll see."

"Thanks," whispered Thorn, and she smothered her tears and crammed cold stew into her face, licking the juice from her fingers.

She thought she saw Brand's eyes gleaming in the dark as he shifted up to leave a space, shoving Odda over and making him mew like a kitten in his fitful sleep. Thorn would have slept happily among corpses then. She didn't even bother to take her boots off as she dropped onto ground still warm from Brand's body.

She was almost asleep when Skifr gently tucked the blanket in around her.

THE GODS'
ANGER

The days were lost in a haze of rowing, and wood creaking, and water slopping against the *South Wind*'s flanks, Thorn's jaw muscles bunching with every stroke, Rulf's eyes narrowed to slits as he gazed upriver, Father Yarvi's withered hand clutched behind his back in his good one, Koll's endless questions and Safrit's scolding, stories told about the fire, shadows shifting over the scarred faces of the crew, the constant muttering of Skifr's instructions and the rattle, grunt and clatter of Thorn's training as Brand drifted off to sleep.

He couldn't say he liked her, but he had to admire the way she kept at it, always fighting no matter the odds, always getting up no matter how often she was put down. That was courage. Made him wish he was more like her.

From time to time they came ashore at villages belonging to no land or lord. Turf-roofed fishers' huts huddling in loops of the river, wattle hovels shepherds shared with their animals under the eaves of the silent forest, which made the one Brand had shared with Rin seem a palace indeed and brought a surge of sappy homesickness welling up in him. Father Yarvi would trade for milk and ale and still-bleating goats, knowing every tongue spoken by men or beasts, it seemed, but there were few smiles traded on either side. Smiles might be free, but they were in short supply out there on the Divine.

They passed boats heading north, and sometimes their crews were dour and watchful, and sometimes they called out cautious greetings. Whichever they did Rulf kept careful eyes on them until they were well out of sight with his black bow ready in one hand, a fearsome thing near as tall as a man, made from the great ridged horns of some beast Brand had never seen and never wanted to.

"They seemed friendly enough," he said, after one almost-merry encounter.

"An arrow from a smiling archer kills you just as dead," said Rulf, setting his bow back beside the steering oar. "Some of these crews will be heading home with rich cargo, but some will have failed, and be looking to make good on their trip by taking a fat ship, and selling her pretty young pair of back oars for slaves."

Thorn jerked her head toward Brand. "They'll only find one pretty back oar on this boat."

"You'd be prettier if you didn't scowl so much," said Rulf, which brought a particularly ugly scowl, just as it was meant to.

"Might be the minister's prow keeps the raiders off," said Brand, wedging his ax beside his sea-chest.

Thorn snorted as she slid her sword back into its sheath. "More likely our ready weapons."

"Aye," said Rulf. "Even law-abiding men forget themselves in lawless places. There's a limit on the reach of the Ministry. But the authority of steel extends to every port. It's a fine sword you have there, Thorn."

"My father's." After a moment of considering, she offered it up to him.

"Must've been quite a warrior."

"He was a Chosen Shield," said Thorn, puffing with pride. "He was the one made me want to fight."

Rulf peered approvingly down the blade, which was well-used and well-kept, then frowned at the pommel, which was a misshapen lump of iron. "Don't reckon this can be its first pommel."

Thorn stared off toward the tangled trees, jaw working. "It had a better, but it's strung on Grom-gil-Gorm's chain."

Rulf raised his brows, and there was an awkward silence as he passed the sword back. "How about you, Brand? Your father a fighting man?"

Brand frowned off toward a heron wading in the shallows of the other bank. "He could give a blow or two."

Rulf puffed out his cheeks, clear that subject was firmly buried. "Let's row, then!"

Thorn spat over the side as she worked her hands about her oar. "Bloody rowing. I swear, when I get back to Thorlby I'll never touch an oar again."

"A wise man once told me to take one stroke at a time." Father Yarvi was just behind them. There were many bad things about being at the back oar, but one of the worst was that you never knew who might be at your shoulder.

"Done a lot of rowing, have you?" Thorn muttered as she bent to the next stroke.

"Oy!" Rulf kicked at her oar and made her flinch. "Pray you never have to learn what he knows about rowing!"

"Let her be." Father Yarvi smiled as he rubbed at his withered wrist. "It's not easy being Thorn Bathu. And it's only going to get harder."

The Divine narrowed and the forest closed in dark about the banks. The trees grew older, and taller, and thrust twisted roots into the slow-flowing water and held gnarled boughs low over it. So while Skifr knocked Thorn over with an oar the rest of the crew rolled up the sail, and took down the mast, and laid it lengthways between the sea-chests on trestles. Unable to climb it, Koll pulled out his knife and set to carving on it. Brand was expecting childish hackings and was amazed to see animals, plants, and warriors all intertwined and beautifully wrought spreading steadily down its length.

"Your son's got talent," he said to Safrit when she brought around the water.

"All kinds of talent," she agreed, "but a mind like a moth. I can't keep it on one thing for two moments together."

"Why is it even called Divine?" grunted Koll, sitting back to stare off upriver, spinning his knife around and around in his fingers and somewhat proving his mother's point. "I don't see much holy about it."

"I've heard because the One God blessed it above all other waters," rumbled Dosduvoi.

Odda raised a brow at the shadowy thicket that hemmed them in on both banks. "This look much blessed to you?"

"The elves knew the true names of these rivers," said Skifr, who'd made a kind of bed among the cargo to drape herself on. "We call them Divine and Denied because those are as close as our clumsy human tongues can come."

The good humor guttered at the mention of elves, and Dosduvoi mumbled a prayer to the One God, and Brand made a holy sign over his heart.

Odda was less pious. "Piss on the elves!" He leapt from his seachest, dragging his trousers down and sending a yellow arc high over the ship's rail. Some laughter, and some cries of upset from men behind who took a spattering as a gust blew up.

One man going often made others feel the need, and soon Rulf was ordering the boat held steady mid-stream while half the crew stood at the rail with hairy backsides on display. Thorn shipped her oar, which meant flinging it in Brand's lap, and worked her trousers down to show a length of muscled white thigh. It was hardly doing good to watch but Brand found it hard not to, and ended up peering out the corner of his eye as she slithered up and wedged her arse over the ship's side.

"I'm all amazement!" called Odda at her as he sat back down.

"That I piss?"

"That you do it sitting. I was sure you were hiding a prick under there." A few chuckles from the benches at that.

"Thought the same about you, Odda." Thorn dragged her trousers back up and hooked her belt. "Reckon we're both disappointed."

A proper laugh swept the ship. Koll gave a whooping snigger, and Rulf thumped at the prow-beast in appreciation, and Odda laughed loudest of all, throwing his head back to show his mouthful of filed teeth. Safrit slapped Thorn on the back as she dropped grinning back on her sea-chest and Brand thought Rulf had been right. There was nothing ugly about her when she smiled.

The gust that wetted Odda's oarmates was the first of many. The heavens darkened and She Who Sings the Wind sent a cold song swirling about the ship, sweeping ripples across the calm Divine and whipping Brand's hair around his face. A cloud of little white birds clattered up, a flock of thousands, twisting and swirling against the bruised sky.

Skifr slid one hand into her ragged coat to rummage through the mass of runes and charms and holy signs about her neck. "That is an ill omen."

"Reckon a storm's coming," muttered Rulf.

"I have seen hail the size of a child's head drop from a sky like that."

"Should we get the boat off the river?" asked Father Yarvi.

"Upend her and get under her." Skifr kept her eyes on the clouds like a warrior watching an advancing enemy. "And quickly."

They grounded the *South Wind* at the next stretch of shingle, Brand wincing as the wind blew colder, fat spots of rain stinging his face.

First they hauled out mast and sail, then stores and sea-chests, weapons and shields. Brand helped Rulf free the prow-beasts with wedges and mallet, wrapped them carefully in oiled cloth while Koll helped Thorn wedge the oars in the rowlocks so they could use them as handles to lift the ship. Father Yarvi unlocked the iron-bound chest from its chains, the veins in Dosduvoi's great neck bulging as he hefted its weight onto his shoulder. Rulf pointed out the spots and six stout barrels were rolled into place around their heaped-up gear, Odda wielding a shovel with marvelous skill to make pits that the tall prow and stern would sit in.

"Bring her up!" bellowed Rulf, Thorn grinning as she vaulted over the side of the ship.

"You seem happy enough about all this," said Brand, gasping as he slid into the cold water.

"I'd rather lift ten ships than train with Skifr."

The rain came harder, so it scarcely made a difference whether they were in the river or not, everyone soaked through, hair and beards plastered, clothes clinging, straining faces beaded with wet.

"Never sail in a ship you can't carry!" growled Rulf through gritted teeth. "Up! Up! Up!"

And with each shout there was a chorus of grunting, growling, groaning. Every man, and woman too, lending all their strength, the cords standing out stark from Safrit's neck and Odda's grooved teeth bared in an animal snarl and even Father Yarvi dragging with his one good hand.

"Tip her!" roared Rulf as they heaved her from the water. "But gently now! Like a lover, not a wrestler!"

"If I tip her like a lover do I get a kiss?" called Odda.

"I'll kiss you with my fist," hissed Thorn through her clenched teeth.

It had grown dark as dusk, and He Who Speaks the Thunder grumbled in the distance as they heaved the *South Wind* over, prow and stern digging deep into the boggy earth. Now they took her under the top rail, upside down, and carried her up the bank, boots mashing the ground to sliding mud.

"Easy!" called Father Yarvi. "Gently! A little toward me! Yes! And down!"

They lowered the ship onto the barrels, and Odda shrieked and flapped his hand because he'd got it caught, but that was the only injury and the *South Wind* was steady on her back. Soaked, sore and gasping they slipped under the hull and crouched huddled in the darkness.

"Good work," said Rulf, his voice echoing strangely. "Reckon we might make a crew of this crowd of fools yet." He gave a chuckle, and others joined him, and soon everyone was laughing, and slapping each other, and hugging each other, for they knew they'd done a fine job, each working for one another, and were bound together by it.

"She makes a noble hall," said Dosduvoi, patting at the timbers above his head.

"One I am exceedingly grateful for in this weather," said Odda.

The rain was pelting now, coming in sheets and curtains, coursing from the *South Wind*'s top rail which had become the eaves of their roof. They heard thunder crackle close by and the wind howled icy-chill around the barrels. Koll huddled up tighter and Brand put his arm around him, like he might've round Rin when they were children and had no roof at all. He felt Thorn pressed tight against him on the other side, the woody hardness of her shoulder against his, shifting as she breathed, and he wanted to put his arm around her too but didn't much fancy her fist in his face.

Probably he should've taken the chance to tell her that he'd been the one went to Father Yarvi. That he'd lost his place on the king's raid over it. Might've made her think twice before digging him with her oar again, at least, or with her insults either.

But the gods knew he wasn't much good at telling things, and the gods knew even better she wasn't easy to tell things to, and the further it all dwindled into the past the harder it got. Didn't seem like doing good, to put her in his debt that way.

So he stayed silent, and let her shoulder press against his instead, then felt her flinch as something heavy banged against the hull.

"Hail," whispered Skifr. The rattling grew louder, and louder yet, blows like axes on shields, and the crew peered fearfully up, or shrank against the ground, or put hands over their heads.

"Look at this." Fror held up a stone that had rolled under the boat, a spiked and knobbled chunk of ice the size of a fist. In the gloom outside the ship Brand could see the hail pounding the wet earth, bouncing and rolling.

"You think the gods are angry with us?" asked Koll.

"It is frozen rain," said Father Yarvi. "The gods hate those who plan badly, and help those with good friends, good swords, and good sense. Worry less about what the gods might do and more about what you can, that's my advice."

But Brand could hear a lot of prayers even so. He'd have given it a go himself, but he'd never been much good at picking out the right gods.

Skifr was yammering away in at least three languages, not one of which he understood. "Are you praying to the One God or the many?" he asked.

"All of them. And the fish god of the Banyas, and the tree spirits of the Shends, and great eight-armed Thopal that the Alyuks think will eat the world at the end of time. One can never have too many friends, eh, boy?"

"I . . . suppose?"

Dosduvoi peered out sadly at the downpour. "I went over to the worship of the One God because her priests said she would bring me better luck."

"How's that worked out?" asked Koll.

"Thus far, unluckily," said the big man. "But it may be that I have not committed myself enough to her worship."

Odda spat. "You can never bow low enough for the One God's taste."

"In that she and Grandmother Wexen are much alike," murmured Yarvi.

"Who are you praying to?" Brand muttered at Thorn, her lips moving silently while she clung to something on a thong around her neck.

He saw her eyes gleam as she frowned back. "I don't pray."

"Why?"

She was silent for a moment. "I prayed for my father. Every morning and every night to every god whose name I could learn. Dozens of the bastards. He died anyway." And she turned her back on him and shifted away, leaving darkness between them.

The storm blew on.

READY OR
DEAD

"Gods," whispered Brand.

The elf-ruins crowded in on both sides of the river, looming towers and blocks and cubes, broken elf-glass twinkling as it caught the watery sun.

The Divine flowed so broad here it was almost a lake, cracked teeth of stone and dead fingers of metal jutting from the shallows. All was wreathed with creeper, sprouting with sapling trees, choked with thickets of ancient bramble. No birds called, not even an insect buzzed over water still as black glass, only the slightest ripple where the oar-blades smoothly dipped, yet Thorn's skin prickled with the feeling of being watched from every empty window.

All her life she had been warned away from elf-ruins. It was the one thing on which her mother and father had always stood united. Men daily risked shipwreck hugging the coast of Gettland to keep their distance from the haunted island of Strokom, where the Ministry had forbidden any man to tread. Sickness lurked there, and death, and things worse than death, for the elves had wielded a magic powerful enough to break God and destroy the world.

And here they went, forty little people in a hollow twig, rowing through the midst of the greatest elf-ruins Thorn had ever seen.

"Gods," breathed Brand again, twisting to look over his shoulder.

There was a bridge ahead, if you could call a thing built on that scale a bridge. It must once have crossed the river in a single dizzying span, the slender roadway strung between two mighty towers, each one dwarfing the highest turret of the citadel of Thorlby. But the bridge had fallen centuries before, chunks of stone big as houses hanging from tangled ropes of metal, one swinging gently with the faintest creak as they rowed beneath.

Rulf gripped the steering oar, mouth hanging wide as he stared up at one of the leaning towers, crouching as if he expected it to topple down and crush the tiny ship and its ant-like crew into nothingness. "If you ever needed reminding how small you are," he muttered, "here's a good spot."

"It's a whole city," whispered Thorn.

"The elf-city of Smolod." Skifr lounged on the steering platform, peering at her fingernails as though colossal elf-ruins were hardly worthy of comment. "In the time before the Breaking of God it was home to thousands. Thousands of thousands. It glittered with the light of their magic, and the air was filled with the song of their machines and the smoke of their mighty furnaces." She gave a long sigh. "All lost. All past. But so it is with everything. Great or small, the Last Door is life's one certainty."

A sheet of bent metal stuck from the river on rusted poles, arrows sweeping across it in flaking paint, bold words written in unknowable elf-letters. It looked uncomfortably like a warning, but of what, Thorn could not say.

Rulf tossed a twig over the side, watched it float away to judge their speed and gave a grudging nod. For once he had to bellow no encouragements—meaning insults—to get the *South Wind* moving at a pretty clip. The ship itself seemed to whisper with the prayers, and oaths, and charms of its crew, spoken in a dozen languages. But

Skifr, who had something for every god and every occasion, for once let the heavens be.

"Save your prayers for later," she said. "There is no danger here."

"No danger?" squeaked Dosduvoi, fumbling a holy sign over his chest and getting his oar tangled with the man in front.

"I have spent a great deal of time in elf-ruins. Exploring them has been one of my many trades."

"Some would call that heresy," said Father Yarvi, looking up from under his brows.

Skifr smiled. "Heresy and progress often look much alike. We have no Ministry in the south to meddle with such things. Rich folk there will pay well for an elf-relic or two. The Empress Theofora herself has quite a collection. But the ruins of the south have often been picked clean. Those about the Shattered Sea have much more to offer. Untouched, some of them, since the Breaking of God. The things one can find there . . ."

Her eyes moved to the iron-shod chest, secured by chains near the setting of the mast, and Thorn thought of the box, and the light from inside it. Had that been dug from the forbidden depths of a place like this one? Was there magic in it that could break the world? She gave a shiver at the thought.

But Skifr only smiled wider. "If you go properly prepared into the cities of elves, you will find less danger than in the cities of men."

"They say you're a witch." Koll blew a puff of wood-chips from his latest patch of carving and looked up.

"They say?" Skifr widened her eyes so the white showed all the way around. "True and false are hard to pick apart in the weave of what *they say*."

"You said you know magic."

"And so I do. Enough to cause much harm, but not enough to do much good. So it is, with magic."

"Could you show it to me?"

Skifr snorted. "You are young and rash and know not what you ask, boy." They rowed in the shadow of a vast wall, its bottom sunk in the river, its top broken off in a skein of twisted metal. Rank upon rank of great windows yawned empty. "The powers that raised this city also rendered it a ruin. There are terrible risks, and terrible costs. Always, there are costs. How many gods do you know the names of?"

"All of them," said Koll.

"Then pray to them all that you never see magic." Skifr frowned down at Thorn. "Take your boots off."

Thorn blinked. "Why?"

"So you can take a well-deserved break from rowing."

Thorn looked at Brand and he shrugged back. Together they pulled their oars in and she worked off her boots. Skifr slipped out of her coat, folded it and draped it over the steering oar. Then she drew her sword. Thorn had never seen it drawn before, and it was long, and slender, and gently curved, Mother Sun glinting from a murderous edge. "Are you ready, my dove?"

The break from rowing suddenly did not seem so appealing. "Ready for what?" asked Thorn, in a voice turned very small.

"A fighter is either ready or dead."

On the barest shred of instinct Thorn jerked her oar up, the blade of Skifr's sword chopping into it right between her hands.

"You're mad!" she squealed as she scrambled back.

"You're hardly the first to say so." Skifr jabbed left and right and made Thorn hop over the lowered mast. "I take it as a compliment." She grinned as she swished her sword back and forth, oarsmen jerking fearfully out of her way. "Take everything as a compliment, you can never be insulted."

She sprang forward again and made Thorn slither under the mast, breath whooping as she heard Skifr's sword rattle against it once, twice.

"My carving!" shouted Koll.

"Work around it!" snarled Skifr.

Thorn tripped on the chains that held the iron-bound chest and toppled into Odda's lap, tore his shield from its bracket, blocked a blow with both hands before Skifr ripped it from her and kicked her over backwards.

Thorn clawed up a coil of rope and flung it in the old woman's face, lunged for Fror's sword but he slapped her hand away. "Find your own!"

"It's in my chest!" she squealed, rolling over Dosduvoi's oar and grabbing the giant from behind, peering over his great shoulder.

"God save me!" he gasped as Skifr's blade darted past his ribs on one side then the other, nicking a hole in his shirt, Thorn dodging desperately, running out of room as the carved prow and Father Yarvi, smiling as he watched the performance, grew mercilessly closer.

"Stop!" shouted Thorn, holding up a trembling hand. "Please! Give me a chance!"

"Do the berserks of the Lowlands stop for their enemies? Does Bright Yilling pause if you say please? Does Grom-gil-Gorm give chances?"

Skifr stabbed again and Thorn leapt past Yarvi, teetered on the top strake, took one despairing stride and sprang, clear off the ship and onto the shaft of the front oar. She felt it flex under her weight, the oarsman straining to keep it level. She tottered to the next, bare foot curling desperately around the slippery wood, arms wide for balance. To hesitate, to consider, to doubt, was doom. She could only run on in great bounds, the water flickering by beneath, oars creaking and clattering in their sockets and the cheering of the crew ringing in her ears.

She gave a shrill whoop at the sheer reckless excitement of it, wind rushing in her open mouth. Running the oars was a noble feat, often sung of but rarely attempted. The feeling of triumph was short-lived, though. The *South Wind* had only sixteen oars a side and she was quickly running out. The last came rushing at her, Brand reaching over the rail, fingers straining. She made a despairing grab at his outstretched hand, he caught her sleeve—

The oar struck her hard in the side, her sleeve ripped and she tumbled headfirst into the river, surfaced gasping in a rush of bubbles.

"A creditable effort!" called Skifr, standing on the steering platform with her arm draped around Rulf's shoulders. "And swimming is even better exercise than rowing! We will make camp a few miles further on and wait for you!"

Thorn slapped her hand furiously into the water. "Miles?"

Her rage did not slow the *South Wind*. If anything it caused it to quicken. Brand stared from the stern with that helpless look, his arm still hanging over the side, and shrugged.

Skifr's voice floated out over the water. "I'll hold on to your boots for you!"

Snarling curses, Thorn began to swim, leaving the silent ruins in her wake.

ITCHING

Brand went down hard, practice sword spinning from his hand, tumbled grunting down the slope and flopped onto his back with a groan, the jeering of the crew echoing in his ears.

Lying there, staring into the darkening sky with his many bruises throbbing and his dignity in shreds, he guessed she must have hooked his ankle. But he'd seen no hint it was coming.

Thorn stuck her own sword point-down in the knobbled turf where they'd set out their training square and offered him her hand. "Is that three in a row now, or four?"

"Five," he grunted, "as you well know." He let her haul him up. He'd never been able to afford much pride and sparring with her was taking an awful toll on what little he had. "Gods, you got quick." He winced as he arched his back, still aching from her boot. "Like a snake but without the mercy."

Thorn grinned wider at that, and wiped a streak of blood from under her nose, the one mark he'd put on her in five bouts. He hadn't meant it as a compliment but it was plain she took it as one, and Skifr did too.

"I think young Brand has taken punishment enough for one day," the old woman called to the crew. "There must be a ring-crusted hero among you with the courage to test themselves against my pupil?"

Wasn't long ago they'd have roared with laughter at that offer. Men who'd raided every bitter coast of the Shattered Sea. Men who'd lived by the blade and the feud and called the shield wall home. Men who'd spilled blood enough between them to float a longship, fighting some sharp-tongued girl.

No one laughed now.

For weeks they'd watched her training like a devil in all weathers. They'd watched her put down and they'd watched her get up, over and over, until they were sore just with the watching of it. For a month they'd gone to sleep with the clash of her weapons as a lullaby and been woken by her warcries in place of a cock's crow. Day by day they'd seen her grow faster, and stronger, and more skillful. Terrible skillful, now, with ax and sword together, and she was getting that drunken swagger that Skifr had, so you could never tell where she or her weapons would be the next moment.

"Can't recommend it," said Brand as he lowered himself wincing beside the fire, pressing gently at a fresh scab on his scalp.

Thorn spun her wooden ax around her fingers as nimbly as you might a toothpick. "None of you got the guts for it?"

"Gods damn it, then, girl!" Odda sprang up from the fire. "I'll show you what a real man can do!"

Odda showed her the howl a real man makes when a wooden sword whacks him right in the groin, then he showed her the best effort Brand had ever seen at a real man eating his own shield, then he showed her a real man's muddy backside as he went sprawling through a bramble-bush and into a puddle.

He propped himself on his elbows, caked head to toe with mud, and blew water out of his nose. "Had enough yet?"

"I have." Dosduvoi stooped slowly to pick up Odda's fallen sword and drew himself up to his full height, great chest swelling. The wooden blade looked tiny in his ham of a fist.

Thorn's jaw jutted as she scowled up at him. "The big trees fall the hardest." Splinter in the world's arse she might be, but Brand found himself smiling. However the odds stood against her, she never backed down.

"This tree hits back," said Dosduvoi as he took up a fighting stance, big boots wide apart.

Odda sat down, kneading at a bruised arm. "It'd be a different story if the blades were sharpened, I can tell you that!"

"Aye," said Brand, "a short story with you dead at the end."

Safrit was busy cutting her son's hair, bright shears click-clicking. "Stop squirming!" she snapped at Koll. "It'll be over the faster."

"Hair has to be cut." Brand set a hand on the boy's shoulder. "Listen to your mother." He almost added *you're lucky to have one,* but swallowed it. Some things are better left unsaid.

Safrit waved the shears toward Brand. "I'll give that beard of yours a trim while I'm about it."

"Long as you don't bring the shears near me," said Fror, fingering one of the braids beside his scar.

"Warriors!" snorted Safrit. "Vainer than maidens! Most of these faces are best kept from the world, but a good-looking lad like you shouldn't be hidden in all that undergrowth."

Brand pushed his fingers through his beard. "Surely has thickened up these past few weeks. Starting to itch a little, if I'm honest."

A cheer went up as Dosduvoi lifted his sword high and Thorn dived between his wide-set legs, spun, and gave him a resounding kick in the arse, sending the big man staggering.

Rulf scratched at a cluster of raw insect bites on the side of his neck. "We're all itching a little."

"No avoiding some passengers on a voyage like this." Odda had a good rummage down the front of his trousers. "They're only striving to find the easiest way south, just as we are."

"They fear a war is brewing with the High King of lice," said Safrit, "and seek allies among the midges." And she slapped one against the back of her neck.

Her son scrubbed a shower of sandy clippings from his hair, which still seemed wild as ever. "Are there really allies to be found out here?"

"The Prince of Kalyiv can call on so many riders the dust of their horses blots out the sun," said Odda.

Fror nodded. "And I hear the Empress of the South has so many ships she can fashion a footbridge across the sea."

"It's not about ships or horses," said Brand, rubbing gently at the callouses on his palms. "It's about the trade that comes up the Divine. Slaves and furs go one way, silver and silk come the other. And it's silver wins wars, just as much as steel." He realized everyone was looking at him and trailed off, embarrassed. "So Gaden used to tell me . . . at the forge . . ."

Safrit smiled, toying with the weights strung about her neck. "It's the quiet ones you have to watch."

"Still pools are the deepest," said Yarvi, his pale eyes fixed on Brand. "Wealth is power. It is Queen Laithlin's wealth that is the root of the High King's jealousy. He can shut the Shattered Sea to our ships. Cut off Gettland's trade. With the Prince of Kalyiv and the empress on his side, he can close the Divine to us too. Throttle us without drawing a blade. With the prince and the empress as our allies, the silver still flows."

"Wealth is power," muttered Koll to himself, as though testing the words for truth. Then he looked over at Fror. "How did you get the scar?"

"I asked too many questions," said the Vansterman, smiling at the fire.

Safrit bent over Brand, tugging gently at his beard, shears snipping. It was strange, having someone so close, fixed on him so carefully, gentle fingers on his face. He always told Rin he remembered their mother, but it was only stories told over and over, twisted out of shape by time until he remembered the stories but not the memories themselves. It was Rin who'd always cut his hair, and he touched the knife she'd made for him then and felt a sudden longing for home. For the hovel they'd worked so hard for, and the firelight on his sister's face, and worry for her rushed in so sharp he winced at the sting of it.

Safrit jerked back. "Did I nick you?"

"No," croaked Brand. "Missing home is all."

"Got someone special waiting, eh?"

"Just my family."

"Handsome lad like you, I can hardly believe it."

Dosduvoi had finally put a stop to Thorn's dodging by grabbing a handful of her unruly hair, and now he caught her belt with his other hand, jerked her up like a sheaf of hay and flung her bodily into a ditch.

"Some of us are cursed with bad love-luck," said Rulf mournfully, as Skifr called a halt to the bout and peered into the ditch after her pupil. "I was gone from my farm too long and my wife married again."

"Bad love-luck for you, maybe," muttered Safrit, tossing a tuft of Brand's beard into the fire, "but good for her."

"Bad love-luck is swearing an oath not to have any love at all." Father Yarvi gave a sigh. "The older I get, the less the tender care of Grandmother Wexen seems a good trade for romance."

"I did have a wife," said Dosduvoi, lowering himself beside the fire and gingerly seeking out a comfortable position for his bruised buttocks, "but she died."

"It's not bad luck if she's crushed by your bulk," said Odda.

"That is not funny," said the giant, though judging from the sniggering many of the crew disagreed.

"No wife for me," said Odda. "Don't believe in 'em."

"I doubt they're any more convinced by you," said Safrit. "Though I feel sorry for your hand, forced to be your only lover all this time."

Odda grinned, filed teeth shining with the firelight. "Don't be. My hand is a sensitive partner, and always willing."

"And, unlike the rest of us, not put off by your monstrous breath." Safrit brushed some loose hairs from Brand's now close-cropped beard and sat back. "You're done."

"Might I borrow the shears?" asked Skifr.

Safrit gave the gray fuzz on her skull a look over. "Doesn't seem you've much to cut."

"Not for me." The old woman nodded at Thorn, who'd dragged herself out of the ditch and was limping over, grimacing as she rubbed at her sore head, loose hair torn free and shooting off at all angles. "I think another of our lambs needs shearing. Dosduvoi has proved that mop a weakness."

"No." Thorn tossed down her battered wooden weapons and ti-died a few strands back behind her ear, a strange gesture from her, who never seemed to care the least for how she looked.

Skifr raised her brows. "I would not have counted vanity among your many shortcomings."

"I made my mother a promise," said Thorn, snatching up a flat loaf and stuffing half of it in her mouth with dirty fingers in one go. She might not have outfought three men at once but Brand had no doubt she could have out-eaten them.

"I had no notion you held your mother in such high regard," said Skifr.

"I don't. She's always been a pain in my arse. Always telling me the right way to do things and it's never the way I want to do them." Thorn ripped at the loaf with her teeth like a wolf at a carcass, eating and speaking at once, spraying crumbs. "Always fussing over what folk think of me, what they'll do to me, how I might be hurt, how I might embarrass her. Eat this way, talk this way, smile this way, piss this way."

All the while she talked Brand was thinking about his sister, left alone with no one to watch over her, and the anger stole up on him. "Gods," he growled. "Is there a blessing made you couldn't treat like a curse?"

Thorn frowned, cheeks bulging as she chewed. "What does that mean?"

He barked the words, suddenly disgusted with her. "That you've a mother who gives a damn about you, and a home waiting where you're safe, and you still find a way to complain!"

That caused an uncomfortable silence. Father Yarvi narrowed his eyes, and Koll widened his, and Fror's brows crept up in surprise. Thorn swallowed slowly, looking as shocked as if she'd been slapped. More shocked. She got slapped all the time.

"I bloody hate *people*," she muttered, snatching another loaf from Safrit's hand.

It was hardly the good thing to say but for once Brand couldn't keep his mouth shut. "Don't worry." He dragged his blanket over one shoulder and turned his back on her. "They feel much the same about you."

DAMN THEM

Thorn's nose twitched at the smell of cooking. She blinked awake, and knew right off something was odd. She could scarcely remember the last time she had woken without the tender help of Skifr's boot.

Perhaps the old witch had a heart after all.

She had dreamt a dog was licking at the side of her head, and she tried to shake the memory off as she rolled from her blankets. Maybe dreams were messages from the gods, but she was damned if she could sieve the meaning from that one. Koll was hunched at the water's edge, grumbling as he washed the pots out.

"Morning," she said, giving an almighty stretch and almost enjoying the long ache through her arms and across her back. The first few days she'd hardly been able to move in the mornings from the rowing and the training together, but she was hardening to the work now, getting tough as rope and timber.

Koll glanced up and his eyes went wide. "Er . . ."

"I know. Skifr let me sleep." She grinned across the river. For the first time, Divine seemed an apt name for it. The year was wearing on and Mother Sun was bright and hot already, birds twittering in the forest and insects floating lazy over the water. The trailing branches of the trees about the bank were heavy with white flowers and Thorn took a long, blossom-scented breath in through her nose and let it sigh away. "I've a feeling it'll be a fine day." And she ruffled Koll's hair, turned around, and almost walked into Brand.

He stared at her, that helpless look of his splattered all over his face. "Thorn, your—"

"Go and die." Half the night she'd been lying awake thinking of harsh things to say to him, but when the moment came that was the best she could manage. She shouldered past and over to the embers of the fire where the crew were gathered.

"Eat well," Rulf was saying. "Might be later today we'll reach the tall hauls. You'll need all the strength you've got and more besides when we carry . . . the . . ." He trailed off, staring, as Thorn walked up, grabbing a spare a bowl and peering into the pot.

"No need to stop for me," she said. They were all staring at her and it was starting to make her nervous.

Then Odda chuckled, spluttering food. "She looks like a brush with half the bristles plucked!"

"A lamb half-sheared," said Dosduvoi.

"A willow with half the branches lopped," murmured Fror.

"I like that one," said Odda. "That has poetry. You should speak more."

"You should speak less, but things are as they are."

A breeze floated up from the river, strangely cold against the side of Thorn's head, and she frowned down, and saw her shoulder was covered in hair. She touched one hand to her scalp, afraid of what she might find. On the right side her hair was muddled into its usual incompetent braid. The left was shaved to patchy stubble, her fingertips trembling as they brushed the unfamiliar knobbles of her skull.

"You sleep on your right." Skifr leaned past her shoulder, plucking a piece of meat from the pot between long thumb and forefinger. "I did the best I could without waking you. You look so peaceful when you sleep."

Thorn stared at her. "You said you wouldn't make me do it!"

"Which is why I did it." And the old woman smiled as though she'd done Thorn quite the favor.

So much for the witch having a heart, and the fine day too. Thorn hardly knew then whether she wanted to weep, scream, or bite Skifr's face. In the end all she could do was stalk off toward the river, the crew's laughter ringing in her ears, clenching her teeth and clutching at her half-tangled, half-bald head.

Her mother's most treasured possession was a little mirror set in silver. Thorn always teased her that she loved it because she was so vain, but knew really it was because it had been a gift from her father, brought back long ago from the First of Cities. Thorn had always hated to look at herself in it. Her face too long and her cheeks too hollow, her nose too sharp and her eyes too angry. But she would happily have traded that reflection for the lopsided mockery that peered from the still water at the river's edge now.

She remembered her mother singing softly as she combed Thorn's hair, her father smiling as he watched them. She remembered the laughter and the warmth of arms about her. Her family. Her home. She gripped the pouch she wore and thought what a pitiful thing it was to carry your father's fingerbones around your neck. But it was all she had left. She bitterly shook her head as she stared at her ruined reflection and another appeared behind her—tall and lean and colorless.

"Why did you bring me out here?" she asked, slapping both reflections angrily from the water.

"To make allies of our enemies," said Father Yarvi. "To bring help to Gettland."

"In case you hadn't noticed, I've no touch for making friends."

"We all have our shortcomings."

"Why bring me, then? Why pay Skifr to teach me?"

The minister squatted beside her. "Do you trust me, Thorn?"

"Yes. You saved my life." Though looking into his pale blue eyes she wondered how far one should trust a deep-cunning man. "And I swore an oath. What choice do I have?"

"None. So trust me." He glanced up at the wreckage of her hair. "It might take a little getting used to, but I think it suits you. Strange and fierce. One of a kind."

She snorted. "It's unusual, that I'll grant you."

"Some of us are unusual. I always thought you were happy to stand out. You seem to thrive on mockery like a flower on dung."

"Harder work than it seems," she muttered. "Always finding a brave face."

"That I know, believe me."

They stayed there, beside the water, for a while, in silence.

"Would you help me shave the other side?"

"I say leave it."

"Like this? Why?"

Yarvi nodded over toward the crew. "Because damn them, that's why."

"Damn them," muttered Thorn, scooping up water with her hand and pushing back the hair she still had. She had to admit she was getting a taste for the idea. Leaving it half-shaved, strange and fierce, a challenge to everyone who looked at her. "Damn them." And she snorted up a laugh.

"It's not as though you'll be the only odd-looking one on this crew. And anyway," Yarvi brushed some of the clippings gently from her shoulder with his withered hand, "hair grows back."

THAT WAS A TOUGH DAY'S WORK at the oar, fighting an angry current as the Divine narrowed and its banks steepened, Rulf frowning as he nudged the ship between rocks frothing with white water. That evening, as the sunset flared pink over the forested hills, they reached the tall hauls.

There was a strange village at the shore where no two houses were the same. Some built of timber, some of stone, some from turf like the barrows of dead heroes. It was home to folk of the Shattered Sea who had stopped on the way south, and folk from Kalyiv and the empire who had stopped on the way north, and folk from the forest tribes and the Horse People too who must have stuck on journeys east or west. Seeds blown from half the world away and chosen by some weird luck to put their roots down here.

Whatever their clothes and their customs, though, however sharp they had grown at spinning coins from passing crews, Father Yarvi had the Golden Queen's blood in his veins and knew the best way to fleece them. He bargained with each in their own tongue, baffled them now with charming smiles and now with stony blankness, until he had them bickering over the chance to offer him the lowest prices. When he finally rented eight great bearded oxen from the village's headwoman, he left her blinking down bewildered at the few coins in her palm.

"Father Yarvi is no fool," said Brand as they watched him work his everyday magic.

"He's the most deep-cunning man I ever met," answered Rulf.

There was a graveyard of abandoned timber by the river—rollers and runners, broken masts and oars, even a warped old keel with some strakes still on it, the bones of a ship that must have come down off the hills too damaged and been broken up for parts. The crew busied themselves with axes and chisels and by the time Father Moon was showing himself they had the *South Wind* ashore with good runners mounted alongside her keel and all her cargo packed on two rented wagons.

"Do we train now?" asked Thorn, as she watched the crew settle to their usual evening merry-making about the fire, Koll causing waves of laughter by copying one of Odda's less-than-likely stories.

Skifr looked at her, one eye gleaming in the fading light. "It is late, and there will be hard work tomorrow. Do you want to train?"

Thorn pushed some wood-shavings around with her toe. "Maybe just a little?"

"We will make a killer of you yet. Fetch the weapons."

———

RULF KICKED THEM ALL grumbling from their beds at the first glimmer of dawn, his breath steaming on the damp air.

"Up, you turds! You've got the hardest day of your lives ahead of you!"

There had been no easy days since they set off from Thorlby, but their helmsman was right. Carrying a ship over a mountain is exactly as hard as it sounds.

They heaved groaning at ropes, dragged snarling at oars switched about to make handles, set their shoulders to the keel when the runners snagged, gripping at each other in a straining, stinking, swearing tangle. Even with four of the oxen yoked to the prow they were soon all bruised from falls and raw from rope, whipped by twigs and riddled with splinters.

Safrit went ahead to clear the track of fallen branches. Koll darted in and out below the keel with a bucket of pitch and pig fat to keep the runners sliding. Father Yarvi shouted to the drovers in their tongue, who never used the goad but only crooned to the oxen in low voices.

Uphill, always uphill, the track faint and full of stones and roots. Some prowled armed through the trees about the ship, watching for bandits who might wait in the woods for crews to ambush, and rob, and sell as slaves.

"Selling a ship's crew is much more profitable than selling things to a ship's crew, that's sure." Odda's sigh implied he spoke from experience.

"Or than dragging a ship through a wood," grunted Dosduvoi.

"Save your breath for the lifting," Rulf forced through clenched teeth. "You'll need it."

As the morning wore on Mother Sun beat down without mercy and fat flies swarmed about the toiling oxen and the toiling crew. The sweat ran down Thorn's stubbled scalp in streaks, dripped from her brows and soaked her vest so that it chafed her nipples raw. Many of the crew stripped to their waists and a few much further. Odda struggled along in boots alone, sporting the hairiest arse ever displayed by man or beast.

Thorn should have been watching where she put her feet but her eyes kept drifting across the boat to Brand. While the others grumbled and stumbled and spewed curses he kept on, eyes ahead and wet hair stuck to his clenched jaw, thick muscles in his sweat-beaded shoulders working as he hefted all that weight with no complaints. That was strength right there. Strength like Thorn's father had, solid and silent and certain as Father Earth. She remembered Queen Laithlin's last words to her. *Fools boast of what they will do. Heroes do it.* And Thorn glanced across at Brand again and found herself wishing she was more like him.

"Yes, indeed," murmured Safrit as she held the waterskin to Thorn's cracked lips so she could drink without letting go her rope. "That is a well-made lad."

Thorn jerked her eyes away, got half her mouthful down her windpipe and near choked on it. "Don't know what you're speaking of."

"Course not." Safrit pushed her tongue into her cheek. "That must be why you keep not looking."

Once they even passed a ship being hauled the other way by a crowd of sweat-bathed Lowlanders, and they nodded to each other but wasted no breath on greetings. Thorn had no breath to spare, chest on fire and every muscle aching. Even her toenails hurt.

"I'm no great enthusiast . . . for rowing," she snarled, "but I'd damn sure rather . . . row a ship . . . than carry it."

With one last effort they heaved the *South Wind* over a stubborn brow and onto the flat, the runners grinding to a halt.

"We'll rest here for now!" called Father Yarvi.

There was a chorus of grateful groans, and men tied their ropes off around the nearest trees, dropping among the knotted roots where they stood.

"Thank the gods," whispered Thorn, pushing her hands into her aching back. "The downslope'll be easier. It has to be."

"Guess we'll see when we get there," said Brand, shading his eyes.

The ground dropped away ahead but, further on, indistinct in the haze, it rose again. It rose in forested slopes, higher, and higher, to a ridge above even the one they stood on now.

Thorn stared at it, jaw hanging open in sick disbelief. "More and more, crushing with stones seems like it might have been the less painful option."

"It's not too late to change your mind," said Father Yarvi. "We may be short of comforts out here, but I'm sure we can find stones."

THE MAN
WHO
FOUGHT A
SHIP

It was a grim and weary crew who struggled groaning from their beds, all wracked with aches and bruises from yesterday's labor and looking forward to as hard a day ahead. Even Odda had no jokes as he contemplated the long drop down the forested hillside, the hint of water glimmering in the misty distance.

"Least it's downhill," said Brand.

Odda snorted as he turned away. "Ha."

Brand soon found out his meaning. Uphill, the challenge had been dragging the *South Wind* on. Downhill, it was stopping her running off, which meant just as much work but a lot more danger. Not enough width on the crooked track for any help from the oxen, a dozen of the crew wrapped rags around sore hands, looped check-ropes around raw forearms and across aching shoulders padded with blankets and struggled along beside the ship, six of them on each side. They strained to keep her straight as she lurched down that lumpy hillside, Koll creeping ahead with his bucket, slipping in to daub the runners whenever they set to smoking.

"Steady," grumbled Rulf, holding up a hand. "Steady!"

"Easier said than bloody done," groaned Brand. He'd been given a rope, of course. The trouble with being able to lift heavy things is that when heavy things need lifting folk step out of the way and smile at you. He'd done some tough jobs to earn a crust for him and Rin but he'd never worked this hard in his life, hemp wet with sweat wound around one forearm, over his shoulders, then around the other, cutting at him with every step, legs all aquiver, boots scuffing at the loose earth and the slick leaves and the fallen pine needles, coughing on the dust Odda scuffled up ahead of him and flinching at the curses of Dosduvoi behind.

"When do we get to that damn river?" snarled Odda over his shoulder as they waited for a fallen tree to be heaved from the path.

"We'll soon be able to float the boat in the one flowing out of me." Brand shook his head and the sweat flew in fat drops from his wet hair.

"As soon as Safrit brings the water it's straight out of my back and down my crack," said Dosduvoi from behind him. "Are you going to tell us how you got the scar, Fror?"

"Cut myself shaving," the Vansterman called from the other side of the ship, then left a long pause before adding, "Never shave with an ax."

Thorn was one of five carrying the part-carved mast. Brand could feel her eyes sharp as arrows in his back and guessed she was still furious over what he'd said about her mother. He hardly blamed her. Wasn't Thorn who'd trotted off and left Rin to fend for herself, was it? Seemed whenever Brand lost his temper it was really himself he was angry at. He knew he ought to say sorry for it but words had never come easy to him. Sometimes he'd spend days picking over the right ones to say, but when he finally got his mouth open the wrong ones came drooling straight out.

"Reckon I'd be better off if I never said another word," he grunted to himself.

"You'd get no bloody complaints from me," he heard Thorn mutter, and was just turning to give her a tongue-lashing he'd no doubt soon regret when he felt a jolt through his rope that dragged him floundering into a heap of leaves, only just keeping his feet.

"Easy!" roared Dosduvoi, and hauled back hard on his own rope. A knot slipped with a noise like a whip cracking and he gave a shocked yelp and went flying over backwards.

Odda squealed out, "Gods!" as he was jerked onto his face, knocking the next man over so he lost his grip on his own rope, the loose end snapping like a thing alive.

There was a flurry of wingbeats as a bird took to the sky and the *South Wind* lurched forward, one of the men on the other side shrieking as his rope tore across his shoulders and spun him around, knocking Fror sideways, the sudden weight dragging the rest of the men over like skittles.

Brand saw Koll leaning in with his pitch, staring up in horror as the high prow shuddered over him. He tried to scramble clear, slipped on his back under the grinding keel.

No time for first thoughts, let alone second ones. Maybe that was a good thing. Brand's father had always told him he wasn't much of a thinker.

He bounded off the track in a shower of old leaves, dragging his rope around the nearest tree, a thick-trunked old beast with gnarled roots grasping deep into the hillside.

Folk were screaming over each other, timbers groaning, wood snapping, but Brand paid them no mind, wedged one boot up against the tree and then the other. With a grunt he forced his legs and his back out straight, leaning into the rope across his shoulders, hauling it taut so he was standing sideways from the trunk like one of the branches.

If only he'd been made of wood too. The rope twanged like a harpstring and his eyes bulged at the force of it, hemp grating against bark, slipping in his hands, biting into his arms. He clenched his teeth and closed his eyes and gripped at the rags around the rope. Gripped them tight as Death grips the dying.

Too much to lift. Way too much, but once the load's on you what choice do you have?

More grinding in his ears as the *South Wind* shifted and the weight grew, and grew, and crushed a slow groan out of him, but he knew if he let his knees, or his back, or his arms bend once the rope would fold him in half.

He opened his eyes for an instant. Sunlight flickered through leaves. Blood on his quivering fists. The rope smoking about the trunk. Voices echoed far away. He hissed as the rope twitched and pinged then slipped again, biting into him surely as a saw.

Couldn't let go. Couldn't fail his crew. Bones creaking as the hemp cut into his shoulders, his arms, his hands, sure to rip him apart, the jagged breath tearing at his chest and snorting from his clenched teeth.

Couldn't let go. Couldn't fail his family. His whole body trembling, every last thread of muscle on fire with the effort.

Nothing in the world but him and the rope. Nothing but effort and pain and darkness.

And then he heard Rin's voice, soft in his ear. "Let go."

He shook his head, whimpering, straining.

"Let go, Brand!"

An ax thudded into wood and he was falling, the world turning over. Strong arms caught him, lowered him, weak as a child, floppy as rags.

Thorn, with Mother Sun behind her, glowing in the fuzz on the side of her head.

"Where's Rin?" he whispered, but the words were just a croak.

"You can let go."

"Uh." His fists were still gripping. Took a mighty effort to make his pulsing fingers come open, enough for Thorn to start unwinding the rope, hemp dark with blood.

She winced, and shrieked out, "Father Yarvi!"

"I'm sorry," he croaked.

"What?"

"Shouldn't have said that . . . about your mother—"

"Shut up, Brand." There was a pause, then, a babble of voices in the distance, a bird sending up a trilling call in the branches above. "Thing that really burns is I'm starting to think you were right."

"I was?"

"Don't get carried away. Doubt it'll happen again."

There were people gathering about them, blurry outlines looking down.

"You ever see the like o' that?"

"He had her whole weight for a moment."

"A feat to sing of, all right."

"Already setting it to a verse," came Odda's voice.

"You saved my life," said Koll, staring down with wide eyes, pitch smeared up his cheek.

Safrit put the neck of the waterskin to Brand's lips. "The ship would have crushed him."

"The ship might've crushed herself," said Rulf. "We'd have brought no help to Gettland then."

"We'd have needed a stack of help ourselves."

Even swallowing was an effort. "Just . . . done what anyone would do."

"You remind me of an old friend of ours," said Father Yarvi. "Strong arm. Strong heart."

"One stroke at a time," said Rulf, voice a little choked.

Brand looked down at what the minister was doing and felt a surge of sickness. The rope-burns coiled up his arms like red snakes around white branches, raw and bloody.

"Does it hurt?"

"Just a tingle."

"Just a damn tingle!" bellowed Odda. "You hear that? What rhymes with tingle?"

"It'll hurt soon enough," said Father Yarvi. "And leave you some scars."

"Marks of a great deed," murmured Fror who, when it came to scars, had to be reckoned an expert. "Hero's marks."

Brand winced as Yarvi wound the bandages around his forearms, the cuts burning like fury now. "Some hero," he muttered, as Thorn helped him sit up. "I fought a rope and lost."

"No." Father Yarvi slid a pin through the bandages and put his withered hand on Brand's shoulder. "You fought a ship. And won. Put this under your tongue." And he slipped a dried leaf into Brand's mouth. "It'll help with the pain."

"The knot slipped," said Dosduvoi, blinking at the frayed end of his rope. "What kind of awful luck is that?"

"The kind that afflicts men who don't check their knots," said Father Yarvi, glaring at him. "Safrit, make space for Brand in the wagon. Koll, you stay with him. Make sure he's moved to perform no further heroics."

Safrit made a bed among the supplies from the crew's blankets. Brand tried to tell her he could walk but they could all see he couldn't.

"You'll lie there and you'll like it!" she snapped, her pointed finger in his face.

So that was that. Koll perched on a barrel beside him and the wagon set lurching off down the slope, Brand wincing at every jolt.

"You saved my life," muttered the lad, after a while.

"You're quick. You'd have got out of the way."

"No I wouldn't. I was looking through the Last Door. Let me thank you, at least."

They looked at each other for a moment. "Fair enough," said Brand. "I'm thanked."

"How did you get that strong?"

"Work, I guess. On the docks. At the oar. In the forge."

"You've done smith work?"

"For a woman named Gaden. She took her husband's forge on when he died and turned out twice the smith he'd been." Brand remembered the feel of the hammer, the ringing of the anvil, the heat of the coals. Never thought he'd miss it, but he did. "It's a good trade, working iron. Honest."

"Why'd you stop?"

"Always dreamed of being a warrior. Winning a place in the songs. Joining a crew." Brand watched Odda and Dosduvoi squabbling under the weight of their ropes, Fror shaking his head in disgust, and smiled. "It was a cleaner crew than this I had in mind, but you have to take the family you're given." The pain was less but it seemed Yarvi's leaf had loosened his tongue. "My mother died when I was little. Told me to do good. My father didn't want me . . ."

"My father died," said Koll. "Long time ago."

"Well, now you've got Father Yarvi. And all these brothers around you." Brand caught Thorn's eye for an instant before she frowned off sideways into the trees. "And Thorn for a sister too, for that matter."

Koll gave his quick grin. "Mixed blessing, that."

"Most blessings are. She's prickly, but I reckon she'd fight to the death for any one of us."

"She certainly does like fighting."

"She certainly does."

The wagon's wheels squealed, the cargo rattled, the straining crew bellowed at one another. Then Koll said, quietly, "Are you my brother, then?"

"Guess so. If you'll have me."

"Reckon I could do worse." The lad shrugged, as if it didn't matter much either way. But Brand got the feeling it did.

WITH ONE LAST HEAVE the *South Wind* slid into the churning waters of the Denied and a ragged cheer went up.

"We made it," said Brand, hardly believing it. "Did we make it?"

"Aye. You can all tell your grandchildren you carted a ship over the tall hauls." Rulf wiped the sweat from his forehead on one thick forearm. "But we've some rowing still to do today!" he called, bringing the celebrations to a quick end. "Let's get her loaded up and make a few miles before sundown!"

"On your feet, idler." Dosduvoi swung Brand down from the wagon and onto his still-shaky legs.

Father Yarvi was talking to the leader of the drovers in the gods knew what strange tongue, then they both broke into laughter and gave each other a long hug.

"What did he say?" asked Brand.

"Beware of the Horse People," said Father Yarvi, "for they are savage and dangerous."

Thorn frowned toward the oxen, finally freed of their burden. "I don't see the joke."

"I asked him what he says to the Horse People, when he trades with them."

"And?"

"Beware of the Boat People, for they are savage and dangerous."

"Who are the Boat People?" asked Koll.

"We are," said Brand, grimacing as he clambered back aboard the *South Wind*. Every joint and sinew was aching and he went stooped in an old man's shuffle to his place at the stern, flopping onto his sea chest the moment Thorn thumped it down for him.

"You sure you can row?"

"I'll keep stroke with you all right," he muttered back at her, though it felt like a hero's effort just to sit up.

"You can barely keep stroke with me healthy," she said.

"We'll see if you can keep stroke with me, you mouthy string of gristle." Rulf was standing behind them. "You're in my place, lad."

"Where do I go?"

Rulf nodded toward the steering oar on its platform above them. "Thought for this evening you might take the helm."

Brand blinked. "Me?"

"Reckon you earned it." And Rulf slapped him on the back as he helped him up.

Grunting at the pain, Brand turned, one arm over the steering oar, and saw the whole crew watching him. Safrit and Koll with the cargo, Odda and Dosduvoi and Fror at their oars, Father Yarvi standing with Skifr near the dove-carved prow and beyond it the Denied flowing away south, Mother Sun scattering gold upon the water.

Brand grinned wide. "I like the view from here."

"Don't get used to it," said Rulf.

And all at once the crew started thumping at their oars, hammering, pounding, a thunder of flesh on wood. A drumming of respect. For him. For him who all his life had been nothing.

"To be fair, it was quite a thing you did up there." Thorn had the hint of a grin, eyes glinting as she slapped at her oar. "Quite a thing."

Brand felt pride swelling in him then like he'd never known before. He'd come a long road since Hunnan left him alone on the beach below Thorlby. He might not have sworn a warrior's oath, but he'd found a crew even so. A family to be part of. He wished Rin was there to see it, and pictured her face if she had been, and had to sniff and pretend he'd got something in his eye. Felt like standing in the light, and no mistake.

"Well don't just hit 'em, you lazy bastards!" he shouted in a broken voice. "Pull 'em!"

The crew laughed as they set to their oars, and the *South Wind* pulled smoothly off into the swift Denied, rowing with the current at last, leaving the oxen and their drivers to wait on the bank for a new burden.

STRANGE TIMES

The forest gave way to the open steppe. Terribly open. Ruthlessly flat. Mile upon mile of lush, green, waving grass.

To Thorn, brought up among the hills and mountains and cliffs of Gettland, there was something crushing in all that emptiness, all that space, stretching off under a bottomless sky to the far, far horizon.

"Why does no one farm it?" asked Koll, straddling the downed mast with the wind whipping the shavings from under his knife.

"The Horse People graze it," said Dosduvoi. "And don't like finding other folk out here."

Odda snorted. "They like it so little they skin 'em alive, indeed."

"A practice the Prince of Kalyiv taught them."

"Who learned it in the First of Cities," said Fror, wiping his misshapen eye with a fingertip.

"Though I understand it was taken there by travellers from Sagenmark," said Rulf.

"Who were taught it when Bail the Builder first raided them," said Yarvi.

"So are the skinners skinned," mused Skifr, watching the wind sweep patterns in the grass, "and the bloody lessons turn in circles."

"Well enough." Rulf scanned the river ahead, and behind, and the flat land around with eyes more fiercely narrowed than ever. "Long as we take no instruction."

"Why are you so worried?" asked Thorn. "We haven't seen a ship for days."

"Exactly. Where are they?"

"Here are two," said Father Yarvi, pointing downriver.

He had sharp eyes. It wasn't until they came much closer that, straining over her shoulder, Thorn could see what the black heaps on the river's bank were. The charred skeletons of a pair of small ships in a wide patch of trampled grass. The blackened circle of a spent fire. A fire just like the one they warmed their hands at every night.

"It doesn't look good for the crews," muttered Brand, with a knack for saying what everyone could already see.

"Dead," said Skifr brightly. "Perhaps some lucky ones are enslaved. Or unlucky ones. The Horse People are not known as gentle masters."

Odda frowned out across the expanse of flat grass. "You think we'll make their acquaintance?"

"Knowing my luck," murmured Dosduvoi.

"From now on we look for high ground to camp on!" bellowed Rulf. "And we double the guard! Eight men awake at all times!"

So it was with everyone nervous, frowning out across the steppe and startling at every sound, that they caught sight of a ship rowing upriver.

She was of a size with the *South Wind*, sixteen oars a side or so. Her prow-beast was a black wolf, so Thorn guessed her crew to be Throvenlanders, and by the scars on the shields at the rail, men ready for a fight. Maybe even hungry for one.

"Keep your weapons close!" called Rulf, his horn bow already in his hand.

Safrit watched nervously as men struggled to manage oar-blades and war-blades at once. "Shouldn't we smooth the path for Father Peace?"

"Of course." Father Yarvi loosened his own sword in its sheath. "But the words of an armed man ring that much sweeter. Well met!" he called across the water.

A mailed and bearded figure stood tall at the prow of the other ship. "And to you, friends!" It would have sounded more peaceable if he hadn't had men with drawn bows on either side of him. "Our ship is the *Black Dog*, come up the Denied from the First of Cities!"

"The *South Wind*, come down the Divine from Roystock!" Yarvi shouted back.

"How were the tall hauls?"

"Thirsty work for those who did the lifting." Yarvi held up his crippled hand. "But I got through it."

The other captain laughed. "A leader should share his men's work, but take a fair share and they'll lose all respect for him! May we draw close?"

"You may, but know we are well armed."

"In these parts it's the unarmed men who cause suspicion." The captain signalled to his crew, a weathered-looking group, all scars, beards, and bright ring-money, who skilfully drew the *Black Dog* into the middle of the current and alongside the *South Wind*, prow to stern.

Their captain burst out in disbelieving laughter. "Who's that old bastard you have at the helm there? Bad Rulf or I'm a side of ham! I was sure you were dead and had lost no sleep over it!"

Rulf barked out a laugh of his own. "A side of ham and a rotten one at that, Blue Jenner! I was sure you were dead and had tapped a keg in celebration!"

"Bad Rulf?" muttered Thorn.

"Long time ago." The old helmsman waved it away as he set his bow down. "Folk generally get less bad with age."

The crew of the *Black Dog* tossed their prow-rope across the water and, in spite of some cursing at their tangling oars, the crews dragged the two ships together. Blue Jenner leaned across and clasped Rulf's arm, both men beaming.

Thorn did not smile, and kept her own hand on her father's sword.

"How the hell did you get clear of that mess Young Halstam got us into?" Rulf was asking.

Jenner pulled off his helmet and tossed it back to his men, scrubbing at a tangle of thin gray hair. "I'm ashamed to say I took my chances with Mother Sea and swam for it."

"You always had fine weaponluck."

"Still took an arrow in my arse, but despite being a bony man I've been blessed with a fleshy arse and it's done no lasting harm. I counted the arrow good luck, for it surely pricked me free of a thrall collar."

Rulf fingered gently at his neck, and Thorn saw marks she'd never noticed there, below his beard. "I was less lucky. But thanks to Father Yarvi I find myself a free man again."

"Father Yarvi?" Jenner's eyes went wide. "Gettland's minister? Who was once the son of the Golden Queen Laithlin?"

"The same," said Yarvi, threading his way between the sea-chests to the back of the boat.

"Then I'm honored, for I've heard you named a deep-cunning man." Blue Jenner raised his brows at Thorn. "You've got women pulling your oars now?"

"I've got whoever moves my boat," said Rulf.

"Why the mad hair, girl?"

"Because damn you," growled Thorn, "that's why."

"Oh, she's a fierce one! Never mind the oar, I daresay she could break a man in half."

"I'm willing to give it a go," she said, not a little flattered.

Jenner showed his teeth, a yellowing set with several gaps. "Were I ten years younger I'd leap at the chance, but age has brought caution."

"The less time you have, the less you want to risk what's left," said Rulf.

"That's the truth of it." Jenner shook his head. "Bad Rulf back from beyond the Last Door and girls pulling oars and heaven knows what else. Strange times, all right."

"What times aren't?" asked Father Yarvi.

"There's the truth of that too!" Blue Jenner squinted up at the muddy sun. "Getting towards dinner. Shall we put ashore and swap news?"

"By swap news do you mean drink?" asked Rulf.

"I do, and that excessively."

THEY FOUND AN EASILY-DEFENDED loop of the river, set a strong guard and built a great fire, the flames whipped sideways by the cease-less wind, showering sparks across the water. Then each crew tapped a keg of their ale and there was much singing of ever more tuneless songs, telling of ever more unbelievable tales, and making of ever more raucous merriment. Someone ill-advisedly gave Koll beer, and he got quite a taste for it, then shortly afterward was sick and fell asleep, much to his mother's profound disgust and everyone else's profound amusement.

Merry-making had never made Thorn especially merry, though. In spite of the smiles everyone kept blades to hand and there were several men who laughed as little as she did. The *Black Dog*'s helms-man, called Crouch and with a white streak in his balding hair, seemed to be nursing some particular grudge against the world. When he got up to piss in the river Thorn noticed him giving the *South Wind*'s contents a thorough look-over, that iron-bound chest of Father Yar-vi's in particular.

"I don't like the look of him," she muttered to Brand.

He peered at her over the rim of his cup. "You don't like the look of anyone."

She'd never had any objection to the look of Brand at all, but she kept that to herself. "I like his look less than most, then. One of those people with nought in them but hard stares and hard words. Face like a slapped arse."

He grinned into his ale at that. "Oh, I hate those people."

She had to grin herself. "Beneath my forbidding exterior I've got hidden depths, though."

"Well hidden," he said, as he lifted his cup. "But I might be starting to plumb 'em."

"Bold of you. Plumbing a girl without so much as a by your leave."

He blew ale out of his nose, fell into a coughing fit and had to be clapped on the back by Odda, who seized the chance to honk out his ill-made verse on Brand lifting the ship. The slope got steeper and the danger greater and the feat more impressive with every telling, Safrit beaming at Brand and saying, "He saved my son's life." The only one to dispute the questionable facts was Brand himself, who couldn't have looked less comfortable at all the praise if he'd been sitting on a spike.

"How are things around the Shattered Sea?" Blue Jenner asked when the song was over. "It's been a year since we've seen home."

"Much as they were," said Yarvi. "Grandmother Wexen makes ever greater demands on behalf of the High King. The latest talk is of taxes."

"A pox on him and his One God!" snapped Jenner. "A fellow should own what he takes, not have to rent it from some other thief just because he has the bigger chair."

"The more some men get the more they want," said Yarvi, and folk on both sides of the fire murmured their agreement.

"Was the Divine clear?"

"We found no trouble, anyway," said Rulf. "And the Denied?"

Jenner sucked at the gaps in his teeth. "The damn Horse People are stirred up like angry bees, attacking boats and caravans, burning steadings within sight of Kalyiv."

"Which tribe?" asked Yarvi. "Uzhaks? Barmeks?"

Jenner stared back blankly. "There are tribes?"

"All with their own ways."

"Well, they mostly shoot the same kind of arrows, far as I can see, and the Prince of Kalyiv isn't making much distinction between 'em either. He's grown sick of their taunting, and means to teach them a bloody lesson."

"The best kind," said Odda, baring his filed teeth.

"Except he's not planning to do it with his own hands."

"Princes rarely do," said Yarvi.

"He's strung a chain across the Denied and is letting no fighting crew pass until we Northerners have helped him give the Horse People their proper chastisement."

Rulf puffed up his broad chest. "Well he won't be stopping the Minister of Gettland."

"You don't know Prince Varoslaf and no sensible man would want to. There's no telling what that bald bastard will do one moment to the next. Only reason we got away is I spun him a tale about spreading the news and bringing more warriors from the Shattered Sea. If I was you I'd turn back with us."

"We're going on," said Yarvi.

"Then the very best of weatherluck to you all, and let's hope you don't need weaponluck." Blue Jenner took a long draft from his cup. "But I fear you might."

"As might anyone who takes the tall hauls." Skifr lay on her back, arms behind her head, bare feet toward the fire. "Perhaps you should test yours while you can?"

"What did you have in mind, woman?" growled Crouch.

"A friendly test of arms with practice blades." Skifr yawned wide. "My pupil has beaten everyone on our crew and needs new opponents."

"Who's your pupil?" asked Jenner, peering over at Dosduvoi, who seemed a mountain in the flickering shadows.

"Oh, no," said the giant. "Not me."

Thorn put on her bravest face, stood, and stepped into the firelight. "Me."

There was a silence. Then Crouch gave a disbelieving cackle, soon joined by others.

"This half-haired waif?"

"Can the girl even heft a shield?"

"She could heft a needle, I reckon. I need someone to stitch a hole in my sock!"

"You'll need someone to stitch a hole in you after she's done," growled Odda.

A lad maybe a year older than Thorn begged for the chance to give her the first beating and the two crews gathered in a noisy circle with torches to light the contest, shouting insults and encouragement, making wagers on their crew-mate. He was a big one with great thick wrists, fierce in the eyes. Thorn's father always said, *fear is a good thing. Fear keeps you careful. Fear keeps you alive.* That was just as well because Thorn's heart was thudding so hard she thought her skull might burst.

"Bet on this scrap of nothing?" yelled Crouch, chopping one of his armrings in half with a hatchet and betting it against Thorn. "Might as well throw your money in the river! You having a piece of this?"

Blue Jenner quietly stroked his beard so his own armrings rattled. "I like my money where it is."

The nerves vanished the moment their wooden blades first clashed and Thorn knew she had the lad well beaten. She dodged his second blow, steered away the third and let him stumble past. He was strong but he came at her angrily, blindly, his weight set all wrong. She ducked under a heedless sweep, almost laughing at how clumsy it was, hooked his shield down and struck him across the face with a sharp smack. He sat down hard in the dirt, blinking stupidly with blood pouring from his nose.

"You are the storm," she heard Skifr murmur over the cheering. "Do not wait for them. Make them fear. Make them doubt."

She sprang screaming at the next man the instant Jenner called for the fight to start, barged him into his shocked friends, chopped him across the stomach with her practice sword, and put a dent in his helmet with a ringing blow of her wooden ax. He stumbled drunkenly for a moment while the *South Wind*'s crew laughed, trying to pry the rim back up over his brows.

"Men used to fighting in the shield wall tend to think only ahead. The shield becomes a weakness. Use the flanks."

The next man was short but thick as a tree-trunk, cautious and watchful. She let him herd her back with his shield long enough for the boos of the *Black Dog*'s crew to turn to cheers. Then she came alive, feinted left and darted right, went high with her sword and, as he raised his shield, hooked his ankle with her ax, dragged him squealing over and left her sword's point tickling at his throat.

"Yes. Be never where they expect you. Always attack. Strike first. Strike last."

"You useless dogs!" snapped Crouch. "I'm shamed to be one of you!" And he snatched up the fallen sword, took up a shield with a white arrow painted on it and stepped into the circle.

He was a vicious one, and fast, and clever, but she was faster and cleverer and far more vicious and Skifr had taught her tricks he never dreamed of. She danced about him, wore him down, rained blows on him until he hardly knew which way he was facing. Finally she slipped around a lunge and gave him a smack across the arse with the flat of her sword they might have heard in Kalyiv.

"This was no fair test," he growled as he stood up. It was plain he desperately wanted to rub his stinging buttocks but was forcing himself not to.

Thorn shrugged. "The battlefield isn't fair."

"On the battlefield we fight with steel, girl." And he flung the practice sword down. "It'd be a different outcome with real blades."

"True," said Thorn. "Rather than nursing a bruised pride and a bruised backside you'd be spilling guts out of your split arse."

Laughter from the *South Wind*'s crew at that, and Jenner tried to calm his helmsman with an offer of more ale but he shook him off. "Get me my ax and we'll see, bitch!"

The laughter guttered out, and Thorn curled her lip and spat at his feet. "Get your ax, sow, I'm ready!"

"No," said Skifr, putting her arm across Thorn's chest. "The time will come for you to face death. This is not it."

"Hah," spat Crouch. "Cowards!"

Thorn growled in her throat, but Skifr pushed her back again, eyes narrowed. "You are a hatful of winds, helmsman. You are a hollow man."

Odda stepped past her. "Far from being hollow, he is full to the crown with turds." Thorn was surprised to see a drawn knife gleaming in his hand. "I never had a braver oarmate, man or woman. At your next insult I will take it upon myself to kill you."

"You'll have to beat me to it," rumbled Dosduvoi, tossing aside his blanket and drawing himself up to his full height.

"And me." And Brand was beside her with his bandaged hand on that fine dagger of his.

Many fingers were tickling at weapons on both sides and—what with the ale, and the injured pride, and the lost silver—things might quickly have turned exceeding ugly. But before a blow was landed Father Yarvi sprang nimbly between the two bristling crews.

"We all have enemies enough without making more among our friends! Blood shed here would be blood wasted! Let us make of the fist an open hand. Let us give the Father of Doves his day. Here!" And he reached into a pocket and tossed something glinting to Crouch.

"What's this?" growled the helmsman.

"Queen Laithlin's silver," said Yarvi, "and with her face upon it." The minister might have been lacking fingers but the ones he had were quick indeed. Coins spun and glittered in the firelight as he flicked them among the *Black Dog*'s crew.

"We don't want your charity," snarled Crouch, though many of his oarmates were already scrambling on their knees for it.

"Consider it an advance, then!" called Yarvi. "On what the queen will pay you when you present yourselves at Thorlby. She and her husband King Uthil are always seeking bold men and good fighters. Especially those who have no great love for the High King."

Blue Jenner raised his cup high. "To the beautiful and generous Queen Laithlin, then!" As his crew cheered, and charged their cups, he added more softly, "and her deep-cunning minister," and even more softly yet, with a wink at Thorn, "not to mention his formidable back oar."

"What's happening?" cried Koll, staggering up wild-eyed, wild-haired and tangled with his blanket, then he fell over and was promptly sick again, to gales of helpless laughter.

Within a few moments the two crews were once more exchanging tales, and finding old comrades in common, and arguing over whose was the better knife while Safrit dragged her son away by the ear and dunked his head in the river. Crouch was left nursing his grudge alone, standing with fists on hips and glaring daggers at Thorn.

"I've a feeling you've made an enemy there," muttered Brand, sliding his dagger back into its sheath.

"Oh, I'm always doing that. What does Father Yarvi say? Enemies are the price of success." She threw one arm around his shoulders, the other about Odda's, and hugged the two of them tight. "The shock is that I've made some friends besides."

A RED DAY

"Shields!" bellowed Rulf.

And Brand was hooked by panic and torn from happy dreams of home, scrambling from the comfort of his blankets and up into a chill dawn the color of blood.

"Shields!"

The crew were stumbling from their beds, bouncing off one another, charging about like startled sheep, half-dressed, half-armed, half-awake. A man kicked the embers of the fire as he ran past and sent sparks whirling. Another bellowed as he tried to struggle into his mail shirt, tangled with the sleeves.

"Arm yourselves!"

Thorn was up beside him. The unshaved side of her head was chaos these days, braids and snarls and matted worms bound up with rings of silver clipped from coins, but her weapons were oiled and polished to a ready gleam and her face was set hard. Made Brand feel braver, to see her brave. The gods knew, he needed courage. He needed courage and he needed to piss.

They'd pitched camp on the only hill for miles, a flat-topped knoll in a bend of the river, broken boulders jutting from its flanks, a few stunted trees clinging to the top. Brand hurried to the eastern crest where the crew were gathering, stared down the slope and across the flat ocean of grass that stretched away into the sunrise. As he scraped sleep from his eyes with trembling fingers he saw figures out there, ghostly riders wriggling in the dawn haze.

"Horse People?" he croaked out.

"Uzhaks, I think," Father Yarvi shaded his pale eyes against Mother Sun, a bloody smudge on the far horizon, "but they live on the shores of the Golden Sea. I don't know what's brought them here."

"A deep desire to kill us?" said Odda as the riders took shape out of the murk, red sun glinting on metal, on the blades of spears and curved swords, on helmets made to look like the heads of beasts.

"How many are there?" muttered Thorn, jaw-muscles working on the shaved side of her head.

"Eighty?" Fror watched them as calmly as a man might watch a neighbor weed his garden. "Ninety?" He opened up a pouch and spat in it, started mixing something inside with a fingertip. "A hundred?"

"Gods," whispered Brand. He could hear the sound of hooves as the Horse People circled closer, yells and yips and strange warbles echoing across the plain, above the rattle and growl of the crew making ready their own war-gear and calling on their chosen gods for weaponluck. One rider swerved close, long hair streaming, to try an arrow. Brand shrank back but it was just a ranging shot, a taunting shot, dropping into the grass halfway up the slope.

"An old friend once told me the greater the odds the greater the glory," said Rulf, plucking at his bowstring with calloused fingers and making it angrily hum.

Dosduvoi slipped the oil-cloth from the head of his great ax. "The chances of death also increase."

"But who wants to meet Death old, beside the fire?" And Odda's teeth shone with spit as he flashed his mad grin.

"Doesn't sound such a bad outcome." Fror pushed his hand into his pouch and pulled it out covered in blue paint, pressed it onto his face with the fingers spread to leave a great palm-print. "But I am ready."

Brand wasn't. He gripped his shield that Rin had painted with a dragon, it seemed a hundred years ago and half the world away. He gripped the haft of his ax, palms still sore with the rope burns underneath their bandages. The Horse People were ever-moving, their troop breaking apart and coming back together, flowing across the plain like swift-running water but always working their way closer, a white banner streaming under a horned skull. He caught glimpses of brave faces, beast faces, battle faces, teeth bared and eyes rolling. So many of them.

"Gods," he whispered. Had he really chosen this? Instead of a nice, safe, boring life at Gaden's forge?

"Skifr!" called Father Yarvi, low and urgent.

The old woman was sitting behind them, crosslegged beneath one of the trees, frowning into the dead fire as though the solution to their troubles might be hidden among the embers. "No!" she snapped over her shoulder.

"Arrows!" someone screeched and Brand saw them, black splinters sailing high, drifting with the wind. One flickered down near him, the feathered flights twitching. What change in the breeze might have wafted that little thing of wood and metal through his chest, and he'd have died out here under a bloody sky and never seen his sister again, or the docks, or the middens of Thorlby. Even things you always hated seem wonderful when you look back on them from a place like this.

"Get a wall together you lazy dogs!" Rulf roared, and Brand scrambled between Odda and Fror, wood and metal grating as they locked their shields together, rim behind the one on the left and in front of the one on the right. A thousand times he'd done it in the training square, arms and legs moving by themselves. Just as well, since his head felt full of mud. Men with spears and bows crowded behind them, thumping the front rank on their backs and snarling encouragements, those without shields waiting to kill anyone who broke through, to plug the gaps when men fell. When men died. Because men would die here, today, and soon.

"Before breakfast too, the bastards!" snapped Odda.

"If I had it in mind to kill a man I'd want him hungry," grunted Fror.

Brand's heart was beating as if it would burst his chest, his knees shaking with the need to run, jaw clenched tight with the need to stand. To stand with his crew, his brothers, his family. He wriggled his shoulders to feel them pressed tight against him. Gods, he needed to piss.

"How did you get the scar?" he hissed.

"Now?" growled Fror.

"I'd like to die knowing something about my shoulder-man."

"Very well." The Vansterman flashed a mad grin, good eye white in the midst of that blue handprint. "When you die, I'll tell you."

Father Yarvi squatted in the shadow of the shield wall, yelling words in the Horse People's tongue, giving Father Peace his chance, but no answer came but arrows, clicking on wood, flickering overhead. Someone cried out as a shaft found his leg.

"Mother War rules today," muttered Yarvi, hefting his curved sword. "Teach them some archery, Rulf."

"Arrows!" shouted the helmsman and Brand stepped back, angling his shield to make a slot to shoot through, Rulf stepping up beside him with his black bow full-drawn, string whining in fury. Brand felt the wind of the flying shaft on his cheek as he stepped back and locked his rim with Fror's again.

A shrill howl echoed out as the arrow found its mark and the crew laughed and jeered, stuck out their tongues and showed their brave faces, beast faces, battle faces. Brand didn't feel much like laughing. He felt like pissing.

The Horse People were known for darting in and out, tricking their enemies and wearing them down with their bows. A well-built shield wall is hard to pierce with arrows alone, though, and that horn bow of Rulf's was even more fearsome than it looked. With the height of their little hill he had the longer reach and, in spite of the years washed by him, his aim was deadly. One by one he sent arrows whistling down the grassy slope, calm as still water, patient as stone. Twice more the crew cheered as he brought down a horse then knocked a rider from his saddle to tumble through the grass. The others fell back out of his bow's reach and began to gather.

"They can't get around us because of the river." Father Yarvi pressed between them to glance over Odda's shield. "Or make use of their horses among the boulders, and we have the high ground. My left hand picked a good spot."

"It's not my first dance," said Rulf, sliding out another arrow. "They'll come on foot, and they'll break on our wall like Mother Sea on the rocks."

Rocks feel no pain. Rocks shed no blood. Rocks do not die. Brand went up on his toes to peer over the wall, saw the Uzhaks sliding from their saddles, readying for a charge. So many of them. The *South Wind*'s crew was outnumbered two to one by his reckoning. Maybe more.

"What do they want?" whispered Brand, scared by the fear in his own voice.

"There is a time for wondering what a man wants," said Fror, no fear at all in his. "And there is a time for splitting his head. This is that second time."

"We hold 'em here!" roared Rulf, "and when I cry 'heave' we drive these bastards down the slope. Drive 'em, and cut 'em down, and trample 'em, and keep mercy for another day, you hear? Arrow."

The shields swung apart and Brand caught a glimpse of men running. Rulf sent his shaft flitting down the hill into the nearest one's ribs, left him crawling, wailing, pleading to his friends as they charged on past.

"Hold now, boys!" called Rulf, tossing aside his bow and lifting a spear. "Hold!"

Around him men growled and spat and muttered prayers to Mother War, breath echoing from the wood in front of them. The odd speckle of rain was falling, a dew on helmets and shield rims, and Brand needed to piss worse than ever.

"Oh, true God!" shouted Dosduvoi, as they heard the quick footsteps of their enemies, howling war cries coming ever closer. "All-powerful! All-knowing God! Smite these heathens!"

"I'll smite the bastards myself!" screamed Odda.

And Brand gasped at the impact, staggered back a half-step, then forwards, putting all his weight to his shield, boots sliding at the wet grass. Metal clanged and rattled and battered against wood. A storm of metal. Something pinged against the rim of his shield and he ducked away, splinters in his face, a devil's broken voice shrieking on the other side.

Fror's misshapen eye bulged as he bellowed words from the *Song of Bail*. "Hand of iron! Head of iron! Heart of iron!" And he lashed blindly with his sword over the shield wall. "Your death comes, sang the hundred!"

"Your death comes!" roared Dosduvoi. Some time for poetry, but others took up the cry, fire in their throats, fire in their chests, fire in their maddened eyes. "Your death comes!"

Whether it was the Horse People's death or theirs they didn't say. It didn't matter. Mother War had spread her iron wings over the plain and cast every heart into shadow. Fror lashed again and caught Brand above the eye with the pommel of his sword, set his ears ringing.

"Heave!" roared Rulf.

Brand ground his teeth as he pushed, shield grinding against shield. He saw a man fall yelling as a spear darted under a rim and ripped into his leg, kept shoving anyway. He heard a voice on the other side, so clear the words, so close the enemy, just a plank's thickness from his face. He jerked up, chopping over his shield with his ax, and again, a grunt and a gurgle, the blade caught on something. A spear jabbed past, scraped against his shield rim and a man howled.

Fror butted someone, their nose popping against his forehead. Men growled and spluttered, stabbing and pushing, all tangled one with another.

"Die, you bastard, die!"

An elbow caught Brand's jaw and made him taste blood. Mud flicked in his face, half-blinded him, and he tried to blink it away, and snarled, and cursed, and shoved, and slipped, and spat salt, and shoved again. The slope was with them and they knew their business and slowly but surely the wall began to shift, driving their enemies back, forcing them down the hill the way they'd come.

"Your death comes, sang the hundred!"

Brand saw an oarsman biting at an Uzhak's neck. He saw Koll stabbing a fallen man with a knife. He saw Dosduvoi fling a figure tumbling with a sweep of his shield. He saw the point of a blade come out of a man's back. Something bounced from Brand's face and he gasped. At first he thought it was an arrow, then realized it had been a finger.

"Heave, I said! Heave!"

They pressed in harder, a hell of snarling and straining bodies, crowded too tight to use his ax and he let it fall, snaked his arm down and slid out the dagger Rin forged for him.

"Hand of iron! Heart of iron!"

The feel of its grip in his hand made him think of Rin's face, firelit in their little hovel. These bastards were between him and her and a rage boiled up in him. He saw a face, rough metal rings in braided hair, and he jerked his shield up into it, snapped a head back, stabbed under the rim, metal squealing, stabbed again, hand sticky-hot. The man fell and Brand trampled over him, stumbling and stomping, dragged up by Odda, spitting through his clenched teeth.

"Your death comes!"

How often had he listened breathless to that song, mouthing the words, dreaming of claiming his own place in the wall, winning his own glory? Was this what he'd dreamed of? There was no skill here, only blind luck. No matching of noble champions, only a contest of madness. No room for tricks or cleverness or even courage, unless courage was to be carried helpless by the surge of battle like a storm washes driftwood. Perhaps it was.

"Kill them!"

The noise of it was horrifying, a clamor of rattling metal and battering wood and men swearing at the tops of their broken voices. Sounds Brand couldn't understand. Sounds that had no meaning. The Last Door stood wide for them all and each of them faced it as best he could.

"Your death comes!"

The rain was getting heavier, boots ripping the grass and churning the red earth to mud and he was tired and sore and aching but there was no stopping. Gods, he needed to piss. Something smashed against his shield, near tore it from his arm. A red blade darted past his ear and he saw Thorn beside him.

The side of her face was spotted with blood and she was smiling. Smiling like she was home.

BATTLE-JOY

Thorn was a killer. That, no one could deny.

The muddied and bloodied and boot-trampled stretch of grass behind the shifting shield wall was her ground, and to anyone who trod there she was Death.

With a hammering louder than the hail on the *South Wind*'s hull the shield wall edged down the hillside, shoving, hacking, trampling over men and dragging them between their shields, swallowing them up like a hungry serpent. One tried to get up and she stabbed him in the back with her father's sword, his bloodied face all fear and pain and panic as he fell.

It should have been harder than with a practice blade, but it was so much easier. The steel so light, so sharp, her arm so strong, so quick. Her weapons had minds of their own. Ruthless minds, fixed on murder.

She was a killer. Skifr had said so and here was the proof, written in blood on the skins of her enemies. She wished her father had been there to see it. Maybe his ghost was, cheering her on at her shoulder.

She wished Hunnan had been there, so she could shove his face in the blood she'd spilled. So she could dare him to deny her a place. So she could kill him too.

The Horse People didn't understand this way of fighting and they swarmed at the wall in a mess, in ones and twos, their own courage their undoing. Thorn saw one clumsily angling a spear over the shields, aiming to stab at Brand. She darted forward, hooked him around the back with her ax, its pointed beard sinking deep into his shoulder, dragged him between the shields and into her arms.

They tottered in a hug, snapping at each other, his long hair in her mouth, digging with knees and elbows, then Father Yarvi slashed him across the back of his legs and she screamed as she tore her ax free, hacked it into the side of his skull, ripping off his helmet and sending it bouncing up the ruined hillside.

She'd heard her father speak of the battle-joy. The red joy Mother War sends her most favored children. She'd listened to his tales wide-eyed and dry-mouthed beside the fire. Her mother had told him those were no stories for a daughter's ear but he'd leaned close and spoken on in a throaty whisper, so close she felt his warm breath on her cheek. She'd heard him speak of the battle-joy, and now she felt it.

The world burned, blazed, danced, her ripping breath a furnace in her throat as she rushed to the end of the wall, which was flexing now, twisting, threatening to break apart. Two Uzhaks had clambered up between the boulders on the hill's flank and got around Dosduvoi. She hacked one in the side, folded him double. The spear of the other seemed to move as slowly as if it came through honey and she laughed as she slipped around it, chopped his legs away with her ax, sent him reeling.

An arrow flickered past her and Dosduvoi snatched her behind his shield, two shafts already lodged near its rim. The wall was buckling in the center, faces twisted as men strained to hold it together. There was a crash, a crewman fell, drooling teeth, and the wall split apart. A huge Uzhak stood in the gap, wearing a mask made from a walrus jaw with the tusks on either side of his leering face, snorting like a bull as he swung a great toothed club in both fists, sending men staggering, tearing the breach wider.

Thorn had no fear in her. Only the battle-joy, fiercer than ever.

She raced at the giant, blood surging like Mother Sea. His maddened eyes rolled toward her and she dropped, slid on her side between his great boots, turned, slashed as his club thudded into the ground behind her, caught him across the back of his leg, blood frozen in black spots as he lurched onto his knees. Fror stepped forward and hacked him down with thudding blows, one, two, three, the blue hand on his face red-speckled.

Thorn saw the Horse People scattering, bounding away down the slope toward the open plain and their waiting horses and she held her weapons high and screamed, burning to the tips of her fingers. Her father's ghost urged her on and she sprang after her fleeing enemies like a hound after hares.

"Stop her!" roared Rulf, and someone dragged her back, cursing and struggling, the hair she still had tangled across her face. It was Brand, his beard scratching her cheek and his left arm under hers so that his shield was across her. Beyond the running Uzhaks she saw others stalking forward through the grass, bows drawn and faces eager. Lots of them, and close behind the ebbing battle-joy a wave of fear washed in on her.

"Close up the wall!" roared Rulf, spit flecking from his teeth. The men edged back, shuffled together, stopping up the gaps, shields wobbling and rattling and the daylight flickering between them. Thorn heard arrows click against lime-wood, saw one spin from the rim of Brand's shield and over his shoulder. Odda was down, a shaft in his side, spewing curses as he dragged himself up the hill.

"Back! Back! Steady, now!"

She caught Odda under his arms and started to haul him away, while he grunted and kicked and blew bloody bubbles. She fell with him on top of her, nearly cut herself with her own ax, struggled up and dragged him on, then Koll was there to help and between them they pulled him back to the crest of the hill, the shield wall edging after them. Back to where they'd stood a few mad moments ago, the river at their backs and the plain stretching away before them.

Thorn stood there dumb, numb, not sure how many of the crew were dead. Three? Four? Everyone had scratches and some were hurt bad. Didn't know if she was hurt. Didn't know whose blood was on her. From the look of that arrow she held no high hopes for Odda. She held no high hopes for anything. Through the gaps in the battered shields she could see the trampled slope scattered with bodies, some still moving, groaning, pawing at their wounds.

"Push it through or pull it out?" snapped Safrit, kneeling beside Odda, gripping his bloody hand tight.

Father Yarvi only stared down, and rubbed at his lean jaw, fingertips leaving red streaks across his cheek.

The fury was gone as though it had never been, the fire in her guttered to ashes. Thorn's father never told her that the battle-joy is borrowed strength and must be repaid double. She gripped the pouch with his fingerbones in it but there was no comfort there. She saw the leaking wounds and the men moaning and the slaughter they'd done. The slaughter she'd done.

She was a killer, that there was no denying.

She hunched over as if she'd been punched in the guts and coughed thin puke into the grass, straightened shivering, and staring, with the world too bright and her knees all a-wobble and her eyes swimming.

She was a killer. And she wanted her mother.

She saw Brand staring at her over his shoulder, his face all grazed down one side and his neck streaked with blood into the collar of his shirt and the tattered bandages flapping about the red dagger in his hand.

"You all right?" he croaked at her.

"Don't know," she said, and was sick again, and if she'd eaten anything she might never have stopped.

"We have to get to the *South Wind*," someone said in a voice squeaky with panic.

Father Yarvi shook his head. "They'd rain down arrows on us from the bank."

"We need a miracle," breathed Dosduvoi, eyes turned toward the pink sky.

"Skifr!" shouted Yarvi, and the old woman winced as though a fly was bothering her, muttering and hunching her shoulders. "Skifr, we need you!"

"They're coming again!" someone called from the ragged wall.

"How many?" asked Yarvi.

"More than last time!" shouted Rulf, nocking an arrow to his black bow.

"How many more?"

"A lot more!"

Thorn tried to swallow but for once could find no spit. She felt so weak she could hardly lift her father's sword. Koll was bringing water to the shield wall and they were drinking, and snarling, and wincing at their wounds.

Fror swilled water around his mouth and spat. "Time to sell our lives dearly, then. Your death comes!"

"Your death comes," a couple of men muttered, but it was more lament than challenge.

Thorn could hear the Horse People coming, could hear their war-cries and their quick footsteps on the hillside. She heard the growling of the crew as they made ready to meet the charge and, weak though she was, she clenched her teeth and hefted her red-speckled ax and sword. She walked toward the wall. Back to that trampled stretch of mud behind it, though the thought gave her anything but joy.

"Skifr!" screamed Father Yarvi.

With a shriek of anger the old woman sprang up, throwing off her coat. "Be damned, then!" And she began to chant, soft and low at first but growing louder. She strode past, singing words Thorn did not understand, had never heard the like of. But she guessed the language and it was no tongue of men.

These were elf-words, and this was elf-magic. The magic that had shattered God and broken the world, and as if at a chill wind every hair on Thorn's body bristled.

Skifr chanted on, higher and faster and wilder, and from the straps about her body she drew two studded and slotted pieces of dark metal, sliding one into the other with a snap like a closing lock.

"What is she doing?" said Dosduvoi but Father Yarvi held him back with his withered hand.

"What she must."

Skifr held the elf-relic at arm's length. "Stand aside!"

The wavering shield wall split in two and Thorn stared through the gap. There were the Horse People, a crawling mass of them, weaving between the bodies of their fallen, springing swift and merciless with death in their eyes.

There was a clap like thunder close at hand, a flash of light and the nearest of the Uzhaks was flung tumbling down the hillside as though flicked by a giant finger. Another crack and a disbelieving murmur went up from the crew, another man sent spinning like a child's toy, his shoulder on fire.

Skifr's wailing went higher and higher, splinters of shining metal tumbling from the elf-relic in her hand and falling to smoke in the grass at her feet. Men whimpered, and gaped, and clutched at talismans, more fearful of this sorcery than they were of the Uzhaks. Six strokes of thunder rolled across the plain and six men were left ruined and burning and the rest of the Horse People ran squealing in terror.

"Great God," whispered Dosduvoi, making a holy sign over his heart.

There was a silence then. The first in some time. Only the whisper of the wind in the grass and the rough clicking of Odda's breath. There was a smell like burning meat. One of the fallen splinters had caught fire in the grass. Skifr stepped forward grimly and ground the flame out under her boot.

"What have you done?" whispered Dosduvoi.

"I have spoken the name of God," said Skifr. "Written in fire and caught in elf-runes before the Breaking of the World. I have torn

Death from her place beside the Last Door and sent her to do my bidding. But there is always a price to be paid."

She walked over to where Odda was slumped pale against one of the stunted trees, Safrit bent over him trying to tease out the arrow.

"The name of God has seven letters," she said, and she pointed that deadly piece of metal at him. "I am sorry."

"No!" said Safrit, trying to put herself between them, but Odda pushed her gently away.

"Who wants to die old?" And he showed his mad grin, the filed lines in his teeth turned red with blood. "Death waits for us all."

There was another deafening crack, and Odda arched his back, trembling, then fell still, smoke rising from a blackened hole in his mail.

Skifr stood looking down. "I said I would show you magic."

NOT LIKE
THE SONGS

"They're running." The wind whipped Thorn's hair about her bloody face as she stared after the Uzhaks, the riders, and the horses without their riders, dwindling specks now far out across the ocean of grass.

"Can't say I blame 'em," muttered Brand, watching Skifr wrap her coat tight about herself and slump again crosslegged, gripping at the holy signs around her neck, glowering at the embers of the fire.

"We fought well," said Rulf, though his voice sounded hollow.

"Hands of iron." Fror nodded as he wiped the paint from his face with a wetted rag. "We won a victory to sing of."

"We won, anyway." Father Yarvi picked up one of the bits of metal Skifr had left in the grass and turned it this way and that so it twinkled in the sun. A hollow thing, still with a little smoke curling out. How could that reach across the plain and kill a man?

Safrit was frowning toward Skifr as she wiped her bloody hands clean. "We won using some black arts."

"We won." Father Yarvi shrugged. "Of the two endings to a fight that is the better. Let Father Peace shed tears over the methods. Mother War smiles upon results."

"What about Odda?" Brand muttered. The little man had seemed invincible, but he was gone through the Last Door. No more jokes.

"He would not have survived the arrow," said Yarvi. "It was him or all of us."

"A ruthless arithmetic," said Safrit, her mouth set in a hard line.

The minister did not look at her. "Such are the sums a leader must solve."

"What if this sorcery brings a curse on us?" asked Dosduvoi. "What if we risk a second Breaking of God? What if we—"

"We won." Father Yarvi's voice was as cold and sharp as drawn steel, and he curled the fingers of his good hand about that little piece of elf-metal and made a white-knuckled fist of it. "Thank whatever god you believe in for your life, if you know how. Then help with the bodies."

Dosduvoi shut his mouth and walked away, shaking his great head.

Brand pried open his sore fingers and let his shield drop, Rin's painted dragon all hacked and gouged, the rim bright with new scratches, the bandages on his palm blood-spotted. Gods, he was bruised and grazed and aching all over. He hardly had the strength to stand, let alone to quibble over the good thing to have done. The more he saw, the less sure he was of what the good thing might be. There was a burning at his neck, wet when he touched it. A scratch there, from friend or enemy he couldn't say. The wounds hurt just as much whoever dealt them.

"Lay them out with dignity," Father Yarvi was saying, "and fell these trees for pyres."

"Those bastards too?" Koll pointed to the Horse People scattered torn and bloody down the slope, several of the crew picking over their bodies for anything worth the taking.

"Them too."

"Why give them a proper burning?"

Rulf caught the lad by the arm. "Because if we beat beggars here, we're no better than beggars. If we beat great men, we're greater still."

"Are you hurt?" asked Safrit.

Brand stared at her as if she was speaking a foreign tongue. "What?"

"Sit down."

That wasn't hard to do. He was so weak at the knees he was near falling already. He stared across the windswept hilltop as the crew put aside their weapons and started dragging the corpses into lines, others setting about the stunted trees with axes to make a great pyre. Safrit leaned over him, probing at the cut on his neck with strong fingers.

"It's not deep. There's plenty worse off."

"I killed a man," he muttered, to no one in particular. Maybe it sounded like a boast, but it surely wasn't meant to be. "A man with his own hopes, and his own worries, and his own family."

Rulf squatted beside him, scratching at his gray beard. "Killing a man is nowhere near so light a matter as the bards would have you believe." He put a fatherly hand on Brand's shoulder. "You did well today."

"Did I?" muttered Brand, rubbing his bandaged hands together. "Keep wondering who he was, and what brought him here, and why we had to fight. Keep seeing his face."

"Chances are you'll be seeing it till you step through the Last Door yourself. That's the price of the shield wall, Brand." And Rulf held out a sword to him. A good sword, with silver on the hilt and a scabbard stained from long use. "Odda's. But he'd have wanted you to take it. A proper warrior should have a proper blade."

Brand had dreamed of having his own sword, now looking at it made him feel sick. "I'm no warrior."

"Yes y'are."

"A warrior doesn't fear."

"A fool doesn't fear. A warrior stands in spite of his fear. You stood."

Brand plucked at his damp trousers. "I stood and pissed myself."

"You won't be the only one."

"The hero never pisses himself in the songs."

"Aye, well." Rulf gave his shoulder a parting squeeze, and stood. "That's why those are songs, and this is life."

Mother Sun was high over the steppe when they set off, the pyre-smoke slowly rising. Though the blood had drained from the sky and left only a clear and beautiful blue, it was still crusted dark under Brand's fingernails, and in his bandages, and at his throbbing neck. It was still a red day. He felt every day he lived would be a red day now.

Four oars lay still beside the mast, the ashes of the men who'd pulled them already whirling out across the plains. Skifr sat brooding among the cargo, hood drawn up, the nearest oarsmen all shuffled as far from her as they could get without falling out of the boat.

Brand glanced across at Thorn as they settled to rowing and she looked back, her face as pale and hollow as Odda's had been when they stacked the wood around him. He tried to smile, but his mouth wouldn't find the shape of it.

They'd fought in the wall. They'd stood at the Last Door. They'd faced Death and left a harvest for the Mother of Crows. Whatever Master Hunnan might've said, they were both warriors now.

But it wasn't like the songs.

WHAT GETTLAND NEEDS

Kalyiv was a sprawling mass, infesting one bank of the Denied and spreading like a muddy sickness onto the other, the bright sky above smudged with the smoke of countless fires and dotted with scavenging birds.

The prince's hall stood on a low hill over the river, gilded horses carved upon its vast roof beams, the wall around it made as much from mud as masonry. Crowding outside that was a riot of wooden buildings ringed by a fence of stout logs, the spears of warriors glinting at the walkway. Crowding outside that, a chaos of tents, yurts, wagons, shacks and temporary dwellings of horrible wretchedness sprawled out over the blackened landscape in every direction.

"Gods, it's vast," muttered Brand.

"Gods, it's ugly," muttered Thorn.

"Kalyiv is as a slow-filling bladder," said Skifr, thoughtfully picking her nose, considering the results, then wiping them on the shoulder of the nearest oarsman so gently he didn't even notice. "In spring it swells with northerners, and folk from the empire, and Horse People from across the steppe all swarming here to trade. In summer it splits its skin and spills filth over the plains. In winter they all move on and it shrivels back to nothing."

"It surely smells like a bladder," grunted Rulf, wrinkling his nose.

Two huge, squat towers of mighty logs had been thrown up on either side of the river and a web of chains strung between them, links of black iron spiked and studded, bowing under the weight of frothing water, snarled up with driftwood and rubbish, stopping dead all traffic on the Denied.

"Prince Varoslaf has fished up quite a catch with his iron net," said Father Yarvi.

Thorn had never seen so many ships. They bobbed on the river, and clogged the wharves, and had been dragged up on the banks in tight-packed rows stripped of their masts. There were ships from Gettland and Vansterland and Throvenland. There were ships from Yutmark and the Islands. There were strange ships which must have come up from the south, dark-hulled and far too fat-bellied for the trip over the tall hauls. There were even two towering galleys, each with three ranks of oars, dwarfing the *South Wind* as they glided toward the harbor.

"Look at those monsters," murmured Brand.

"Ships from the Empire of the South," said Rulf. "Crews of three hundred."

"It's the crews he's after," said Father Yarvi. "To fight his fool's war against the Horse People."

Thorn was far from delighted at the thought of fighting more Horse People. Or for that matter of staying in Kalyiv for the summer. It had smelled a great deal better in her father's stories. "You think he'll want our help?"

"Certainly he'll want it, as we want his." Yarvi frowned up toward the prince's hall. "Will he demand it, is the question."

He had demanded it of many others. The harbor thronged with sour-faced men of the Shattered Sea, all mired in Kalyiv until Prince Varoslaf chose to loosen the river's chains. They lazed in sullen groups about slumping tents and under rotten awnings, and played loaded dice, and drank sour ale, and swore at great volume, and stared at everything with hardened eyes, the newest arrivals in particular.

"Varoslaf had better find enemies for these men soon," murmured Yarvi, as they stepped from the *South Wind*. "Before they find some nearer to hand."

Fror nodded as he made fast the prow-rope. "Nothing more dangerous than idle warriors."

"They're all looking at us." Brand's bandages had come off that morning and he kept picking nervously at the rope-scabs snaking up his forearms.

Thorn dug him with her elbow. "Maybe your hero's fame goes ahead of us, Ship-lifter."

"More likely Father Yarvi's does. I don't like it."

"Then pretend you do," said Thorn, putting her bravest face on and meeting every stare with a challenge. Or the most challenge she could manage with a hot wind whipping grit in her eyes and flapping her shirt against her sweaty back.

"Gods, it stinks," choked Brand as they made it off the creaking wharves and onto Father Earth, and Thorn could not have disagreed even if she could have taken a full breath to do it. The crooked streets were scattered with baking dung, dogs squabbling over rubbish, dead animals skewered on poles beside doorways.

"Are they selling those?" muttered Brand.

"They're offering them up," answered Father Yarvi, "so their gods can see which houses have made sacrifices and which have not."

"What about those?" Thorn nodded toward a group of skinned carcasses dangling from a mast raised in the middle of a square, gently swinging and swarming with flies.

"Savages," murmured Rulf, frowning up at them.

With an unpleasant shifting in her stomach, Thorn realized those glistening bodies were man-shaped. "Horse People?" she croaked.

Father Yarvi grimly shook his head. "Vanstermen."

"What?" The gods knew there were few people who liked Vanstermen less than Thorn, but she could see no reason for the Prince of Kalyiv to skin them.

Yarvi gestured toward some letters scraped into a wooden sign. "A crew that defied Prince Varoslaf's wishes and tried to leave. Other men of the Shattered Sea are discouraged from following their example."

"Gods," whispered Brand, only just heard over the buzzing of the flies. "Does Gettland want the help of a man who does this?"

"What we want and what we need may be different things."

A dozen armed men were forcing their way through the chaos of the docks. The prince might have been at war with the Horse People, but his warriors did not look much different from the Uzhaks Thorn had killed higher up the Denied. There was a woman in their midst, very tall and very thin, coins dangling from a silk headscarf wound around her black, black hair.

She stopped before them and bowed gracefully, a satchel swinging from her slender neck. "I am servant to Varoslaf, Great Prince of Kalyiv."

"Well met, and I am—"

"You are Father Yarvi, Minister of Gettland. The prince has given me orders to conduct you to his hall."

Yarvi and Rulf exchanged a glance. "Should I be honored or scared?"

The woman bowed again. "I advise you to be both, and prompt besides."

"I have come a long way for an audience and see no reason to dawdle. Lead on."

"I'll pick out some men to go with you," growled Rulf, but Father Yarvi shook his head.

"I will take Thorn and Brand. To go lightly attended, and by the young, is a gesture of trust in one's host."

"You trust Varoslaf?" muttered Thorn, as the prince's men gathered about them.

"I can pretend to."

"He'll know you pretend."

"Of course. On such twisted foundations are good manners built."

Thorn looked at Brand, and he stared back with that helpless expression of his.

"Have a care," came Skifr's voice in her ear. "Even by the ruthless standards of the steppe Varoslaf is known as a ruthless man. Do not put yourself in his power."

Thorn looked to the great chains strung across the river, then to those dangling bodies swinging, and could only shrug. "We're all in his power now."

THE PRINCE OF KALYIV'S HALL seemed even bigger on the inside, its ribs fashioned from the trunks of great trees still rooted in the hard-packed earth, shafts of sunlight filled with floating dust spearing down from windows high above. There was a long firepit but the flames burned low and the echoing space seemed almost chill after the heat outside.

Varoslaf, Prince of Kalyiv, was much younger than Thorn had expected. Only a few years older than Yarvi, perhaps, but without a hair on his head, nor his chin, nor even his brows, all smooth as an egg. He was not raised up on high, but sat on a stool before the firepit. He was not a big man, and he wore no jewels and boasted no weapon. He had no terrible frown upon his hairless face, only a stony blankness. There was nothing she could have described to make him seem fearsome to a listener, and yet he was fearsome. More so, and more, the closer they were led across that echoing floor.

By the time she and Brand stood at Father Yarvi's shoulders a dozen strides from his stool, Thorn feared Prince Varoslaf more than anyone she had ever met.

"Father Yarvi." His voice was dry and whispery as old papers and sent a sweaty shiver down her back. "Minister of Gettland, high is our honor at your visit. Welcome all to Kalyiv, Crossroads of the World."

His eyes moved from Brand, to Thorn, and back to Yarvi, and he reached down to stroke the ears of a vast hound curled about the legs of his stool. "It is a well-judged compliment that a man of your standing comes before me so lightly attended."

Thorn did indeed feel somewhat lonely. As well as that bear of a dog there were many guards scattered about the hall, with bows and curved swords, tall spears and strange armor.

But if Yarvi was overawed, the minister did not show a grain of it. "I know I will want for nothing in your presence, great prince."

"Nor will you. I hear you have that witch Scarayoi with you, the Walker in the Ruins."

"You are as well-informed as a great lord should be. We call her Skifr, but she is with us."

"Yet you keep her from my hall." Varoslaf's laugh was harsh as a dog's bark. "That was well-judged too. And who are these young gods?"

"The back oars of my crew. Thorn Bathu, who killed six Uzhaks in a skirmish on the Denied, and Brand who took the whole weight of our ship across his shoulders as we crossed the tall hauls."

"Slayer of Uzhaks and Lifter of Ships." Brand shifted uncomfortably as the prince gave the two of them a searching gaze. "It warms me to see such strength, and skill, and bravery in those so young. One could almost believe in heroes, eh, Father Yarvi?"

"Almost."

The prince jerked his head toward his willow-thin servant. "A token for tomorrow's legends."

She drew something from the satchel around her neck and pressed it into Brand's palm, then did the same to Thorn. A big, rough coin, crudely stamped with a prancing horse. A coin of red gold. Thorn swallowed, trying to judge its value, and guessed she had never held so much in her hand before.

"You are too generous, great prince," croaked Brand, staring down with wide eyes.

"Great deeds deserve great rewards from great men. Or else why raise men up at all?" Varoslaf's unblinking gaze shifted back to Yarvi. "If they are your back oars what wonders might the others perform?"

"I daresay some of them could make the rest of your gold vanish before your eyes."

"No good crew is without a few bad men. We cannot all be righteous, eh, Father Yarvi? Those of us who rule especially."

"Power means having one shoulder always in the shadows."

"So it does. How is the jewel of the north, your mother, Queen Laithlin?"

"She is my mother no more, great prince, I gave up my family when I swore my oath to the Ministry."

"Strange customs, you northerners have," and the prince fiddled lazily with the ears of his hound. "I think the bonds of blood cannot be severed with a word."

"The right words can cut deeper than swords, and oaths especially. The queen is with child."

"An heir to the Black Chair perhaps? News rich as gold in these unhappy times."

"The world rejoices, great prince. She speaks often of her desire to visit Kalyiv again."

"Not too soon, I pray! My treasury still bears the scars of her last visit."

"Perhaps we can forge an agreement that will mend those scars and make your treasury swell besides?"

A pause. Varoslaf looked to the woman and she shook herself gently, the coins dangling from her scarf twisting and twinkling on her forehead. "Is that why you have come so far, Father Yarvi? To make my treasury swell?"

"I have come seeking help."

"Ah, you too desire the bounty of great men." Another pause. Thorn felt a game was played between these two. A game of words, but no less skillful than the exercises in the training square. And even more dangerous. "Only name your desire. As long as you do not seek allies against the High King in Skekenhouse."

Father Yarvi's smile did not slip by so much as a hair. "I should have known your sharp eyes would see straight to the heart of the matter, great prince. I—and Queen Laithlin, and King Uthil—fear Mother War may spread her wings across the Shattered Sea in spite of all our efforts. The High King has many allies, and we seek to balance the scales. Those who thrive on the trade down the Divine and the Denied may need to pick a side—"

"And yet I cannot. As you have seen I have troubles of my own, and no help to spare."

"Might I ask if you have help to spare for the High King?"

The prince narrowed his eyes. "Ministers keep coming south with that question."

"I am not the first?"

"Mother Scaer was here not a month ago."

Father Yarvi paused at that. "Grom-gil-Gorm's minister?"

"On behalf of Grandmother Wexen. She came before me with a dozen of the High King's warriors and warned me not to paddle in the Shattered Sea. One might almost say she made threats." The hound lifted its head and gave a long growl, a string of drool slipping from its teeth and spattering the ground. "Here. In my hall. I was sore tempted to have her skinned in the public square but . . . it did not seem politic." And he stilled his dog with the slightest hiss.

"Mother Scaer left with her skin, then?"

"It would not have fit me. She headed southward in a ship bearing the High King's prow, bound for the First of Cities. And though I much prefer your manners to hers, I fear I can only give you the same promise."

"Which was?"

"To help all my good friends about the Shattered Sea equally."

"Meaning not at all."

The Prince of Kalyiv smiled, and it chilled Thorn even more than his frown. "You are known as a deep-cunning man, Father Yarvi. I am sure you need no help to sift out my meaning. You know where I sit. Between the Horse People and the great forests. Between the High

King and the empress. At the crossroads of the world and with perils all about me."

"We all have perils to contend with."

"But a prince of Kalyiv must have friends in the east, and the west, and the north, and the south. A prince of Kalyiv thrives on balance. A prince of Kalyiv must keep a foot over every threshold."

"How many feet do you have?"

The dog pricked up its ears and gave another growl. Varoslaf's smile faded as slowly as melting snow. "A word of advice. Stop this talk of war, Father Yarvi. Return to Gettland and smooth the way for Father Peace, as I understand a wise minister should."

"I and my crew are free to leave Kalyiv, great prince?"

"Force Uthil's minister to stay against his will? That would not be politic either."

"Then I thank you humbly for your hospitality and for your advice, well meant and gratefully received. But we cannot turn back. We must go on with all haste to the First of Cities, and seek help there."

Thorn glanced across at Brand, and saw him swallow. To go on to the First of Cities, half the world away from home. She felt a flicker of excitement at that thought. And a flicker of fear.

Varoslaf merely snorted his disdain. "I wish you luck. But I fear you will get nothing from the empress. She has grown ever more devout in her old age, and will have no dealings with those who do not worship her One God. The only thing she hungers after more than priest-babble is spilled blood. That and elf-relics. But it would take the greatest ever unearthed as a gift to win her favor."

"Oh, great prince, wherever would I find such a thing?" Father Yarvi bowed low, all innocence and humility.

But Thorn saw the deep-cunning smile at the corner of his mouth.

III.

FIRST OF CITIES

LUCK

The gods knew, there'd been a stack of disappointments on that journey high as Brand's head. Plenty of things sadly different from the tales whispered and the songs sung back in Thorlby. And plenty of things folk tended to leave out altogether.

The vast bogs about the mouth of the Denied, for one—clouds of stinging insects haunting banks of stinking sludge where they'd woken to gray mornings soaked with marshwater and bloated with itching bites.

The long coast of the Golden Sea, for another—mean little villages in mean little fences where Father Yarvi argued in strange tongues with shepherds whose faces were tanned to leather by the sun. Beaches of pebbles where the crew pitched rings of spitting torches and lay watching the night, startling at every sound, sure bandits were waiting just beyond the light.

The memory of the battle with the Horse People prowled in their wake, the face of the man Brand killed haunting his thoughts, the hammering of steel on wood finding him in his sleep.

"Your death comes!"

Jerking awake in the sticky darkness to nothing but the quick thud of his heart and the slow chirp of crickets. There was nothing in the songs about regrets.

The songs were silent on the boredom too. The oar, the oar, and the buckled shoreline grinding by, week after week. The homesickness, the worry for his sister, the weepy nostalgia for things he'd always thought he hated. Skifr's endless barking and Thorn's endless training and the endless beatings she gave out to every member of the crew and Brand especially. Father Yarvi's endless answers to Koll's endless questions about plants, and wounds, and politics, and history, and the path of Father Moon across the sky. The chafing, the sickness, the sunburn, the heat, the flies, the thirst, the stinking bodies, the worn-through seat of his trousers, Safrit's rationing, Dosduvoi's toothache, the thousand ways Fror got his scar, the bad food and the running arses, the endless petty arguments, the constant fear of every person they saw and, worst of all, the certain knowledge that, to get home, they'd have to suffer through every mile of it again the other way.

Yes, there'd been a stack of frustrations, hardships, hurts, and disappointments on that journey.

But the First of Cities exceeded every expectation.

It was built on a wide promontory that jutted miles out into the straits, covered from sea to sea with buildings of white stone, with proud towers and steep roofs, with lofty bridges and strong walls within strong walls. The Palace of the Empress stood on the highest point, gleaming domes clustered inside a fortress so massive it could have held the whole of Thorlby with room for two Roystocks left over.

The whole place blazed with lights, red and yellow and white, so many they tinged the blue evening clouds with welcoming pink and set a thousand thousand reflections dancing in the sea, where ships from every nation of the world swarmed like eager bees.

Perhaps they'd seen greater buildings up there on the silence of the Divine, but this was no elf-ruin but the work of men alone, no crumbling tomb to lost glories but a place of high hopes and mad dreams, bursting with life. Even this far distant Brand could hear the city's call. A hum at the edge of his senses that set his very fingertips tingling.

Koll, who'd swarmed up the half-carved mast to cling to the yard for the best view, started flailing his arms and whooping like a madman. Safrit clutched her head below muttering, "I give up. I give up. He can plunge to his death if he wants to. Get down from there, you fool!"

"Did you ever see anything like it?" Brand whispered.

"There is nothing like it," said Thorn, a crazy grin on a face grown leaner and tougher than ever. She had a long pale scar through the stubble on the shorn side of her head, and rings of red gold to go with the silver in her tangled hair, clipped from the coin Varoslaf had given her. A hell of an indulgence to wear gold on your head, Rulf had said, and Thorn had shrugged and said it was as good a place to keep your money as any.

Brand kept his own in a pouch around his neck. It was a new life for Rin, and he didn't plan on losing that for anything.

"There she is, Rulf!" called Father Yarvi, clambering between the smiling oarsmen toward the steering platform. "I've a good feeling."

"Me too," said the helmsman, a cobweb of happy lines cracking the skin at the corners of his eyes.

Skifr frowned up at the wheeling birds. "Good feelings, maybe, but poor omens." Her mood had never quite recovered from the battle on the Denied.

Father Yarvi ignored her. "We will speak to Theofora, the Empress of the South, and we will give her Queen Laithlin's gift, and we shall see what we shall see." He turned to face the crew, spreading his arms, tattered coat flapping in the breeze. "We've come a long and dangerous way, my friends! We've crossed half the world! But the end of the road is ahead!"

"The end of the road," murmured Thorn as the crew gave a cheer, licking her cracked lips as if she was a drunk and the First of Cities a great jug of ale on the horizon.

Brand felt a childish rush of excitement and he splashed water from his flask all over Thorn, spray sparkling as she slapped it away and shoved him off his sea-chest with her boot. He punched her on the shoulder, which these days was like punching a firmly-held shield, and she caught a fistful of his frayed shirt, the two of them falling in a laughing, snarling, sour-smelling wrestle in the bottom of the boat.

"Enough, barbarians," said Rulf, wedging his foot between them and prying them apart. "You are in a civilized place, now! From here on we expect civilized behavior."

THE DOCKS WERE ONE vast riot.

Folk shoved and tugged and tore at each other, lit by garish torch-light, the crowd surging like a thing alive as fights broke out, fists and even blades flashing above the crowd. Before a gate a ring of warriors stood, dressed in odd mail like fishes' scales, snarling at the mob and occasionally beating at them with the butts of their spears.

"Thought this was a civilized place?" muttered Brand as Rulf guided the *South Wind* toward a wharf.

"The most civilized place in the world," murmured Father Yarvi. "Though that mostly means folk prefer to stab each other in the back than the front."

"Less chance of getting blood on your fine robe that way," said Thorn, watching a man hurry down a wharf on tiptoe holding his silken skirts above his ankles.

A huge, fat boat, timbers green with rot, was listing badly in the harbor, half its oars clear of the water, evidently far overloaded and with panicked passengers crammed at its rail. While Brand pulled in his oar two jumped—or were pushed—and tumbled flailing into the sea. There was a haze of smoke on the air and a smell of charred wood, but stronger still was the stink of panic, strong as hay-reek and catching as the plague.

"This has the feel of poor luck!" called Dosduvoi as Brand clambered onto the wharf after Thorn.

"I'm no great believer in luck," said Father Yarvi. "Only in good planning and bad. Only in deep cunning and shallow." He strode to a grizzled northerner with a beard forked and knotted behind his neck, frowning balefully over the loading of a ship much like theirs.

"A good day to—" the minister began.

"I don't think so!" the man bellowed over the din. "And you won't find many who do!"

"We're with the *South Wind*," said Yarvi, "come down the Denied from Kalyiv."

"I'm Ornulf, captain of the *Mother Sun*." He nodded toward his weatherbeaten vessel. "Came down from Roystock two years hence. We were trading with the Alyuks in spring, and had as fine a cargo as you ever saw. Spices, and bottles, and beads, and treasures our womenfolk would've wept to see." He bitterly shook his head. "We had a storehouse in the city and it was caught up in the fire last night. All gone. All lost."

"I'm sorry for that," said the minister. "Still, the gods left you your lives."

"And we're quitting this bloody place before we lose those too."

Yarvi frowned at a particularly blood-curdling woman's shriek. "Are things usually like this?"

"You haven't heard?" asked Ornulf. "The Empress Theofora died last night."

Brand stared at Thorn, and she gave a grimace and scratched at the scar on her scalp.

The news sucked a good deal of the vigor from Father Yarvi's voice. "Who rules, then?"

"I hear her seventeen-year-old niece Vialine was enthroned as thirty-fifth Empress of the South this morning." Ornulf snorted. "But I received no invitation to the happy event."

"Who rules, then?" asked Yarvi, again.

The man's eyes swiveled sideways. "For now, the mob. Folk taking it upon themselves to settle scores while the law sleeps."

"Folk love a good score down here, I understand," said Rulf.

"Oh, they hoard 'em up for generations. That's how that fire got started, I hear, some merchant taking vengeance on another. I swear they could teach Grandmother Wexen a thing or two about old grudges here."

"I wouldn't bet on that," muttered Father Yarvi.

"The young empress's uncle, Duke Mikedas, is having a stab at taking charge. The city's full of his warriors. Here to keep things calm, he says. While folk adjust."

"To having him in power?"

Ornulf grunted. "I thought you were new here."

"Wherever you go," murmured the minister, "the powerful are the powerful."

"Perhaps this duke'll bring order," said Brand, hopefully.

"Looks like it'd take five hundred swords just to bring order to the docks," said Thorn, frowning toward the chaos.

"The duke has no shortage of swords," said Ornulf, "but he's no lover of northerners. If you've a license from the High King you're among the flowers but the rest of us are getting out before we're taxed to a stub or worse."

Yarvi pressed his thin lips together. "The High King and I are not on the best of terms."

"Then head north, friend, while you still can."

"Head north now you'll find yourself in Prince Varoslaf's nets," said Brand.

"He's still fishing for crews?" Ornulf grabbed his forked beard with both fists as though he'd tear it from his jaw. "Gods damn it, so many wolves! How's an honest thief to make a living?"

Yarvi passed him something and Brand saw the glint of silver. "If he has sense, he presents himself to Queen Laithlin of Gettland, and says her minister sent him."

Ornulf stared down at his palm, then at Yarvi's shrivelled hand, then up, eyes wide. "You're Father Yarvi?"

"I am." The line of warriors had begun to spread out from their gate, shoving folk ahead of them though there was nowhere to go. "And I have come for an audience with the empress."

Rulf gave a heavy sigh. "Unless Theofora can hear you through the Last Door, it'll have to be this Vialine we speak to."

"The empress dies the very day we turn up," Brand leaned close to mutter. "What do you think about luck now?"

Father Yarvi gave a long sigh as he watched a loaded cart heaved off the docks and into the sea, the uncoupled horse kicking out wildly, eyes rolling with terror. "I think we could use some."

BEHIND THE
THRONE

"I look like a clown," snapped Thorn, as she wove through the teeming streets after Father Yarvi.

"No, no," he said. "Clowns make people smile."

He'd made her wash, and put some bitter-smelling herb in the searing water to kill off her lice, and she felt as raw under her chafing new clothes as the skinned men on the docks of Kalyiv. Safrit had clipped half her hair back to stubble, then hacked at the matted side with a bone comb but given up in disgust once she broke three teeth off it. She'd given Thorn a tunic of some blood-colored cloth with gold stitching about the collar, so fine and soft it felt as if you were wearing nothing, then when Thorn demanded her old clothes back Safrit had pointed out a heap of burning rags in the street and asked if she was sure.

Thorn might've been a head taller but Safrit was as irresistible as Skifr in her way and would not be denied. She had ended up with jingling silver rings on her arms and a necklace of red glass beads wound around and around her neck. The sort of things that would have made her mother clasp her hands with pride to see her daughter wearing, but had always felt as comfortable as slave's chains to Thorn.

"People here expect a certain . . ." Yarvi waved his crippled hand at a group of black-skinned men whose silks were set with flashing splinters of mirror. "Theater. They will find you fascinatingly fearsome. Or fearsomely fascinating. You look just right."

"Huh." Thorn knew she looked an utter fool because when she finally emerged in all her perfumed absurdity Koll had sniggered, and Skifr had puffed out her cheeks, and Brand had just stared at her in silence as if he'd seen the dead walk. Thorn's face had burned with the humiliation and had hardly stopped burning since.

A man in a tall hat gaped at her as she passed. She would have liked to show him her father's sword but foreigners weren't allowed to carry weapons in the First of Cities. So she leaned close and snapped her teeth at him instead, which proved more than enough armament to make him squeak in fear and scurry off.

"Why haven't you made any effort?" she asked, catching up to Yarvi. He seemed to have a knack of slipping unnoticed through the press while she had to shoulder after him leaving a trail of anger in her wake.

"I have." The minister brushed down his plain black coat, not a trace of adornment anywhere. "Among these gaudy crowds I will stand out for my humble simplicity, a trustworthy servant of the Father of Doves."

"You?"

"I said I'd look like one, not that I'd be one." Father Yarvi shook his head as she dragged at the over-tight seat of her new trousers yet again. "Honestly, Brand was right when he said there is no blessing you cannot treat like a curse. Most people would be thankful for fine new clothes. I can scarcely take you to the palace reeking like a beggar, can I?"

"Why are you taking me to the palace at all?"

"Should I go alone?"

"You could take someone who won't say the worst thing at the worst time. Safrit, or Rulf, or Brand, even? He's got one of those faces folk trust."

"He's got one of those faces folk take advantage of. And not to dismiss the towering diplomatic talents of Safrit, or Rulf, or Brand, but there's always the chance the young Empress Vialine will warm to a woman her own age."

"Me? Folk never warm to me!" Thorn remembered the contempt of the girls in Thorlby, the dagger-stares and the poison-laughter and, even though she'd killed eight men, she shivered at the thought. "Women my age least of all."

"This will be different."

"Why?"

"Because you will be keeping your tongue still and smiling ever so sweetly."

Thorn raised her brows at that. "Doesn't sound much like me. You sure?"

Yarvi's narrowed eyes slid across to hers. "Oh, I am sure. Wait, now."

Thorn's jaw dropped at the sight of six strange monsters crossing the street, each fastened to the one behind by a silver chain, necks long as a man was tall swaying mournfully.

"We're a long way from Gettland," she muttered as she watched them plod off between white buildings so high the crooked lane was like a shadowy canyon. She remembered the damp, dark stone of Gettland, the morning mist over gray Mother Sea, her breath smoking on the dawn chill, huddling about the fire for warmth in the long evening, her mother's voice crooning out the night prayer. It seemed another life. It seemed another world. One Thorn had never thought she might miss.

"Yes we are," said Yarvi, setting briskly off through the sticky, stinking heat of the First of Cities. Thorn knew the year was wearing on, but autumn here was far hotter than midsummer in Thorlby.

She thought of the hard miles they'd traveled. The months of rowing. The slaving over the tall hauls. The constant danger of the steppe. Not to mention the brooding presence of Prince Varoslaf across the path. "Could the empress give us any help even if she chose to try?"

"Perhaps not in steel, but in silver, most definitely." Yarvi murmured an apology in some unknown language as he stepped around a group of women in dark veils, their paint-rimmed eyes following Thorn as if she was the strange one.

"The odds at home will still be long." Thorn counted the enemies off on her calloused fingers. "The High King's own men in Yutmark, and the Inglings, and the Lowlanders, and the Vanstermen, and the Islanders—"

"You may be surprised to learn I had thought of this already."

"And we've got only the Throvenlanders on our side."

Yarvi snorted. "That alliance is milk left in the noon heat."

"Eh?"

"Won't last."

"But King Fynn said—"

"King Fynn is a bloated bag of guts with little authority even in his own kingdom. Only his vanity will bind him to us, and that will melt before Grandmother Wexen's wrath in due course like snow before Mother Sun. That little trick only bought us time."

"Then . . . we'll stand alone."

"My uncle Uthil would stand alone against the world and insist that steel is the answer."

"That sounds brave," said Thorn.

"Doubtless."

"But . . . not wise."

Yarvi gave her a smile. "I'm impressed. I expected you to learn swordsmanship, but never prudence. Don't worry, though. I hope to find other ways to shorten the odds."

AS SOON AS THEY stepped through the towering bronze doors of the palace Thorn went from embarrassment at being dressed like a princess to shame at being dressed like a peasant. The slaves here looked like queens, the guards like heroes of legend. The hall in which they were received was crowded with jewel-encrusted courtiers as brightly colored, as pompous and, as far as Thorn could tell, every bit as useless the peacocks that swaggered about the immaculate gardens outside.

She would happily have shrivelled away into her new boots but they had great thick soles, and she had grown the past few months, and she stood taller than Father Yarvi now, who was taller than most himself. As always she was left with no choice but to push her shoulders back and her chin up and put on that bravest face of hers, however much the coward behind it might be sweating through her absurd crimson tunic.

Duke Mikedas sat above them in a golden chair on a high dais, one leg slung casually over its carven arm, his fabulous armor covered with gilded swirls. He was one of those handsome men who fancies himself more handsome than he is, dark-skinned and with a twinkling eye, his black hair and beard streaked with silver.

"Greetings, friends, and *welcome* to the First of Cities!" He flashed a winning smile, though it won nothing from Thorn but the deepest suspicion. "How is my mastery of your tongue?"

Father Yarvi bowed low and Thorn followed. Bow when I bow, he had said, and that seemed to mean whenever possible. "Flawless, your grace. A most welcome and impressive—"

"Remind me of your names again, I have the most *abysmal* memory for names."

"He is Father Yarvi, Minister of Gettland."

The woman who spoke was long and lean and very pale, her head close shaven. Elf-bangles rattled on one tattooed forearm, ancient steel, and gold, and broken crystal glittering. Thorn curled her lips back from her teeth, and only just remembered in time not to spit on the highly polished floor.

"Mother Scaer," said Yarvi. "Every time our paths cross it is a fresh delight."

The Minister of Vansterland, who whispered in the ear of Grom-gil-Gorm, and had been sent south by Grandmother Wexen to warn Prince Varoslaf not to paddle in the Shattered Sea.

"I wish I could say the same," said Mother Scaer. "But none of our three meetings has been altogether pleasant." She moved her ice-blue gaze to Thorn. "This woman I do not know."

"In fact you met in Skekenhouse. She is Thorn Bathu, daughter of Storn Headland."

Thorn was somewhat gratified to see Mother Scaer's eyes widen. "Whatever have you been feeding her?"

"Fire and whetstones," said Yarvi, smiling, "and she has quite the appetite. She is a proven warrior now, tested against the Uzhaks."

"What curious warriors you have!" Duke Mikedas sounded more amused than impressed and his courtiers tittered obediently. "I'd like to see her matched against a man of my household guard."

"How about two of 'em?" snapped Thorn, before she even realized her mouth was open. The voice hardly sounded like hers, a grating challenge echoing loud and savage from the silver-fretted marble walls.

But the duke only laughed. "Wonderful! The exuberance of the young! My niece is the same. She thinks anything can be done, in spite of tradition, in spite of the feelings of others, in spite of . . . *realities*."

Yarvi bowed again. "Those who rule, and those beside them, must be always mindful of realities."

The duke wagged his finger. "I like you already."

"I believe, in fact, we have a friend in common."

"Oh?"

"Ebdel Aric Shadikshirram."

The duke's eyes widened, and he swung his leg down from the chair and sat forward. "How is she?"

"I am sorry to tell you she has passed through the Last Door, your grace."

"Dead?"

"Killed by a treacherous slave."

"Merciful God." The duke slumped back. "She was a singular woman. I asked her to marry me, you know. I was a young man then, of course, but . . ." He shook his head in wonderment. "She *refused* me."

"A singular woman indeed."

"The years trickle like water through our fingers. It seems only yesterday . . ." The duke gave a long sigh, and his eyes hardened. "But, to the matter."

"Of course, your grace." Father Yarvi bowed again. His head was bobbing like an apple in a bucket. "I come as emissary from Queen Laithlin and King Uthil of Gettland, and seek an audience with her radiance Vialine, Empress of the South."

"Hmmmm." The duke propped himself on one elbow and rubbed unhappily at his beard. "Where is Guttland again?"

Thorn ground her teeth but Father Yarvi's patience was steel-forged. "Gettland is on the western shore of the Shattered Sea, your grace, north of the High King's seat at Skekenhouse."

"So many little countries up there it takes a scholar to keep track of them!" A tinkling of laughter from the courtiers and Thorn felt a powerful urge to put her fist in their faces. "I wish I could honor *every* supplicant with an audience, but you must understand this is a difficult time."

Yarvi bowed. "Of course, your grace."

"So many enemies to be tamed and friends to be reassured. So many alliances to tend to and some . . . less important than others, no disrespect intended." His brilliant smile exuded disrespect like the stink from an old cheese.

Yarvi bowed. "Of course, your grace."

"The Empress Vialine is not a woman of . . ." he gestured at Thorn as if at an unpromising horse in his stable, "*this* type. She is little more than a girl. Impressionable. Innocent. She has so very much to learn about how things truly *are*. You understand I must be cautious. You understand you must be patient. For a nation as wide and varied as ours to ford the river from one ruler to another is always . . . a *bumpy* crossing. But I will send for you in due course."

Yarvi bowed. "Of course, your grace. Might I ask when?"

The duke waved him away with a flourish of his long fingers. "Due course, Father, er . . ."

"Yarvi," hissed out Mother Scaer.

Thorn was no diplomat, but she got the strong impression due course meant never.

Mother Scaer was waiting for them in the statue-lined hallway outside with two warriors of her own, a scowling Vansterman and a great Lowlander with a face like a stone slab. Thorn was in a black mood and set straight away to bristling, but neither seemed willing to be stared down.

Nor did their mistress. "I am surprised to see you here, Father Yarvi."

"And I you, Mother Scaer." Though neither of them looked surprised in the least. "We both find ourselves half the world from our proper places. I thought you would be beside your king, Grom-gil-Gorm. He needs you to speak for Father Peace, before Mother War drags him to ruin against Gettland."

Mother Scaer's look grew even icier, if that was possible. "I would be with him, had Grandmother Wexen not chosen me for this mission."

"A high honor." The slightest curl at the corner of Yarvi's mouth suggested it was closer to a sentence of exile, and they both knew it. "You must truly have delighted Grandmother Wexen to earn it. Did you speak up for your country? Did you stand for your king and his people, as a minister should?"

"When I make an oath I keep it," snapped Scaer. "A loyal minister goes where her grandmother asks her."

"Just like a loyal slave."

"You are the expert there. Does your neck still chafe?"

Yarvi's smile grew strained at that. "The scars are quite healed."

"Are they?" Scaer leaned close, her thin lips curling from her teeth. "If I were you, I would return to the Shattered Sea before you pick up some more." And she brushed past, Thorn and the Vansterman exchanging one more lingering scowl before he strode away.

"She's trouble," whispered Thorn once they were out of earshot.

"Yes."

"And she's close with the duke."

"Yes."

"And was sent here ahead of us."

"Yes."

"So . . . Grandmother Wexen guessed what you'd do long before you did it."

"Yes."

"I've a feeling we're not going to get an audience with anything this way."

Yarvi looked sourly across at her. "See? You're a diplomat after all."

OLD FRIENDS

Gods, she was quick now. Brand was twice the fighter he'd been when they left Thorlby just from fighting her, but every day he was less her equal. He felt like a lumbering hog against her, always three steps behind. Alone he had no chance at all, whatever the ground. Even with two comrades beside him he was starting to feel outnumbered. Less and less she was on the defensive, more and more she was the hunter and they the helpless prey.

"Koll," called Brand, jerking his head, "take the left." They started to spread out about the courtyard of the crumbling palace Yarvi had found for them, trying to trap her, trying to tempt her with the gaps between them. "Dosduvoi, get—"

Too late he realized Thorn had lured the big man into the one bright corner of the yard and Dosduvoi cringed as Mother Sun stabbed him suddenly in the eyes.

Thorn was on him like lightning, staggered him in spite of his size with a splintering ax-blow on the shield, slid her sword under the rim and rammed the point into his considerable gut. She reeled away laughing as Brand lashed at the air where she'd stood a moment before, making sure one of the flaking pillars that ringed the yard was between her and Koll.

"Oh, God," wheezed Dosduvoi as he folded up, clutching at his belly.

"Promising," said Skifr, circling them with her hands clasped behind her back. "But don't let your own wind sweep you away. Treat every fight as if it is your last. Every enemy as though they are your worst. The wise fighter seems less than they are, however mean the opposition."

"Thanks for that," Brand forced through gritted teeth, trying to wipe some trickling sweat off on his shoulder. Gods, it was hot. Sometimes it didn't seem there was a breath of wind anywhere in this cursed city.

"My father used to say never get proud." Thorn's eyes darted from Brand to Koll and back as they tried to herd her into a corner. "He said great warriors start believing their own songs, start thinking it'll have to be a great thing that kills them. But a little thing can kill anyone."

"Scratch gone bad," said Safrit, watching with hands on hips.

"Frayed shield strap," grunted Brand, trying to keep his eyes on Thorn's weapons but finding her clinging vest something of a distraction.

"Slip on a sheep's turd," said Koll, nipping in and jabbing at Thorn but giving her the chance to land a crashing blow on his shield and slip around him into space again.

"Your father sounds a sensible man," said Skifr. "How did he die?"

"Killed in a duel with Grom-gil-Gorm. By all accounts, he got proud."

Thorn changed direction in an instant and, fast as Koll was getting, she was far faster. Fast as a scorpion and less merciful. Her ax thudded into the lad's leg, made it buckle and he gasped as he staggered sideways. Her sword slapped into his side and he went tumbling across the courtyard with a despairing cry.

But that gave Brand his chance. Even off-balance she managed to turn his sword away so it thudded hard into her shoulder. Gods, she was tough, she didn't even flinch. He crashed into her with his shield, drove her snarling back against the wall, rim gouging out a shower of loose plaster. They staggered in an ungainly tussle and, for a moment, he was sure he had her. But even as he was forcing her back she somehow twisted her foot behind his, growled as she switched her weight and sent him tumbling over it.

They went down hard, him on the bottom. Gods, she was strong. It was like Bail wrestling the great eel in the song, but more than likely with a worse outcome.

"You're supposed to be killing him!" called Skifr, "not coupling with him! That you can do on your own time."

They rolled in a tangle and came out with Thorn on top, teeth bared as she tried to work her forearm up under his jaw to choke him, he with a grip on her elbow, straining to twist it away, both snarling in each other's faces.

So close her two eyes blurred into one. So close he could see every bead of sweat on her forehead. So close her chest pressed against him with each quick, hot, sour-sweet breath.

And for a moment it felt as if they weren't fighting at all, but something else.

Then the heavy door shuddered open and Thorn sprang off him as quickly as if she'd been slapped.

"Another win?" snapped Father Yarvi, stepping over the threshold with Rulf frowning at his shoulder.

"Of course," said Thorn, as if there was nothing in her mind but giving Brand a beating. What else would there be?

He clambered up, brushing himself off, pretending his skin wasn't burning from his face to his toes. Pretending he was hunching over because of an elbow in the ribs rather than any swelling lower down. Pretending everything was the same as ever. But something had changed that day she stepped into the courtyard in her new clothes, the same but so, so different, the light catching the side of her frown and making one eye gleam, and he couldn't speak for staring at her. Everything had fallen apart all of a sudden. Or maybe it had fallen together. She wasn't just his friend or his rival or his oarmate any more, one of the crew. She still was, but she was something else as well, something that excited and fascinated but mostly scared the hell out of him. Something had changed in the way he saw her and now when he looked at her he couldn't see anything else.

They were sleeping on the floor of the same crumbling room. Hadn't seemed anything strange about it when they moved in, they'd been sleeping on top of each other for months. Only now he lay awake half the sticky-hot night thinking about how close she was. Listening to the endless sounds of the city and trying to make out her slow breath. Thinking how easy it would be to reach out and touch her . . .

He realized he was looking sidelong at her arse again, and forced his eyes down to the floor. "Gods," he mouthed, but he'd no idea which one you prayed to for help with a problem like this.

"Well I'm tremendously glad someone's winning," snapped Yarvi.

"No luck at the palace?" croaked out Brand, still bent over and desperate to find a distraction.

"The palace has no luck in it at all," said Rulf.

"Another day wasted." Yarvi sank down on a bench with his shoulders slumped. "We'll be lucky if we get another chance to be insulted by Duke Mikedas, let alone his niece."

"I thought you didn't believe in luck?" asked Thorn.

"Right now, I'm down to hoping it believes in me."

Father Yarvi looked rattled, and Brand had never seen that before. Even when they fought the Horse People, he had always seemed certain of what to do. Now Brand wondered whether that was a mask the minister had made himself. A mask which was starting to crack. For the first time he was painfully aware Yarvi was only a few years older than he was, and had the fate of Gettland to carry, and only one good hand to do it.

"I wonder what they're doing in Thorlby right now?" murmured Koll wistfully, shaking out his hurt leg.

"Coming close to harvest time, I reckon," said Dosduvoi, who'd rolled his shirt up to check his own bruises.

"Fields golden with swaying barley," said Skifr.

"Lots of traders coming to the markets." Safrit toyed with the merchant's weights around her neck. "Docks swarming with ships. Money being made."

"Unless the crops have been burned by the Vanstermen's raids," snapped Yarvi. "And the merchants have been held at Skekenhouse by Grandmother Wexen. Fields black stubble and the docks sitting empty. She could have roused the Lowlanders by now. The Inglings too, with Bright Yilling at their head. Thousands of them, marching on Gettland."

Brand swallowed, thinking of Rin in their fragile little hovel outside the walls. "You think so?"

"No. Not yet. But soon, maybe. Time drains away and I do nothing. There's always a way." The minister stared down at the ground, good fingers fussing with the nail on his twisted thumb. "Half a war is fought with words, won with words. The right words to the right people. But I don't have either."

"It'll come right," muttered Brand, wanting to help but with no idea what he could do.

"I wish I could see how." Yarvi put his hands over his pale face, the bad one like a twisted toy next to the good. "We need a damn miracle."

And there was a thumping knock on the door.

Skifr raised an eyebrow. "Are we by any chance expecting visitors?"

"We're hardly overburdened with friends in the city," said Thorn.

"You're hardly overburdened with friends anywhere," said Brand.

"It could be that Mother Scaer has sent a welcoming party," said Yarvi.

"Weapons," growled Rulf. He tossed Thorn's sword to her and she snatched it from the air.

"By God, I'm happy to fight anyone," said Dosduvoi, seizing a spear, "as long as it's not her."

Brand drew the blade that had been Odda's, the steel frighteningly light after the practice sword. Fear had quickly solved the problem in his trousers, if nothing else.

The door shuddered from more knocks, and it was not a light door.

Koll crept over to it, going up on tiptoe to peer through the spyhole.

"It's a woman," he hissed. "She looks rich."

"Alone?" asked Yarvi.

"Yes, I'm alone," came a muffled voice through the door. "And I'm a friend."

"That's just what an enemy would say," said Thorn.

"Or a friend," said Brand.

"The gods know we could use one," said Rulf, but nocking an arrow to his black bow even so.

"Open it," said Yarvi.

Koll whipped back the bolt as though it might burn him and sprung away, a knife at the ready in each hand. Brand crouched behind his shield, fully expecting a flight of arrows to come hissing through the archway.

Instead the door creaked slowly open and a face showed itself at the crack. A woman's face, dark-skinned and dark-eyed with black hair loosely twisted up and held with jewelled pins. She had a little scar through her top lip, a notch of white tooth showing as she smiled.

"Knock, knock," she said, slipping through and pushing the door shut behind her. She wore a long coat of fine white linen and around her neck a golden chain, each link worked to look like an eye. She raised one brow at all the sharpened steel and slowly put up her palms. "Oh, I surrender."

Rulf gave a great whoop, and flung his bow skittering across the floor, rushed over to the woman and gathered her in a great hug.

"Sumael!" he said, squeezing her tight. "Gods, how I've missed you!"

"And I you, Rulf, you old bastard," she wheezed, slapping him on the back, then groaning as he lifted her off her feet. "Had my suspicions when I heard a ship called the *South Wind* had landed. Nice touch, by the way."

"It reminds us where we came from," said Yarvi, good hand rubbing at his neck.

"Father Yarvi," said Sumael, slipping free of the helmsman's embrace. "Look at you. Lost at sea and desperately in need of someone to pick out the course."

"Some things never change," he said. "You look . . . prosperous."

"You look awful."

"Some things never change."

"No hug for me?"

He gave a snort, almost a sob. "I'm worried if I do I might never let go."

She walked over, their eyes fixed on each other. "I'll take the risk." And she put her arms around him, going up on her toes to hold him close. He put his head on her shoulder, and tears glistened on his gaunt cheeks.

Brand stared at Thorn, and she shrugged back. "I guess now we know who Sumael is."

"SO THIS IS THE EMBASSY of Gettland?" Sumael poked at a lump of mold-speckled plaster and it dropped from the wall and scattered across the dusty boards. "You've an eye for a bargain."

"I am my mother's son," said Yarvi. "Even if she's not my mother anymore." The crumbling hall they ate in could have seated forty but most of the crew had gone their own ways and the place had a hollow echo to it now. "What are you doing here, Sumael?"

"Apart from catching up with old friends?" She sat back in her chair and let one stained boot, strangely at odds with her fine clothes, drop onto the scarred tabletop. "I helped my uncle build a ship for the Empress Theofora and one thing led to another. Much to the annoyance of several of her courtiers, she made me inspector of her fleet." A strand of hair fell across her face and she stuck her bottom lip out and blew it back.

"You always had a touch with boats." Rulf was beaming at her as if at a favorite daughter unexpectedly come home. "And annoying people."

"The empire's boats were rotting in the harbor of Rugora, down the coast. Which, as it happens, was also where the empress's niece Vialine was being educated." That strand of hair fell loose again and she blew it back again. "Or imprisoned, depending how you look at it."

"Imprisoned?" asked Brand.

"There's little trust within the royal family here." Sumael shrugged. "But Vialine wanted to understand the fleet. She wants to understand everything. We became friends, I suppose. When Theofora fell ill and Vialine was called back to the First of Cities, she asked me to go with her, and . . ." She lifted the chain of eyes with a fingertip and let it fall clinking. "By some strange magic I find myself counselor to the Empress of the South."

"Talent floats to the top," said Rulf.

"Like turds," grunted Thorn.

Sumael grinned back. "You must be buoyant, then."

Brand laughed, and Thorn gave him a glare, and he stopped.

"So you sit at the right hand of the most powerful woman in the world?" asked Rulf, shaking his balding head.

"By no means alone." That strand fell again and Sumael gave a twitch of annoyance and started pulling the pins from her hair. "There's a council of dozens, and most of them belong to Duke Mikedas. Vialine may be empress in name but he holds the power, and has no intention of sharing."

"He shared nothing with us," said Yarvi.

"I heard." The hair fell in a black curtain across half of her face, the other eye twinkling. "At least you came away with your heads."

"You think we'll keep them if we stay?" asked Yarvi.

Sumael's eye slid across to Thorn. "That depends on how diplomatic you can be."

"I can be diplomatic," snarled Thorn.

Sumael only smiled the wider. She seemed immune to intimidation. "You remind me of a ship's captain Yarvi and I used to sail with."

Yarvi burst out laughing, and so did Rulf, and Thorn frowned through it. "Is that an insult or a compliment?"

"Call it a little of both." Yarvi sat forward, elbows on the table and his shrivelled hand clasped in the other. "The High King is making ready for war, Sumael. Who knows, war might already have started."

"What allies do you have?" she asked, sweeping her hair up with both hands and gathering it in a knot.

"Fewer than we need."

"Some things never change, eh, Yarvi?" Sumael slid the pins back with nimble fingers. "The duke is not so taken with the One God as Theofora was, but he means to honor the alliance with Grandmother Wexen, even so. He can pick a winner."

"We shall see," said Yarvi. "I need to speak to the empress."

Sumael puffed out her cheeks. "I can try. But more than a hearing I cannot promise."

"You don't owe me anything."

She held his eye as she flicked the last pin home, its jewelled end glittering. "It's not a question of debts. Not between us."

Yarvi looked to be caught between laughing and crying, and in the end he sat back, and gave a ragged sigh. "I thought I'd never see you again."

Sumael smiled, that notch of white tooth showing, and Brand found he was starting to like her. "And?"

"I'm glad I was wrong."

"So am I." That strand of hair fell into her face again and she frowned cross-eyed at it a moment, and blew it back.

HOPES

Thorn pushed through a grumbling throng flooding into a temple for prayers. So many temples here, and so much crowding into them to pray.

"Worshipping this One God takes up a lot of time," grunted Brand, trying to work his broad shoulders through the press.

"The tall gods and the small gods have their own business to be about. The One God only seems to care for meddling in everyone else's."

"And bells." Brand winced at another clanging peel from a white tower just above them. "If I never hear another bloody bell I won't complain." He leaned close to whisper. "They bury their dead unburned. Bury them. In the ground. Unburned."

Thorn frowned at the overgrown yard beside the temple, crammed with marking stones wonky as a beggar's teeth, each one, she guessed, with a corpse beneath it, rotting. Hundreds of them. Thousands. A charnel pit right inside the city.

She gave a sweaty shudder at the thought, squeezing at the pouch that held her father's fingerbones. "Damn this city." He might have loved talking about the place, but she was starting to hate it. Far too big, the size of it was crushing. Far too noisy so you couldn't think straight. Far too hot, always sticky and stinking day or night. Rubbish and flies and rot and beggars everywhere, it made her dizzy. So many people, and all of them passing through, no one knowing each other, or wanting anything from each other but to claw out a profit.

"We should go home," she muttered.

"We only just got here."

"Best time to leave a place you hate."

"You hate everything."

"Not everything." She glanced sideways and caught Brand looking at her, and felt that tingling in her stomach again as he quickly looked away.

Turned out he didn't just have the puzzled look and the helpless look, he had another, and now she was catching it all the time. Eyes fixed on her, bright behind a few stray strands of hair. Hungry, almost. Scared, almost. The other day, when they'd been pressed together on the ground, so very close, there'd been . . . something. Something that brought the blood rushing to her face, and not just her face either. In her guts she was sure. Just below her guts, even more so. But the doubts crowded into her head like the faithful into their temples at prayer time.

Could you just ask? I know we used to hate each other but I've come to think I might like you quite a lot. Any chance you like me, at all? Gods, it sounded absurd. All her life she'd been pushing folk away, she had no idea where to start at pulling one in. What if he looked at her as if she was mad? The thought yawned like a pit at her feet. What do you mean *like*? Like, *like* like? Should she just take hold of him and kiss him? She kept thinking about it. She hardly thought about anything else anymore. But what if a look was just a look? What if it was like her mother said—what man would want someone as strange and difficult and contrary as she was? Not one like Brand who was well-made and well-liked and what a man should be and could have anyone he wanted—

Suddenly his arm was around her, herding her back into a door-way. Her heart was in her mouth, she even gave a little girlish squeak as he pressed up tight against her. Then everyone was scrambling to the sides of the lane as horses clattered by, feathers on their bridles thrashing and gilded armor glinting and tall riders in tall helmets caring nothing for those who cowered to either side. Duke Mikedas's men, no doubt.

"Someone could get hurt," Brand muttered, frowning after them.

"Aye," she croaked. "Someone could."

She was fooling herself. Had to be. They were friends. They were oarmates. That was all they needed to be. Why ruin it by pushing for something she couldn't have, didn't deserve, wouldn't get . . . then she caught his eye, and there was that damn look again that set her heart going as if she'd rowed a hard mile. He jerked away from her, gave an awkward half-smile, strode on as the crowds pressed back in after the horsemen.

What if he felt the same as her, wanting to ask but scared to ask and not knowing how to ask? Every conversation with him felt dangerous as a battle. Sleeping in the same room was torture. They'd just been oarmates on one floor when they first threw their blankets down, laughing at the state of the great ruin Yarvi had bought, daylight showing through the roof. But now she only pretended to sleep while she thought about how close he was, and sometimes she thought he was pretending too, could swear his eyes were open, watching her. But she was never sure. The thought of sleeping next to him made her miserable, and the thought of not sleeping next to him made her miserable.

Do you . . . *like* me? Like? *Like?*

The whole thing was a bloody riddle in a language she couldn't speak.

Brand puffed out his cheeks and wiped sweat from his forehead, no doubt blissfully unaware of the trouble he was causing. "Guess we'll be gone soon as we strike a deal with the empress."

Thorn tried to swallow her nerves and talk normally, whatever that meant. "I'm thinking that won't happen."

Brand shrugged. Calm and solid and trusting as ever. "Father Yarvi'll find a way."

"Father Yarvi's deep-cunning all right but he's no sorcerer. If you'd been at the palace, seen that duke's face . . ."

"Sumael will find a way for him, then."

Thorn snorted. "You'd think Mother Sun was up that woman's arse for the light she's shining into everyone's lives."

"Not yours, I reckon."

"I don't trust her."

"You don't trust anyone."

She almost said, "I trust you," but swallowed it at the last moment and settled for a grunt.

"And Rulf trusts her," Brand went on. "With his life, he told me. Father Yarvi too, and he's hardly the trusting type."

"Wish I knew more about what happened with those three," said Thorn. "There's a story there."

"Sometimes you'll be happier for knowing less."

"That's you. Not me." She glanced over at him and caught him looking back. Hungry almost, scared almost, and she felt that tingle deep in her stomach and would have been off on a mad argument with herself yet again if they hadn't come to the market.

One of the markets, anyway. The First of Cities had dozens, each one big as Roystock. Places of mad bustle and noise, cities of stalls choked with people of every shape and color. Great scales clattered and abacuses rattled and prices were screamed in every tongue over the braying and clucking and honking of the livestock. There was a choking reek of cooking food and sickly-sweet spice and fresh dung and the gods knew what else. Everything else. Everything in the world for sale. Belt buckles and salt. Purple cloth and idols. Monstrous, sad-eyed fishes. Thorn squeezed her eyes shut and forced them open, but the every-colored madness still boiled before her.

"Just meat," said Thorn plaintively, weighing Father Yarvi's purse in her hand. "We just want meat." Safrit hadn't even asked for a certain kind. She dodged as a woman in a stained apron strode past with a goat's head under her arm. "Where the hell do we start?"

"Hold up." Brand had stopped at a stall where a dark-skinned merchant was selling strings of glass beads and lifting one so Mother Sun sparkled through the yellow glass. "Pretty, ain't they? Sort of thing a girl likes as a gift."

Thorn shrugged. "I'm no expert on pretty. Girls neither, for that matter."

"You are one, aren't you?"

"So my mother tells me." She added in a mutter, "Opinion's divided."

He held up another necklace, green and blue this time. "Which ones would you want?" And he grinned sideways. "For a gift?"

Thorn felt that tingling in her stomach, stronger than ever. Close to actual vomiting. If ever she was going to get proof then here it was. A gift. For her. Hardly the one she would have chosen but with luck that might be next. If she picked out the right words. What to say? Gods, what to say? Her tongue seemed twice its usual size of a sudden.

"Which ones would I want, or . . ." She kept her eyes on him and let her head drop to one side, tried to make her voice soft. Winsome, whatever that sounded like. She couldn't have been soft more than three times in her life and winsome never, and it came out a clumsy growl. "Which ones *do* I want?"

The puzzled look, now. "I mean, which ones would you want brought back? If you were in Thorlby."

And in spite of the cloying heat a coldness spread out, starting in Thorn's chest and creeping slowly to her very fingertips. Not for her. For someone back in Thorlby. Of course they were. She'd let herself get blown away on her own wind, in spite of Skifr's warnings.

"Don't know," she croaked, trying to shrug as if it was nothing, but it wasn't nothing. "How should I know?" She turned away, her face burning as Brand talked prices with the merchant, and she wished the ground would open up and eat her unburned like the southern dead.

She wondered what girl those beads were for. Wasn't as if there were that many in Thorlby the right age. More than likely Thorn knew her. More than likely Thorn had been laughed at and pointed at and sneered at by her. One of the pretty ones her mother always told her to be more like. One of the ones who knew how to sew, and how to smile, and how to wear a key.

She thought she'd made herself tough right through. Slaps and punches and shield blows hardly hurt her. But everyone has chinks in their armor. Father Yarvi might have stopped them crushing her with stones, but casually as that Brand crushed her just as flat with a string of beads.

He was still grinning as he slipped them into a pocket. "She'll like them, I reckon."

Thorn's face twisted. Never even occurred to him she might think they were for her. Never even occurred to him to think of her the way she'd come to think of him. It was as if all the color had drained out of the world. She'd spent a lot of her life feeling shamed and foolish and ugly, but never so much as this.

"I'm such a stupid shit," she hissed.

Brand blinked at her. "Eh?"

The helpless look, this time, and the temptation to sink her fist into it was almost overpowering, but she knew it wasn't his fault. It was no one's fault but her own, and punching yourself never solves anything. She tried to put a brave face on but she couldn't find it right then. She wanted just to get away. To get anywhere, and she took one step and stopped dead.

The scowling Vansterman who had stood beside Mother Scaer in the palace was blocking her path, his right hand hidden in a rolled up cloak where, she had no doubt, it held a blade. There was a rat-faced little man at his shoulder and she could feel someone moving over on her left. The big Lowlander, she guessed.

"Mother Scaer wants a word with you," said the Vansterman, showing his teeth, and far from a pretty set. "Be best if you came quietly."

"Better yet, we'll go our own way quietly," said Brand, plucking at Thorn's shoulder.

She shook him off, hot shame turned to chill rage in an instant. She needed to hurt someone, and these idiots had come along at just the right moment.

Right for her. Wrong for them.

"I'll be doing nothing quietly." And she flicked one of Father Yarvi's silver coins to the holder of the nearest stall, covered in tools and timber.

"What's this for?" he asked as he caught it.

"The damage," said Thorn, and she snatched up a hammer, flung it underhand so it bounced from the Vansterman's skull, sending him stumbling back, all amazement.

She grabbed a heavy jug from another stall and smashed it over his head before he could get his balance, spraying them both with wine. She caught him as he fell and dug the jagged remains of the handle into his face.

A knife came at her and she dodged it on an instinct, jerking back from the waist so the blade hissed by her, eyes wide as she followed the flashing metal. The rat-faced man stabbed again and she reeled sideways, lurched over a stall, its owner wailing about his goods. She came up clutching a bowl of spice, flung it at Rat-face in a sweet-smelling orange cloud. He coughed, spat, lunged at her blindly. She used the bowl like a shield, the knife-blade buried itself in the wood and she wrenched it from his hand.

He came at her with a clumsy punch but she got her arm inside it, felt his fist scuff her cheek as she stepped in and kneed him full in the gut, then again between the legs and made him squeal. She caught him around the jaw, arching back, and butted him with all her strength in his rat face. The jolt of it dizzied her for a moment, but not half as much as it did him. He flopped onto his hands and knees, drooling blood, and she stepped up with a wild swing of her boot and kicked him onto his back, a table going over and half-burying him in an avalanche of glistening fish.

She turned, saw Brand being forced backward over a stall stacked with fruit, the big Lowlander trying to push a knife into his face, Brand's tongue wedged between his teeth, eyes crossed as he stared at the bright point.

When you're training, fighting your oarmates, there's always a little held back. Thorn held back nothing now. She caught the Lowlander's thick wrist with one hand and hauled his arm straight behind him, screamed as she drove the heel of her other hand down into his elbow. There was a crunch and his arm bent the wrong way, knife tumbling from his flopping hand. He screamed until Thorn chopped him in the neck just the way Skifr taught her and he fell jerking onto the next stall, sending broken pottery flying.

"Come on!" she spat, but there was no one left to fight. Only the shocked stall-holders and the scared bystanders and a mother holding her hand over her daughter's eyes. "Go quietly, will I?" she shrieked, lifting her boot to stomp on the Lowlander's head.

"No!" Brand caught her under the arm and dragged her through the wreckage, folk scrambling to give them room as they half-walked, half-ran into the mouth of a side-street.

"Did you kill them?" he was squeaking.

"With any luck," snarled Thorn, tearing herself free of him. "Why? Did you plan to buy 'em beads, did you?"

"What? We were sent to get meat, not make corpses!" They took a quick turn, past a group of surprised beggars and on through the shadows of a rotten alley, the commotion fading behind them. "Don't want to cause trouble for Father Yarvi. Don't want to see you crushed with rocks either if I can help it."

She saw he was right, and that made her angrier than ever. "You're such a coward," she hissed, which surely wasn't fair but she wasn't feeling very fair right then. There was something tickling her eye, and she wiped it, and her hand came away red.

"You're bleeding," he said, reaching out, "here—"

"Get your hand off me!" She shoved him against the wall, then, when he bounced off, shoved him again even harder. He shrank back, one hand up as she stood over him with her fists clenched, and he looked confused, and hurt, and scared.

It was a look that gave her a tingle, all right, but not in a good way. In that look she saw her silly bloody hopes as twisted and broken as she'd left that Lowlander's arm, and it was no one's fault but her own. She shouldn't have let herself hope, but hopes are like weeds: however often you root them out they keep on springing up.

She gave a growl of frustration, and stalked off down the alleyway.

RUINS

He'd ruined it.

Brand leant against the crumbling wall of the courtyard between Rulf and Father Yarvi, watching Thorn give Fror a pasting. He'd spent half his time watching her, since they reached the First of Cities. But now he did it with the mournful longing of an orphan at a baker's stall, taunting himself with the sight of treats he knows he'll never have. A feeling Brand knew all too well. A feeling he'd hoped never to have again.

There'd been something good between them. A friendship, if nothing else. A friendship a long, hard time in the making.

Like the blundering oaf he was, he'd ruined it.

He'd come back to their room and her things were gone and she was sleeping with Safrit and Koll and she hadn't said why. She hadn't said one word to him since that day in the market. She must've seen how he was looking at her, guessed what he was thinking. Wasn't as though he was any good at hiding it. But judging by the way she looked at him now, or rather the way she didn't, the thought made her flesh crawl. Of course it did.

Why would someone like her—so strong, and sharp, and confident—want a dullard like him? Anyone could see at one glance she was something truly special and he was nothing, and would always be nothing, just like his father used to tell him. A cringing dunce who'd begged for scraps, and picked through rubbish, and dragged sacks around the docks for a pittance and been grateful to get it.

He wasn't sure exactly how he'd done it, but he'd found a way to let everyone down. His crew. His family. Himself. Thorn. He'd ruined it.

Koll slid back the bolt on the door and Sumael stepped into the courtyard. She had two others with her: a small servant in a hooded cloak and a big-shouldered man with a watchful frown and a scar through one gray brow.

The servant pushed her hood back. She was slight and dark-haired, with quick eyes that missed no detail as she watched the fight. If you could call it a fight. Fror was one of the best warriors on the crew, but it only took Thorn a few more moments to put him down and she wasn't even breathing hard afterward.

"I'm done," he groaned, clutching at his ribs with one hand while he held the other up for mercy.

"Most encouraging," said Skifr, catching the wooden blade of Thorn's ax before she could hit him again regardless. "I delight in the way you are fighting today, my dove. No doubts, no conscience, no mercy. Who will be next to face you . . . ?"

Dosduvoi and Koll found the corners of the courtyard suddenly fascinating. Brand held up helpless palms as Skifr's eyes fell on him. The mood Thorn was in, he wasn't sure he'd come through a bout alive. The old woman gave a sigh.

"I fear you have nothing left to learn from your oarmates. The time has come for stiffer opposition." She pulled her coat off and tossed it over Fror's back. "How did you get that scar, Vansterman?"

"I kissed a girl," he grunted, crawling toward the wall, "with a very sharp tongue."

"Further proof that romance can be more dangerous than sword-play," said Skifr, and Brand could only agree with that. She pulled out a wooden sword and ax of her own. "Now, my dove, we shall truly see what you have learned—"

"Before you begin," said Sumael, "I've—"

"Red-toothed war waits for nothing!" Skifr sprang, weapons darting out quick and deadly as striking snakes, Thorn twisting and writhing as she dodged and parried. Brand could hardly count how many crashing blows they traded in the time it took him to take a breath. Eight? Ten? They broke apart as suddenly as they met, circling each other, Thorn weaving between the columns in a prowling crouch, Skifr swaggering sideways, weapons drifting in lazy circles.

"Oh, this is something," murmured Rulf, grinning wide.

Fror winced as he rubbed at his ribs. "It's a lot more fun than fighting her yourself, that's sure."

Sumael's frowning companion murmured something under his breath, and Father Yarvi smiled.

"What did he say?" whispered Brand.

"He said the girl is extraordinary."

Brand snorted. "That's bloody obvious."

"Very good," Skifr was saying. "But do not wait for me to hand you an opening. I am no gift-giver."

"I'll cut my own, then!" Thorn darted forward so fast Brand took a wobbly step back, her ax and sword flashing in circles, but Skifr twisted, reeled, somehow finding a path between them and away to safety.

"Please," said Sumael, louder. "I need to—"

"There is no place for please on the battlefield!" screamed Skifr, unleashing another blinding flurry, wood clattering on wood, herding Thorn into the corner of the yard then her blade raking stone as Thorn ducked under it, rolled away and came up swinging. Skifr gasped as she stumbled back, Thorn's sword missing the end of her nose by a finger's breadth.

Koll gave a disbelieving titter. Father Yarvi puffed out his cheeks, eyes bright. Rulf shook his balding head in disbelief. "I never saw the like."

"Excellent," said Skifr, eyes narrowed. "I am glad to see my wisdom has not been wasted." She spun her ax in her fingers so quickly it became a blur. "Truly excellent, but you will find—"

"Stop!" screamed Sumael, dragging every face sharply toward her. To Brand's surprise she sank to one knee, sweeping her arm toward her servant. "May I present her radiance Vialine, Princess of the Denied, Grand Duke of Napaz, Terror of the Alyuks, Protector of the First of Cities and Thirty-fifth Empress of the South."

For a moment Brand thought it some elaborate joke. Then he saw Father Yarvi drop to one knee, and everyone else in the yard just afterward, and any hint of laughter quickly died.

"Gods," he whispered, getting his own knee to the paving so fast it hurt.

"Sorry," croaked Thorn, hastily doing the same.

The empress stepped forward. "Don't be. It was a most instructive display." She spoke the Tongue with a heavy accent, but her voice was rich and full of confidence.

"Your radiance—" said Yarvi.

"Do I seem all that radiant to you?" The empress laughed. An open, friendly laugh that echoed about the courtyard. "I would rather we speak plainly. I get very little plain speaking at the palace. Except from Sumael, of course."

"I find Sumael's speaking just a little too plain at times." Father Yarvi brushed off his knees as he stood. "We are truly honored by your visit."

"It is I who should be honored. You have traveled across half the world to speak with me, after all. I would hate to be the sort of person who would not walk half a mile from my palace gate to speak with you."

"I will try not to waste your time, then, empress." The minister took a step toward her. "Do you understand the politics of the Shattered Sea?"

"I know a little. Sumael has told me more."

Yarvi took another step. "I fear Mother War will soon spread her bloody wings across its every shore."

"And you seek my help. Even though we pray to different gods? Even though my aunt made an alliance with the High King?"

"Her alliance, not yours."

The empress folded her arms and stepped sideways. She and the minister began to circle each other warily, very much as Thorn and Skifr had done a few moments before. "Why should I forge a new one with Gettland?"

"Because you wish to favor the winning side."

Vialine smiled. "You are too bold, Father Yarvi."

"King Uthil would say there is no such thing as *too* bold."

"Gettland is a small nation, surrounded by enemies—"

"Gettland is a rich nation surrounded by paupers. Queen Laithlin has made sure of it."

"The Golden Queen," murmured Vialine. "Her fame as a merchant has spread even this far. Is it true she has found a way to catch gold and silver in paper?"

"She has. One of many wonders, the secrets of which she would happily share with her allies."

"You offer me gold and silver, then?"

"The High King offers nothing but prayers."

"Is gold and silver everything to you, Father Yarvi?"

"Gold and silver is everything to everyone. Some of us have enough of it to pretend otherwise."

The empress gave a little gasp at that.

"You asked for honesty." Yarvi snapped his fingers toward Thorn and she stood up. "But as it happens my mother has sent something made of neither gold nor silver. A gift, brought the long, hard road down the Divine and the Denied from the darkest corners of the Shattered Sea." And he slid the black box from inside his coat and handed it to Thorn.

"An elf-relic?" said the empress, scared and curious at once.

The frowning man moved closer to her, frowning even deeper.

Thorn held the box out awkwardly. They might have been of an age, but Vialine looked like a child next to her. Her head barely came to Thorn's chest, let alone her shoulder. As though realizing how strange a pair they made, Thorn dropped to one knee so she could hold the gift at a more fitting angle, the elf-letters etched on the lid glinting as they caught the light. "Sorry."

"Don't be. I wish I was tall." Vialine pushed back the lid of the box, and that pale light flooded out, and her eyes went wide. Brand felt Rulf stiffen beside him, heard Koll give a gasp of amazement, Fror murmuring a breathless prayer. He'd seen the light before and still he strained forward, longing to see what made it. The lid of the box was in the way, though.

"It is beautiful," breathed the empress, reaching out. She gasped as she touched whatever was inside, the light on her face shifting from white to pink and back as she jerked her hand away. "Great God! It still turns?"

"It does," said Skifr. "It senses you, Empress, and shifts to match your mood. It was brought from the elf-ruins of Strokom, where no man has trodden since the Breaking of God. There may not be another like it in the world."

"Is it . . . safe?"

"No truly wonderful thing can be entirely safe. But it is safe enough."

Vialine stared into the box, her wide eyes reflecting its glow. "It is too grand a gift for me."

"How could any gift be too grand for the Empress of the South?" asked Yarvi, taking a gentle step toward her. "With this upon your arm, you will seem radiant indeed."

"It is beautiful beyond words. But I cannot take it."

"It is a gift freely given—"

Vialine looked up at him through her lashes. "I asked you to speak honestly, Father Yarvi." And she snapped the box shut, and put the light out with it. "I cannot help you. My aunt Theofora made promises I cannot break." She lifted her small fist high. "I am the most powerful person in the world!" Then she laughed, and let it fall. "And there is nothing I can do. Nothing I can do about anything. My uncle has an understanding with Mother Scaer."

"A ruler must plow her own furrow," said Yarvi.

"Easier said than done, Father Yarvi. The soil is very stony hereabouts."

"I could help you dig it over."

"I wish you could. Sumael says you are a good man."

"Above average." Sumael had a little smile at the corner of her mouth. "I've known worse men with both their hands."

"But you cannot help me. No one can." Vialine drew up her hood, and with one last glance toward Thorn, still kneeling in the middle of the courtyard with the box in her hand, the Empress of the South turned to leave. "And I am sorry, but I cannot help you."

It was hardly what they'd all been hoping for. But so it goes, with hopes.

SOME BLOODY DIPLOMAT

Skifr came at her again but this time Thorn was ready. The old woman grunted in surprise as Thorn's ax caught her boot and sent her lurching. She parried the next blow but it rocked her on her heels and the one after tore her sword from her hand and knocked her clean on her back.

Even on the ground Skifr was dangerous. She kicked dust in Thorn's face, rolled and flung her ax with deadly accuracy. But Thorn was ready for that too, hooked it from the air with her own and sent it skittering into the corner, pressing on, teeth bared, and pinning Skifr against one of the pillars, the point of her sword tickling the old woman's sweat-beaded throat.

Skifr raised her gray brows. "Auspicious."

"I won!" bellowed Thorn, shaking her notched wooden weapons at the sky. It had been months since she dared hope she might ever get the better of Skifr. Those endless mornings being beaten with the oar as Mother Sun rose, those endless evenings trying to hit her with the bar by the light of Father Moon, those endless blows and slaps and slides into the mud. But she had done it. "I beat her!"

"You beat her," said Father Yarvi, nodding slowly.

Skifr winced as she clambered up. "You have beaten a grand-mother long years past her best. There will be sterner challenges ahead for you. But . . . you have done well. You have listened. You have worked. You have become deadly. Father Yarvi was right—"

"When am I wrong?" The minister's smile vanished at a hammering on the door. He jerked his head toward Koll and the boy slid back the bolt.

"Sumael," said Yarvi, smiling as he did whenever she visited. "What brings—"

She was breathing hard as she stepped over the threshold. "The empress wishes to speak to you."

Father Yarvi's eyes widened. "I'll come at once."

"Not you." She was looking straight at Thorn. "You."

BRAND HAD SPENT MOST of his life feeling out of place. Beggar among the rich. Coward among the brave. Fool among the clever. But a visit to the Palace of the Empress opened up whole new gulfs of crippling inadequacy.

"Gods," he whispered, every time he crept around another corner after Thorn and Sumael into some new marbled corridor, or gilded stairway, or cavernous chamber, each richer than the last. He tiptoed down a hallway lit with candles tall as a man. Dozens of them, each worth more in Thorlby than he was, left burning on the chance that someone might happen by. Everything was jewelled or silvered, panelled or painted. He looked at a chair inlaid with a dozen kinds of wood, and thought how much more it must have cost than everything he had earned in his life. He wondered if he was dreaming it, but knew he didn't have a good enough imagination.

"Wait here," said Sumael, as they reached a round room at the top of a flight of steps, every bit of the marble walls carved as finely as Koll's mast with scenes from some story. "Touch nothing." And she left Brand alone with Thorn. The first time since that day in the market.

And look how that turned out.

"Quite a place," he muttered.

Thorn stood with her back to him, turning her head to show a sliver of frown. "Is that why Father Yarvi sent you along? To say what anyone could see?"

"I don't know why he sent me along." Chill silence stretched out. "I'm sorry if I dragged you back. The other day. You're far the better fighter, I should've let you take the lead."

"You should've," she said, without looking at him.

"Just . . . seems like you're angry with me, and whatever I—"

"Does now seem like the time?"

"No." He knew some things were better left unsaid but he couldn't stand thinking she hated him. He had to try and put things right. "I just—" He glanced across at her, and she caught him looking, the way she had dozens of times the last few weeks, but now her face twisted.

"Just shut your bloody mouth!" she snarled, white with fury, and looked ready to give him a bloody mouth as well.

He looked down at the floor, so highly polished he could see his own stricken face staring stupidly back, and had nothing to say. What could you say to that?

"If you love-birds are quite finished," said Sumael from the doorway, "the empress is waiting."

"Oh, we're finished," snapped Thorn, stalking off.

Sumael shrugged her shoulders at Brand, and two frowning guards shut the doors on him with a final-sounding *click*.

THE GARDENS WERE LIKE something from a dream, all lit in strange colors by the purple sunset and the shifting torchlight, flames flickering from cages of coals that sent sparks dancing with every breath of wind. Nothing was the way the gods had made it, everything tortured by the hands of man. Grass shaved as carefully as a romancer's jaw. Trees clipped into unnatural shapes and bowing under the weight of their own bloated, sweet-smelling blossom. Birds too, twittering from the twisted branches, and Thorn wondered why they didn't fly away until she saw they were all tethered to their perches with silver chains fine as spider's threads.

Paths of white stone twisted between statues of impossibly stern, impossibly slender women wafting scrolls, books, swords. Empresses of the past, Thorn reckoned, and all wondering why this half-shaved horror had been allowed among them. The guards looked as if they had the same question. Lots of guards, every mirror-bright sword and spear making her acutely aware of how unarmed she was. She sloped after Sumael around a star-shaped pool, crystal water tinkling into it from a fountain carved like snakes coiled together, up to the steps of a strange little building, a dome set on pillars with a curved bench beneath it.

On the bench sat Vialine, Empress of the South.

She had undergone quite a transformation since she visited Father Yarvi's crumbling house. Her hair was twisted into a shining coil netted with golden wire and hung with jewels. Her bodice was set with tiny mirrors that twinkled blue and pink with the fading light, red and orange with the torch-flames. From a streak of dark paint across the bridge of her nose, her eyes gleamed brightest of all.

Thorn wasn't sure she'd ever felt so far out of her depth. "What do I say?"

"She's just a person," said Sumael. "Talk to her like she's a person."

"What the hell do I know about talking to a person?"

"Just be honest." Sumael slapped Thorn on the back and sent her stumbling forward. "And do it now."

Thorn edged onto the lowest stair. "Your radiance," she croaked out, trying to go down on one knee then realizing it couldn't really be done on a set of steps.

"Vialine, and please don't kneel. A week ago I was nobody much. It still makes me nervous."

Thorn froze awkwardly halfway down, and wobbled back to an uncertain stoop. "Sumael says you sent for—"

"What is your name?"

"Thorn Bathu, your—"

"Vialine, please. The Thorn seems self-explanatory. The Bathu?"

"My father won a famous victory there the day I was born."

"He was a warrior?"

"A great one." Thorn fumbled for the pouch about her neck. "Chosen Shield to a queen of Gettland."

"And your mother?"

"My mother . . . wishes I wasn't me." Sumael had told her to be honest, after all.

"My mother was a general who died in battle against the Alyuks."

"Good for her," said Thorn, then instantly thought better of it. "Though . . . not for you." Worse and worse. "I suppose, your radiance . . ." She trailed off into mortified silence. Some bloody diplomat.

"Vialine." The empress patted the bench beside her. "Sit with me."

Thorn stepped up into the little pavilion, around a table, a silver platter on it heaped with enough perfect fruit to feed an army, and to a waist-high rail.

"Gods," she breathed. She had scarcely thought about how many stairs she climbed, but now she saw they were on the palace roof. There was a cliff-like drop to more gardens far below. The First of Cities was spread out under the darkening sky beyond, a madman's maze of buildings, lights twinkling in the blue evening, as many as stars in the sky. In the distance, across the black mirror of the straight, other clusters of lights. Other towns, other cities. Strange constellations, faint in the distance.

"And all this is yours," Thorn whispered.

"All of it and none of it." There was something in the set of Vialine's jaw, jutting proudly forward, that Thorn thought she recognized. That she had seen in her mother's mirror, long ago. That made her think the empress was used to wearing a brave face of her own.

"That must be quite a weight to carry," she said.

Vialine's shoulders seemed to sag a little. "Something of a burden."

"Empress, I don't know anything about politics." Thorn perched
herself on the bench in a manner she hoped was respectful, whatever
that looked like, she'd never been too comfortable sitting unless it was
at an oar. "I don't know anything about anything. You'd be much better talking to Father Yarvi—"

"I don't want to talk about politics."

Thorn sat in prickling awkwardness. "So . . ."

"You're a woman." Vialine leaned forward, her hands clasped in
her lap and her eyes fixed on Thorn's face. Disarmingly close. Closer
than Thorn was used to having anyone, let alone an empress.

"So my mother tells me," she muttered. "Opinion's divided . . ."

"You fight men."

"Yes."

"You beat men."

"Sometimes . . ."

"Sumael says you beat them three at a time! Your crew respect
you. I could see it in their faces. They *fear* you."

"Respect, I don't know. Fear, maybe, your—"

"Vialine. I never saw a woman fight like you. Can I?" Before
Thorn could answer the empress had put her hand on Thorn's shoulder and squeezed at it. Her eyes went wide. "Great God, you're like
wood! You must be so strong." She let her hand drop, much to Thorn's
relief, and stared down at it, small and dark on the marble between
them. "I'm not."

"Well, you won't beat a strong man with strength," murmured
Thorn.

The empress's eyes flickered to hers, white in the midst of that
black paint, torch flames gleaming in the corners. "With what, then?"

"You must be quicker to strike and quicker when you do. You must
be tougher and cleverer, you must always look to attack, and you
must fight without honor, without conscience, without pity." Skifr's
words, and Thorn realized only then how completely she had learned

them, how totally she had taken them in, how much the old woman had taught her. "So I'm told, anyway—"

Vialine snapped her fingers. "*That* is why I sent for you. To learn how to fight strong men. Not with swords, but the principles are the same." She propped her chin on her hands, a strangely girlish gesture in a woman who ruled half the world. "My uncle wants me to be nothing more than prow-beast for his ship. Less, if anything. The prow-beast at least goes at the keel."

"Our ships have one at the stern as well."

"Marvelous. He wants me to be that one, then. To sit in the throne and smile while he makes the choices. But I refuse to be his puppet." Vialine clenched her fist and thumped the table, scarcely even making the tiny fruit knife rattle on the platter. "I refuse, do you hear me?"

"I do, but . . . I'm not sure my hearing will make much difference."

"No. It's my uncle's ears I need to open." The empress glared off across the darkening gardens. "I stood up to him again in the council today. You should have seen his face. He couldn't have been more shocked if I'd stabbed him."

"You can't know that for sure until you stab him."

"Great God, I'd like to!" Vialine grinned across at her. "I bet no one makes a puppet of you, do they? I bet no one dares! Look at you." She had an expression Thorn wasn't used to seeing. Almost . . . admiring. "You're, you know—"

"Ugly?" muttered Thorn.

"No!"

"Tall?"

"No. Well, yes, but, *free*."

"Free?" Thorn gave a disbelieving snort.

"Aren't you?"

"I'm sworn to serve Father Yarvi. To do whatever he thinks necessary. To make up for . . . what I did."

"What did you do?"

Thorn swallowed. "I killed a boy. Edwal was his name, and I don't reckon he deserved to die, but . . . I killed him, all right."

Vialine was just a person, as Sumael had said and, in spite of her clothes and her palace, or maybe because of them, there was something in her even, earnest gaze that drew the words out.

"They were all set to crush me with stones for it, but Father Yarvi saved me. Don't know why, but he did. It was Skifr taught me to fight." Thorn smiled as she touched her fingers to the shaved side of her head, thinking how strong she'd thought herself back then and how weak she'd been. "We fought Horse People on the Denied. Killed a few of them, then I was sick. And we fought men in the market, the other day. Me and Brand. Not sure whether I killed those, but I wanted to. Angry, about those beads . . . I reckon . . ." She trailed off, realizing she'd said a lot more than she should have.

"Beads?" asked Vialine, the painted bridge of her nose crinkled with puzzlement.

Thorn cleared her throat. "Wouldn't worry about it."

"I suppose freedom can be dangerous," said the empress.

"I reckon."

"Perhaps we look at others and see only the things we don't have."

"I reckon."

"Perhaps we all feel weak, underneath."

"I reckon."

"But you fight men and win, even so."

Thorn sighed. "At that, I win."

Vialine counted the points off on her small fingers. "So, quickness to strike, and cleverness, and aggression without conscience, honor or pity."

Thorn held up her empty hands. "They've got me everything I have."

The empress laughed. A big laugh, from such a small woman, loud and joyous with her mouth wide open. "I like you, Thorn Bathu!"

"You're joining a small group, then. Sometimes feels like it's shrinking all the time." And Thorn eased out the box, and held it between them. "Father Yarvi gave me something for you."

"I told him I could not take it."

"He told me I had to give it to you even so." Thorn bit her lip as she eased the box open and the pale light spilled out, more strange and more beautiful than ever in the gathering darkness. The perfect edges of the elf-bangle gleamed like dagger-blades, glittering metal polished and faceted, winking with the lamplight, dark circles within circles shifting in the impossible depths beneath its round window. A relic from another world. A world thousands of years gone. A thing beside which the priceless treasures of the palace seemed petty baubles, worthless as mud.

Thorn tried to make her voice soft, persuasive, diplomatic. It came out rougher than ever. "Father Yarvi's a good man. A deep-cunning man. You should speak to him."

"I did." Vialine looked from the bangle to Thorn's eyes. "And you should be careful. Father Yarvi is a man like my uncle, I think. They give no gift without expecting something in return." She snapped the box closed, then took it from Thorn's hand. "But I will take it, if that is what you want. Give Father Yarvi my thanks. But tell him I can give him no more."

"I will." Thorn looked out at the garden as it sank into gloom, fumbling for something else to say, and noticed that where the guard had stood beside the fountain there were only shadows. All of them were gone. She and the empress were alone. "What happened to your guards?"

"That's odd," said Vialine. "Ah! But here are more."

Thorn counted six men climbing the steps at the far end of the gardens. Six imperial soldiers, fully armed and armored, clattering quickly down the path through pools of orange torchlight toward the empress's little house. Another man followed them. A man with gold on his breastplate and silver in his hair and a smile brighter than either upon his handsome face.

Duke Mikedas, and as he saw them he gave a jaunty wave.

Thorn had a feeling, then, as though the guts were draining out of her. She reached for the silver plate and slipped the little fruit knife between her fingers. A pitiful weapon, but better than none at all.

She stood as the soldiers stepped smartly around the fountain and between two statues, felt Vialine stand at her shoulder as they spread out. Thorn recognized one of them as the breeze caught the glowing coals and light flared across his face. The Vansterman she had fought in the market, cuts and purple bruises down one cheek and a heavy ax in his fist.

Duke Mikedas bowed low, but with a twist to his mouth, and his men did not bow at all. Vialine spoke in her own language and the duke answered, waving a lazy hand toward Thorn.

"Your grace," she forced through clenched teeth. "What an honor."

"My apologies," he said in the Tongue. "I was telling her radiance that I simply *could* not miss your visit. A gift, indeed, to find the two of you alone!"

"How so?" asked Vialine.

The duke raised his brows high. "Northern interlopers have come to the First of Cities! *Barbarians,* from Guttland, or wherever. Set on exporting their petty squabbles to our shores! They have tried to drive a wedge between us and our ally, the High King, who has accepted our One God into his heart. When that failed . . ." He sternly shook his head. "They have sent an *assassin* to the palace. An unnatural murderer, hoping to prey upon the innocent good nature of my idiot niece."

"I suppose that'd be me?" growled Thorn.

"Oh, *fiend* in woman's shape! Roughly woman's shape, anyway, you're rather too . . . muscular for my taste. I seem to remember you wanted to try two of my guards?" Mikedas grinned, and all the while his men edged forward, steel glimmering as it caught the light. "How d'you feel about six of 'em?"

Always look less than you are. Thorn cringed back, hunched her shoulders, made herself look small and full of fear even though a strange calm had come on her. As if the Last Door did not yawn at her heels, but she saw it all from outside. She judged the distances, noted the ground, the statues, the torches, the table, the pillars, the steps, the long drop behind them.

"An empress really shouldn't take such chances with her safety," the duke was saying, "but do not despair, my dear niece, I shall avenge you!"

"Why?" whispered Vialine. Thorn could feel her fear, and that was useful. Two weak, and scared, and helpless girls, and behind her back she curled her fingers tight around that tiny knife.

The duke's lip curled. "Because you prove to be an utter pain in my arse. We all like a girl with spirit, don't we?" He stuck out his bottom lip and shook his head in disappointment. "But there is a limit. Really there is."

Thorn's father used to tell her, *if you mean to kill, you kill, you don't talk about it.* But fortunately for her the duke was no killer, prating and boasting and savoring his power, giving Thorn time to judge her enemy, time to choose her best chance.

She reckoned the duke himself a small threat. He wore a sword and dagger but she doubted they had ever been drawn. The others knew their business, though. Good swords out, and good shields on their arms, and good daggers at their belts. Good armor too, scaled mail twinkling in the twilight, but weak at the throat. The insides of the elbows. The backs of the knees. That was where she had to strike.

She alone, against seven. She almost laughed then. Absurd odds. Impossible odds. But the only ones she had.

"Theofora could never do as she was told," the duke blathered on, "but then she was too old a horse to learn obedience. I really had hoped a seventeen-year-old empress could be led by the nose." He gave a sigh. "Some ponies just chafe at the bridle, though. They kick and bite and refuse to be ridden. Better to destroy them before they throw their master. The throne will pass to your cousin Asta next." He showed those perfect teeth of his. "She's four. Now that's a woman you can work with!" Finally tiring of his own cleverness, he sent two of his men forward with a lazy gesture. "Let's get it done."

Thorn watched them come. One had a big, often-broken nose. The other a pocked and pitted face, smiling in a faintly uninterested way. Swords drawn but not raised as they came onto the first step. You couldn't blame them for being confident. But they were so confident they never even considered she might give them a fight.

And Thorn would give them a fight.

"Careful, your grace," said the Vansterman. "She's dangerous."

"Please," scoffed the duke, "she's just a girl. I thought you northerners were all fire and—"

The wise wait for their moment, as Father Yarvi had often told her, but never let it pass. The big-nosed man took the next step, squinting as the light from the torches in the pavilion shone into his eyes, then looking mildly surprised when Thorn darted forward and slit his throat with the fruit knife.

She angled the cut so blood sprayed the pock-faced man beside and he flinched. Just for an instant, but long enough for Thorn to jerk Big Nose's knife from his belt as he stumbled backward and ram it under the rim of Pockmark's helmet, into the shadow between his neck and his collarbone, all the way to the grip.

She planted her boot against his chest as he made a strangled groan and kicked him back, toppling from the first step and tangling with the two men behind. She caught his sword, cutting her hand on the blade but tearing it from his slack grip, bloody fingers around the crosspiece so she held it overhand like a dagger. She screamed as she ripped it upward, scraping the rim of the next man's shield and catching him under the jaw, the point raking across his face and knocking his helmet askew.

He reeled away screeching, blood bubbling between his clutching fingers, tottering into the duke who gasped and shoved him into the bushes, staring at the black specks down his breastplate as though they were a personal affront.

Big Nose was stumbling drunkenly back, looking even more surprised than before, desperately trying to hold his neck together but his whole left side was already dark with blood. Thorn reckoned she could put him out of her mind.

To deal with three that quickly was fine weaponluck indeed, but surprise had been her one advantage. It was spent, and the odds still four to one.

"God damn it!" bellowed the duke, wiping at his blood-spattered cloak. "Kill them!"

Thorn shuffled back, keeping a pillar close on her left like a shield, eyes darting back and forth as the men closed in, shields and swords and axes plenty ready now, hard steel and hard eyes all gleaming red with the torchlight. She could hear Vialine behind her, almost whimpering with each breath.

"Brand!" she screamed at the top of her lungs. "Brand!"

RAGE

Brand stood there, staring at the jug of water on the table, and the goblets beside it, thinking they must be there for visitors but not daring to touch them even though he was thirsty as a man lost in the desert.

What if they were meant for better visitors than him?

He twisted his shoulders in a vain effort to peel his clinging shirt from his sticky skin. Gods, the heat, the endless, strangling heat, even as night crept in. He went to the window, closed his eyes and took a long breath, feeling the warm breeze on his face and wishing it was the salt wind of Thorlby.

He wondered what Rin was doing now. Rolled his eyes to the twilit skies and sent a prayer up to Father Peace to keep her well. In his eagerness to be a warrior, and find a crew, and make himself a new family he'd forgotten about the one he had. He was a man you could rely on, all right. To make a damn mess of things. He heaved up a heavy sigh.

And then he heard it, faint. Like someone calling his name. Thought he was dreaming it at first, then it came again, and he was sure. It sounded like Thorn, and the way things were between them she wouldn't be calling him without a reason.

He shoved the door open, thinking to rouse the guards.

But the guards were gone. Only the empty corridor, shadowy steps up at the far end. He thought he heard fighting, felt a stab of worry. Metal, and cries, and his name screamed out again.

He started running.

THORN SNATCHED UP THE SILVER PLATTER, fruit tumbling, shrieked as she flung it at the Vansterman and he ducked behind his big ax, stumbling away as the plate bounced from his shoulder and spun off into the bushes.

Tethered songbirds flapped and squawked and fluttered in a helpless panic and Thorn wasn't much better off, penned behind the pillars of the pavilion as if it was a cage. Beside the Vansterman there were two soldiers still standing—one tall and rangy with a hell of a reach, one short and beefy with a neck thick as a tree. The duke loitered at the back, pointing at Thorn with his dagger and shouting in a broken voice. A clever man, maybe, but a man used to everything going his way.

"Got blood on your shoes have I?" she snarled at him. "Y'old bastard?"

She made a grab for one of the torches, ripping it from its sconce, ignoring the sparks that scattered searing up her arm.

Thick Neck darted toward her and she blocked his sword with hers, steel clashing, chopped at him and struck splinters from his shield, stepped away, trying to give herself room to think of something, slipped on fallen fruit in the darkness and lurched against the table. A sword chopped into her leg. The meat of her left thigh, above the knee. She gave a kind of swallowing yelp as the tall soldier pulled it free of her, readying for a thrust.

You will be struck, and when you are the force of it must not stagger you, the pain of it must not slow you, the shock of it must not cause you to doubt. She lashed at the tall soldier with the torch and he brought his shield up just in time, tottering down the steps as red coals spilled from the cage and across his back in a shower of glowing dust.

She ducked on an instinct, Thick Neck's sword whistling by and clanging against the nearest pillar, splinters of marble spinning, fighting shadows flickering, dodging, stabbing all around them. Thorn swung for him but her leg had no strength in it, her sword bounced from his armored shoulder, only checked him for a moment.

She saw her blood, gleaming black in the torchlight, a trail of spots and spatters leading to the point of the tall man's sword. She saw the duke's face twisted with rage. She heard the empress screaming something over the rail. Calling for help, but there was no help coming. Thick Neck had his front foot on the top step, hard eyes fixed on her over his shield rim. Tall was clawing at his back, trying to brush the coals from his smoldering cloak.

She had to fight, while she still had blood to fight with. Had to attack, and it had to be now.

She shoved herself from the table as Thick Neck stabbed at her and sprang down the steps, over a fallen body. Her wounded thigh gave as she came down but she was ready for that, fell forward, rolled under Tall's hard-swung sword, the wind from the blade catching her hair, came up on her good side, slashing at him as she passed.

She caught Tall behind the knee and he grunted, trying to turn and falling to all fours in front of her. She lifted the sword high, arching back, brought it crashing down on his helmet. The force of it jolted her arm so hard it made her teeth buzz. The blade shattered, shards of steel bouncing away. But it left a mighty dent, one of Tall's legs kicking wildly as he flopped on his face, mouth open in a silent yawn. Thorn tottered against a statue, broken sword still clutched in her fist.

Good weaponluck, Odda would've said, because the Vansterman chose that moment to swing his ax and it missed her by a hair, heavy blade knocking a great chunk of marble loose. Thorn shoved him away with the torch, a few last sparks whirling on the breeze. Her leg was throbbing, pulsing, no strength in it at all.

Thick Neck stepped carefully toward her, shield up. There's always a way, Father Yarvi used to say, but Thorn couldn't see it. She was too hurt. The odds were too long. She clutched hard to that broken sword, bared her teeth, showed him her bravest face. She could smell flowers. Flowers and blood.

"Your death comes," she whispered.

Vialine shrieked as she leapt between the pillars and onto the short man's back, grabbing him around his bull neck, clutching at the wrist of his sword arm. He tried to throw her off, shield flailing, but that left a gap. Thorn dived at him, her left knee buckled, pain stabbing through her leg but she caught his armor as she fell and dragged herself up, snarled as she drove the broken sword blade up under his jaw. He spoke blood, the empress squealing as they crashed down on top of her.

Thorn rolled just in time, the Vansterman's heavy ax flashing past, thudding through Thick Neck's mail and deep into his chest. Thorn half-scrambled, half hopped up as he struggled to drag his ax free, the breath burning in her heaving chest.

"Brand!" she screamed in a broken voice. She heard a step behind her, lurched around and saw a flash of metal. The duke punched her in the cheek, made her head jolt, but it was a feeble sort of blow, barely even staggering her.

She clutched at his gilded breastplate. "That your best?" she hissed, but the words were blood, drooling down her chin. There was something in her mouth. Cold, and hard, across her tongue. That was when she realized he'd stabbed her. He'd stabbed her and the dagger was right through her face, between her jaws, his hand still around the grip.

They stared at each other in the darkness, neither quite believing what had happened. Neither quite believing she was still standing. Then, by the glimmering of torchlight, she saw his eyes go hard.

She felt the blade shift in her mouth as he tried to tear it free and she bit down on it, kneed him in his side with her wounded leg, twisted her head, twisting the bloody grip of the dagger out of his limp hand. She shoved him clumsily away, staggering sideways as the Vansterman swung at her, his ax grazing her shoulder and ripping a shower of leaves from the bushes as she hopped back toward the fountain.

Everyone's got a plan until they start bleeding and she was bleeding now. Her leg was hot with it, her face sticky with it. No plans any more. She snorted and blew a red mist.

She caught the grip and dragged the dagger out of her face. Came out easy enough. Might have been a tooth came with it, though. Gods, she was dizzy. Her leg had stopped throbbing. Just numb. Numb and wet and her knee trembling. She could hear it flapping inside her blood-soaked trousers.

Drowsy.

She shook her head, trying to shake the dizziness out but it only made things worse, the blurry gardens tipping one way then back the other.

Duke Mikedas had drawn his sword, was dragging the corpse of the thick-necked man away so he could get at the empress.

Thorn waved the knife around but it was so heavy. As if there was an anvil hanging off the point. The torches flashed and flickered and danced.

"Come on," she croaked, but her tongue was all swollen, couldn't get the words around it.

The Vansterman smiled as he herded her back toward the fountain.

She tripped, clutched at something, knee buckling, just staying upright.

Kneeling in water. Fish flitting in the darkness.

Vialine screamed again. Her voice was getting hoarse from it.

The Vansterman wafted his ax back and forward and the big blade caught the light and left orange smears across Thorn's blurred sight.

The empress said *don't kneel* but she couldn't get up.

She could hear her own breath, wheezing, wheezing.

Didn't sound too good.

Gods, she was tired.

"Brand," she mumbled.

HE CAME UP THE steps running.

Caught a glimpse of a darkened garden, a path of white stones between flowering trees, and statues, and dead men scattered in the shadows about a torchlit fountain—

He saw Thorn kneeling in it, clutching at wet stone carved like snakes, a dagger in her other hand. Her face was tattered red and her clothes torn and stuck to her dark and the water pink with blood.

A man stood over her with an ax in his hand. The Vansterman from the market.

Brand made a sound like a boiling kettle. A sound he never made before and never heard a man make.

He tore down that path like a charging bull and as the Vansterman turned, eyes wide, Brand caught him, snatched him off his feet like the north gale snatches up a leaf and rammed him at a full sprint into a statue.

They hit it so hard the world seemed to shake. So hard it rattled Brand's teeth in his head. So hard the statue broke at the waist and the top fell in dusty chunks across the grass.

Brand might've heard the Vansterman's shattered groan if it wasn't for the blood pounding in his skull like Mother Sea on a storm day, blinding him, deafening him. He seized the Vansterman's head with both hands and rammed it into the marble pedestal, two times, three, four, chips of stone flying until his skull was bent and dented and flattened and Brand flung him down ruined onto the path.

Thorn was slumped against the fountain, her face all the wrong colors, skin waxy pale and streaked with blood and her torn cheeks and her mouth and her chin all clotted black.

"Stay back!" someone shrieked. An older man in a gilded breast-plate with a sheen of sweat across his face. He had the Empress Vialine about the neck, a jewelled sword to her throat, but it was too long for the task. "I am Duke Mikedas!" he bellowed, as if the name was a shield.

But a name's just a name. Brand's lips curled back and he took a step forward, the growling in his throat hot as dragon's fire, kicking a corpse out of his way.

The duke whipped the sword from Vialine's neck and pointed it wobbling toward Brand. "I'm warning you, stay——"

The empress grabbed his hand and bit it, twisting free as he screamed. He raised his sword but Brand was on him, making that sound again, that shrieking, keening, gurgling sound, not thinking of doing good, or of standing in the light, or anything but breaking this man apart with his hands.

The sword grazed his head and bounced off his shoulder. Maybe it cut him and maybe it didn't and Brand didn't care. His arms closed tight about the duke like a lock snapping shut. He was a big man, but Brand once held the weight of a ship across his shoulders. He hoisted Duke Mikedas into the air as if he was made of straw.

Four charging steps he took, thudding across the dark lawn, lifting the duke higher and higher.

"You can't——" he screeched, then Brand flung him into space. Over the stone rail he tumbled. He seemed to hang there for a moment against the dusky sky, astonished, sword still in his hand. His screech turned to a coughing gurgle and he plummeted flailing out of sight.

"God," croaked Vialine.

There was a crunch far below as her uncle hit the ground. Then a long clatter.

Then silence.

DEBTS AND PROMISES

Thorn's eyes opened and it was dark.

The darkness beyond the Last Door?

She tried to move, and gasped at the pain.

Surely the one good thing about death was that the pain stopped?

She felt bandages across her face, remembered the jolt as Duke Mikedas's knife punched through her mouth, gave a rusty groan, her throat dry as old bones.

She squinted toward a slit of brightness, fumbled back blankets and slowly, ever so slowly, swung her legs down, everything bruised and battered and stabbed through with cramps. She moaned as she tried to put weight on her left leg, pain catching fire in her thigh, creeping up into her back, down through her knee.

She hopped and she shuffled, clutching at the wall. Gods, the pain in her leg, but when she winced at that, gods, the pain in her face, and when she whimpered at that, gods, the pain in her chest, up her throat, in her eyes as the tears flowed, and she made it to that strip of light, the light under a door, and pawed it open.

She shuffled forward with one hand up to shield her sore eyes, like

staring into the blinding sun even though it was only a single candle.
A thick candle with long, jewelled pins stuck into the wax. She saw
crumbling plaster, fallen clothes casting long shadows across the
boards, the dark folds on a rumpled bed—

She froze. A dark-skinned back, a bare back, lean muscles shifting.
She heard a slow grunting, a woman's voice and a man's, together,
and Thorn saw a pale arm slip up that back, a long, wasted arm and
on the end was a shrivelled hand with just one stump of a finger.

"Uh," she croaked, eyes wide, and the woman's head jerked
around. Black hair across her face, and a scar through her top lip, and
a notch of white tooth showing. Sumael, and with Father Yarvi underneath her.

"Uh." Thorn couldn't go forward, couldn't go back, and she
stared at the floor, burning with pain and embarrassment, trying to
swallow but feeling as if she'd never have spit again in the aching hole
of her mouth.

"You're awake." Father Yarvi scrambled from the bed and into his
trousers.

"Am I?" she wanted to ask, but it came out, "Uh."

"Back to bed before you set that leg bleeding." And the minister
slipped his arm around her and started helping her to hop and shuffle
back toward the dark doorway.

Thorn couldn't help glancing over her shoulder as they passed the
threshold, saw Sumael stretched out naked as though nothing could
be more ordinary, looking sideways at her through narrowed eyes.

"In pain?" asked Father Yarvi as he lowered her onto the bed.

"Uh," she grunted.

Water sloshed into a cup, a spoon rattled as he mixed something in.
"Drink this."

It tasted beyond foul and her ripped mouth and her swollen tongue
and her dry throat burned from it, but she fought it down, and at least
she could make words afterward.

"I thought," she croaked, as he swung her legs back into the bed
and checked the bandages around her thigh, "you swore . . . an oath."

"I swore too many. I must break some to keep another."

"Who decides which ones you keep?"

"I'll keep my first one." And he closed the fingers of his good hand and made a fist of it. "To be revenged upon the killers of my father."

She was growing drowsy. "I thought . . . you did that . . . long ago."

"On some of them. Not all." Yarvi pulled the blankets over her. "Sleep, now, Thorn."

Her eyes drifted closed.

"DON'T GET UP."

"Your radiance—"

"For God's sake: Vialine." The empress had some scratches across her cheek, but no other sign of her brush with Death.

"I should—" Thorn winced as she tried to sit and Vialine put her hand on her shoulder, and gently but very firmly pushed her back onto the bed.

"Don't get up. Consider that an imperial edict." For once, Thorn decided not to fight. "Are you badly hurt?"

She thought about saying no, but the lie would hardly have been convincing. She shrugged, and even that was painful. "Father Yarvi says I'll heal."

The empress looked down as though she was the one in pain, her hand still on Thorn's shoulder. "You will have scars."

"They're expected on a fighter."

"You saved my life."

"They would have killed me first."

"Then you saved both our lives."

"Brand played his part, I hear."

"And I have thanked him. But I have not thanked you." Vialine took a long breath. "I have dissolved the alliance with the High King. I have sent birds to Grandmother Wexen. I have let her know that, regardless of what gods we pray to, the enemy of Gettland is my enemy, the friend of Gettland is my friend."

Thorn blinked. "You're too generous."

"I can afford to be, now. My uncle ruled an empire within the empire, but without him it has fallen like an arch without its keystone. I have taken your advice. To strike swiftly, and without mercy. Traitors are being weeded out of my council. Out of my guard." There was a hardness in her face, and just then Thorn was glad she was on Vialine's right side. "Some have fled the city, but we will hunt them down."

"You will be a great empress," croaked Thorn.

"If my uncle has taught me anything, it is that an empress is only as great as those around her."

"You have Sumael, and you—"

Vialine's hand squeezed her shoulder, and she looked down with that earnest, searching gaze. "Would you stay?"

"Stay?"

"As my bodyguard, perhaps? Queens have them, do they not, in the North? What do you call them?"

"A Chosen Shield," whispered Thorn.

"As your father was. You have proved yourself more than qualified."

A Chosen Shield. And to the Empress of the South. To stand at the shoulder of the woman who ruled half the world. Thorn fumbled for the pouch around her neck, felt the old lumps inside, imagining her father's pride to hear of it. What songs might be sung of that in the smoky inns, and in the narrow houses, and in the high Godshall of Thorlby?

And at that thought a wave of homesickness surged over Thorn, so strong she nearly choked. "I have to go back. I miss the gray cliffs. I miss the gray sea. I miss the *cold*." She felt tears in her eyes, then, and blinked them away. "I miss my mother. And I swore an oath."

"Not all oaths are worth keeping."

"You keep an oath not for the oath but for yourself." Her father's words, whispered long ago beside the fire. "I wish I could split myself in half."

Vialine sucked at her teeth. "Half a bodyguard would be no good to me. But I knew what your answer would be. You are not one to be held, Thorn Bathu, even with a gilded chain. Perhaps one day you will come back of your own accord. Until then, I have a gift for you. I could only find one worthy of the service you have done me."

And she brought out something that cast pale light across her face, and struck a spark in her eyes, and stopped Thorn's breath in her throat. The elf-bangle that Skifr had dug from the depths of Strokom, where no man had dared tread since the Breaking of God. The gift the *South Wind* had carried all the long road down the Divine and the Denied. A thing too grand for an empress to wear.

"Me?" Thorn wriggled up the bed in an effort to get away from it. "No! No, no, no!"

"It is mine to give, well-earned and freely given."

"I can't take it—"

"One does not refuse the Empress of the South." Vialine's voice had iron in it, and she raised her chin and glared down her nose at Thorn with an authority that was not to be denied. "Which hand?"

Thorn mutely held out her left, and Vialine slipped the elf-bangle over it and folded the bracelet shut with a final sounding click, the light from its round window glowing brighter, shifting to blue-white, metal perfect as a cut jewel gleaming, and circles within circles slowly shifting beneath the glass. Thorn stared at it with a mixture of awe and horror. A relic beyond price. Beautiful beyond words. Sitting now, on her ridiculous bony wrist, with the bizarre magnificence of a diamond on a dung-heap.

Vialine smiled, and finally let go of her shoulder. "It looks well on you."

THE SHEARS CLICK-CLICKED OVER the left side of Thorn's scalp and the hair fluttered down onto her shoulder, onto her bandaged leg, onto the cobbles of the yard.

"Do you remember when I first clipped your head?" asked Skifr. "You howled like a wolf cub!"

Thorn picked up a tuft of hair and blew it from her fingers. "Seems you can get used to anything."

"With enough work." Skifr tossed the shears aside and brushed the loose hair away. "With enough sweat, blood, and training."

Thorn worked her tongue around the unfamiliar inside of her mouth, rough with the stitches, and leaned forward to spit pink. "Blood I can give you." She grimaced as she stretched her leg out, the elf-bangle flaring angry purple with her pain. "But training might be difficult right now."

Skifr sat, one arm about Thorn's shoulders, rubbing her hand over her own stubbled hair. "We have trained for the last time, my dove."

"What?"

"I have business I must attend to. I have ignored my own sons, and daughters, and grandsons, and granddaughters too long. And only the most wretched of fools would dare now deny that I have done what Father Yarvi asked of me, and made you deadly. Or helped you make yourself deadly, at least."

Thorn stared at Skifr, an empty feeling in her stomach. "You're leaving?"

"Nothing lasts forever. But that means I can tell you things I could not tell you before." Skifr folded her in a tight, strange-smelling hug. "I have had twenty-two pupils in all, and never been more proud of one than I am of you. None worked so hard. None learned so fast. None had such courage." She leaned back, holding Thorn at arm's length. "You have proved yourself strong, inside and out. A loyal companion. A fearsome fighter. You have earned the respect of your friends and the fear of your enemies. You have demanded it. You have *commanded* it."

"But . . ." muttered Thorn, rocked far more by compliments than blows, "I've still got so much to learn . . ."

"A fighter is never done learning. But the best lessons one teaches oneself. It is time for you to become the master." And Skifr held out her ax, letters in five languages etched on the bearded blade. "This is for you."

Thorn had dreamed of owning a weapon like that. A thing fit for a hero's song. Now she took it numbly, and laid it on her lap, and looked down at the bright blade. "To the fighter, everything must be a weapon," she muttered. "What will I do without you?"

Skifr leaned close, her eyes bright, and gripped her tight. "Anything! Everything! I am no mean prophet and I foresee great things for you!" Her voice rose higher and higher, louder and louder, and she pointed one clawing finger toward the sky. "We will meet again, Thorn Bathu, on the other side of the Last Door, if not on this one, and I will thrill to the tales of your high deeds, and swell with pride that I played my own small part in them!"

"Damn right you will," said Thorn, sniffing back her tears. She had held this strange woman in contempt. She had hated her, and feared her, and cursed her name all down the Divine and the Denied. And now she loved her like a mother.

"Be well, my dove. Even more, be ready." Skifr's hand darted out but Thorn caught it by the wrist before it could slap her and held it trembling between them.

Skifr smiled wide. "And always strike first."

FATHER YARVI SMILED AS he peeled away the bandages. "Good. Very good." He pressed gently at the sore flesh of her cheeks with his fingertips. "You are healing well. Walking already."

"Lurching like a drunk already."

"You are lucky, Thorn. You are very lucky."

"Doubtless. Not every girl gets to be stabbed through the face."

"And by a duke of royal blood too!"

"The gods have smiled on me, all right."

"It could have been through your eye. It could have been through your neck." He started to bathe her face with a flannel that smelled of bitter herbs. "On the whole I would prefer to be scarred than dead, wouldn't you?"

Thorn pushed her tongue into the salty hole her missing tooth had left. It was hard to think of herself as lucky just then. "How are the scars? Tell me the truth."

"They will take time to heal, but I think they will heal well. A star on the left and an arrow on the right. There must be some significance in that. Skifr might have told us, she had an eye for portents—"

Thorn did not need Skifr to see into her face's future. "I'll be monstrous, won't I?"

"I know of people with uglier deformities." And Yarvi put his withered hand under her nose and let the one finger flop back and forth. "Next time, avoid the blade."

She snorted. "Easily said. Have you ever fought seven men?"

Drops trickled into the steaming bowl as he wrung out the flannel, the water turning a little pink. "I could never beat one."

"I saw you win a fight once."

He paused. "Did you indeed?"

"When you were king, I saw you fight Keimdal in the square." He stared at her for a moment, caught for once off-balance. "And when you lost, you asked to fight him again, and sent your mother's Chosen Shield in your place. And Hurik ground Keimdal's face into the sand on your behalf."

"A warrior fights," murmured Yarvi. "A king commands."

"So does a minister."

He started to smear something on her face that made the stitches sting. "I remember you now. A dark-haired girl, watching."

"Even then you were a deep-cunning man."

"I have had to be."

"Your trip to the First of Cities has turned out better than anyone could've hoped."

"Thanks to you." He unwound a length of bandage. "You have

done what no diplomat could achieve, and made an ally of the Empire of the South. Almost enough to make me glad I didn't crush you with rocks. And you have your reward." He tapped at the elf-bangle, its faint light showing through her sleeve.

"I'd give it back if I could open it."

"Skifr says it cannot be opened. But you should wear it proudly. You have earned it, and more besides. I may not be my mother's son any longer, but I still have her blood. I remember my debts, Thorn. Just as you remember yours."

"I've had a lot of time for remembering, the last few days. I've been remembering Throvenland."

"Another alliance that no one could have hoped for."

"You have a habit of coming away with them. I've been thinking about the man who poisoned the water."

"The man you killed?"

Thorn fixed his pale blue eye with hers. "Was he your man?"

Father Yarvi's face showed no surprise, no confirmation and no denial. He wound the bandages around her head as if she had not spoken.

"A deep-cunning man," she went on, "in need of allies, knowing King Fynn's ready temper, might have staged such a thing."

He pushed a pin gently through the bandages to hold them firm. "And a hot-headed girl, a thorn in the world's arse, not knowing anything, might have got herself caught up in the gears of it."

"It could happen."

"You are not without some cunning of your own." Father Yarvi put the bandages and the knife carefully away in his bag. "But you must know a deep-cunning man would never lay bare his schemes. Not even to his friends." He patted her on the shoulder, and stood. "Keep your lies as carefully as your winter grain, my old teacher used to tell me. Rest, now."

"Father Yarvi?" He turned back, a black shape in the bright outline of the door. "If I hadn't killed that poisoner . . . who would have drunk the water?"

A silence, then, and with the light behind him she could not see his face. "Some questions are best not asked, Thorn. And certainly best not answered."

"RULF'S BEEN GETTING THE CREW back together." Brand pushed some invisible dust around with the toe of his boot. "Few new men but mostly the same old faces. Koll can't wait to get started carving the other side of the mast, he says. And Dosduvoi's thinking of preaching the word of the One God up north. Fror's with us too."

Thorn touched a finger to her bandages. "Reckon folk'll be asking me how I got the scars, now, eh?"

"Hero's marks," said Brand, scratching at the ones that snaked up his own forearms. "Marks of a great deed."

"And it's hardly like my looks were ever my strongest point, is it?" Another awkward silence. "Father Yarvi says you killed Duke Mikedas."

Brand winced as though the memory was far from pleasant. "The ground killed him. I just made the introduction."

"You don't sound proud of it."

"No. Not sure I'm touched by Mother War like you are. Don't have your . . ."

"Fury?"

"I was going to say courage. Anger I've got plenty of. Just wish I didn't."

"Father Yarvi says you carried me back. He says you saved my life."

"Just what an oarmate does."

"Thanks for doing it, even so."

He stared at the ground, chewing at his lip, and finally looked up at her. "I'm sorry. For whatever I did. For . . ." He had that helpless look of his again, but rather than making her want to hold him, it made her want to hit him. "I'm sorry."

"Not your fault," she grated out. "Just the way things are."

"I wish they were a different way."

"So do I." She was too tired, too sore, too hurting inside and out to try and make it pretty. "Not as if you can make yourself like someone, is it?"

"Guess not," he said in a meek little voice that made her want to hit him even more. "Been through a lot together, you and me. Hope we can be friends, still."

She made her voice cold. Cold and sharp as a drawn blade. It was that or she might set to crying and she wouldn't do it. "Don't think that'll work for me, Brand. Don't see how this just goes back the way it was."

His mouth gave a sorry twist at that. As if he was the one hurt. Guilt, more than likely, and she hoped it stung. Hoped it stung half as much as she did. "Up to you." He turned his back on her. "I'll be there. If you need me."

The door shut, and she bared her teeth at it, and that made her face ache, and she felt tears in her eyes, and dashed them hard away. Wasn't fair. Wasn't fair at all, but she guessed love's even less fair than the battlefield.

To fool herself once was once too often. She had to rip those hopes up before they could take root. She had to kill the seeds. As soon as she could she limped off to find Rulf and asked for a different oar to pull on the way back home.

Owed her that much, didn't they?

STRANGE
BEDFELLOWS

"So you're leaving?" asked Sumael, her heavy footsteps echoing down the corridor.

"Within the week," said Father Yarvi. "We may not make it home before the Divine freezes as it is. You could always come with us. Don't pretend you don't miss the northern snows."

She laughed. "Oh, every balmy day here I wish I was frozen near to death again. You could always stay with us. Don't you enjoy the southern sun?"

"I am a little too pale. I burn before I brown." He gave a ragged sigh. "And I have an oath to keep."

Her smile faded. "I didn't think you took your oaths that seriously."

"This one I do," said Father Yarvi.

"Will you break the world to keep it?"

"I hope it won't come to that."

Sumael snorted. "You know how it is, with hopes."

"I do," murmured Brand. He got the feeling there were two conversations going on. One in plain sight and one hidden. But he'd never been much good with conversations, or with things he couldn't see, so he said no more.

Sumael swung a gate open with a squealing of rusted hinges, rough steps dropping into darkness. "She's down there."

The vaulted passage at the bottom was caked with mold, something scurrying away from the flickering light of Brand's torch.

"Just follow my lead," said Yarvi.

Brand gave a weary nod. "What else would I do?"

They stopped before a barred opening. Brand saw the glimmer of eyes in the shadows and stepped close, raising his torch.

Mother Scaer, once minister of Vansterland, then emissary of Grandmother Wexen, now sat against a wall of mossy rock with her shaved head on one side, her tattooed forearms on her knees and her long hands dangling. She had five elf-bangles stacked on one wrist, gold and glass and polished metal glinting. Brand would've been awestruck at the sight of them once but now they seemed petty, gaudy, broken things beside the one Thorn wore.

"Ah, Father Yarvi!" Scaer stretched a long leg toward them, chains rattling from an iron band about her bare ankle. "Have you come to gloat?"

"Perhaps a little. Can you blame me? You did conspire to murder the Empress Vialine, after all."

Mother Scaer gave a hiss. "I had no part of that. Grandmother Wexen sent me here to stop that puffed-up bladder of arrogance Duke Mikedas from doing anything foolish."

"How did that work out?" asked Yarvi.

Mother Scaer held up a length of chain to show them, and let it drop in her lap. "You should know better than anyone, a good minister gives the best advice they can, but in the end the ruler does what the ruler does. Did you bring this one to frighten me?" Mother Scaer's blue eyes fell on Brand, and even through the bars he felt a chill. "He is not frightening."

"On the contrary, I brought him to make you feel comfortable. My frightening one picked up a scratch killing seven men when she saved the empress and ruined all your plans." Brand didn't point out that he'd killed two of those men. He took no pride in it, and he was getting the feeling that wasn't the story everyone wanted to tell. "But she's healing nicely. Perhaps she can frighten you later."

Mother Scaer looked away. "We both know there is no later for me. I should have killed you at Amwend."

"You wanted to leave my guts for the crows, I remember. But Grom-gil-Gorm said, why kill what you can sell?"

"His first mistake. He made a second when he trusted you."

"Well, like King Uthil, Gorm is a warrior, and warriors tend to prefer action to thought. That is why they need ministers. That is why he needs your advice so very badly. That, I suspect, is why Grandmother Wexen was so keen to prize you from his side."

"He will get no help from me now," said Mother Scaer. "You, and Grandmother Wexen, and Duke Mikedas between you have made sure of that."

"Oh, I don't know," said Yarvi. "I am heading back up the Divine within the week. Back to the Shattered Sea." He pushed out his lips and tapped at them with his forefinger. "To send a passenger on to Vulsgard would not be too much trouble, eh, Brand?"

"Not too much," said Brand.

Yarvi raised his brows as though the idea had just occurred. "Perhaps we could find room for Mother Scaer?"

"We've lost one mysterious bald woman." Brand shrugged. "We've space for another."

Gorm's minister frowned up at them. Interested, but not wanting to seem interested. "Don't toy with me, boy."

"Never been much good at toying," said Brand. "I had a short childhood."

Mother Scaer slowly unfolded her long limbs and stood, bare feet flapping on damp stone as she walked to the bars until the chains were taut, then leaned a little farther, shadows shifting in the hollows of her gaunt face.

"Are you offering me my life, Father Yarvi?"

"I find it in my hands, and have no better use for it."

"Huh." Mother Scaer raised her brows very high. "What tasty bait. And no hook in it, I suppose?"

Yarvi leaned closer to the bars himself, so the two minister's faces were no more than a foot's length apart. "I want allies."

"Against the High King? What allies could I bring you?"

"There is a Vansterman on our crew. A good man. Strong at the oar. Strong in the wall. Would you say so, Brand?"

"Strong at the oar." Brand remembered Fror bellowing out the *Song of Bail* on that hill above the Denied. "Strong in the wall."

"Seeing him fight beside men of Gettland made me realize again how much alike we are," said Yarvi. "We pray to the same gods under the same skies. We sing the same songs in the same tongue. And we both struggle under the ever-weightier yoke of the High King."

Mother Scaer's lip curled. "And you would free Vansterland from her bondage, would you?"

"Why not? If at the same time I can free Gettland from hers. I did not enjoy wearing a galley captain's thrall-collar. I enjoy being slave to some drooling old fool in Skekenhouse no more."

"An alliance between Gettland and Vansterland?" Brand grimly shook his head. "We've been fighting each other since before there was a High King. Since before there was a Gettland. Madness, surely."

Yarvi turned to look at him, a warning in his eye. "The line between madness and deep-cunning has ever been a fine one."

"The boy is right." Mother Scaer pushed her arms through the bars and let them dangle. "There are ancient feuds between us, and deep hatreds—"

"There are petty squabbles between us, and shallow ignorance. Leave the wrathful words to the warriors, Mother Scaer, you and I know better. Grandmother Wexen is our true enemy. She is the one who tore you from your place to do her slave-work. She cares nothing for Vansterland, or Gettland, or any of us. She cares only for her own power."

Mother Scaer let her head fall on one side, blue eyes narrowed. "You will never win. She is too strong."

"Duke Mikedas was too strong, and both his power and his skull lie in ruins."

They narrowed further. "King Uthil will never agree."

"Let me worry about King Uthil."

Further still. "Grom-gil-Gorm will never agree."

"Do not underestimate yourself, Mother Scaer, I do not doubt your own powers of persuasion are formidable."

Blue slits, now. "Less so than yours, I think, Father Yarvi." Of a sudden she opened her eyes wide, and pushed her hand out through the bars so fast that Brand flinched back and nearly dropped his torch. "I accept your offer."

Father Yarvi took her hand and, stronger than she looked, she pulled him close by it. "You understand I can promise nothing."

"I am less interested in promises than I used to be. The way to bend someone to your will is to offer them what they want, not to make them swear an oath." Yarvi twisted his hand free. "It will be cold on the Divine, as the year grows late. I'd pack something warm."

As they walked off into the darkness, Father Yarvi put his hand on Brand's shoulder. "You did well."

"I scarcely said a thing."

"No. But the wise speaker learns first when to stay silent. You'd be surprised how many clever people never take the lesson."

Sumael was waiting for them at the gate. "Did you get what you wanted?"

Yarvi stopped in front of her. "Everything I wanted and far more than I deserved. But now it seems I must leave it behind."

"Fate can be cruel."

"It usually is."

"You could stay."

"You could come."

"But in the end we must all be what we are. I am counselor to an empress."

"I am minister to a king. We both have our burdens."

Sumael smiled. "And when you've a load to lift . . ."

"You're better lifting than weeping."

"I will miss you, Yarvi."

"It will be as if I left the best piece of myself behind."

They looked at each other for a moment longer, then Sumael dragged in a sharp breath. "Good luck on the journey." And she strode away, shoulders back.

Father Yarvi's face twisted and he leaned against the gate as if he might fall. Brand was on the point of offering his hand, but the wise speaker learns first when to stay silent. Soon enough the minister drew himself up without help.

"Gather the crew, Brand," he said. "We've a long way to go."

IV.

HIGH DEEDS

FAREWELLS

Thorn gently slid her oar from its port and gave the sweat-polished wood a fond final stroke with her fingertips.

"Fare you well, my friend." The oar was all indifference, though, so with a parting sigh she hefted her sea-chest rattling onto the wharf and sprang up after it.

Mother Sun smiled down on Thorlby from a clear sky, and Thorn closed her eyes and tipped her face back, smiling as the salt breeze kissed her scarred cheeks.

"Now that's what weather should be," she whispered, remembering the choking heat of the First of Cities.

"Look at you." Rulf paused in tying off the prow-rope to shake his balding head in wonder. "Hard to believe how you've grown since you first sat at my back oar. And not just in height."

"From girl to woman," said Father Yarvi, clambering from the *South Wind*.

"From woman to hero," said Dosduvoi, catching Thorn in a crushing hug. "Remember that crew of Throvenmen singing a song about you on the Divine? The she-devil who killed ten warriors and saved the Empress of the South! A woman who breathes fire and looks lightning!"

"Snake for a tail, wasn't it?" grunted Fror, winking his smaller eye at her.

"All that time spent staring at your arse," mused Koll, "and I never noticed the tail—ow!" As his mother clipped him around the head.

Dosduvoi was still chuckling over the Throvenmen. "Their faces when they realized you were sitting right in front of them!"

"And then they begged to fight you." Rulf laughed with him. "Bloody fools."

"We warned 'em," grunted Fror. "What did you say, Safrit?"

"She might not breathe fire, but you'll get burned even so."

"And she kicked their white arses one after another and dumped their captain in the river!" shouted Koll, springing up onto the ship's rail and balancing there with arms spread wide.

"Lucky he didn't drown with all that ice," said Rulf.

In spite of the warmth, Thorn shivered at the memory. "Gods, but it was cold up there on the Divine."

The ice had come early, crackling against the keel, and just a week north of the tall hauls it had locked the river tight. So they'd dragged the *South Wind* over and made a hall of her again, and lived there huddled like a winter flock for two freezing months.

Thorn still trained as hard as if she could hear Skifr's voice. Harder, maybe. She fought Dosduvoi and Fror and Koll and Rulf, but though she saw him watching, she never asked for Brand.

She still woke when Skifr would've woken her. Earlier, maybe. She'd look down in the chill darkness through the smoke of her breath and see him lying, chest slowly shifting, and wish she could drop down beside him in the warmth the way she used to. Instead she'd force herself out into the bitter chill, teeth clenched against the aching in her leg as she ran across a white desert, the elf-bangle glowing chill white at her wrist, the streak of the crew's campfire the one feature in the great white sky.

She had what she'd always wanted. Whatever Hunnan and his like might say she had proved herself a warrior, with a favored place on a minister's crew and songs sung of her high deeds. She had sent a dozen men through the Last Door. She had won a prize beyond price from the most powerful woman in the world. And here was the harvest.

A thousand miles of lonely nothing.

Thorn had always been happiest in her own company. Now she was as sick of it as everyone else was. So she stood on the docks of Thorlby and hugged Safrit tight, and dragged Koll down from the rail and scrubbed his wild hair while he squirmed in embarrassment, then caught Rulf and kissed him on his balding pate, and seized hold of Dosduvoi and Fror and hauled them into a struggling, sour-smelling embrace. A frowning giant and a scarred Vansterman, foul as dung and frightening as wolves when she met them, grown close to her as brothers.

"Gods damn it but I'll miss you horrible bastards."

"Who knows?" said Mother Scaer, still stretched out among their supplies where she had spent most of the homeward voyage. "Our paths may cross again before too long."

"Let's hope not," Thorn muttered under her breath, looked over those familiar faces, and gave it one last try. "How'd you get the scar, Fror?"

The Vansterman opened his mouth as if to toss out one of his jokes. He always had one ready, after all. Then his eyes flickered to her scarred cheeks and he stopped short, thinking. He took a long breath, and looked her straight in the eye.

"I was twelve years old. The Gettlanders came before dawn. They took most of the villagers for slaves. My mother fought and they killed her. I tried to run, and their leader cut me with his sword. Left me for dead with nothing but this scar."

There was the truth, then, and it was ugly enough. But there was something else in the way Fror looked at her. Something that made the hairs stand on Thorn's neck. Her voice cracked a little when she asked the question. "Who was their leader?"

"They called him Headland."

Thorn stared down at the sword she wore. The sword that had been her father's. "This sword, then?"

"The gods cook strange recipes."

"But you sailed with Gettlanders! You fought beside me. Even though you knew I was his daughter?"

"And I'm glad I did." Fror shrugged. "Vengeance only walks a circle. From blood, back to blood. Death waits for us all. You can follow your path to her bent under a burden of rage. I did, for many years. You can let it poison you." He took a long breath, and let it sigh away. "Or you can let it go. Be well, Thorn Bathu."

"You too," she muttered, hardly knowing what to say. Hardly knowing what to think.

She took a last look at the *South Wind,* tame now, at the wharf, the paint flaking on the white doves mounted at prow and stern. That ship had been her home for a year. Her best friend and her worst enemy, every plank and rivet familiar. Seemed a different ship to the one they set out in. Weathered and worn, scarred and seasoned. A little bit like Thorn. She gave it a final, respectful nod, jerked her sea-chest up onto her shoulder, turned—

Brand stood behind her, close enough that she could almost smell his breath, sleeves rolled up to show the snaking scars about his forearms, stronger and quieter and better-looking than ever.

"Reckon I'll be seeing you, then," he said.

His eyes were fixed on her, gleaming behind those strands of hair across his face. It seemed she'd spent most of the last six months trying not to think about him, which was every bit as bad as thinking about him but with the added frustration of failing not to. Hard to forget someone when they're three oars in front of you. His shoulder moving with the stroke. His elbow at his oar. A sliver of his face as he looked back.

"Aye," she muttered, putting her eyes to the ground. "I reckon." And she stepped around him, and down the bouncing planks of the wharf, and away.

Maybe it was hard, to leave it at that after all they had been through. Maybe it was cowardly. But she had to put him behind her, and leave her disappointment and her shame and her foolishness along with him. When something has to be done, there's nothing to be gained by putting it off but pain.

Damn, but she was starting to sound like Skifr.

That thought rather pleased her.

Thorlby was changed. Everything so much smaller than she remembered. Grayer. Emptier. The wharves were nowhere near so crowded as they used to be, a sorry few fisherman working at their squirming catches, scales flashing silver. Warriors stood guard on the gate, but young ones, which made Thorn wonder what the rest were busy at. She knew one from the training square, his eyes going wide as ale cups as she strutted past.

"Is that her?" she heard someone mutter.

"Thorn Bathu," a woman whispered, voice hushed as if she spoke a magic spell.

"The one they're singing of?"

Her legend had marched ahead of her, would you believe? So Thorn put her shoulders back, and her bravest face on, and she let her left arm swing, the elf-bangle shining. Shining in the sunlight, shining with its own light.

Up the Street of Anvils she went, and the customers turned to stare, and the hammering ceased as the smiths looked out, and Thorn whistled a song as she walked. The song those Throvenmen had sung, about a she-devil who saved the Empress of the South.

Why not? Earned it, hadn't she?

Up the steep lanes she'd walked down with Father Yarvi when he led her from the citadel's dungeons and off to Skekenhouse, to Kalyiv, to the First of Cities. A hundred years ago it seemed, as she turned down a narrow way where every stone was familiar.

She heard muttering behind and saw she'd picked up a little gaggle of children, peering awestruck from around the corner. Just like the ones that had followed her father when he was in Thorlby. Just as he used to she gave them a cheery wave. Then just as he used to she bared her teeth and hissed, scattered them screaming.

Skifr always said that history turns in circles.

The narrow house, the step worn in the middle, the door her father badly carved, all the same, yet somehow they made her nervous. Her heart was hammering as she reached up to shove the door wide, but at the last moment she bunched her fist and knocked instead. She stood waiting, awkward as a beggar even though this was her home, fingers clutched tight around the pouch at her neck, thinking about what Fror had told her.

Maybe her father hadn't been quite the hero she always reckoned him. Maybe her mother wasn't quite the villain either. Maybe no one's all one or all the other.

It was her mother who answered. Strange, to see her looking just the same after all that had happened. Just another hair or two turned gray, and for a moment Thorn felt like a child again, clamping a brave face over her anger and her fear.

"Mother . . ." She tried to tame the tangled side of her head, plucking at the gold and silver rings bound up in her matted hair. A fool's effort, as she couldn't have combed that thicket with an ax. She wondered what her mother's tongue would stab at first: the madness of her hair or the ugliness of her scars or the raggedness of her clothes, or the—

"Hild!" Her face lit up with joy and she caught Thorn in her arms and held her so tight she made her gasp. Then she jerked her out to arm's length and looked her up and down, beaming, then clutched her tight again. "I'm sorry, Thorn—"

"You can call me Hild. If you like." Thorn snorted out a laugh.

"It's good to hear you say it."

"You never used to like it."

"There's a lot changed this past year."

"Here too. War with the Vanstermen, and the king ill, and Grandmother Wexen keeping ships from the harbor . . . but there'll be time for that later."

"Aye." Thorn slowly pushed the door shut and leaned back against it. It was only then she realized how tired she was. So tired she nearly slid down onto her arse right there in the hall.

"You were expected back weeks ago. I was starting to worry. Well, I started worrying the day you left—"

"We got caught in the ice."

"I should've known it would take more than half the world to keep my daughter away. You've grown. Gods, how you've grown!"

"You're not going to say anything about my hair?"

Her mother reached out, and tidied a loose worm of it behind Thorn's ear, touched her scarred cheek gently with her fingertips. "All I care about is that you're alive. I've heard some wild stories about— Father Peace, what's that?" Her mother caught Thorn's wrist and lifted it, the light from the elf-bangle falling across her face, eyes glittering with golden reflections as she stared down.

"That . . ." muttered Thorn, "is a long story."

GREETINGS

Brand said he'd help them unload.

Maybe because that was the good thing to do. Maybe because he couldn't bear to leave the crew quite yet. Maybe because he was scared to see Rin. Scared she'd come to harm while he was gone. Scared she might blame him for it.

So he said as long as he didn't have to lift the ship he'd help them unload it, and told himself it was the good thing to do. There aren't many good things don't have a splinter of selfishness in them somewhere, after all.

And when the unloading was done and half the crew already wandered their own ways he hugged Fror, and Dosduvoi, and Rulf, and they laughed over things Odda had said on the way down the Divine. Laughed as Mother Sun sank toward the hills behind Thorlby, shadows gathering in the carvings that swirled over the whole mast from its root to its top.

"You did one hell of a job on that mast, Koll," said Brand, staring up at it.

"It's the tale of our voyage." Koll had changed a deal since they set out, twitchy-quick as ever but deeper in the voice, stronger in the face, surer in the hands as he slid them gently over the carved trees, and rivers, and ships, and figures all wonderfully woven into one another. "Thorlby's here at the base, the Divine and Denied flow up this side and down the other, the First of Cities at the mast-head. Here we cross the Shattered Sea. There Brand lifts the ship. There we meet Blue Jenner."

"Clever boy, isn't he?" said Safrit, hugging him tight. "Just as well you didn't fall off the bloody yard and smash your brains out."

"Would've been a loss," murmured Brand, gazing up at the mast in more wonder than ever.

Koll pointed out more figures. "Skifr sends Death across the plain. Prince Varoslaf chains the Denied. Thorn fights seven men. Father Yarvi seals his deal with the empress, and . . ." He leaned close, made a few more cuts to a kneeling figure at the bottom with his worn-down knife and blew the chippings away. "Here's me, now, finishing it off." And he stepped back, grinning. "Done."

"It's master's work," said Father Yarvi, running his shrivelled hand over the carvings. "I've a mind to have it mounted in the yard of the citadel, so every Gettlander can see the high deeds done on their behalf, and the high deed of carving it not least among them."

The smiles faded then and left them dewy-eyed, because they all saw the voyage was over, and their little family breaking up. Those whose paths had twined so tight together into one great journey would each be following their own road now, scattered like leaves on a gale to who knew what distant ports, and it was in the hands of the fickle gods whether those paths would ever cross again.

"Bad luck," murmured Dosduvoi, slowly shaking his head. "You find friends and they wander from your life again. Bad, bad luck—"

"Oh, stop prating on your luck you huge fool!" snapped Safrit. "My husband had the poor luck to be stolen by slavers but he never stopped struggling to return to me, never gave up hope, died fighting to the last for his oarmates."

"That he did," said Rulf.

"Saved my life," said Father Yarvi.

"So you could save mine and my son's." Safrit gave Dosduvoi's arm a shove which made the silver rings on his wrist rattle. "Look at all you have! Your strength, and your health, and your wealth, and friends who maybe one day wander back into your life!"

"Who knows who you'll pass on this crooked path to the Last Door?" murmured Rulf, rubbing thoughtfully at his beard.

"That's good luck, damn it, not bad!" said Safrit. "Give praise to whatever god you fancy for every day you live."

"I never thought of it like that before," said Dosduvoi, forehead creased in thought. "I'll endeavor to think on my blessings." He carefully rearranged the ring-money on his great wrist. "Just as soon as I've had a little round of dice. Or two." And he headed off toward the town.

"Some men never bloody learn," muttered Safrit, staring after him with hands on hips.

"None of 'em do," said Rulf.

Brand held out his hand to him. "I'll miss you."

"And I you," said the helmsman, clasping him by the arm. "You're strong at the oar, and strong at the wall, and strong there too." And he thumped Brand on his chest, and leaned close. "Stand in the light, lad, eh?"

"I'll miss all of you." Brand looked toward Thorlby, the way that Thorn had gone, and had to swallow the lump in his throat. To walk off with scarcely a word that way, as if he was nothing and nobody. That hurt.

"Don't worry." Safrit put her hand on his shoulder and gave it a squeeze. "There are plenty of other girls about."

"Not many like her."

"That's a bad thing?" asked Mother Scaer. "I know of a dozen back in Vulsgard who'd tear each other's eyes out for a lad like you."

"That's a good thing?" asked Brand. "On balance, I'd prefer a wife with eyes."

Mother Scaer narrowed hers, which made him more nervous still. "That's why you pick the winner."

"Always sensible," said Father Yarvi. "It is time you left us, Mother

Scaer." He frowned toward the warriors standing at the city's gate. "Vanstermen are less popular even than usual in Thorlby, I think."

She growled in her throat. "The Mother of Crows dances on the border once again."

"Then it is our task as ministers to speak for the Father of Doves, and make of the fist an open hand."

"This alliance you plan." Scaer scrubbed unhappily at her shaved head. "To sponge away a thousand years of blood is no small deed."

"But one that will be worth singing of."

"Men prefer to sing of the making of wounds, fools that they are." Her eyes were blue slits as she stared into Yarvi's. "And I fear you stitch one wound so you can carve a deeper. But I gave my word, and will do what I can."

"What else can any of us do?" The elf-bangles rattled on Mother Scaer's long arm as Yarvi clasped her hand in farewell. Then his eyes moved to Brand, cool and level. "My thanks for all your help, Brand."

"Just doing what you paid me for."

"More than that, I think."

"Just trying to do good, then, maybe."

"The time may come when I need a man who is not so concerned about the greater good, but just the good. Perhaps I can call on you?"

"It'd be my honor, Father Yarvi. I owe you for this. For giving me a place."

"No, Brand, I owe you." The minister smiled. "And I hope soon enough to pay."

BRAND HEADED ACROSS THE hillside, threading between the tents and shacks and ill-made hovels sprouted up outside the gates like mushrooms after the rains. Many more than there used to be. There was war with the Vanstermen, and folk had fled homes near the border to huddle against Thorlby's walls.

Lamplight gleamed through chinks in wattle, voices drifting into the evening, a fragment of a sad song echoing from somewhere. He passed a great bonfire, pinched faces of the very old and very young lit by whirling sparks. The air smelled strong of smoke and dung and unwashed bodies. The sour stink of his childhood, but it smelled sweet to him then. He knew this wouldn't be his home much longer.

As he walked he felt the pouch shifting underneath his shirt. Heavy it was, now. Red gold from Prince Varoslaf and yellow gold from the Empress Vialine and good silver with the face of Queen Laithlin stamped upon it. Enough for a fine house in the shadow of the citadel. Enough that Rin would never want for anything again. He was smiling as he shoved the door of their shack rattling open.

"Rin, I'm—"

He found himself staring at a clutch of strangers. A man, a woman, and how many children? Five? Six? All crushed tight about the firepit where he used to warm his aching feet and no sign of Rin among them.

"Who the hell are you?" Fear clutched at him, and he put his hand on his dagger.

"It's all right!" The man held up his palms. "You're Brand?"

"Damn right I am. Where's my sister?"

"You don't know?"

"If I knew would I be asking? Where's Rin?"

IT WAS A FINE HOUSE in the shadow of the citadel.

A rich woman's house of good cut stone with a full second floor and a dragon's head carved into its roof beam. A homely house with welcoming firelight spilling around its shutters and into the evening. A handsome house with a stream gurgling through a steep channel beside it and under a narrow bridge. A well-kept house with a door new-painted green, and hanging over the door a shingle in the shape of a sword, swinging gently with the breeze.

"Here?" Brand had labored up the steep lanes with crates and barrels to the homes of the wealthy often enough, and he knew the street. But he'd never been to this house, had no notion why his sister might be inside.

"Here," answered the man, and gave the door a beating with his knuckles.

Brand stood there wondering what sort of pose to strike, and was caught by surprise halfway between two when the door jerked open.

Rin was changed. Even more than he was, maybe. A woman grown, she seemed now, taller, and her face leaner, dark hair cut short. She wore a fine tunic, clever stitching about the collar, like a wealthy merchant might.

"You all right, Hale?" she asked.

"Better," said the man. "We had a visitor." And he stepped out of the way so the light fell across Brand's face.

"Rin . . ." he croaked, hardly knowing what to say, "I'm—"

"You're back!" And she flung her arms around him almost hard enough to knock him over, and squeezed him almost hard enough to make him sick. "You just going to stand on the step and stare?" And she bundled him through the doorway. "Give my love to your children!" she shouted after Hale.

"Be glad to!"

Then she kicked the door shut and dragged Brand's sea-chest from his shoulder. As she set it on the tiled floor a chain hung down, a silver chain with a silver key gleaming on it.

"Whose key's that?" he muttered.

"Did you think I'd get married while you were gone? It's my own key to my own locks. You hungry? You thirsty? I've got—"

"Whose house is this, Rin?"

She grinned at him. "It's yours. It's mine. It's ours."

"This?" Brand stared at her. "But . . . how did—"

"I told you I'd make a sword."

Brand's eyes went wide. "Must've been a blade for the songs."

"King Uthil thought so."

Brand's eyes went wider still. "King Uthil?"

"I found a new way to smelt the steel. A hotter way. The first blade cracked when we quenched it, but the second held. Gaden said we had to give it to the king. And the king stood up in the Godshall and said steel was the answer, and this was the best steel he ever saw. He's carrying it now, I hear." She shrugged, as if King Uthil's patronage was no great honor. "After that, everyone wanted me to make them a sword. Gaden said she couldn't keep me. She said I should be the master and she the apprentice." Rin shrugged. "Blessed by She who Strikes the Anvil, like we used to say."

"Gods," whispered Brand. "I was going to change your life. You did it by yourself."

"You gave me the chance." Rin took his wrist, frowning down at the scars there. "What happened?"

"Nothing. Rope slipped going over the tall hauls."

"Reckon there's more to that story."

"I've got better ones."

Rin's lip wrinkled. "Long as they haven't got Thorn Bathu in 'em."

"She saved the Empress of the South from her uncle, Rin! The Empress! Of the South."

"That one I've heard already. They're singing it all over town. Something about her beating a dozen men alone. Then it was fifteen. Might've even been twenty last time I heard it. And she threw some duke off a roof and routed a horde of Horse People and won an elf-relic and lifted a ship besides, I hear. Lifted a ship!" And she snorted again.

Brand raised his brows. "I reckon songs have a habit of outrunning the truth."

"You can tell me the truth of it later." Rin took down the lamp and drew him through another doorway, stairs going up into the shadows. "Come and see your room."

"I've got a room?" muttered Brand, eyes going wider than ever. How often had he dreamed of that? When they hadn't a roof over their heads, or food to eat, or a friend in the world besides each other?

She put her arm around his shoulders and it felt like home. "You've got a room."

WRONG
IDEAS

"Reckon I need a new sword."

Thorn sighed as she laid her father's blade gently on the table, the light of the forge catching the many scratches, glinting on the deep nicks. It was worn almost crooked from years of polishing, the binding scuffed to greasy shreds, the cheap iron pommel rattling loose.

The apprentice gave Thorn's sword one quick glance and Thorn herself not even that many. "Reckon you're right." She wore a leather vest scattered with burns, gloves to her elbow, arms and shoulders bare and beaded with sweat from the heat, hard muscles twitching as she turned a length of metal in the glowing coals.

"It's a good sword." Thorn ran her fingers down the scarred steel. "It was my father's. Seen a lot of work. In his day and in mine."

The apprentice didn't so much as nod. Somewhat of a gritty manner she had, but Thorn had one of those herself, so she tried not to hold it too much against her.

"Your master about?" she asked.

"No."

Thorn waited for more, but there wasn't any. "When will he be back?"

The girl just snorted, slid the metal from the coals, looked it over, and rammed it hissing back in a shower of sparks.

Thorn decided to try starting over. "I'm looking for the blade-maker on Sixth Street."

"And here I am," said the girl, still frowning down at her work.

"You?"

"I'm the one making blades on Sixth Street, aren't I?"

"Thought you'd be . . . older."

"Seems thinking ain't your strength."

Thorn spent a moment wondering whether to be annoyed by that, but decided to let it go. She was trying to let things go more often. "You're not the first to say so. Just not common, a girl making swords."

The girl looked up then. Fierce eyes, gleaming with the forge-light through the hair stuck across her strong-boned face, and some-thing damned familiar about her but Thorn couldn't think what. "Almost as uncommon as one swinging 'em."

"Fair point," said Thorn, holding out her hand. "I'm—"

The sword-maker slid the half-made blade from the forge, glow-ing metal passing so close Thorn had to snatch her hand back. "I know who y'are, Thorn Bathu."

"Oh. Course." Thorn guessed her fame was running off ahead of her. She was only now starting to see that wasn't always a good thing.

The girl took up a hammer and Thorn watched her knock a fuller into the blade, watched her strike the anvil-music, as the smiths say, and quite a lesson it was. Short, quick blows, no wasted effort, all au-thority, all control, each one perfect as a master's sword thrust, glow-ing dust scattering from the die. Thorn knew a lot more about using swords than making them, but an idiot could've seen this girl knew her business.

"They say you make the best swords in Thorlby," said Thorn.

"I make the best swords in the Shattered Sea," said the girl, hold-ing up the steel so the glow from it fell across her sweat-shining face.

"My father always told me never get proud."

"Ain't a question of pride. It's just a fact."

"Would you make me one?"

"No. Don't think I will."

Folk who are the best at what they do sometimes forego the niceties, but this was getting strange. "I've got money."

"I don't want your money."

"Why?"

"I don't like you."

Thorn wasn't usually slow to rise to an insult but this was so unexpected she was caught off-guard. "Well . . . I guess there are other swords to be found."

"No doubt there are."

"I'll go and find one, then."

"I hope you find a long one." The swordmaker on Sixth Street leaned down to blow ash from the metal with a gentle puff from her pursed lips. "Then you can stick it up your arse."

Thorn snatched her old sword up, gave serious thought to clubbing the girl across the head with the flat, decided against and turned for the door. Before she quite made it to the handle, though, the girl spoke again.

"Why'd you treat my brother that way?"

She was mad. Had to be. "Who's your damn brother?"

The girl frowned over at her. "Brand."

The name rocked Thorn surely as a kick in the head. "Not Brand who was with me on—"

"What other Brand?" She jabbed at her chest with her thumb. "I'm Rin."

Thorn surely saw the resemblance, now, and it rocked her even more, so it came out a guilty squeak when she spoke. "Didn't know Brand had a sister . . ."

Rin gave a scornful chuckle. "Why would you? Only spent a year on the same boat as him."

"He never told me!"

"Did you ask?"

"Of course! Sort of." Thorn swallowed. "No."

"A year away." Rin rammed the blade angrily back into the coals. "And the moment he sees me, do you know what he sets to talking about?"

"Er . . ."

She started pounding at the bellows like Thorn used to pound Brand's head in the training square. "Thorn Bathu ran the oars in the middle of an elf-ruin. Thorn Bathu saved his life in the shield wall. Thorn Bathu made an alliance that'll put the world to rights. And when I could've bitten his face if I heard your name one more time, what do you think he told me next?"

"Er . . ."

"Thorn Bathu scarcely spoke a word to him the whole way back. Thorn Bathu cut him off like you'd trim a blister. I tell you what, Thorn Bathu sounds something of a bloody bitch to me, after all he's done for her and, no, I don't much fancy making a sword for—"

"Hold it there," snapped Thorn. "You don't have the first clue what happened between me and your brother."

Rin let the bellows be and glared over. "Enlighten me."

"Well . . ." Last thing Thorn needed was to rip that scab off again just when there was a chance of letting it heal. She wasn't about to admit that she made a fool's mistake, and burned herself bad, and had to make herself not look at Brand or talk to Brand or have anything to do with Brand every moment of every day in case she burned herself again. "You got it back to front is all!"

"Strange how people are always getting the wrong idea about you. How often does that have to happen, 'fore you start thinking maybe they got the right idea?" And Rin dragged the iron from the forge and set it back on the anvil.

"You don't know me," growled Thorn, working up the bellows on some anger of her own. "You don't know what I've been through."

"No doubt we've all had our struggles," said Rin, lifting her hammer. "But some of us get to weep over 'em in a big house our daddy paid for."

Thorn threw up her hands at the fine new forge behind the fine home near the citadel. "Oh, I see you and Brand have barely been scraping by!"

Rin froze, then, muscles bunching across her shoulders, and her eyes flicked over, and she looked angry. So angry Thorn took a little step back, a cautious eye on that hovering hammer.

Then Rin tossed it rattling down, pulled her gloves off and flung them on the table. "Come with me."

"MY MOTHER DIED WHEN I was little."

Rin had led them outside the walls. Downwind, where the stink of Thorlby's rubbish wouldn't bother the good folk of the city.

"Brand remembers her a little. I don't."

Some of the midden heaps were years covered over and turned to grassy mounds. Some were open and stinking, spilling bones and shells, rags and the dung of men and beasts.

"He always says she told him to do good."

A mangy dog gave Thorn a suspicious eye, as though it considered her competition, and went back to sniffing through the rot.

"My father died fighting Grom-gil-Gorm," muttered Thorn, trying to match ill-luck for ill-luck. Honestly, she felt a little queasy. From the look of this place, and the stink of it, and the fact she had scarcely even known it was here because her mother's slaves had always carted their rubbish. "They laid him out in the Godshall."

"And you got his sword."

"Less the pommel," grunted Thorn, trying not to breathe through her nose. "Gorm kept that."

"You're lucky to have something from your father." Rin didn't seem bothered by the stench at all. "We didn't get much from ours. He liked a drink. Well. I say *a* drink. He liked 'em all. He left when

Brand was nine. Gone one morning, and maybe we were better off without him."

"Who took you in?" asked Thorn in a small voice, getting the sense she was far outclassed in the ill-luck contest.

"No one did." Rin let that sink in a moment. "There were quite a few of us living here, back then."

"Here?"

"You pick through. Sometimes you find something you can eat. Sometimes you find something you can sell. Winters." Rin hunched her shoulders and gave a shiver. "Winters were hard."

Thorn could only stand there and blink, feeling cold all over even if summer was well on the way. She'd always supposed she'd had quite the tough time growing up. Now she learned that while she raged in her fine house because her mother didn't call her by the name she liked, there had been children picking through the dung for bones to chew. "Why are you telling me this?"

"Cause Brand didn't say and you didn't ask. We begged. I stole." Rin gave a bitter little smile. "But Brand said he had to do good. So he worked. He worked at the docks and the forges. He worked anywhere folk would give him work. He worked like a dog and more than once he was beaten like one. I got sick and he got me through it and I got sick again and he got me through it again. He kept on dreaming of being a warrior, and having a place on a crew, a family always around him. So he went to the training square. He had to beg and borrow the gear, but he went. He'd work before he trained and he'd work after, and even after that if anyone needed help he'd be there to help. Do good, Brand always said, and folk'll do good for you. He was a good boy. He's become a good man."

"I know that," growled Thorn, feeling the hurt all well up fresh, sharper than ever for the guilt that welled up with it, now. "He's the best man I know. This isn't bloody news to me!"

Rin stared at her. "Then how could you treat him this way? If it wasn't for him I'd be gone through the Last Door, and so would you, and this is the thanks—"

Thorn might have been wrong about a few things, and she might not have known a few others she should have, and she might have been way too wrapped up in herself to see what was right under her nose, but there was a limit on what she'd take.

"Hold on, there, Brand's secret sister. No doubt you've opened my eyes wider than ever to my being a selfish arse. But me and him were oarmates. On a crew you stand with the men beside you. Yes, he was there for me, but I was there for him, and—"

"Not that! Before. When you killed that boy. Edwal."

"What?" Thorn felt queasier still. "I remember that day well enough and all Brand did was bloody stand there."

Rin gaped at her. "Did you two talk at all that year away?"

"Not about Edwal, I can tell you that!"

"Course you didn't." Rin closed her eyes and smiled as though she understood it all. "He'd never take the thanks he deserves, the stubborn fool. He didn't tell you."

Thorn understood nothing. "Tell me what, damn it?"

"He went to Father Yarvi." And Rin took Thorn gently but firmly by the shoulder and let the words fall one by one. "He told him what happened on the beach. Even though he knew it'd cost him. Master Hunnan found out. So it cost him his place on the king's raid, and his place as a warrior, and everything he'd hoped for."

Thorn made a strange sound then. A choked-off cluck. The sound a chicken makes when its neck gets wrung.

"Brand went to Father Yarvi," she croaked.

"Yes."

"Brand saved my life. And lost his place for it."

"Yes."

"Then I mocked him over it, and treated him like a fool the whole way down the Divine and the Denied and the whole way back up again."

"Yes."

"Why didn't he just bloody *say*—" And that was when Thorn saw something gleaming just inside the collar of Rin's vest. She reached out, hooked it with a trembling finger, and eased it into the light.

Beads. Glass beads, blue and green.

The ones Brand bought that day in the First of Cities. The ones she'd thought were for her, then for some other lover back in Thorlby. The ones she now saw were for the sister she'd never bothered to ask if he had.

Thorn made that squawking sound again, but louder.

Rin stared at her as if she'd gone mad. "What?"

"I'm such a stupid shit."

"Eh?"

"Where is he?"

"Brand? At my house. Our house—"

"Sorry." Thorn was already backing away. "I'll talk to you about the sword later!" And she turned and started running for the gate.

HE LOOKED BETTER THAN ever. Or maybe she just saw him differently, knowing what she knew.

"Thorn." He looked surprised to see her and she could hardly blame him. Then he looked worried. "What's wrong?"

She realized she must look worse even than usual and wished she hadn't run all the way, or at least waited to knock until she'd caught her breath and wiped the sweat from her forehead. But she'd been dancing around this far too long. Time to face it, sweaty or not.

"I talked to your sister," she said.

He looked more worried. "What about?"

"About you having a sister, for one thing."

"That's no secret."

"That might not be."

He looked even more worried. "What did she tell you?"

"That you saved my life. When I killed Edwal."

He winced. "I told her not to say anything!"

"Well, that didn't work."

"Reckon you'd best come in. If you want to." He stepped back from the door and she followed him into the shadowy hallway, heart pounding harder than ever. "You don't have to thank me."

"Yes," she said. "I do."

"I wasn't trying to do anything noble, just . . . something good. And I wasn't sure, and it took me too long, and I made a bloody mess of it—"

She took a step toward him. "Did you go to Father Yarvi?"

"Yes."

"Did Father Yarvi save my life?"

"Yes."

"Did you lose your place because of it?"

He worked his mouth as though looking for a way to deny it, but couldn't. "I was going to tell you, but . . ."

"I'm not easy to tell things to."

"And I'm not much good at telling." He pushed his hair back and scrubbed at his head as though it hurt. "Didn't want you feeling in my debt. Wouldn't have been fair."

She blinked at that. "So . . . you didn't just risk everything for my sake, you kept it to yourself so I wouldn't feel bad about it."

"One way of putting it . . . maybe." And he looked at her from under his brows, eyes gleaming in the shadows. That look, as if there was nothing he would rather be looking at. And however she'd tried to weed those hopes away they blossomed in a riot, and the want came up stronger than ever.

She took another little step toward him. "I'm so sorry."

"You don't have to be."

"But I am. For how I treated you. On the way back. On the way out, for that matter. I'm sorry, Brand. I've never been sorrier. I've never been sorry at all, really. Got to work on that. Just . . . I got the wrong idea about . . . something."

He stood there, silent. Waiting. Looking. No bloody help at all.

Just say it. How hard could it be? She'd killed men. Just say it. "I stopped talking to you . . . because . . ." But getting the words out was like hauling anvils out of a well. "I . . . like . . ." It was as if she tottered out onto a frozen lake, not knowing whether the next step might send her plunging to an icy doom. "I've always . . . liked . . ." She couldn't make the "you." She couldn't have made the "you" if it was that or die. She squeezed her eyes shut. "What I'm trying to say is—Whoa!"

She snapped her eyes open. He'd touched her cheek, fingertips brushing the scar there.

"You've got your hand on me." Stupidest thing she'd ever said and that with some fierce competition. They could both see he had his hand on her. Wasn't as if it fell there by accident.

He jerked it away. "I thought—"

"No!" She caught his wrist and guided it back. "I mean . . . Yes." His fingertips were warm against her face, hers sliding over the back of his hand, pressing it there and it felt . . . Gods. "This is happening, is it?"

He stepped a little closer, the knobble on his neck bobbing as he swallowed. "I reckon." He was looking at her mouth. Looking at it as though there was something really interesting in there and she wasn't sure she'd ever been so scared.

"What do we do?" she found she'd squeaked out, voice running away from her, higher and higher. "I mean, I know what we *do* . . . I guess." Gods, that was a lie, she hadn't a clue. She wished now Skifr had taught her a little less about swords and a bit more about the arts of love, or whatever. "I mean, what do we do *now* we know that, you know—"

He put his thumb gently across her lips. "Shut up, Thorn."

"Right," she breathed, and she realized she had her hand up between them, as if to push him away. So used to pushing folk away, and him in particular, and she forced it to go soft, laid it gently on his chest, hoped he couldn't feel it trembling.

Closer he came, and she was taken suddenly with an urge to run for it, and then with an urge to giggle, and she made a stupid gurgle swallowing her laughter, and then his lips were touching hers. Gently, just brushing, one way, then the other, and she realized she had her eyes open and snapped them shut. Couldn't think what to do with her hands. Stiff as a woman made of wood, she was, for a moment, but then things started to go soft.

The side of his nose nudged hers, ticklish.

He made a noise in his throat, and so did she.

She caught his lip between hers, tugged at it, slipped that hand on his chest up around his neck, and pulled him closer, their teeth knocked awkwardly together and they broke apart.

Not much of a kiss, really. Nothing like she'd imagined it would be, and the gods knew she'd imagined it enough, but it left her hot all over. Maybe that was just the running, but she'd done a lot of running and never felt quite like this.

She opened her eyes and he was looking at her. That look, through the strands of hair across his face. Wasn't the first kiss she ever had, but the others had felt like children playing. This was as different from that as a battle from the training square.

"Oh," she croaked. "That . . . wasn't so bad."

She let go of his hand and caught a fistful of his shirt, started dragging him back toward her, caught the smile at the corner of his mouth and smiled herself—

There was a rattle outside the door.

"Rin," muttered Brand, and as if that was the starting word on a race they both took off running. Pelted down the corridor like thieves caught in the act, tangling on a stairway, giggling like idiots as they scrambled into a room and Brand wrestled the door shut, leaning back against it as if there were a dozen angry Vanstermen outside.

They hunched in the shadows, their breath coming quick.

"Why did we run?" he whispered.

"I don't know," Thorn whispered back.

"You think she can hear us?"

"What if she can?" asked Thorn.

"I don't know."

"So this is your room, is it?"

He straightened up, grinning like a king who'd won a victory. "I have a room."

"Quite the distinguished citizen," she said, strolling around in a circle, taking it in. Didn't take long. There was a pallet bed in one corner with Brand's worn-out old blanket on it, and his sea chest sitting open in another, and the sword that used to be Odda's leaning against the wall, and aside from that just bare boards and bare walls and a lot of shadows. "Ever wonder if you've overdone the furniture?"

"It's not quite finished."

"It's not quite started," she said, the circle taking her back toward him.

"If it's not what you were used to at the empress's palace, I won't keep you."

She snorted. "I lived under a boat with forty men in it. Reckon I can stand this a while."

His eyes were on her as she came close. That look. Little bit hungry, little bit scared. "Staying, then?"

"I've got nothing else pressing."

And they were kissing again, harder this time. She wasn't worrying about Brand's sister anymore, or about her mother, or about anything. There was nothing on her mind but her mouth and his. Not to begin with, at least. But soon enough some other parts started making themselves known. She wondered what was prodding at her hip and stuck her hand down there to check and then she realized what was prodding at her hip and had to break away she felt so foolish, and scared, and hot, and excited, and hardly knew what she felt.

"Sorry," he muttered, bending over and lifting one leg as if he was trying to hide the bulge and looking so ridiculous she spluttered with laughter.

He looked hurt. "Ain't funny."

"It is kind of." She took his arm and pulled him close, then she hooked her leg around his and he gasped as she tripped him, put him down hard on his back with her on top, straddling him. Familiar territory in its way, but everything was different now.

She pressed her hips up against his, rocking back and forward, gently at first, then not so gently. She had her hand tangled in his hair, dragging his face against hers, his beard prickling at her chin, their open mouths pressed together so her head seemed to be full of his rasping breath, hot on her lips.

She was fair grinding away at him now and liking the feel of it more than a bit, then she was scared she was liking the feel of it, then she decided just to do it and worry later. She was grunting in her throat with each breath and one little part of her thinking that must sound pretty foolish but a much bigger part not caring. One of his hands slipped up her back under her shirt, the other up her ribs, one by one, and made her shiver. She pulled away, breathing hard, looking down at him, propped up on one elbow.

"Sorry," he whispered.

"For what?" She ripped her shirt open and dragged it off, got it caught over the elf-bangle on her wrist, finally tore it free and flung it away.

She felt a fool for a moment, knew she was nothing like a woman should be, knew she was pale and hard and nothing but gristle. But he looked anything but disappointed, slid his hands up her sides and around her back, pulled her down against him, kissing at her, nipping at her lips with his teeth. The pouch with her father's fingerbones fell in his eye and she slapped it back over her shoulder. She set to pulling his shirt open, pushing her hand up his stomach, fingers through the hairs on his chest, the bangle glowing soft gold, reflected in the corners of his eyes.

He caught her hand. "We don't have to . . . you know . . ."

No doubt they didn't have to, and no doubt there were a hundred reasons not to, and right then she couldn't think of one she gave a damn about.

"Shut up, Brand." She twisted her hand free and started dragging his belt open. She didn't know what she was doing, but she knew some right idiots who'd done it.

How hard could it be?

SORT OF ALONE

They'd gone to sleep holding each other but it hadn't lasted long. Brand never knew anyone to thrash about so much in the night. She twitched and twisted, jerked and shuddered, kicked and rolled until she kicked him awake and rolled him right out of his own bed.

So he was left sitting on his sea chest, the lid polished to a comfortable gloss by hundreds of miles of his own rowing backside, watching her.

She'd ended up facedown with her arms spread wide, a strip of sunlight from the narrow window angled across her back, one hand hanging off the bed and the elf-bangle casting a faint glow on the floor. One long leg poked out from under the blanket, a puckered scar across the thigh, hair bound with rings of silver and gold, tangled across her face so all he could see was half of one shut eye and a little piece of cheek with that arrow-shaped mark on it.

To begin with he'd sat with a stupid smile on his face, listening to her snore. Thinking how she'd snored in his ear all the way down the Divine and the Denied. Thinking how much he liked hearing it. Hardly able to believe his luck that she was there, now, naked, in his bed.

Then he'd started worrying.

What would people think when they found out they'd done this? What would Rin say? What would Thorn's mother do? What if a child came? He'd heard it wasn't likely but it happened, didn't it? Sooner or later she'd wake. What if she didn't want him anymore? How could she want him anymore? And, lurking at the back of his mind, the darkest worry of all. What if she woke and she did want him still? What then?

"Gods," he muttered, blinking up at the ceiling, but they'd answered his prayers by putting her in his bed, hadn't they? He could hardly pray for help getting her out.

With a particularly ripping snort Thorn jerked, and stretched out, clenching her fists, and stretching her toes, her muscles shuddering. She blew snot out of one nostril, wiped it on the back of her hand, rubbed her eyes on the back of the other and dragged her matted hair out of her face. She froze, and her head jerked around, eyes wide.

"Morning," he said.

She stared at him. "Not a dream, then?"

"I'm guessing no." A nightmare, maybe.

They looked at each other for a long moment. "You want me to go?" she asked.

"No!" he said, too loud and too eager. "No. You want to go?"

"No." She sat up slowly, dragging the blanket around her shoulders, knobbled knees toward him, and gave a huge yawn.

"Why?" he found he'd said. She stopped halfway through, mouth hanging open. "Wasn't like last night went too well did it?"

She flinched at that like he'd slapped her. "What did I do wrong?"

"You? No! You didn't . . . it's me I'm talking of." He wasn't sure what he was talking of, but his mouth kept going even so. "Rin told you, didn't she?"

"Told me what?"

"That my own father didn't want me. That my own mother didn't want me."

She frowned at him. "I thought your mother died."

"Same bloody thing isn't it?"

"No. It isn't."

He was hardly listening. "I grew up picking through rubbish. I had to beg to feed my sister. I carted bones like a slave." He hadn't meant to say any of it. Not ever. But it just came puking out.

Thorn shut her mouth with a snap. "I'm an arse, Brand. But what kind of arse would I be if I thought less of you for that? You're a good man. A man who can be trusted. Everyone who knows you thinks so. Koll worships you. Rulf respects you. Even Father Yarvi likes you, and he doesn't like anyone."

He blinked at her. "I never speak."

"But you listen when other people speak! And you're handsome and well-made as Safrit never tired of telling me."

"She did?"

"She and Mother Scaer spent a whole afternoon discussing your arse."

"Eh?"

"You could have anyone you wanted. Specially now you don't live in a midden. The mystery is why you'd want me."

"Eh?" He'd never dreamed she had her own doubts. Always seemed so damn sure about everything.

But she drew the blanket tight around her shoulders and looked down at her bare feet, mouth twisted with disgust. "I'm selfish."

"You're . . . ambitious. I like that."

"I'm bitter."

"You're funny. I like that too."

She rubbed gently at her scarred cheek. "I'm ugly."

Anger burned up in him then, so hot it took him by surprise. "Who bloody said so? Cause first they're wrong and second I'll punch their teeth out."

"I can punch 'em myself. That's the problem. I'm not . . . you know." She stuck a hand out of the blanket and scrubbed her nails against the shaved side of her head. "I'm not how a girl should be. Or a woman. Never have been. I'm no good at . . ."

"What?"

"Smiling or, I don't know, sewing."

"I don't need anything sewed." And he slid off his sea chest and knelt down in front of her. His worries had faded. Things had got ruined before somehow and he wouldn't let them get ruined again. Not for lack of trying. "I've wanted you since the First of Cities. Since before, maybe." He reached out and put his hand on hers where it rested on the bed. Clumsy, maybe, but honest. "Just never thought I'd get you." He looked into her face, groping for the right words. "Looking at you, and thinking you want me, makes me feel like . . . like I won."

"Won something no one else would want," she muttered.

"What do I care what they want?" he said, that anger catching fire again and making her look up. "If they're too damn stupid to see you're the best woman in the Shattered Sea that's my good luck, isn't it?" He fell silent, and felt his face burning, and thought for sure he'd ruined the whole thing again.

"That might be the nicest thing anyone ever said to me." She reached up and pushed the hair out of his face. Gentle as a feather, her touch. He hadn't realized she could be so gentle. "No one ever says anything nice to me, but even so." The blanket slipped off her bare shoulder and he set his hand on it, slid it down her side and around her back, skin hissing on skin, warm, and smooth, her eyes closing, and his—

A thumping echoed through the house. Someone beating on the front door, and knocks that weren't to be ignored. Brand heard the bolt drawn back, voices muttering.

"Gods," said Thorn, eyes wide. "Could be my mother."

They hadn't moved so fast even when the Horse People came charging across the steppe, grabbing up clothes and tossing them to each other, pulling them on, him fumbling with his belt and getting it all messed up because he was watching her wriggle her trousers over her arse out of the corner of his eye.

"Brand?" came his sister's voice.

They both froze, he with one boot on, she with none, then Brand called out a cracked, "Aye?"

"You all right?" Rin's voice coming up the steps.

"Aye!"

"You alone?" Just outside the door now.

"Course!" Then, when he realized she might come in, he followed up with a guilty, "Sort of."

"You're the worst liar in Gettland. Is Thorn Bathu in there with you?"

Brand winced. "Sort of."

"She's in there or she's not. Are you bloody in there, Thorn Bathu?"

"Sort of?" said Thorn at the door in a tiny voice.

A long pause. "That was Master Hunnan."

The name was like a bucket of cold water down Brand's trousers and no mistake.

"He said a dove came with news of a raid at Halleby, and with all the men gone north to fight, he's gathering what's left to go and see to it. Some who are training, some who are wounded, some who failed a test. They're meeting on the beach."

"He wants me?" called Brand, a quiver in his voice.

"He says Gettland needs you. And he says for any man who does his duty there'll be a warrior's place."

A warrior's place. Always to have brothers at your shoulder. Always to have something to fight for. To stand in the light. And quick as that the ashes of old dreams that had seemed for months burned out flared up hot and bright again. Quick as that he was decided.

"I'll be down," called Brand, heart suddenly beating hard, and he heard his sister's footsteps move away.

"You're going with that bastard?" asked Thorn. "After what he did to you? What he did to me?"

Brand pulled the blanket off the bed. "Not for his sake. For Gettland."

She snorted. "For you."

"All right, for me. Don't I deserve it?"

Her jaw worked for a moment. "I notice he didn't ask for me."

"Would you have followed him?" he asked, putting his few things onto the blanket and making a bundle of it.

"Course I would. Then I'd have kicked his face in."

"Maybe that's why he didn't ask for you."

"Hunnan wouldn't ask for me if I was holding a bucket of water and he was on fire. None of them would. Warriors of Gettland. There's a bloody joke! Not a funny one, mind." She paused halfway through dragging one boot on. "You're not so keen to go just so you can get away from me, are you? Cause if you're thinking better of this just tell me. I reckon we've had enough secrets—"

"That's not it," he said, even though he wondered if it was part of it. Just get some room to breathe. Just get some time to think.

"Sometimes I wish I'd stayed in the First of Cities," she said.

"You'd never have bedded me then."

"When I died rich and storied that could've been my life's one great regret."

"Just give me a week," he said, strapping on Odda's sword. "I'm not thinking better of anything, but I have to do this. I might never get another chance."

She curled her lips back and made a long hiss. "One week. Then I go after the next man I find who can lift a ship."

"Done." And he kissed her one more time. Her lips were scummy, and her mouth was sour, and he didn't care. He slung his shield over his shoulder, and hefted the little bundle he'd made with his blanket, and he took a long breath, and headed off to the iron embrace of Mother War.

Something stopped him in the doorway, though, and he took one last look back. As if to make sure she was really there. She was, and smiling at him. They were rare, her smiles, but that made them precious. Precious as gold, it seemed, and he was mightily pleased with himself for being the cause of it.

THE CHOSEN
SHIELD

The citadel of Thorlby had not been happy ground for Thorn. The last time she visited it had been as a murderer, herded in chains to the cells. The time before it had been to see her father laid out in the Godshall, pale and cold beneath the dome, her mother sobbing beside her, and she'd looked up at the hard faces of the tall gods and known her prayers had all been wasted. She had to swallow a shadow of the anger she'd felt then, the anger that had burned at her ever since, gripping at the pouch that held her father's fingerbones as she frowned toward the great doors of the Godshall.

There were boys training in the yard, beneath the ancient cedar. Training in the square, the way Thorn used to, their master-at-arms barking out orders as they scrambled into a rickety shield wall. They seemed so young now. So slow and so clumsy. She could hardly believe she had ever been one of them as Koll led her past.

"You are Thorn Bathu?"

An old man sat at the corner of the square, swathed in a thick black fur in spite of the warmth, a drawn sword cradled in his arms. He seemed so withered, and hunched, and pale, that even with the golden circle on his brow it took Thorn a moment to recognize him.

She wobbled down onto one knee beside Koll, staring at the grass. "I am, my king."

King Uthil cleared his throat. "I hear unarmed you killed seven men, and forged an alliance with the Empress of the South. I did not believe it." He narrowed his watery eyes as he looked her up and down. "Now I begin to."

Thorn swallowed. "It was only five men, my king."

"Only five, she says!" And he gave a throaty chuckle to the old warriors about him. A couple just about cracked smiles. The faces of the others grew more dour with every word. No deed would ever be high enough to raise her in their estimation: she was as much an object of contempt as ever. "I like you, girl!" said the king. "We should practice together."

So she could practice with him, as long as she didn't presume to fight for him. Thorn lowered her eyes in case she let her anger show and ended up visiting the citadel's dungeons for a second time. "That would be a high honor," she managed to say.

Uthil broke into a coughing fit, and drew his cloak tight about his shoulders. "Once my minister's potions have worked their magic and I am past this illness. I swear those dung-tasting brews only make me weaker."

"Father Yarvi is a deep-cunning healer, my king," said Thorn. "I would have died without his wisdom."

"Aye," murmured Uthil, staring off into the distance. "I hope his wisdom works soon for me. I must go north, and teach these Vanstermen a lesson. The Breaker of Swords has questions for us." His voice had withered to a crackling wheeze. "What should be our answer?"

"Steel!" hissed Thorn, and the other warriors about the king murmured the word as one.

Uthil's pale hand trembled as he clutched his drawn sword close, and Thorn did not think she would be practicing with the king any time soon. "Steel," he breathed, and settled slowly into his fur, wet eyes fixed on the boys in the square, as if he had forgotten Thorn was there.

"Father Yarvi's waiting," murmured Koll. He led her away across the grass, into a shadowy hall and up a long flight of steps, the scraping of their boots echoing in the darkness, the shouts of the training boys fading behind them.

"Is Brand all right?"

"How the hell should I know?" Thorn snapped, and felt guilty right away. "I'm sorry. I hope he is."

"Are you and him . . ." Koll peered at her sideways. "You know."

"I don't know what me and him are," she snapped, another wave of temper and another slow wash of guilt. "Sorry."

"You're bored."

"I'm idle," she growled, "while high deeds are being done."

Her mood had been filthy for days and the scorn of Uthil's warriors hadn't helped. She had nothing to do but worry. Worry that Brand wouldn't want her when he came back or that she wouldn't want him when he came back or that he wouldn't come back at all. She had more doubts and frustrations spinning faster around her head than before she'd bedded him and there was nothing she could do about any of it.

"Bloody men," she muttered. "We'd be better off without them."

"What did I do?" asked Koll.

"You don't count." She grinned, and ruffled his hair. "Yet."

A heavy door squealed open on a cave of wonders. A round room, ill-lit by flickering lamps, smelling of spice and fust and lined with shelves, the shelves stacked with books, with jars of dried leaves and colored dust, with animals' skulls and broken sticks, with bunches of herbs and stones glittering with crystals.

Safrit stood in there, beckoning Thorn up some steps toward another archway. She leaned close to whisper. "Don't worry."

"Eh?"

"It'll work out fine, whatever you decide."

Thorn stared at her. "Now I'm worried."

Father Yarvi sat on a stool by a firepit in the room beyond, the elf-metal staff that leaned beside him gleaming with reflected fire.

Safrit knelt so low at the threshold she nearly butted the floor, but Thorn snorted as she swaggered forward.

"Having good folk kneel before you, Father Yarvi? I thought you gave up being a king—" The rest of the room came into view and Thorn saw Queen Laithlin sitting on the other side of the fire. Her robe was shrugged back, one pale shoulder bare, and she clasped a bundle of fur to her chest. Prince Druin, Thorn realized, heir to the Black Chair.

"Gods." Thorn was being ambushed by royalty around every corner. She scrambled down to one knee, knocked a jar off a shelf with her elbow, dislodged another when she shot out a hand to catch it, ended up clumsily crowding the clinking mess back with her chest. "Sorry, my queen. I've never been much good at kneeling." She remembered she had said the very same thing the last time they met, on the docks of Thorlby before the *South Wind* left, and she felt her face burning just as hot as it had then.

But Laithlin did not seem to notice. "The best people aren't." She gestured to another stool beside the firepit. "Sit instead."

Thorn sat, but that was no more comfortable. Queen and minister both tipped their heads back and looked at her through narrowed gray eyes. The resemblance between them was uncanny. Mother and son still, whatever oaths he might have sworn to give up all family but the Ministry. They both gazed at her in calm silence. A double assessment that made Thorn feel the size of a pinhead, and all the while the infant prince sucked, sucked, sucked, and a tiny hand slipped from the fur and pulled at a strand of yellow hair.

"Last time we met," said Laithlin, in the end, "I told you that fools boast of what they will do, while heroes do it. It seems you took my words to heart."

Thorn tried to swallow her nerves. Thorlby might have seemed smaller after all she had seen, famed warriors feeble after all she had done, but the Golden Queen was as awe-inspiring as ever. "I've tried to, my queen."

"Father Yarvi tells me you have become most deadly. He tells me you killed six Horse People in battle on the Denied. That seven men came for the Empress of the South and you fought them alone, unarmed, and won."

"I had help. The best of teachers, and a good man beside me—men, that is. Good men beside me."

Laithlin gave the slightest smile. "You have learned humility, then."

"Thanks to Father Yarvi I've learned many things, my queen."

"Tell me about the Empress of the South."

"Well . . ." All Thorn could think of then was how very different she was from Queen Laithlin. "She is young, and small, and clever—"

"And generous." The queen glanced down at the elf-bangle on Thorn's wrist, which flared with it own pink as she blushed again.

"I tried not to take it, my queen, but—"

"It was meant to break an alliance. It helped forge a new one. I could not have hoped for a better return on my investment. Do you wish you had stayed in the First of Cities?"

Thorn blinked. "I . . ."

"I know the empress asked you to. To stand at her shoulder, and protect her from her enemies, and help steer the course of a great nation. Few indeed will ever receive such an offer."

Thorn swallowed. "Gettland is my home."

"Yes. And here you languish in Thorlby while Grandmother Wexen closes the Shattered Sea to our ships and the Vanstermen swarm across the border, a storied warrior sitting on her strong hands while unripe boys and doddering old men are called upon to fight. My husband the king must seem quite a fool to you. Like a man who goes to mow his meadow with a spoon, and leaves his fine new scythe to rust upon the shelf." The queen peered down at her infant son. "The world changes. It must. But Uthil is a man of iron, and iron does not bend easily to new ways."

"He does not seem himself," murmured Thorn.

The minister and queen exchanged a glance she could not plumb the meaning of. "He is not well," said Yarvi.

"And he must soothe the feelings of older and even more rigid men," said Laithlin.

Thorn licked her lips. "I've done too many foolish things to accuse anyone else of folly, least of all a king."

"But you would like to fight?"

Thorn lifted her chin and held the queen's eye. "It's what I'm made for."

"It must grate on your warrior's pride to be ignored."

"My father told me never to get proud."

"Fine advice." The prince had fallen asleep and Laithlin eased him from her breast and passed him up to Safrit, shrugging her robe closed. "Your father was a Chosen Shield for a time, I understand."

"To King Uthil's mother," murmured Yarvi.

"What became of him?" asked the queen, while Safrit rocked the prince in her arms and gently cooed to him.

Thorn felt the pouch weigh against her chest as she shifted uncomfortably. "He was killed in a duel with Grom-gil-Gorm."

"The Breaker of Swords. A fearsome warrior. A terrible enemy to Gettland. And now we face him again. I once had a Chosen Shield of my own."

"Hurik," said Thorn. "I saw him fight in the training square. He was a great warrior."

"He betrayed me," said the queen, her cold eyes on Thorn. "I had to kill him."

She swallowed. "Oh . . ."

"I have never found one worthy to take his place." There was a long and pregnant silence. "Until now."

Thorn's eyes went wide. She looked at Yarvi, and back to the queen. "Me?"

Yarvi held up his crippled hand. "Not me."

Thorn's heart was suddenly hammering. "But . . . I never passed my warrior's test. I never swore a warrior's oath—"

"You've passed far sterner tests," said the queen, "and the only oath a Chosen Shield must swear is to me."

Thorn slid off her stool and knelt at Laithlin's feet, this time without knocking anything into the fire. "Tell me the words, my queen."

"You are a brave one." Laithlin leaned forward, putting her fingertips gently on Thorn's scarred cheek. "But you should not be rash."

"You should be careful what oaths you swear," said Father Yarvi.

"This is a burden as well as an honor. You might have to fight for me. You might have to die for me."

"Death waits for us all, my queen." Thorn did not have to think. It felt more right than anything she had ever done. "I've dreamed of this since I could hold a sword. I am ready. Tell me the words."

"Father Yarvi?" Koll hurried into the room, flushed with excitement and greatly out of breath.

"Not now, Koll—"

"A crow's come!" And he held out a little scrap of paper, tiny marks scrawled across it.

"Mother Scaer replies, at last." Yarvi spread it out upon his knees, eyes flickering over the signs. Thorn watched in wonder. To capture words in lines on a scrap of nothing seemed like magic to her as surely as what Skifr had done out on the steppe.

"What does it say?" asked Laithlin.

"Grom-gil-Gorm accepts King Uthil's challenge. His raids will cease until midsummer's day. Then the warriors of Vansterland and Gettland will meet in battle at Amon's Tooth." Yarvi turned the paper over, and narrowed his eyes.

"What else?"

"The Breaker of Swords makes a challenge of his own. He asks if King Uthil will meet him in the square, man against man."

"A duel," said Laithlin.

"A duel."

"The king is not well enough to fight." Laithlin looked over at her son. Her minister. "He cannot be well enough to fight."

"With the favor of Father Peace, it will never come to that."

"Your circles move, Father Yarvi."

He crumpled up the paper and tossed it into the firepit. "They move."

"Then we must be ready to ride north within the week." Queen Laithlin stood, tall and stern, wise and beautiful, and kneeling at her feet Thorn thought there could never have been a woman more worth following. "Teach her the words."

HALLEBY

It had rained, and the fire was gone. Everything was gone, more or less. A few charred uprights. A few tottering chimney stacks. The rest of the village of Halleby was mud-churned ash and splinters. A few people picking through for anything worth saving and not finding much. A few others gathered around some fresh turned earth, heads hanging.

"A sorry place at the best of times," muttered Brand.

"And these ain't them," said Rauk.

An old man knelt in the wreckage of a house, all smeared with soot and his wispy hair blowing, croaking at the sky, "They took my sons. They took my sons. They took my sons," over and over.

"Poor bastard." Rauk wiped his running nose on the back of one hand and winced again as he hefted his shield. He'd been wincing ever since they left Thorlby.

"Your arm hurt?" asked Brand.

"Took an arrow a few weeks back. I'm all right." He didn't look all right. He looked thin, and drained out, and his watery eyes held none of the challenge they used to. Brand would never have thought he might miss that. But he did.

"You want me to haul your shield awhile?"

A flicker of that old pride, then Rauk seemed to sag. "Thanks." He let his shield drop, groaned through clenched teeth as he worked his arm around in a circle. "Didn't look much of a wound but, gods, it hurts."

"No doubt it's on the mend already," said Brand, swinging the extra shield across his back.

Didn't look like they'd need it today, the Vanstermen were long gone. Just as well, because it was some sorry scrapings Hunnan had gathered. A couple dozen boys with gear that didn't fit, hardly older than Koll and a lot less use, staring at the burned-out wreckage with big, scared eyes. A handful of greybeards, one without a tooth in his head, another without a hair on his, a third with a sword speckled hilt to blunt point with rust. Then there were the wounded. Rauk, and a fellow who'd lost an eye whose bandages kept leaking, and another with a bad leg who'd slowed them down the whole way, and Sordaf, who'd nothing wrong with him at all far as Brand could tell. Apart from being as big an idiot as ever, of course.

He puffed his cheeks out and gave a weary sigh. He'd left Thorn. Naked. In his bed. No clothes at all. For this. The gods knew he'd made some awful decisions but that had to be the worst. Damn standing in the light, he should've been lying in the warm.

Rauk was kneading his shoulder with his pale hand. "Hope it heals soon. Can't stand in the shield wall with a bad arm. You stood in the wall?" There'd have been a barb in that question, once, but now there was only a hollow dread in his voice.

"Aye, on the Denied." There'd have been a pride in that, once, but now all Brand could think of was the feel of his dagger sinking into flesh and he'd a dread of his own as he spoke. "We fought the Horse People there. Don't know why, really, but . . . we fought 'em. You?"

"I have. A skirmish against some Vanstermen, few months back."

Rauk gave another long sniff, both of 'em chewing at memories they didn't much like the taste of. "You kill anyone?"

"I did." Brand thought of the man's face, still so clear. "You?"

"I did," said Rauk, frowning at the ground.

"Thorn killed six." Brand said it far too loud and far too jolly, but desperate to talk about anything but his own part in it. "Should have seen her fight! Saved my life."

"Some folk take to it." Rauk's watery eyes were still fixed on the mud. "Seemed to me most just get through it though, best they can."

Brand frowned at the burned out wreckage that used to be a village. Used to be some folks' lives. "Being a warrior . . . not all brotherhood and back-slapping, is it?"

"It's not like the songs."

"No." Brand pulled the two shields higher up his shoulder. "No it isn't."

"They took my sons. They took my sons. They took my sons . . ."

Master Hunnan had been talking to a woman who'd got away when the Vanstermen came. Now he strode back over with the thumb of his sword-hand tucked in his belt, gray hair flicked by the wind about a frown harder even than usual.

"They came at sunset two days ago. She thinks two dozen but she's not sure and I reckon fewer. They had dogs with 'em. They killed two men, took ten for slaves, and five or so were sick or old they let burn in their houses."

"Gods," whispered one of the boys, and he made a holy sign over his chest.

Hunnan narrowed his eyes. "This is what war is, boy. What were you expecting?"

"They've been gone two days, then." Brand cast an eye over the old men, and that young lad with the bad leg. "And we're not the fastest moving crew you ever saw. We'll never catch 'em now."

"No." Hunnan's jaw worked as he stared off hard-eyed toward the north. Toward Vansterland. "But we can't let this pass either. There's a Vanstermen's village not far from here. Just over the river."

"Rissentoft," said Sordaf.

"You know it?"

He shrugged. "It's got a good sheep-market. Used to drive lambs there with my uncle in the spring. I know a ford nearby."

"Won't it be watched?" asked Brand.

"We weren't watching it."

"There we go, then." Hunnan worked his sword hilt from the sheath then slapped it back in. "We cross at this ford and head for Rissentoft. Get your skinny arses moving!" And the master-at-arms put his head down and started walking.

Brand hurried after him, speaking low, not wanting to start an argument in front of the others, they'd got doubts enough as it was. "Master Hunnan, wait. If it was wrong when they did it to us, how's it right if we do it to them?"

"If we can't hurt the shepherds, we'll have to hurt the flock."

"It wasn't sheep did this, nor shepherds neither. It was warriors."

"This is war," said Hunnan, his mouth twisting. "Right's got nothing to do with it. King Uthil said steel is the answer, so steel it has to be."

Brand waved his hand toward the miserable survivors, picking over the wreckage of their homes. "Shouldn't we stay and help them? What good will burning some other village do just 'cause it's across a river—"

Hunnan rounded on him. "Might help the next village, or the one after that! We're warriors not nursemaids! You got a second chance, boy, but I'm starting to think I was right after all, and you've got more Father Peace than Mother War in you." Looking at Mother War's handiwork behind them, Brand wondered whether that was such a bad thing. "What if it was your family died here, eh? Your house burned? Your sister made some Vansterman's slave? Would you be for vengeance then?"

Brand looked over his shoulder toward the other lads, following in a meager straggle. Then he gave a sigh and hefted the two shields.

"Aye," he said. "I guess I would."

But he couldn't see how any good would come of this.

FIRE

"Reckon I need a new sword."

Thorn tossed her father's rattling down on the table.

Rin gave the blade she was working on another grating stroke with the polishing stone and frowned over at her. "This seems familiar."

"Very. But I'm hoping for a different answer this time around."

"Because you bedded my brother?"

"Because there's going to be a battle, and Queen Laithlin wants her Chosen Shield suitably armed."

Rin set her stone aside and walked over, slapping dust from her hands. "The Queen's Chosen Shield? You?"

Thorn raised her chin and stared back. "Me."

They watched each other for a long moment, then Rin picked up Thorn's sword, spun it over, rubbed at the cheap pommel with her thumb, laid it back down and planted her hands on her hips. "If Queen Laithlin says it's so, I guess it's so."

"It's so," said Thorn.

"We'll need some bone."

"What for?"

"To bind with the iron and make steel." Rin nodded over at the bright blade clamped to the bench, gray steel-dust gathered under it. "I used a hawk's for that one. But I've used a wolf's. A bear's. Do it right, you trap the animal's spirit in the blade. So you pick something strong. Something deadly. Something that means something to you."

Thorn thought about that for a moment, then the idea came and she started to smile. She pulled the pouch from around her neck and tipped the smooth and yellowed little lumps out across the table. She'd worn them long enough. Time to put them to better use. "How about a hero's bones?"

Rin raised her brows at them. "Even better."

THEY STOPPED IN AN ash-scattered clearing by the river, a ring of stones in the center blackened as if it had held one hell of a fire.

Rin swung the big bag of tools down from her shoulder. "We're here."

"Did we have to come so far?" Thorn dumped the coal sacks, stretching out her back and wiping her sweating face on her forearm.

"Don't want my secrets stolen. Talking of which, tell anyone what happens here I'll have to kill you." Rin tossed Thorn a shovel. "Now get in the river and dig out some clay."

Thorn frowned sideways, sucking at the hole in her teeth. "I'm starting to think Skifr was an easier master."

"Who's Skifr?"

"Never mind."

She waded out to her waist in the stream, the water so cold it made her gasp in spite of the summer warmth, and set to cutting clay from the bed and slopping it onto the bank in gray shovelfuls.

Rin put some dull lumps of iron-stone in a jar, along with the black ash of Thorn's father's bones, and a sprinkle of sand, and two glass beads, then she started smearing clay around the lid, sealing it shut.

"What's the glass for?" asked Thorn.

"To trick the dirt out of the iron," murmured Rin, without looking up. "The hotter we get the furnace the purer the steel and the stronger the blade."

"How did you learn all this?"

"I was apprentice to a smith called Gaden. I watched some others. I talked to some sword-merchants from down the Divine." Rin tapped at the side of her head and left a smear of clay there. "The rest I worked out for myself."

"You're a clever girl, aren't you?"

"When it comes to steel." Rin set the clay jar carefully in the middle of the ring of stones. "Back in the river, then."

So Thorn sloshed out shivering into the stream again while Rin built the furnace. She heaped coal up inside, stones outside, and mortared them with clay until she'd built a thing looked like a great domed bread-oven, chest high, with an opening at the bottom.

"Help me seal it." Rin dug up clay with her hands and Thorn did the same, smearing it thick over the outside. "What's it like? Being a Chosen Shield?"

"Dreamed of it all my life," said Thorn, puffing herself up. "And I can't think of anyone I'd rather serve than Queen Laithlin."

Rin nodded. "They don't call her the Golden Queen for nothing."

"It's a high honor."

"No doubt. But what's it like?"

Thorn sagged. "So far, boring. Since I swore the oath I've spent most of my time standing in the queen's counting house, frowning at merchants while they ask her for favors that might as well be in a foreign tongue for all I understand them."

"Wondering if you made a mistake?" asked Rin, digging up another handful of gray mush.

"No," snapped Thorn, and then, after a moment spent squashing more clay into the cracks, "Maybe. It'd hardly be my first."

"You ain't at all as tough you make out, are you?"

Thorn took a long breath. "Who is?"

———

RIN BLEW GENTLY ON her shovel, the coals rustling as they glowed bright, then she got on her belly and rammed them deep into the mouth of the furnace, puffing out her cheeks as she blew hard, over and over. Finally she rocked back on her heels, watching the fire taking the coal, flame flickering orange inside the vent.

"What's happening between you and Brand?" she asked.

Thorn had known it was coming, but that didn't make it any more comfortable. "I don't know."

"Not that complicated a question, is it?"

"You wouldn't think so."

"Well, are you done with him?"

"No," said Thorn, surprised by how firm she sounded.

"Did he say he was done with you?"

"We both know Brand's not much at saying things. But I wouldn't be surprised. Not exactly what men dream of, am I?"

Rin frowned at her for a moment. "I reckon different men dream of different things. Just like different women."

"Couldn't have taken off running much sooner, though, could he?"

"He's wanted to be a warrior a long time. That was his chance."

"Aye." Thorn took a long breath. "Thought it'd get simpler when . . . you know."

"But it didn't get simpler?"

Thorn scrubbed at her shaved head, feeling the bald scar in the stubble. "No, it bloody didn't. I don't know what we're doing, Rin. I wish I did but I don't. I've never been any good at anything but fighting."

"You never know. You might find a talent at working bellows too." And Rin dropped them beside the mouth of the furnace.

"When you've a load to lift," muttered Thorn as she knelt, "you're better lifting than weeping." And she gritted her teeth and made those bellows wheeze until her shoulders were aching and her chest was burning and her vest was soaked through with sweat.

"Harder," said Rin. "Hotter." And she started singing out prayers, soft and low, to He Who Makes the Flame, and She Who Strikes the Anvil, and Mother War too, the Mother of Crows, who gathers the dead and makes the open hand a fist.

Thorn worked until that vent looked like a gate to hell in the gathering darkness, like a dragon's maw in the twilight. Worked until, even though she'd helped carry a ship each way over the tall hauls, she wasn't sure she'd ever worked harder.

Rin snorted. "Out of the way, killer, I'll show you how it's done."

And she set to, as calm and strong and steady at the bellows as her brother at the oar. The coals glowed up hotter yet as the stars came out above, and Thorn muttered out a prayer of her own, a prayer to her father, and reached for the pouch around her neck but his bones were gone into the steel, and that felt right.

She sloshed out into the river and drank, soaked to the skin, and sloshed back out to take another turn, imagining the bellows were Grom-gil-Gorm's head, on and on until she was dried out by the furnace then soaked with sweat again. Finally they worked together, side by side, the heat like a great hand pressing on Thorn's face, red-blue flames flickering from the vent and smoke pouring from the baked clay sides of the furnace and sparks showering up into the night where Father Moon sat big and fat and white above the trees.

Just when it seemed Thorn's chest was going to burst and her arms come right off her shoulders Rin said, "Enough," and the pair of them flopped back, soot-smeared and gasping.

"What now?"

"Now we wait for it to cool." Rin dragged a tall bottle out of her pack and pulled out the stopper. "And we get a little drunk." She took a long swig, soot-smeared neck shifting as she swallowed, then handed the bottle to Thorn, wiping her mouth.

"You know the way to a woman's heart." Thorn closed her eyes, and smelled good ale, and soon after tasted it, and soon after swallowed it, and smacked her dry lips. Rin was setting the shovel in the shimmering haze on top of the furnace, tossed bacon hissing onto the metal.

"You've got all kinds of skills, don't you?"

"I've done a few jobs in my time." And Rin cracked eggs onto the shovel that straight away began to bubble. "There's going to be a battle, then?"

"Looks that way. At Amon's Tooth."

Rin sprinkled salt. "Would Brand fight in it?"

"I guess we both would. Father Yarvi's got other ideas, though. He usually does."

"I hear he's a deep-cunning man."

"No doubt, but he's not sharing his cleverness."

"Deep-cunning folk don't tend to," said Rin, flipping the bacon with a knife blade.

"Gorm's offered a challenge to King Uthil to settle it."

"A duel? There's never been a finer swordsman than Uthil, has there?"

"Not at his best. But he's far from his best."

"I heard a rumor he was ill." Rin pulled the shovel from the furnace and dropped down on her haunches, laying it between them, the smell of meat and eggs making Thorn's mouth flood with spit.

"Saw him in the Godshall yesterday," said Thorn. "Trying to look like he was made of iron but, in spite of Father Yarvi's plant-lore, I swear, he could hardly stand."

"Doesn't sound good, with a battle coming." Rin pulled a spoon out and offered it to Thorn.

"No. It doesn't sound good."

They started stuffing food in and, after all that work, Thorn wasn't sure she'd ever tasted better. "Gods," she said around a mouthful, "a woman who can make fine eggs and fine swords *and* brings fine ale with her? It doesn't work out with Brand I'll marry you."

Rin snorted. "If the boys show as much interest as they've been doing I might count that a fine match."

They laughed together at that, and ate, and got a little drunk, the furnace still hot on their faces.

"YOU SNORE, DO YOU know that?"

Thorn jerked awake, rubbing her eyes, Mother Sun just showing herself in the stony sky. "It has been commented on."

"Time to break this open, I reckon. See what we've got."

Rin set to knocking the furnace apart with a hammer, Thorn raking the still smoking coals away, hand over her face as a tricking breeze sent ash and embers whirling. Rin delved in with tongs and pulled the jar out of the midst, yellow hot. She swung it onto a flat stone, broke it open, knocking white dust away, pulling something from inside like a nut from its shell.

The steel bound with her father's bones, glowing sullen red, no bigger than a fist.

"Is it good?" asked Thorn.

Rin tapped it, turned it over, and slowly began to smile. "Aye. It's good."

RISSENTOFT

In the songs, Angulf Clovenfoot's Gettlanders fell upon the Vanstermen like hawks from an evening sky.

Master Hunnan's misfits fell on Rissentoft like a herd of sheep down a steep flight of steps.

The lad with the game leg could hardly walk by the time they reached the river and they'd left him sore and sorry on the south bank. The rest of them got soaked through at the ford and one lad had his shield carried off by the current. Then they got turned around in an afternoon mist and it wasn't until near dark, all worn-out, clattering and grumbling, that they stumbled on the village.

Hunnan cuffed one boy around the head for quiet then split them up with gestures, sent them scurrying in groups of five down the streets, or down the hardened dirt between the shacks, at least.

"Stay close!" Brand hissed to Rauk, who was straggling behind, shield dangling, looking more pale and tired than ever.

"The place is empty," growled the toothless old-timer, and he looked to have the right of it. Brand crept along a wall and peered through a door hanging open. Not so much as a dog moving anywhere. Apart from the stink of poverty, an aroma he was well familiar with, the place was abandoned.

"They must've heard us coming," he muttered.

The old man raised one brow. "You think?"

"There's one here!" came a scared shriek, and Brand took off running, scrambled around the corner of a wattle shack, shield up.

An old man stood at the door of a house with his hands raised. Not a big house, or a pretty house. Just a house. He had a stoop to his back, and gray hair braided beside his face the way the Vanstermen wore it. Three of Hunnan's lads stood in a half-circle about him, spears levelled.

"I'm not armed," he said, holding his hands higher. They had something of a shake to them and Brand hardly blamed him. "I don't want to fight."

"Some of us don't," said Hunnan, stepping between the lads with his sword drawn. "But sometimes a fight finds us anyway."

"I got nothing you want." The old man stared about nervously as they gathered around him. "Please. Just don't want my house burned. Built it with my wife."

"Where's she?" asked Hunnan.

The old man swallowed, his gray-stubbled throat shifting. "She died last winter."

"What about those in Halleby? You think they wanted their houses burned?"

"I knew folk in Halleby." The man licked his lips. "I didn't have nought to do with that."

"Not surprised to hear about it, though, are you?" And Hunnan hit him with his sword. It opened a great gash in his arm and he yelped, staggered, clutched at his doorframe as he fell.

"Oh," said one of the boys.

Hunnan stepped up with a snarl and chopped the old man in the back of the head with a sound like a spade chopping earth. He rolled over, shuddering, tongue stuck out rigid. Then he lay still, blood spreading across his door-stone, pooling in the deep-cut runes of the gods that guarded his house.

Same gods that guarded the houses in Thorlby. Seemed they weren't watching right then.

Brand stared, cold all over. Happened so fast he'd no time to stop it. No time to think about whether he wanted to stop it, even. Just happened, and they all stood there and watched.

"Spread out," said Hunnan. "Search the houses, then burn 'em. Burn 'em all." The bald old man shook his head, and Brand felt sick inside, but they did as they were bid.

"I'll stay here," said Rauk, tossing down his shield and sitting on it.

Brand shouldered open the nearest door and froze. A low room, much like the one he and Rin used to share, and by the firepit a woman stood. A skinny woman in a dirty dress, couple of years older than Brand. She stood with one hand on the wall, staring at him, breathing hard. Scared out of her wits, he reckoned.

"You all right?" called Sordaf from outside.

"Aye," said Brand.

"Well, bloody hell!" The fat lad grinned as he ducked his head under the low doorway. "Not quite empty, I reckon." He uncoiled some rope, sawed off a length with his knife, and handed it over. "Reckon she'll get a decent price, you lucky bastard."

"Aye," said Brand.

Sordaf went out shaking his head. "War's all bloody luck, I swear . . ."

The woman didn't speak and neither did Brand. He tied the rope around her neck, not too tight, not too loose, and she didn't so much as twitch. He made the other end fast around his wrist, and all the while he felt numb and strange. This was what warriors did in the songs, wasn't it? Take slaves? Didn't seem much like doing good to Brand. Didn't seem anywhere near it. But if it wasn't him took her it'd be one of the others. That was what warriors did.

Outside they were already torching the houses. The woman made a sort of moan when she saw the dead old man. Another when the thatch on her hovel went up. Brand didn't know what to say to her, or to anyone else, and he was used to keeping silent, so he said nothing. One of the boys had tears streaking his face as he set his torch to the houses, but he set it to them all the same. Soon the air was thick with the smell of burning, wood popping and crackling as the fire spread, flaming straw floating high into the gloom.

"Where's the sense in this?" muttered Brand.

But Rauk just rubbed at his shoulder.

"One slave." Sordaf spat with disgust. "And some sausages. Not much of a haul."

"We didn't come for a haul," said Master Hunnan, frown set tight. "We came to do good."

And Brand stood, holding on to a rope tied around a woman's neck, and watched a village burn.

THEY ATE STALE BREAD in silence, stretched out on the chill ground in silence. They were still in Vansterland and could afford no fire, every man alone with his thoughts, all darkling strangers to each other.

Brand waited for the faintest glimmer of dawn, gray cracks in the black cloud overhead. Wasn't as if he'd been sleeping, anyway. Kept thinking about that old man. And the boy crying as he set fire to the thatch. Kept listening to the woman breathing who was now his slave, his property, because he'd put a rope around her neck and burned her house.

"Get up," hissed Brand, and she slowly stood. He couldn't see her face but there was a slump to her shoulders like nothing mattered any more.

Sordaf was on watch, now, blowing into his fat hands and rubbing them together and blowing into 'em again.

"We're going off a bit," said Brand, nodding toward the treeline not far away.

Sordaf gave him a grin. "Can't say I blame you. Chilly night."

Brand turned his back on him and started walking, tugged at the rope and felt the woman shuffling after. Under the trees and through the undergrowth they went, no words said, sticks cracking under Brand's boots, until the camp was far behind. An owl hooted somewhere and he dragged the woman down into the brush, waiting, but there was no one there.

He wasn't sure how long it took them to reach the far side of the wood, but Mother Sun was a gray smudge in the east when they stepped from the trees. He pulled out the dagger Rin made for him and cut the rope carefully from around the woman's neck.

"Go, then," he said. She just stood staring. He pointed out the way. "Go."

She took one step, and looked back, then another, as if she expected some trick. He stood still.

"Thanks," she whispered.

Brand winced. "I don't deserve thanking. Just go."

She took off fast. He watched her run back the way they'd come, through the wet grass, down the gentle slope. As Mother Sun crawled higher he could see Rissentoft in the distance, a black smear on the land, still smoldering.

He reckoned it must've looked a lot like Halleby before the war started.

Now it did again.

FROZEN LAKES

The king's household halted in the spitting rain above the camp, a thousand fires sprawling under the darkening sky, pinprick torches trickling into the valley as the warriors of Gettland gathered. Thorn sprang down and offered the queen her hand. Not that Laithlin needed any help, she was twice the rider Thorn was. But Thorn was desperate to be useful.

In the songs, Chosen Shields protected their queens from assassins, or carried secret messages into the mouth of danger, or fought duels on which the fates of nations rested. Probably she should have learned by now not to take songs too seriously.

She found herself lost among an endlessly shifting legion of slaves and servants, trailing after the Golden Queen like the tail after a comet, besieging her with a thousand questions to which, whether she was nursing the heir to the throne at the time or not, she always had the answers. King Uthil might have sat in the Black Chair but, after a few days in Laithlin's company, it was plain to Thorn who really ruled Gettland.

There was no trace of the easy companionship she'd had with Vi-aline. No earnest talks or demands to be called by her first name. Laithlin was more than twice Thorn's age: a wife and mother, a peerless merchant, the mistress of a great household, as beautiful as she was deep-cunning as she was masterfully controlled. She was everything a woman should be and more. Everything Thorn wasn't.

"My thanks," Laithlin murmured, taking Thorn's hand and making even sliding down from a saddle look graceful.

"I want only to serve."

The queen did not let go of her hand. "No. You were not born to stand in dusty meetings and count coins. You want to fight."

Thorn swallowed. "Give me the chance."

"Soon enough." Laithlin leaned close, gripping Thorn's hand tight. "An oath of loyalty cuts both ways. I forgot that once, and never will again. We shall do great things together, you and I. Things to sing of."

"My king?" Father Yarvi's voice, and sharp with worry.

Uthil had stumbled climbing from his own saddle and now he was leaning heavily on his minister, gray as a ghost, chest heaving as he clutched his drawn sword against it.

"We will speak later," said Laithlin, letting go of Thorn's hand.

"Koll, boil water!" called Father Yarvi. "Safrit, bring my plants!"

"I saw that man walk a hundred miles through the ice and never falter," said Rulf, standing beside Thorn with his arms folded. "The king is not well."

"No." Thorn watched Uthil shamble into his tent with one arm over his minister's shoulders. "And with a great battle coming. Poor luck indeed."

"Father Yarvi doesn't believe in luck."

"I don't believe in helmsmen, but they dog me even so."

Rulf chuckled at that. "How's your mother?"

Thorn frowned across at him. "Unhappy with my choices, as always."

"Still striking sparks from each other?"

"Since you ask, not near so much as we used to."

"Oh? I reckon one of you must have grown up a little."

Thorn narrowed her eyes. "Maybe one of us had a wise old warrior to teach them the value of family."

"Everyone should be so lucky." Rulf peered down at the ground, rubbing at his beard. "I've been thinking, perhaps . . . I should pay her a visit."

"You asking my permission?"

"No. But I'd like to have it, still."

Thorn gave a helpless shrug. "Far be it from me to come between a pair of young lovers."

"Or me." Rulf gave a meaningful look past her from under his brows. "Which is why I'll be dwindling into the west, I think . . ."

Thorn turned, and Brand was walking toward her.

She had been hoping she might see him, but as soon as she did she felt a surge of nerves. As if she was stepping into the training square for the first time and he was her opponent. They should have been familiar to each other now, surely? But of a sudden she had no idea how to be with him. Prickly-playful, like one oar-mate with another? Simpering soft, like a maiden with a suitor? Frosty-regal, like Queen Laithlin with a debtor? Creepy-cautious, like a clever gambler keeping her dice well hidden?

Each step he came closer felt like a step back out onto that frozen lake, ice creaking under her weight, no notion what the next footfall might bring.

"Thorn," he said, looking her in the eye.

"Brand," she said, looking back.

"Couldn't stand to wait for me any longer, eh?"

Prickly-playful, then. "The suitors were queued up outside my house all the way to the bloody docks. There's only so much of men weeping over my beauty I can stand." And she pressed a fingertip to one side of her nose and blew snot into the mud out of the other.

"You've a new sword," he said, looking down at her belt.

She hooked a finger under the plain crosspiece and drew it halfway so he could draw it the rest with the faintest ringing. "From the best blade-maker in the Shattered Sea."

"Gods, she's got good." He brushed Rin's mark on the fuller with his thumb, swished the blade one way and the other, lifted it to peer with one eye down the length, Mother Sun flashing along the bright steel and glinting on the point.

"Didn't have time to do anything fancy with it," said Thorn, "but I'm getting to like it plain."

Brand softly whistled. "That is fine steel."

"Cooked with a hero's bones."

"Is that so?"

"Reckon I'd had my fathers fingers about my neck for long enough."

He grinned as he offered the sword back to her, and she found she was grinning too. "I thought Rin said no to you?"

"No one says no to Queen Laithlin."

Brand had that old puzzled look of his. "Eh?"

"She wanted her Chosen Shield suitably armed," she said, slapping the sword back into its scabbard.

He gaped at her in silence while that sank in.

"I know what you're thinking." Thorn's shoulders slumped. "I don't even have a shield."

He snapped his mouth shut. "I'm thinking you are the shield, and none better. If I was a queen I'd pick you."

"Hate to crush your hopes, but I doubt you'll ever be queen."

"None of the gowns would suit me." He slowly shook his head, starting to smile again. "Thorn Bathu, Chosen Shield."

"What about you? Did you save Gettland, yet? Saw you gathering on the beach. Quite the crowd of young champions. Not to mention a couple of ancient ones."

Brand winced. "Can't say we saved much of anything. We killed an old farmer. We stole some sausages. We burned a village 'cause it was on the wrong side of a river. We took a slave." Brand scratched at his head. "I let her go."

"You just can't help doing good, can you?"

"Don't think Hunnan sees it that way. He'd like to tell everyone I'm a disgrace but he'd have to admit his raid was a disgrace, so . . ." He puffed out his cheeks, looking more puzzled than ever. "I'm swearing my warrior's oath tomorrow. Along with some lads never swung a blade in anger."

Thorn put on Father Yarvi's voice. "Let Father Peace spill tears over the methods! Mother War smiles upon results! You must be pleased."

He looked down at the ground. "I suppose so."

"You're not?"

"Do you ever feel bad? About those men you've killed?"

"Not a lot. Why should I?"

"I'm not saying you should. I'm just asking if you do."

"I don't."

"Well, you're touched by Mother War."

"Touched?" Thorn snorted. "She's slapped me purple."

"Being a warrior, brothers at my shoulder, it's what I always wanted . . ."

"There's no disappointment like getting what you've always wanted."

"Some things are worth the wait," he said, looking her in the eye.

She had no doubts at all what that look meant now. She was starting to wonder if getting across this frozen lake of theirs might not be so hard. Maybe you just took one step at a time, and tried to enjoy the thrill of it. So she took a little pace closer to him. "Where are you sleeping?"

He didn't back off. "Under the stars, I reckon."

"A Chosen Shield gets a tent."

"You trying to make me jealous?"

"No, it's only a small one." She moved another little step. "But it's got a bed."

"I'm getting to like this story."

"Bit cold, though." She moved another little step, and they were both smiling. "On my own."

"I could have a word with Sordaf for you, reckon he could warm a blanket with one fart."

"Sordaf's everything most women could ask for, but I've always had odd tastes." She reached up, using her fingers like a comb, and pushed the hair out of his face. "I had someone else in mind."

"There's a lot of folk watching," said Brand.

"Like I care a damn."

COWARDICE

They knelt in a line. Three of the young lads and Brand. Two had pointed spears at an old farmer. One had cried as he set fire to some houses. The last had let the only slave they took go.

Some warriors.

Yet here they were, with the fighting men of Gettland gathered about them in an armed and armored crowd, ready to welcome them into their brotherhood. Ready to have them at their shoulders when they met Grom-gil-Gorm and his Vanstermen at the appointed place. Ready to carry them into the iron embrace of Mother War.

King Uthil had changed a lot in the year since Brand saw him last, and not for the better. His skin had turned the same iron-gray as his hair, rheumy eyes sunken in dark shadows. He seemed shrivelled in his chair, scarcely moving, as though the King's Circle on his brow was a crushing weight, hands trembling as he hugged his naked sword.

Father Yarvi perched on a stool at the king's side, Queen Laithlin sat bolt upright on the other, shoulders back, fists clenched on her knees, sweeping the crowd with her pale stare as though she could make up for her husband's weakness with her strength.

Thorn stood at the queen's shoulder, pointed chin up and with a challenge in her eyes, arms folded and the elf-bangle burning a chill white on her wrist. She looked like something from the songs, a Chosen Shield from her toes to her half-shaved scalp. Brand could hardly believe he'd clambered out of her bed an hour before. At least he had one thing to feel pleased about.

The king looked slowly down the line of boys to Brand, and cleared his throat.

"You are young," he said, voice so crackly quiet it could hardly be heard over the wind flapping the tent cloth. "But Master Hunnan has judged you worthy, and Gettland is beset by enemies." He raised himself a little in his seat, a glimpse of the man whose speech Brand had thrilled to on the beach before Thorlby. "We march to Amon's Tooth to meet the Vanstermen in battle, and we need every shield!" He was caught by a coughing fit, and croaked out, "Steel is the answer." Then slumped back in his chair, Father Yarvi leaning close to whisper in his ear.

Master Hunnan stepped up with sword in hand and frown on face to stand over the first of the boys. "Do you swear loyalty to Gettland?"

The lad swallowed. "I do."

"Do you swear to serve your king?"

"I do."

"Do you swear to stand by your shoulder-man in the shield wall, and obey your betters?"

"I do."

"Then rise a warrior of Gettland!"

The boy did, looking a lot more scared than happy, and all about him men drummed fists on their chests, clattered ax-hafts on shield rims, thumped boots on the earth in approval.

It took a moment's struggle for Brand to swallow. Soon it would be his turn. Should have been the proudest day of his life. But as he thought of the ashes of Halleby and Rissentoft, of the old man bleeding on his doorstep and the woman with the rope around her neck, pride wasn't his first feeling.

The crowd cheered as the second boy said his third "I do" and the man behind jerked him to his feet like a fish from a pond.

Brand caught Thorn's eye, and her mouth curled up in the faintest smile. He would've smiled back, if he hadn't been churning with doubts. Do good, his mother told him with her dying breath. What good had they done at Rissentoft the other night?

The third lad had tears in his eyes again as he swore his oaths, but the warriors took them for tears of pride and gave him the loudest cheer so far, the clashing of weapons cutting at Brand's jangling nerves.

Hunnan worked his jaw, frown hardening even further as Brand stepped up to him, and the men fell silent.

"Do you swear loyalty to Gettland?"

"I do," croaked Brand, his mouth dry.

"Do you swear to serve your king?"

"I do," croaked Brand, heart thumping in his ears.

"Do you swear to stand by your shoulder-man in the shield wall, and obey your betters?"

Brand opened his mouth, but the words didn't come. Silence stretched out. Smiles faded. He felt every eye on him. There was a faint scraping of metal as warriors stirred uneasily.

"Well?" snapped Hunnan.

"No."

The silence stretched for a pregnant moment longer, like the silence before a cloudburst, then a disbelieving mutter started up.

Hunnan stared down, astonished. "What?"

"Stand, boy," came the king's rasping voice, the noise growing angrier as Brand got to his feet. "I never heard of such a thing before. Why will you not swear your oath?"

"Because he's a coward," snarled Hunnan.

More muttering, angrier still. The boy beside Brand stared at him with wide eyes. Rulf bunched his fists. Father Yarvi raised one brow. Thorn took a step forward, her mouth twisting, but the queen stopped her with a raised finger.

With a wincing effort the king held up one bony hand, eyes on Brand, and his warriors fell silent. "I asked him."

"Maybe I am a coward," said Brand, though his voice sounded out a good deal more boldly than usual. "Master Hunnan killed an old farmer the other night, and I was too coward to stop him. We burned a village and I was too coward to speak out. He set three students on one as a test and I was too coward to stand for the one. Standing for the weak against the strong. Isn't that what a warrior should be?"

"Damn you for a liar!" snarled Hunnan, "I'll—"

"You'll hold your tongue!" growled Father Yarvi, "until the king asks you to speak."

The master-at-arms' frown was murderous, but Brand didn't care. He felt as if a load was lifted. As if he'd had the *South Wind*'s weight across his shoulders again, and suddenly let go. He felt, for the first time since he left Thorlby, as if he was standing in the light.

"You want someone with no fear?" He stuck his arm straight out. "There she stands. Thorn Bathu, the Queen's Chosen Shield. In the First of Cities she fought seven men alone and saved the Empress of the South. They're singing songs of it all about the Shattered Sea! And yet you'd rather take boys who scarcely know which end of a spear to hold. What mad pride is that? What foolishness? I used to dream of being a warrior. To serve you, my king. To fight for my country. To have a loyal brother always at my shoulder." He looked Hunnan right in the eye, and shrugged. "If this is what it means to be a warrior, I want no part of it."

The anger burst out once again, and once again King Uthil had to lift a trembling hand for silence.

"Some here might not care for your words," he said. "But they are not the words of a coward. Some men are touched by Father Peace." His tired eyes swiveled toward Yarvi, and then toward Thorn, and one eyelid began to flicker. "Just as some women are touched by Mother War. Death . . . waits for us all." The hand upon his sword was suddenly trembling worse than ever. "We each must find our own . . . right path . . . to her door . . ."

He keeled forward. Father Yarvi darted from his stool and caught the king before he fell, his sword sliding from his lap and clattering in the mud. Between him and Rulf they lifted Uthil from his chair and walked him back into his tent. His head lolled. His feet dragged in the dirt. The muttering came up stronger than ever, but shocked and fearful now.

"The king dropped his sword."

"An ill omen."

"Poor weaponluck."

"The favor of the gods is elsewhere . . ."

"Calm yourselves!" Queen Laithlin stood, sweeping the crowd with icy scorn. "Are these warriors of Gettland or prattling slave-girls?" She had taken the king's sword from the dirt, hugging it to her chest as he had done, but there was no quiver to her hand, no dampness in her eye, no weakness in her voice. "This is no time for doubts! The Breaker of Swords waits for us at Amon's Tooth! The king may not be with us, but we know what he would say."

"Steel is the answer!" barked Thorn, the elf-bangle flaring hot red.

"Steel!" roared Master Hunnan, holding high his sword, and metal hissed as more blades were drawn, and stabbed toward the sky.

"Steel! Steel! Steel!" came the chant from a hundred throats.

Brand was the only one who stayed silent. He'd always thought doing good meant fighting alongside his brothers. But maybe doing good meant not fighting at all.

THE APPOINTED PLACE

The armies of Vansterland and Gettland glared at each other across a shallow valley of lush, green grass.

"A fine spot to graze a herd of sheep," said Rulf.

"Or to fight a battle." Thorn narrowed her eyes and scanned the ridge opposite. She had never in her life seen a host half the size, the warriors picked out black on the crest against the bright sky, here or there a blade flashing as it caught the light of Mother Sun. The Vanstermen's shield wall was drawn up loose, their shields blobs of bright-painted color and their spears a bristling forest behind. Grom-gil-Gorm's dark banner hung limp over the center, a dusting of archers thrust out in front, more lightly armed skirmishers on each wing.

"So like our own army we might be looking in a great mirror," murmured Yarvi.

"Apart from that damn elf-tower," said Thorn.

Amon's Tooth rose from a rocky outcrop at the far end of the Vanstermen's line, a hollow tower thirty times a man's height, tall and slender as a tapering sword blade, made from hollow cobwebs of elf-metal bars.

"What did it used to be?" asked Koll, gazing up at it in wonder.

"Who can say now?" said the minister. "A signal tower? A monument to the arrogance of the elves? A temple to the One God they broke into many?"

"I can tell you what it will be." Rulf gazed grimly at the host gathered in its shadow. "A grave-marker. A grave for many hundreds."

"Many hundreds of Vanstermen," snapped Thorn. "I reckon our host the larger."

"Aye," said Rulf. "But it's seasoned warriors win battles, and the numbers there are much the same."

"And Gorm is known for keeping some horsemen out of sight," said Father Yarvi. "Our strength is closely matched."

"And only one of us has our king." Rulf glanced back toward the camp. Uthil had not left his sick bed since the previous evening. Some said the Last Door stood open for him, and Father Yarvi had not denied it.

"Even a victory will leave Gettland weakened," said the minster, "and Grandmother Wexen well knows it. This battle is all part of her design. She knew King Uthil could never turn down a challenge. The only victory here is if we do not fight at all."

"What elf-spell have you worked to make that happen?" asked Thorn.

Father Yarvi gave his brittle smile. "I hope a little minister's magic may do the trick."

Koll plucked at his sparse shadow of a beard as he looked across the valley. "I wonder if Fror's among them."

"Maybe," said Thorn. A man they had trained with, laughed with, fought beside, rowed beside.

"What will you do if you meet him in the battle?"

"Probably kill him."

"Let's hope you don't meet, then." Koll lifted an arm to point. "They're coming!"

Gorm's banner was on the move, a party of horsemen breaking from the center of his host and coming down the slope. Thorn nudged her way through the king's most favored warriors to Laithlin's side, but the queen waved her away. "Keep to the back, Thorn, and stay hooded."

"My place is beside you."

"Today you are not my shield but my sword. Sometimes a blade is best hidden. If your moment comes, you will know it."

"Yes, my queen."

Reluctantly, Thorn pulled up her hood, waited until the rest of the royal party had set off, then slouching in her saddle like a thief, in a place no songs are sung of, followed at the back. Down the long slope they trotted, hooves flicking mud from the soft ground. Two standard-bearers went with them, Laithlin's gold and Uthil's iron-gray bravely snapping as the breeze took them.

Closer drew the Vanstermen, and closer. Twenty of their most storied warriors, high-helmed, stern-frowned, braids in their hair and gold rings forged into their mail. And at the fore, the necklace of pommels twisted from the swords of his fallen enemies four-times looped about his great neck, came the man who killed Thorn's father. Grom-gil-Gorm, the Breaker of Swords, in his full battle glory. On his left rode his standard-bearer, a great Shend slave with a garnet-studded thrall collar, black cloth flapping behind him. On his right rode two stocky white-haired boys, one with a mocking smile and Gorm's huge shield upon his back, the other with a warlike sneer and Gorm's great sword. Between them and the king, her jaw working so hard that her shaved scalp squirmed, rode Mother Scaer.

"Greetings, Gettlanders!" The hooves of Gorm's towering horse squelched as he pulled it up in the valley's marshy bottom and grinned into the bright sky. "Mother Sun smiles upon our meeting!"

"A good omen," said Father Yarvi.

"For which of us?" asked Gorm.

"For both of us, perhaps?" Laithlin nudged her own mount forward. Thorn itched to ride up close beside where she could protect her, but forced her heels to be still.

"Queen Laithlin! How can your wisdom and beauty so defy the passing years?"

"How can your strength and courage?" asked the queen.

Gorm scratched thoughtfully at his beard. "When last I was in Thorlby I did not seem to be held in such high regard."

"The gods give no finer gift than a good enemy, my husband always says. Gettland could ask for no better enemy than the Breaker of Swords."

"You flatter me, and I enjoy it hugely. But where is King Uthil? I was so looking forward to renewing the friendship we forged in his Godshall."

"I fear my husband could not come," said Laithlin. "He sends me in his place."

Gorm gave a disappointed pout. "Few warriors so renowned. The battle will be the lesser for his absence. But the Mother of Crows waits for no man, whatever his fame."

"There is another choice." Yarvi eased his horse up beside the queen's. "A way in which bloodshed could be spared. A way in which we of the north could free ourselves from the yoke of the High King in Skekenhouse."

Gorm raised a brow. "Are you a magician as well as a minister?"

"We both pray to the same gods, both sing of the same heroes, both endure the same weather. Yet Grandmother Wexen turns us one against the other. If there is a battle at Amon's Tooth today, whoever is the victor, only she will win. What could Vansterland and Gettland not achieve together?" He leaned eagerly forward in his saddle. "Let us make of the fist an open hand! Let there be an alliance between us!"

Thorn gave a gasp at that, and she was not alone. A muttering went through the warriors on both sides, breathed oaths and angry glances, but the Breaker of Swords held up his hand for quiet.

"A bold idea, Father Yarvi. No doubt you are a deep-cunning man. You speak for Father Peace, as a minister should." Gorm worked his mouth unhappily, took a long breath through his nose, and let it sigh away. "But I fear it cannot be. My minister is of a different mind."

Yarvi blinked at Mother Scaer. "She is?"

"My new minister is."

"Greetings, Father Yarvi." Gorm's young white-haired sword-and shield-bearers parted to let a rider through, a cloaked rider upon a pale horse. She pushed her hood back and the wind blew up chill, lashing the yellow hair about her gaunt face, eyes fever-bright as she smiled. A smile so twisted with bitterness it was hard to look upon.

"You know Mother Isriun, I think," murmured Gorm.

"Odem's brat," hissed Queen Laithlin, and it was plain from her voice that this was no part of her plans.

"You are mistaken, my queen." Isriun gave her a crooked smile. "My only family now is the Ministry, just as Father Yarvi's is. Our only parent is Grandmother Wexen, eh, *brother*? After her abject failure in the First of Cities, she did not feel Sister Scaer could be trusted." Scaer's face twitched at that title. "She sent me to take her place."

"And you allowed it?" muttered Yarvi.

Gorm worked his tongue sourly around his mouth, clearly a long stride from pleased. "I have an oath to the High King to consider."

"The Breaker of Swords is wise as well as strong," said Isriun. "He remembers his proper place in the order of things." Gorm looked sourer yet at that, but kept a brooding silence. "Something you of Gettland have forgotten. Grandmother Wexen demands you be chastised for your arrogance, your insolence, your disloyalty. Even now the High King raises a great army of Lowlanders and Inglings in their countless thousands. He summons his champion, Bright Yilling, to command them! The greatest army the Shattered Sea has ever seen! Ready to march on Throvenland for the glory of the One God!"

Yarvi snorted. "And you stand with them, do you, Grom-gil-Gorm? You kneel before the High King? You prostrate yourself before his One God?"

The long hair fluttered across Gorm's scarred face in the wind, his frown carved from stone. "I stand where my oaths have put me, Father Yarvi."

"Still," said Isriun, her thin hands twisting eagerly together, "the

Ministry speaks always for peace. The One God offers always for-giveness, however little it may be deserved. To spare bloodshed is a noble desire. We stand by our offer of a duel of kings to settle the issue." Her lip curled. "But I fear Uthil is too old, and weak, and riddled with sickness to fight. No doubt the One God's punishment for his disloyalty."

Laithlin glanced across at Yarvi, and the minister gave the slightest nod. "Uthil sends me in his place," she said, and Thorn felt her heart, already beating hard, begin to thud against her ribs. "A challenge to a king must be a challenge to his queen also."

Mother Isriun barked scornful laughter. "Will you fight the Breaker of Swords, gilded queen?"

Laithlin's lip curled. "A queen does not fight, child. My Chosen Shield will stand for me."

And Thorn felt a terrible calm settle upon her, and inside her hood she began to smile.

"This is trickery," snapped Isriun, her own smile vanished.

"This is law," said Yarvi. "As minister to a king you should under-stand it. You gave the challenge. We accept."

Gorm waved a great hand as though at a bothersome fly. "Trick-ery or law, it is the same. I will fight anyone." He sounded almost bored. "Show me your champion, Laithlin, and at dawn tomorrow we will meet on this ground, and I will kill him, and break his sword, and add its pommel to my chain." He turned his dark eyes on the warriors of Gettland. "But your Chosen Shield should know that Mother War breathed on me in my crib, and it has been foreseen no man can kill me."

Laithlin gave a chill smile, and it was as if all things slotted smoothly into place like the workings of a lock, and the gods' purpose for Thorn Bathu was suddenly revealed.

"My Chosen Shield is not a man."

So it was time for the sword to be drawn. Thorn pulled off the cloak and flung it away. In silence Gettland's warriors parted and she nudged her horse between them, her gaze fixed on the King of Vansterland.

And as he saw her come his great brow furrowed with doubt.

"Grom-gil-Gorm," she said softly as she rode between Laithlin and Yarvi. "Breaker of Swords." Mother Isriun's horse shied back out of her way. "Maker of Orphans." Thorn reined in beside him, his frowning face lit red by the blazing light of her elf-bangle, and she leaned from her saddle to whisper.

"Your death comes."

A BRAVE
FACE

For a while afterward they didn't move. Her hair tickling his face, her ribs pressing on his with each hot breath. She kissed his open mouth, nuzzled his face, and he lay still. She slid off him, stretched out beside him with a contented grunt, and he lay still. She wriggled against him, working her head into his shoulder, breath getting slower, softer, and he lay still.

No doubt he should've been holding her like a miser clutches his gold, making the most of every moment they had.

But instead Brand felt sore, and surly, and scared. Instead her clammy skin against his felt as if it was trapping him, her heat smothering him, and he twisted free of her and stood, caught his head on the canvas in the darkness and thrashed it away with his hand, cursing, making the fabric flap and wobble.

"You surely taught my tent a lesson," came Thorn's voice.

He could hardly see any sign of her. Maybe a little crescent of light on her shoulder as she propped herself on one elbow. A gleam at the corners of her eyes. A glint of gold in her hair.

"You're going to fight him, then?" he said.

"I reckon."

"Grom-gil-Gorm."

"Unless he's so scared he decides not to turn up."

"The Breaker of Swords. The Maker of Orphans." The names dropped dead in the darkness. Names great warriors quailed at. Names mothers scared their children with. "How many duels has he fought?"

"They say a score."

"How many have you?"

"You know how many, Brand."

"None."

"It's around that number."

"How many men has he killed?"

"Pits full of them." Her voice was getting hard, now, a fiery glow under the blanket from her elf-bangle. "More than any man around the Shattered Sea, maybe."

"How many pommels on that chain of his? A hundred? Two?"

"And my father's is one of them."

"You looking to follow in his footsteps?"

That glow grew brighter, showing him the lines of her scowl. "Since you ask, I'm hoping to kill the big bastard and leave his corpse for the crows."

Silence between them, and someone passed outside with a torch, orange flaring across the side of Thorn's face, the star-shaped scar on her cheek. Brand knelt, level with her. "We could just go."

"No, we can't."

"Father Yarvi, he twisted you into this. A trick, a gamble, like that poisoner in Yaletoft. This is all his plan—"

"What if it is? I'm not a child, Brand, my eyes were open. I swore an oath to him and another to the queen and I knew what they meant. I knew I might have to fight for her. I knew I might have to die for her."

"If we took horses we could be ten miles off by dawn."

She kicked angrily at the blanket and lay back, hands over her face. "We're not running, Brand. Neither one of us. I told Gorm his death comes. Be a bit of a let-down for everyone if I never even arrived, wouldn't it?"

"We could go south to Throvenland, join a crew and go down the Divine. On to the First of Cities. Vialine would give us a place. For the gods' sake, Thorn, he's the Breaker of Swords—"

"Brand, stop!" she snarled, so suddenly that he jerked back. "You think I don't know all this? You think my head isn't buzzing with it already like a nest of bloody wasps? You think I don't know everyone in our camp is working at the same sums and coming to the same answer?" She leaned farther forward, eyes gleaming. "I'll tell you what you could do for me, Brand. You could be the one man in fifty miles who thinks I can win. Or at least pretends I can. This isn't your choice, it's mine, and I've made it. Your choice is to be my shoulder-man or go."

He knelt there naked, blinking for a moment as if he'd been slapped. Then he took a long, shuddering breath, and blew it out. "I'll always be your shoulder-man. Always."

"I know you will. But I'm meant to be the one terrified."

"I'm sorry." He reached out, touched her face in the darkness and she pressed her cheek into his hand. "It's just . . . It took us a long time getting here. I don't want to lose you."

"I don't want to be lost. But you know I was born to do this."

"If anyone can beat him, you can." He wished he believed it.

"I know. But I might not have much time left." She took his wrist, and dragged him into the bed. "I don't want to spend it talking."

BRAND SAT WITH THORN'S sword across his knees and polished it.

He'd polished it plain hilt to bright point a dozen times already. As the stars were snuffed out, and the sky brightened, and Mother Sun showed herself behind Amon's Tooth. The steel couldn't be any cleaner, the edge any keener. But still he scrubbed, muttering prayers to Mother War. Or the same prayer, over and over.

". . . let her live, let her live, let her live . . ."

You want a thing when you can't have it. When you get it you suddenly sprout doubts. Then when you think you might lose it you find you need it worse than ever.

Father Yarvi was muttering some prayers of his own while he tended to a pot over the fire, from time to time tossing a few dried leaves from one pouch or another into a brew that smelled like feet.

"You could probably stop polishing," he said.

"I can't stand in the square with her." Brand flipped the sword over and set furiously to work on the other side. "All I can do is polish and pray. I plan to do both the best I can."

Brand knew Thorn would show no fear. But she even had the hint of a smile as she sat, elbows on her knees and her hands calmly dangling, the elf-bangle on her wrist glowing bright. She had a steel guard on her left arm but otherwise no armor, just leather stitched in places with steel rings, bound tight with straps and belts so there was nothing left loose to catch a hold of. Queen Laithlin stood at her side, binding her tangled hair tight against her skull, fingers moving sure and steady as if it was for a wedding feast rather than a duel. Two brave faces there, and no mistake. The bravest in the camp, for all they were the two with most to lose.

So when Thorn glanced over at him, Brand did his best to nod back with a brave face of his own. That much he could do. That, and polish, and pray.

"Is she ready?" murmured Father Yarvi.

"It's Thorn. She's always ready. Whatever these idiots might think."

The warriors had been gathering since first light and now there was a whispering crowd looking on, pressed in about the tents, peering over one another's shoulders. Master Hunnan was in the front rank, and couldn't have frowned any harder without tearing the deep-creased skin on his forehead. Brand could see the dismay and disgust on their faces. That some girl should be fighting for Gettland's honor while the sworn warriors stood idle. A girl who'd failed a test and been named a murderer. A girl who wore no mail and carried no shield.

Thorn showed no sign of giving a damn for their opinion as she stood, though. She looked as long and lean as a spider, the way Skifr used to but taller, and broader, and stronger, and she spread her arms wide and worked the fingers, her jaw set hard and her narrowed eyes fixed on the valley.

Queen Laithlin set a hand on her shoulder. "May Mother War stand with you, my Chosen Shield."

"She always has, my queen," said Thorn.

"It's nearly time." Father Yarvi poured some of his brew into a cup and held it out with his good hand. "Drink this."

Thorn sniffed at it and jerked back. "Smells foul!"

"The best brews do. This will sharpen your senses, and quicken your hands and dull any pain."

"Is that cheating?"

"Mother Isriun will be using every trick she can devise." And Yarvi held out the steaming cup again. "A champion must win, the rest is dust."

Thorn held her nose, swallowed it down, and spat with disgust.

Rulf stepped up, shield held like a tray with two knives laid on it, freshly sharpened. "Sure you don't want mail?"

Thorn shook her head. "Speed will be my best armor and my best weapon. Speed, and surprise, and aggression. These might come in handy too, though." She took the blades and slid them into sheaths at her chest and her side.

"One more for luck." Brand held out the dagger that Rin made him, the one he'd carried up and down the Divine and the Denied. The one that saved his life out on the steppe.

"I'll keep it safe." Thorn slid it through her belt at the small of her back.

"I'd rather it kept you safe," murmured Brand.

"A lot of blades," said Father Yarvi.

"Got caught without any once and didn't enjoy the experience," said Thorn. "I won't be dying for lack of stabbing back, at least."

"You won't be dying." Brand made sure his voice held no doubts, even if his heart was bursting with them. "You'll be killing the bastard."

"Aye." She leaned close. "I feel like my guts are going to drop out of my arse."

"I'd never know."

"Fear keeps you careful," she muttered, hands opening and closing. "Fear keeps you alive."

"No doubt."

"I wish Skifr was here."

"You've got nothing left to learn from her."

"A little of that elf-magic might not hurt, though. Just in case."

"And rob you of the glory? No." Brand showed her both sides of the sword, a frosty glint to the edges he'd been polishing since the first hint of light. "Don't hesitate."

"Never," she said, as she slid the blade through the clasp at her side and held her hand out for the ax. "Why did you? That day on the beach?"

Brand thought back, back down a long, strange year to the training square on the sand. "I was thinking about doing good." He spun the ax around, steel etched with letters in five tongues flashing. "Looking at both sides of the case, like the fool I am."

"You'd have beaten me if you hadn't."

"Maybe."

Thorn slid the ax through its loop. "I would've failed my test and Hunnan would never have given me another. I wouldn't have killed Edwal. I wouldn't have been called a murderer. I wouldn't have been trained by Skifr, or rowed down the Divine, or saved the empress, or had songs sung of my high deeds."

"I wouldn't have lost my place on the king's raid," said Brand. "I'd be a proud warrior of Gettland now, doing just as Master Hunnan told me."

"And my mother would have married me off to some old fool, and I'd be wearing his key all wrong and sewing very badly."

"You wouldn't be facing Grom-gil-Gorm."

"No. But we'd never have had . . . whatever we've got."

He looked into her eyes for a moment. "I'm glad I hesitated."

"So am I." She kissed him, then. One last kiss before the storm. Her lips soft against his. Her breath hot in the dawn chill.

"Thorn?" Koll was standing beside them. "Gorm's in the square."

Brand wanted to scream, then, but he forced himself to smile instead. "The sooner you start, the sooner you kill him."

He drew Odda's sword and started beating on Rulf's shield with the hilt, and others did the same with their own weapons, their own armor, noise spreading out through the ranks, and men began to shout, to roar, to sing out their defiance. She was nowhere near the champion they'd have picked, but she was Gettland's champion even so.

And Thorn strode tall through a thunder of clashing metal, the warriors parting before her like the earth before the plow.

Striding to her meeting with the Breaker of Swords.

STEEL

"I have been waiting for you," said Grom-gil-Gorm in his sing-song voice.

He sat upon a stool with his white-haired blade- and shield-bearers kneeling to either side, one of them smiling at Thorn, the other scowling as if he might fight her himself. Behind them, along the eastern edge of the square, twenty of Gorm's closest warriors were ranged, Mother Isriun glaring from their midst, hair stirred about her gaunt face by a breath of wind, Sister Scaer sullen beside her. Behind them were hundreds more fighting men, black outlines along the top of the ridge, Mother Sun bright as she rose beyond Amon's Tooth.

"Thought I'd give you a little more time alive." Thorn put on her bravest face as she stepped between Queen Laithlin and Father Yarvi. Stepped out in front of Gettland's twenty best and into that little plot of close-cut grass. A square just like the many she'd trained in, eight strides on a side, a spear driven into the ground at each corner.

A square where either she or Grom-gil-Gorm would die.

"No gift to me." The Breaker of Swords shrugged his great shoulders and his heavy mail, forged with zigzag lines of gold, gave an iron whisper. "Time drags when the Last Door stands so near."

"Perhaps it stands nearer for you than for me."

"Perhaps." He toyed thoughtfully with one of the pommels on his chain. "You are Thorn Bathu, then?"

"Yes."

"This one they sing the songs of?"

"Yes."

"The one who saved the Empress of the South?"

"Yes."

"The one who won a priceless relic from her." Gorm glanced down at the elf-bangle, glowing red as a burning coal on Thorn's wrist, and raised his brows. "I had taken those songs for lies."

She shrugged. "Some of them."

"However grand the truth, it is never enough for the skalds, eh?" Gorm took his shield from the smiling boy, a mighty thing, painted black with a rim scored and dented by a hundred old blows. Gifts from the many men he had killed in squares like this one. "I think we met before."

"In Skekenhouse. Where you knelt before the High King."

His cheek gave the faintest twitch of displeasure. "We all must kneel to someone. I should have known you sooner, but you have changed."

"Yes."

"You are Storn Headland's daughter."

"Yes."

"That was a glorious duel." The frowning boy offered Gorm's sword and he curled his great fingers about the grip and drew it. A monstrous blade, Thorn would have needed both hands to swing it but he carried it lightly as a willow switch. "Let us hope ours will make as jolly a song."

"Don't count on the same outcome," said Thorn, watching Mother Sun's reflection flash down his steel. He would have the reach, the strength, the armor but, weighed down by all that metal, she would have the speed. She would last the longer. Who would have the upper hand in the contest of wits, it remained to be seen.

"I have fought a score of duels, and put a score of brave men in their howes, and learned one thing. Never count on the outcome." Gorm's eyes moved over her clothes, her weapons, judging her as she was judging him. She wondered what strengths he saw. What weaknesses. "I never fought a woman before, though."

"Nor will you again. This is your last fight." She raised her chin at him. "Mother War's breath will not shield you from me."

She had hoped for anger, some sign he might be taunted into rashness, but all the King of Vansterland gave her was a sad little smile. "Ah, the confidence of the young. It was foreseen no man could kill me." And he stood, his great shadow stretching toward her across the stubbled grass, a giant stepped out from the songs. "Not that you could."

"MOTHER WAR, LET HER LIVE," mouthed Brand, both fists clenched aching tight. "Mother War, let her live . . ."

An eerie silence fell across the valley as the fighters took their places. Only the stirring of the wind in the grass, a bird calling high and harsh in the iron sky, the faint jingle of war-gear as one man or another shifted nervously. Mother Isriun stepped out into the lonely space between the two champions.

"Are you ready to kill? Are you ready to die?" She held up her hand, a curl of white goose-down in her fingers. "Are you ready to face the One God's judgment?"

Gorm stood straight and tall, huge as a mountain, his broad shield held before him, his long sword out behind. "Mother War will be my judge," he growled.

Thorn crouched low, teeth bared in a vicious grin, tense as a full-bent bow. "Whichever." She turned her head and spat. "I'm ready."

"Then begin!" called Mother Isriun, and let the feather fall, and hurried back, out of the short grass and into the rank of warriors opposite.

Down that feather drifted, slow, slow, every eye on both sides fixed upon it. It was caught by an eddy, whirled and spun. Down it drifted, and down, every breath on both sides held.

"Mother War, let her live, Mother War, let her live . . ."

THE INSTANT THAT SCRAP of down touched the close-cropped grass Thorn sprang. She had not forgotten Skifr's lessons. They were in her flesh. Always attack. Strike first. Strike last.

One stride and the wind rushed at her. Gorm stayed rigid, watching. Two strides and she crushed the feather into the dirt beneath her heel. Still he was frozen. Three strides and she was on him, screaming, swinging high with Skifr's ax, low with the sword forged from her father's bones. Now he moved, moved to meet her, and her blade crashed on his, and the ax chopped splinters from his shield.

In that instant she knew she had never fought anyone so strong. She was used to a shield giving when she hit it, used to staggering a man with the weight of her blows. But striking Gorm's shield was like striking a deep-rooted oak. Striking his sword jarred her from her palm to the tip of her nose and left her bared teeth rattling.

Thorn had never been one to get discouraged at the first reverse, though.

Gorm had thrust his heavy left boot recklessly forward and she dropped low, trying to hook it with her ax and bring him down. He stepped back nimbly for all his mountainous bulk and she heard him grunt, felt the great sword coming, whipping at her like a scorpion's tail. She only just lurched under as it ripped past at a vicious angle, a blow to split shields, to split helms, to split heads, the wind of it cold on her face.

She twisted, watching for the opening a swing like that must leave, but there was none. Gorm handled that monstrous blade as neatly as

Thorn's mother might a needle, no rage or madness in it, all control. His eyes stayed calm. His door of a shield never drifted.

That first exchange she judged a draw, and she danced back into room to wait for another chance. To seek out a better opening.

Slowly, carefully, the Breaker of Swords took one step toward the center of the square, twisting his great left boot into the sod.

"YES!" HISSED RULF AS Thorn darted in, letting go a flurry of blows. "Yes!" Blades clattered as they scarred Gorm's shield, Brand clenching his fists so tight the nails bit at his palms.

He gasped as Thorn rolled under the shining arc of Gorm's sword, came up snarling to hack at his shield, pushed a great thrust scornfully away and danced back out of range, using the full width of the square. She went in a drunken swagger, weapons drifting, the way that Skifr used to, and Gorm studied her over the rim of his shield, trying to find some pattern in the chaos.

"He is cautious," hissed Queen Laithlin.

"Stripped of the armor of his prophecy," muttered Father Yarvi. "He fears her."

The King of Vansterland took one more slow step, twisting his boot into the ground again as though he were laying the foundation stone of a hero's hall. He was all stillness, Thorn all movement.

"Like Mother Sea against Father Earth," murmured Rulf.

"Mother Sea always wins that battle," said Laithlin.

"Given time," said Father Yarvi.

Brand winced, unable to look, unable to look away. "Mother War, let her live . . ."

GORM'S SHIELD WAS SOLID as a citadel's gate. Thorn couldn't have broken it down with a ram and twenty strong men. And getting around it would hardly be easier. She'd never seen a shield handled so cleverly. Quick to move it, he was, and even quicker to move behind it, but he held it high. Each step he took that big left boot of his crept too far forward, more of his leg showing below the bottom rim than was prudent. Each time she saw it happen it seemed more a weakness.

Tempting. So tempting.

Too tempting, maybe?

Only a fool would think a warrior of his fame would have no tricks, and Thorn was no one's fool. Be quicker, tougher, cleverer, Skifr said. She had tricks of her own.

She let her eyes rest on that boot, licking her lips as if she watched the meat brought in, long enough to make sure he saw her watching, then she moved. His sword darted out but she was ready, slipped around it, Skifr's ax whipping across, but shoulder-high, not low where he expected it. She saw his eyes go wide. He lurched back, jerking up the shield, caught her ax with the rim, but the bearded blade still thudded into his shoulder, mail rings flying like dust from a beaten carpet.

She expected him to drop back, maybe even fall, but he shrugged her ax off as if it was a harsh word, pressed forward, too close for his sword or hers. The rim of his shield caught her in the mouth as she tumbled away and sent her staggering. No pain, no doubt, no dizziness. The shock of it only made her sharper. She heard Gorm roar, saw Mother Sun catch steel and dodged back as his blade whistled past.

That exchange she had to judge a draw as well, but they were both marked now.

Blood on his mail. Blood on his shield rim. Blood on her ax. Blood in her mouth. She bared her teeth at him in a fighting snarl and spat red onto the grass between them.

BLOOD

Like a pack of dogs, the sight of blood brought the gathered warriors suddenly to life, and the noise couldn't have been more deafening if they'd had the battle after all.

From the ridge in front the Vanstermen screeched prayers and bellowed curses, from the ridge behind the Gettlanders roared out futile encouragements, pointless advice. They rattled axes on shields, swords on helmets, sent up a din of lust and fury to wake the dead in their howes, to wake the gods from slumber.

Of all things, men most love to watch others face Death. It reminds them they yet live.

Across the square, among the snarling, snapping Vanstermen, Brand saw Mother Isriun, livid with fury, and Mother Scaer beside her, eyes calmly narrowed as she watched the contest.

Gorm swung a great overhead and Thorn twitched away, his sword missing her by a hand's breadth and opening a huge wound in the ground, grass and earth showering up. Brand bit his knuckle, painful hard. It would only take one of those to find her and that heavy steel could cut her clean in half. It felt as if it was a day since the fight began and he hadn't taken a breath the whole time.

"Mother War, let her live . . ."

THORN STRUTTED ABOUT THE SQUARE. It was her grass. She owned it. Queen of this mud. She hardly heard the screaming warriors on the high ground, barely saw Laithlin, or Isriun, or Yarvi, or even Brand. The world had shrunk to her, and the Breaker of Swords, and the few short strides of short grass between them, and she was starting to like what she saw.

Gorm was breathing hard, sweat across his furrowed forehead. The weight of all that gear was bound to tell, but she hadn't hoped it would be so soon. His shield was beginning to droop. She almost laughed. She could have done this for hours. She had done it for hours, for days, for weeks, down the Divine and the Denied and back.

She sprang in, aiming high with her sword. Too high, so he could duck, and duck he did, but just as she had planned his shield tipped forward. It was an easy thing to step around it, hook the top rim with the bearded head of Skifr's ax, marked with letters in five tongues. She meant to drag it down, leave him open, maybe tear it from his arm altogether, but she misjudged him. He roared, ripping his shield upwards, tearing the ax from her grip and sending it spinning high into the air.

That left his body unguarded for a moment, though, and Thorn had never been one to hesitate. Her sword hissed in below his shield and struck him in the side. Hard enough to fold him slightly, to make him stumble. Hard enough to cut through mail and find the flesh beneath.

Not hard enough to stop him, though.

He snarled, swung once and made her stagger back, thrust and made her dance away, chopped again, even harder, steel hissing at the air, but she was already backing off, watchful, circling.

As he turned toward her she saw the ragged tear in his mail, links flapping free, blood glistening. She saw how he favored that side as he took up his stance, and she began to smile as she filled her empty left hand with her longest dagger.

She might have lost her ax, but that round was hers.

NOW, THORN WAS ONE of them. Now she'd bloodied Grom-gil-Gorm and Master Hunnan thrust his fist in the air, roared his support. Now the warriors who'd sneered at her made a deafening din in admiration of her prowess.

No doubt those with the gift were already setting the song of her triumph in verse. They tasted victory, but all Brand could taste was fear. His heart thudded as loud as Rin's hammer. He twitched and gasped with every movement in the square. He'd never felt so helpless. He couldn't do good. He couldn't do bad. He couldn't do anything.

Thorn darted forward, going low with her sword, so fast Brand could hardly follow it. Gorm dropped his shield to block but she was already gone, slashing across the top of his shield with her dagger. Gorm jerked his head back, staggered a step, a red line across his cheek, across his nose, under his eye.

THE BATTLE JOY WAS on her now. Or maybe Father Yarvi's brew was.

The breath ripped at her chest, she danced on air. The blood sweet in her mouth, her skin on fire. She smiled, smiled so wide it seemed her scarred cheeks might split.

The cut below Gorm's eye was leaking, streaks of blood down his face, out of his slit nose, into his beard.

He was tiring, he was hurt, he was growing careless. She had his measure and he knew it. She could see the fear in his eyes. Could see the doubt, ever growing.

His shield had drifted up even higher to guard his wounded face.

His stance had loosened, his heavy sword wilting in his grip. That left leg slipped still farther forward, all exposed, knee wobbling.

Perhaps it had been a trick, in the beginning, but what trick could stop her now? She breathed fire and spat lightning. She was the storm, always moving. She was Mother War made flesh.

"Your death comes!" she screamed at him, words even she could hardly hear over the noise.

She would kill the Breaker of Swords, and avenge her father, and prove herself the greatest warrior about the Shattered Sea. The greatest warrior in the world! The songs they would sing of this!

She led him in a circle, led him around until her back was to the Vanstermen, until her back was to the east. She saw Gorm narrow his eyes as Mother Sun stabbed at them, twisting away, leaving his leg unguarded. She feinted high, tightening her fingers about the grip, ducked under an ill-timed chop and screamed out as she swept her sword in a great, low circle.

The blade forged with her father's bones struck Gorm's leg above the ankle with all Thorn's strength, and anger, and training behind it. The moment of her victory. The moment of her vengeance.

But instead of slicing through flesh and bone the bitter edge clanged on metal, jarred in Thorn's hand so badly she stumbled forward, off-balance.

Hidden armor. Steel glinting beneath the slit leather of Gorm's boot.

He moved quick as a snake, not near so tired nor so hurt as he had made her think, chopping down, catching her blade with his and tearing it from her numbed fingers.

She lashed at him with her knife but he caught it on his shield and rammed the boss into her ribs. It was like being kicked by a horse and she tottered back, only just staying on her feet.

Gorm glared at her over his shield rim, and it was his turn to smile. "You are a worthy opponent," he said. "As dangerous as any I have fought." He stepped forward, planting that armored boot on her fallen sword and grinding it into the sod. "But your death comes."

—

"OH, GODS," CROAKED BRAND, cold right through to his bones.

Thorn was fighting with two knives now, no reach, and Gorm was herding her around the square with shining sweeps of his great sword, seeming stronger than ever.

The men of Gettland had fallen suddenly quiet, while the noise from across the valley redoubled.

Brand prayed Thorn would stay away but knew her only chance was to close with him. Sure enough, she ducked under a high cut and flung herself forward, stabbed with her right, a vicious, flashing overhand, but Gorm heaved his shield up, her blade thudding deep between two boards and lodging tight.

"Kill him!" hissed Queen Laithlin.

Thorn slashed at Gorm's sword-arm with her left as he brought it back, dagger scraping down his mail and catching his hand, blood spattering as the great sword tumbled from his grip.

Or perhaps he let it fall. As she stabbed at him again he caught her arm, his fingers closing about her wrist with a smack that was like a punch in Brand's stomach.

"Oh, gods," he croaked.

BREATH

Thorn snatched for Brand's dagger but her elbow tangled with Gorm's loose shield and he stepped close, smothering her. He had her left wrist tight and he wrenched it up, the elf-bangle grinding into her flesh. He let go the handle of his shield and caught her right sleeve.

"I have you!" he snarled.

"No!" She twisted back as if she was trying to wriggle free and he dragged her closer. "I have you!"

She jerked forward, using his strength against him, butted him full in the jaw and snapped his head up. She set her knee against his ribs, screamed as she ripped her right arm free.

He kept his crushing grip on her left wrist, though. She had one chance. Just one. She tore Brand's dagger from the small of her back, stabbed at Gorm's neck as his eyes came back toward her.

He jerked his shield hand up to ward her off and the blade punched through the meat of it, snake-worked crosspiece smacking against his palm. She snarled as she drove his hand back, his shield flopping loose on the straps, but with a trembling effort he stopped the bright point just short of his throat, held it there, pink spit flecking from his bared teeth.

Then, even though his hand was stabbed right through, the great fingers closed about her right fist and trapped her tight.

Thorn strained with every fiber to push the red blade into his neck, but you will not beat a strong man with strength, and there was no man as strong as the Breaker of Swords. He had both her hands pinned and he set his shoulder, let go a growl, and pressed her trembling back, back toward the edge of the square, hot blood leaking from his punctured palm and down the hilt of the dagger, wetting her crushed fist.

BRAND GAVE A SICK GROAN as Gorm forced Thorn down onto her knees in front of the jeering warriors of Vansterland.

Her elf-bangle glowed red through the flesh of his clutching sword hand, bones showing black inside, squeezing, squeezing. She gasped through her gritted teeth as the knife toppled from the loose fingers of her left hand, bounced from her shoulder and away into the grass, and Gorm let go her wrist and caught her tight around the throat.

Brand tried to take a step into the square but Father Yarvi had him by one arm, Rulf by the other, wrestling him back.

"No," hissed the helmsman in his ear.

"Yes!" shrieked Mother Isriun, staring down in delight.

NO BREATH.

Thorn's every hard-trained muscle strained but Gorm was too strong, and back he twisted her, and back. His grip crushed her right hand around the handle of Brand's dagger, bones groaning. She fumbled in the grass with the other for her knife but couldn't find it, punched at his knee but there was no strength in it, tried to reach his face but could only tear weakly at his bloody beard.

"Kill her!" shouted Mother Isriun.

Gorm forced Thorn toward the ground, blood dripping from his snarl and pattering on her cheek. Her chest heaved, but all that happened was a dead squelching in her throat.

No breath. Her face was burning. She could hardly hear the storm of voices for the surging of blood in her head. She plucked at Gorm's hand with her numb fingertips, tore at it with her nails but it was forged from iron, carved from wood, ruthless as the roots of trees that over years will burst the very rock apart.

"Kill her!" Even though she could see Mother Isriun's face, twisted in triumph above her, she could only just hear her shriek. "The High King decrees it! The One God ordains it!"

Gorm's eyes flickered sideways to his minister, his cheek twitching. His grip seemed to loosen, but perhaps that was Thorn's grip on life, slipping, slipping.

No breath. It was growing dark. She faced the Last Door, no tricks left to play. Death slid the bolt, pushed it wide. She teetered on the threshold.

But Gorm did not push her over.

As if through a shadowy veil she saw his forehead crease.

"Kill her!" screeched Mother Isriun, her voice going higher and higher, wilder and wilder. "Grandmother Wexen demands it! Grandmother Wexen *commands* it!"

And Gorm's bloody face shuddered again, a spasm from his eye down to his jaw. His lips slipped back over his teeth and left his mouth a straight, flat line. His right hand relaxed, and Thorn heaved in a choking breath, the world tipping over as she flopped onto her side.

BRAND WATCHED IN DISBELIEF as Gorm let Thorn fall and turned slowly to stare at Isriun. The hungry snarls of his warriors began to fade, the crowds above fell silent, the noise all guttering out to leave a shocked quiet.

"I am the Breaker of Swords." Gorm put his right hand ever so gently on his chest. "What madness makes you speak to me in such a fashion?"

Isriun pointed down at Thorn, rolling onto her face, coughing puke into the grass. "Kill her!"

"No."

"Grandmother Wexen commands—"

"I tire of Grandmother Wexen's commands!" roared Gorm, eyes near-popping from his bloody face. "I tire of the High King's arrogance! But most of all, Mother Isriun . . ." He bared his teeth in a horrible grimace as he twisted Brand's dagger from his shield hand. "I tire of your voice. Its constant bleating grates upon me."

Mother Isriun's face had turned deathly pale. She tried to shrink back but Scaer's tattooed arm snaked about her shoulders and held her tight. "You would break your oaths to them?" muttered Isriun, eyes wide.

"Break my oaths?" Gorm shook the scarred shield from his arm and let it clatter down. "There is less honor in keeping them. I shatter them. I spit on them. I shit on them." He loomed over Isriun, the knife glinting red in his hand. "The High King decrees, does he? Grandmother Wexen commands, does she? Old goat and old sow, I renounce them! I defy them!"

Isriun's thin neck fluttered as she swallowed. "If you kill me there will be war."

"Oh, there will be war. The Mother of Crows spreads her wings, girl." Grom-gil-Gorm slowly raised the knife that Rin had forged, Isriun's eyes rooted to the bright point. "Her feathers are swords! Hear them rattle?" And a smile spread across his face. "But I do not need to kill you." He tossed the knife skittering through the grass to end beside Thorn where she hunched on hands and knees, retching. "After all, Mother Scaer, why kill what you can sell?"

Gorm's old minister, and now his new one, gave a smile chill as the winter sea. "Take this snake away and put a collar on her."

"You'll pay!" shrieked Isriun, eyes wild. "You'll pay for this!" But Gorm's warriors were already dragging her up the eastern slope.

The Breaker of Swords turned back, blood dripping from the dangling fingers of his wounded hand. "Does your offer of alliance still stand, Laithlin?"

"What could Vansterland and Gettland not achieve together?" called the Golden Queen.

"Then I accept."

A stunned sigh rippled around the square, as if the held breath of every man was suddenly let out.

Brand twisted free of Rulf's limp hands and ran.

"THORN?"

The voice seemed to echo from a long way away, down a dark tunnel. Brand's voice. Gods, she was glad to hear it.

"You all right?" Strong hands at her shoulder, lifting her.

"I got proud," she croaked, throat raw, mouth stinging. Tried to get to her knees, so weak and dizzy she nearly fell again, but he caught her.

"But you're alive."

"I reckon," she whispered, more than a little surprised as Brand's face drifted gradually out of the bright blur. Gods, she was glad to see it.

"That's enough." He stretched her arm over his shoulders and she groaned as he lifted her gently to her feet. She couldn't have taken a step on her own, but he was strong. He wouldn't let her fall. "You need me to carry you?"

"It's a fine thought." She winced as she looked toward the warriors of Gettland gathered on the crest ahead of them. "But I'd better walk. Why didn't he kill me?"

"Mother Isriun changed his mind."

Thorn took one look back as they shuffled up the slope toward the camp. Grom-gil-Gorm stood in the middle of the square, bloodied but unbeaten. Mother Scaer was already working at his wounded shield hand with needle and thread. His sword-hand was gripping

Queen Laithlin's, sealing the alliance between Vansterland and Gettland. Bitter enemies made friends. At least for now.

Beside them, with arms folded, Yarvi smiled.

In spite of all the prayers to Mother War, it seemed Father Peace made the judgment that day.

IN THE LIGHT

Brand gave the billet a few more ringing blows with his hammer then shoved it back into the coals in a shower of sparks.

Rin gave a disgusted click of her tongue. "You've not got what they call a gentle touch, have you?"

"That's what you're here for." Brand grinned at her. "Got to make you feel special, don't I?"

But she was looking past him, toward the door. "You've a visitor."

"Father Yarvi, what an honor." Brand set down his hammer and wiped his forehead on his forearm. "Come to buy a blade?"

"A minister should stand for Father Peace," said Yarvi as he stepped into the forge.

"A good one stays friendly with Mother War too," said Rin.

"Wise words. And now more than ever."

Brand swallowed. "It's going to be war, then?"

"The High King will take time gathering his warriors. But I think it will be war. Still. War is a fine thing for a swordsmith's business."

Rin raised her brows at Brand. "We'd settle for a poorer peace, I reckon. I hear King Uthil's on the mend, at least."

"His strength rushes back," said Yarvi. "Soon he will be terrorizing his warriors once again at sword practice, and using your fine steel to do it."

"Father Peace be praised," said Rin.

"Father Peace and your skills," said Brand.

Yarvi humbly bowed. "I do what I can. And how do the gods treat you, Brand?"

"Well enough." He nodded at his sister. "If it wasn't for my tyrant of a master I'd be enjoying the job. Turns out I like working with metal a lot more than I remembered."

"Easier than working with people."

"Steel is honest," said Brand.

Father Yarvi looked sideways at him. "Is there somewhere we can speak alone?"

Brand looked over at Rin, already pounding at the bellows. She shrugged. "Steel is patient too."

"You're not, though."

"Go have your talk." She narrowed her eyes at him. "Before I change my mind."

Brand pulled his gloves off and led Yarvi out into the little yard, noisy with the sound of running water. He sat on the bench Koll had carved for them in the dappled shade of the tree, breeze cool on his sweat-sheened face, and offered Father Yarvi the place beside him.

"A pleasant spot." The minister smiled up at Mother Sun, flashing and flickering through the leaves. "It's a fine life you and your sister have made for yourselves."

"She made it. I just happened along."

"You've always played your part. I remember you taking the weight of the *South Wind* across your shoulders." Yarvi looked down at the scars snaking up Brand's forearms. "There was a feat to sing of."

"I find I care less for songs than I used to."

"You are learning. How is Thorn?"

"Already back to training three-quarters of every day."

"She is carved from wood, that one."

"No woman firmer touched by Mother War."

"And yet she has been the needle that stitched two great alliances together. Perhaps she was touched by Father Peace too."

"Don't tell her that."

"The two of you are still . . . together?"

"Aye." Brand had a sense the minister knew these answers, but that every question had another hidden in it. "You could call it that."

"Good. That's good."

"I suppose so," he said, thinking of the screaming argument they'd had that morning.

"It's not good?"

"It's good," he said, thinking of how they'd made up afterward. "It's just . . . I always thought of being together as the end of the work. Turns out it's where the work starts."

"No road worth traveling is easy," said Father Yarvi. "Each of you has strengths the other lacks, weaknesses the other makes up for. It is a fine thing, a rare thing, to find someone who . . ." He frowned up at the shifting branches, as though he thought of something far away, and the thought was painful. "Makes you whole."

Took a little while for Brand to gather the courage to speak. "I've been thinking about melting down that coin Prince Varoslaf gave me."

"To make a key?"

Brand pushed a couple of fallen leaves around with the side of his boot. "Probably she'd prefer a dagger but . . . a key's traditional. What do you think Queen Laithlin would think of it?"

"The queen has had three sons and no daughters. I think she is becoming very much attached to her Chosen Shield. But I'm sure she could be persuaded."

Brand gave those leaves another push. "No doubt folk think I'm the one should wear the key. I'm none too popular in Thorlby."

"The king's warriors are not all admirers of yours, it is true. Master Hunnan in particular. But I have heard it said enemies are the price of success. Perhaps they are the price of conviction too."

"The price of cowardice, maybe."

"Only a fool would reckon you a coward, Brand. To stand up before the warriors of Gettland and speak as you did?" Father Yarvi put his lips together and gave a faint whistle. "People may sing no hero's songs of it, but that was rare courage."

"You think so?"

"I do, and courage is not your only admirable quality."

Brand hardly knew what to say to that, so he said nothing.

"Did you know Rulf melted down his earnings from our voyage and made a key of his own?"

"For who?"

"Thorn's mother. They are being married in the Godshall next week."

Brand blinked. "Oh."

"Rulf is getting old. He would never say so, but he is keen to step back." Yarvi looked sideways. "I think you would do well in his place."

Brand blinked again. "Me?"

"I told you once that I might need a man beside me who thinks of doing good. I think so more than ever."

"Oh." Brand couldn't think of anything else to say.

"You could join Safrit, and Koll, and be part of my little family." Every word Father Yarvi let drop was carefully weighed out and these did not fall by accident. He knew just what to offer. "You would be close to me. Close to the queen. Close to the queen's Chosen Shield. The helmsman of a minister's ship." He remembered that day on the steering platform, the crew thumping at their oars, the sunlight bright on the water of the Denied. "You would stand at the right hand of the man who stands at the right hand of the king."

Brand paused, rubbing at his fingertips with his thumbs. No doubt he should've leapt at the chance. A man like him couldn't expect too many like it. Yet something held him back. "You're a deep-cunning man, Father Yarvi, and I'm not known for my wits."

"You could be, if you used them. But it's your strong arm and your strong heart I want you for."

"Can I ask you a question?"

"You can ask. But make sure you want the answer."

"How long had you planned for Thorn to fight a duel with Grom-gil-Gorm?"

Yarvi narrowed his pale eyes a little. "A minister must deal in like-lihoods, in chances, in possibilities. That one occurred to me long ago."

"When I came to you in the Godshall?"

"I told you then the good thing is a different thing for every man. I considered the possibility that a woman who could use a sword might one day find a way to challenge Gorm. Great and storied warrior that he is, he would not be able to turn down a woman's challenge. And yet he would fear one. More than any man."

"You believe that prophecy?"

"I believe that he believes it."

"That was why you had Skifr train her."

"One reason. The Empress Theofora loved rare things, and also loved to watch blood spilled, and I thought a fighting girl from the far north might excite her curiosity long enough for me to speak to her, and present my gift. Death ushered Theofora through the Last Door before I got the chance." Yarvi gave a sigh. "A good minister strives to look ahead, but the future is a land wrapped in fog. Events do not always flow down the channel you dig for them."

"Like your deal with Mother Scaer."

"Another hope. Another gamble." Father Yarvi sat back against the trunk of the tree. "I needed an alliance with the Vanstermen, but Mother Isriun spoiled that notion. She gave the challenge, though, and a duel was better than a battle." He spoke calmly, coldly, as though he spoke of pieces on a board rather than people he knew.

Brand's mouth felt very dry. "If Thorn had died, what then?"

"Then we would have sung sad songs over her howe, and happy songs over her high deeds." Yarvi's were the eyes of a butcher who looks at livestock, judging where the profit is. "But we and the Vanstermen would not have wasted our strength fighting each other. Queen Laithlin and I would have prostrated ourselves at the feet of Grandmother Wexen and made golden apologies. King Uthil would have recovered, free of dishonor. In time we might have thrown the dice again."

Something in Father Yarvi's words niggled at Brand, like a hook in his head, tickling, tickling. "We all thought King Uthil was at the Last Door. How could you be sure he'd recover?"

Yarvi paused for a moment, his mouth half-open, then carefully shut it. He looked toward the doorway, the clanging of Rin's hammer echoing from beyond, and back to Brand. "I think you are a more cunning man than you pretend."

Brand had a feeling he stood on spring ice, cracks spreading beneath his boots, but there was no going back, only forward. "If I'm to stand at your shoulder I should know the truth."

"I told you once that the truth is like the good thing, each man has his own. My truth is that King Uthil is a man of iron, and iron is strong, and holds a fine edge. But iron can be brittle. And sometimes we must bend."

"He would never have made peace with the Vanstermen."

"And we had to make peace with the Vanstermen. Without them we stand alone against half the world."

Brand slowly nodded, seeing the pieces of it slide into place. "Uthil would have accepted Gorm's duel."

"He would have fought Gorm in the square, for he is proud, and he would have lost, for each year leaves him weaker. I must protect my king from harm. For his good, and the good of the land. We needed allies. We went seeking allies. I found allies."

Brand thought of the minister bent over the fire, throwing dried leaves into the brew. "You poisoned him. Your own uncle."

"I have no uncle, Brand. I gave my family up when I joined the

Ministry." Yarvi's voice held no guilt. No doubt. No regret. "Sometimes great rights must be stitched from little wrongs. A minister does not have the luxury of doing what is simply good. A minister must weigh the greater good. A minister must choose the lesser evil."

"Power means having one shoulder always in the shadows," muttered Brand.

"It does. It must."

"I understand. I don't doubt you, but . . ."

Father Yarvi blinked, and Brand wondered whether he'd ever seen him look surprised before. "You refuse me?"

"My mother told me to stand in the light."

They sat there for a moment, looking at one another, then Father Yarvi slowly began to smile. "I admire you for it, I truly do." He stood up, laying his good hand on Brand's shoulder. "But when Mother War spreads her wings, she may cast the whole Shattered Sea into darkness."

"I hope not," said Brand.

"Well." Father Yarvi turned away. "You know how it goes, with hopes." And he walked into the house, and left Brand sitting in the shade of the tree, wondering, as ever, if he'd done a good thing or a bad.

"A little help here!" came his sister's voice.

Brand started up. "On my way!"

A STORM
COMING

Thorn strode across the sand with her stool on her shoulder. The tide was far out and the wind blew hard over the flats, tattered clouds chasing each other across a bruised sky.

They were packed in tight about the training square, the shouts turning to grunts as she pushed through the warriors, the grunts to silence as she set her stool next to the spear that marked one corner. Even the two lads who were meant to be sparring came to an uncertain halt, staring at her as she stepped over her stool and planted her arse on it.

Master Hunnan frowned over. "I see the queen's Chosen Shield is among us."

Thorn held up one hand. "Don't worry, you needn't all applaud."

"The training square is for warriors of Gettland, and for those who would be warriors."

"Aye, but there's probably some half-decent fighters down here even so. Don't let me stop you."

"You won't," snapped Hunnan. "Heirod, you're next." It was a great big lad that stood, pink blotches on his fat cheeks. "And you,

Edni." She was maybe twelve years old, and a skinny scrap, but she sprang up bravely enough, her chin thrust out as she took her mark, even though the shield was way too big for her and wobbled in her hand.

"Begin!"

There was no art to it at all. The boy went charging in, puffing like a bull, shrugged Edni's sword off his thick shoulder, barrelled into her and sent her sprawling, the shield coming off her arm and rolling away on its edge.

The boy looked at Hunnan, waiting for him to call the bout, but the master-at-arms only stared back. Heirod swallowed, and stepped forward, and gave Edni a couple of reluctant kicks before Hunnan raised his hand for a halt.

Thorn watched the girl clamber up, wiping blood from under her nose, clinging tight to her brave face, and thought of all the beatings she'd taken in this square. Thought of all the kicks and the scorn and the sand she'd eaten. Thought of that last day, and Edwal with her wooden sword through his neck. No doubt nudging her memory had been what Master Hunnan had in mind.

He gave a rare, thin little smile. "What did you think of that?"

"I think the boy's a clumsy thug." She pressed her thumb on one side of her nose and blew snot onto the sand. "But it's not his fault. He learned from one, and so did she. The one who got shamed in that bout was their teacher."

A muttering went through the warriors, and Hunnan's smile sprang back into a frown. "If you think you know better, why don't you give a lesson?"

"That's why I'm here, Master Hunnan. I've nothing to learn from you, after all." She pointed to Edni. "I'll take her," Then she pointed out an older girl, big and solemn. "And her." And then another with pale, pale eyes. "And her. I'll give them a lesson. I'll give them one a day, and in a month we'll come back, and we'll see what we'll see."

"You can't just come here and take my pupils where you please!"

"Yet here I am, and with King Uthil's blessing."

Hunnan licked his lips, wrong-footed, but he soon rallied, and fixed on attack. "Hild Bathu," his lip curled with disgust. "You failed your test in this square. You failed to become a warrior. You lost to the Breaker of Swords—"

"I lost to Gorm, true." Thorn rubbed at one scarred cheek as she grinned up at him. "But he never broke my sword." She stood, one hand slack on the pommel. "And you're not Gorm." She stepped across the sand toward him. "Reckon you're better than me?" And she stepped so close she almost planted her boots on his. "Fight me." She leaned in, so their noses were near touching, and hissed it over and over. "Fight me. Fight me. Fight me. Fight me. Fight me. Fight me. Fight me."

Hunnan flinched each time she said it, but he kept his silence.

"Good choice," she said. "I'd snap you like an old twig."

She shouldered past him, calling out to the rest of the warriors. "Maybe you're thinking that wasn't fair. The battlefield isn't fair, but I'll grant you old Hunnan's a few years past his best. So anyone thinks he can fill Gorm's boots, I'll fight him. I'll fight any of you." She swaggered in a circle, taking in each side of the square, staring the warriors in their eyes one after another.

Silence. Only the wind sighing across the beach.

"No one?" She snorted. "Look at you, sulking because you didn't get a battle. There'll be more battle than you know what to do with soon enough. I hear the High King gathers his warriors. Lowlanders, and Islanders, and Inglings. Thousands of them. There's a storm coming, and Gettland will need every man. Every man and every woman. You three, come with me. We'll be back in a month." She lifted her arm to point at Hunnan. "And your boys better be ready."

Thorn swung the stool up onto her shoulder and stalked from the square, off across the sand toward Thorlby. She didn't look back.

But she heard the footsteps of the girls behind her.

ACKNOWLEDGMENTS

As always, four people without whom:
Bren Abercrombie, whose eyes are sore from reading it.
Nick Abercrombie, whose ears are sore from hearing about it.
Rob Abercrombie, whose fingers are sore from turning the pages.
Lou Abercrombie, whose arms are sore from holding me up.

Then, because no man is an island, especially this one, my heartfelt
    thanks:
For planting the seed of this idea: Nick Lake.
For making sure the sprout grew to a tree: Robert Kirby.
For making sure the tree bore golden fruit: Jane Johnson.

Then, because the fruit metaphor has run its course, all those who've
    helped make, market, publish, publicize, illustrate, translate and
    above all *sell* my books wherever they may be around the world
    but, in particular: Natasha Bardon, Emma Coode, Ben North,
    Jaime Frost, Tricia Narwani, Jonathan Lyons, and Ginger Clark.

To the artists and designers somehow rising to the impossible challenge of making me look classy: Nicolette and Terence Caven,
Mike Bryan and Dominic Forbes.

For endless enthusiasm and support in all weathers: Gillian Redfearn.

And to all the writers whose paths have crossed mine on the Internet,
at the bar, or in some cases even on the printed page, and who've
provided help, advice, laughs and plenty of ideas worth the
stealing.

You know who you are . . .

ABOUT THE AUTHOR

JOE ABERCROMBIE is the *New York Times* bestselling author of *Half a King*, *Red Country*, and the First Law trilogy: *The Blade Itself*, *Before They Are Hanged*, and *Last Argument of Kings*. He spent ten years as a freelance film editor, but is now a full-time writer who lives in Bath, England, with his wife, two daughters, and son.

joeabercrombie.com

Facebook.com/joeabercrombieauthor

@LordGrimdark

ABOUT THE TYPE

This book was set in Fournier, a typeface named for Pierre-Simon Fournier (1712–68), the youngest son of a French printing family. He started out engraving woodblocks and large capitals, then moved on to fonts of type. In 1736 he began his own foundry and made several important contributions in the field of type design; he is said to have cut 147 alphabets of his own creation. Fournier is probably best remembered as the designer of St. Augustine Ordinaire, a face that served as the model for the Monotype Corporation's Fournier, which was released in 1925.